I0614492

Blues at 11

by

Rebecca Grace

The Blues Series

This is a work of fiction. Names, characters, places, and incidents are either the product of the author's imagination or are used fictitiously, and any resemblance to actual persons living or dead, business establishments, events, or locales, is entirely coincidental.

Blues at 11

COPYRIGHT © 2015 by Rebecca G. Martinez

All rights reserved. No part of this book may be used or reproduced in any manner whatsoever without written permission of the author or The Wild Rose Press, Inc. except in the case of brief quotations embodied in critical articles or reviews.
Contact Information: info@thewildrosepress.com

Cover Art by *Debbie Taylor*

The Wild Rose Press, Inc.
PO Box 708
Adams Basin, NY 14410-0708
Visit us at www.thewildrosepress.com

Publishing History
First Crimson Rose Edition, 2015
Print ISBN 978-1-62830-721-4
Digital ISBN 978-1-62830-722-1

The Blues Series
Published in the United States of America

"Someone needs to find the killer. What if he's after me too? Think about Lindy's accident. She was driving my car. The hit and run driver might have been after me."

Hank waved an impatient hand. "From what I've heard, she was driving too fast and may have been racing the other car."

"She told me she was careful."

"You think she'd tell the truth if she was racing? Look, I would appreciate it if you hired a PI and left my dad out of this."

"All you're worried about is looking bad for your mayor and rich people like the Brookings family. I'm sure they'll give you a nice contribution to your next campaign for providing personal attention."

"I am not elected," he said through gritted teeth.

"But you are worried about your job and appearances. Isn't that why you were making such a big deal out of my 'security arrangement' with your dad?" It was my turn to hold up the quote fingers.

The coldness that grew in his eyes was like an approaching glacier. "Look, I know what's happening. You're doing your normal Kimberly crap."

His harsh words smacked into me like a slap of hard wind to my face. "My what?"

He unloaded on me with the force of a blizzard. "You're a pampered princess who is so damned used to getting your own way that you can't handle it when the real world invades your private fantasy life! Well, it's here, lady, and it's real. But I won't stand by and let you hurt my father by getting him involved."

Praise for Rebecca Grace and...

SHADOWS FROM THE PAST
"Mystery and romance come together in this hauntingly beautiful tale of love and hope... I recommend this to fans of mystery/suspense with an unforgettable love story."

~*The Romance Reviews (4 Stars)*

"*SHADOWS FROM THE PAST* is a great story that pulled me in immediately. It's haunting, suspenseful and enjoyable. Rebecca Grace has created a thrilling ride with this story. I had no idea what I would find out next... If you're a fan of romantic suspense, *SHADOWS FROM THE PAST* is top notch!"

~*Siren Book Reviews (5 Stones)*

"*SHADOWS FROM THE PAST* is an enjoyable read... a good story. I recommend it for people who like a little mystery and suspense in their story..."

~*Sizzling Hot Book Reviews*

DEADLY MESSAGES
"The action and suspense in this book will truly keep you on your toes. A roller-coaster ride of scenes set the stages as Mitch and Connie come together to find out whether they are hunting for one killer or two. A romance blossoms and they learn to rely on each other. A very balanced narrative combined with a solid mystery make this a must read!"

~*Rt Book Reviews (4 Stars)*

Dedication

To my family and my friends in TV news business—
and no, this is not based on anyone I know.

Chapter One

Saturday afternoon

"Rick Wells needs to die."

When I made that pronouncement to my best friend Delia Lindsay while sitting at the Geneva bar on a Saturday afternoon, I had no idea how much I would regret saying those words. It seemed like a good idea. Later I wanted to go back and swallow that comment quicker than the martinis I guzzled. As television anchor Kimberly delaGarza, I made factual statements all the time. This was pure commentary.

I punctuated my proclamation by piercing the air with the plastic pink spear from my martini. "If I had a full-sized one of these, I'd run it through the prick. Damn lying weasel."

"Awfully messy, all that blood." Delia shook her brassy blonde curls. She twisted red lips, puffy from a recent collagen injection. "I wouldn't want him bleeding all over my new imported rugs."

I dropped my plastic weapon. Blood didn't appeal to me either. "Good point."

Delia and I sat at the end of the black marble bar, partaking in our once-a-month martini ritual. Halfway between my beach-front townhouse in the south bay city of Mira Loma and Delia's rambling mountainside mansion in Malibu, Geneva offered a casual atmosphere and chic California cuisine served in an airy dining room or shaded patio. Delia and I seldom ventured beyond the bar with floor-to-ceiling windows that provided a breathtaking view of the Pacific Coast.

During the week, Geneva was a crowded lunch spot for Hollywood power players. On weekends, only locals visited before sunset. We sat alone at the bar. Two couples occupied separate tables near the windows.

I sipped my second drink, but I was in a mood to line 'em up and knock 'em back. My insides were wound tighter than a stopwatch. Thank goodness Delia let me vent my anger toward that ungrateful, lousy SOB.

"How about this?" I swirled the liquid at the bottom of my glass. "We shoot him in a dark alley and bury his body in the desert. There's plenty of open land outside Palm Springs."

"Too much work." Delia studied her bright red nails. "All that lifting and digging."

"Fuck!" I tossed back the rest of my drink and slammed the glass on the bar.

The loud crack caught the attention of a young bartender polishing glasses a few feet away. "Do you need another, Miss delaGarza?"

Even though we frequented Geneva, I didn't know him. Felipe, the usual bartender, refilled our drinks before we re-ordered. This guy required Delia's instructions to perfect our second round. Blond, blue-eyed and big shouldered, he resembled dozens of bartenders awaiting a call from Hollywood.

I hadn't given my name, but the recognition didn't surprise me. My face was plastered on billboards and buses from Santa Barbara to San Diego. *"James Kent and Kimberly delaGarza, the TV8 news team you can trust at 6 and 11."*

Lifting my glass, I flashed my best anchor smile. "Why not?"

Delia patted my hand. "I'm paying today. You deserve special treatment."

"Special" was what Rick Wells used to call me. Before last weekend. Before he transformed into a weasel by admitting he'd been seeing someone else. Someone half his age. My lips pressed together as my fists clenched. He'd broken up with me after ten years. Ten fucking years! For that, the jerk deserved to die, didn't he?

My gaze caught sight of the ocean in the mirror behind the bar. It appeared to wink, ready to help. "Let's rent a yacht and shove his sorry ass overboard. No body, no blood. We can feed the sharks."

Delia cocked a waxed brow. She'd been listening to my tirades for the past week. She didn't look surprised by this deadly turn in my thinking.

The bartender placed fresh martinis on the bar and Delia lifted her glass in a toast. Gold bracelets jangled against her tanned wrist. "To the end of Rick the Weasel."

Sliding a fresh olive into my mouth, I nodded and bit it. After a couple of vicious chomps, I swallowed and flicked my hand as though swatting away a pesky fly. "Poof. Gone!"

The bartender hadn't moved, watching me but giving no indication he'd heard our morbid conversation. "Is the drink okay?"

Delia took a sip and winked a cobalt eyelid.

"Perfect! And keep them coming. We're trying to decide the best way to kill a guy and get away with it."

The towheaded bartender drew back as we burst into delirious giggles. "Why would you wanna kill someone? Miss delaGarza, you're like, ya know, queen of L.A. news."

I laughed harder. Today I felt like an evil queen.

"Boyfriend troubles." Delia wrinkled her nose, made perfect by Dr. Chou in Beverly Hills. She looked from side to side, as though eavesdroppers lurked behind the potted plants. "Don't tell anyone, but the Queen got dumped by her boyfriend."

I glared at her. "Let's tell the whole damn town."

"You're the one planning to kill him."

I couldn't face the bartender. I didn't want to witness his attitude sliding from awe for the TV Queen to pity for an old lady dumped for a young chick. It happened all the time in L.A.

"What's your name, kid?" Delia loved introducing herself to bartenders and waiters and bringing them into our conversations. Exactly what I didn't want today.

"Toby. I'm filling in for Felipe."

"Good to meet you, Toby. I'm Delia Lindsay and you know Kimmie."

I sneaked a peek in his direction. To my surprise, his look of admiration hadn't diminished. I rewarded him with a queenly smile. "It's a pleasure meeting you. I hope you keep watching TV8."

His head bobbed like an eager puppy. "I'm thinking of going into broadcasting. Maybe you can give me pointers."

Ah, the real reason for his adoration. Ambition. Before I could respond, the outer door opened, drawing his attention.

I lifted my drink, wishing I could leap into the clear liquid and emerge devoid of feelings. The worst thing was I didn't know what I felt—sadness, betrayal, hurt, anger? Emotions swirled inside me like a mixed drink.

We couldn't kill Rick, but plotting his demise felt better than feeling sorry for myself. Rick claimed he was going to marry his Gen X or Gen Y babe. Whatever "Gen" she was, she wasn't part of our "Gen".

"I may be forty-three, but I look damn good in a short skirt." I smoothed my thigh-high skirt, and stretched to show off my legs and new Dior sandals. Brushing away a drop of liquor that splashed onto my low-cut top, I studied the hint of cleavage visible over a rounded neckline. "And at least my boobs are real."

I was getting wound up. Yanking off the Hermes' scarf that held back my shoulder length hair, I tilted my head forward, shaking it. "This black hair is natural. Look for one damn white hair."

"Calm down, babe. I'd give anything for your smooth skin and cheekbones that look so great on camera. I'll bet you haven't gained five pounds since college."

I winked at her. "Dad's tall, lean genes and Mom's perfect skin. What can I say?"

"Bitch!" She slapped my arm in a playful gesture. "I could spend thousands and you'd still look better."

Delia confessed to only the nose job and minor plastic surgery, but I suspected she *had* spent thousands. She just wouldn't admit it.

"My point is that it's all real." I retied the scarf.

She eyed me over the top of her glass. "Be honest. You won't miss Rick. You haven't loved him in years."

"Maybe not, but didn't you hear? I'm Queen of L.A. TV. This is no way to treat a queen."

"Unless you're Henry the Eighth."

I picked up a plastic pink saber and whacked at the air. "Off with his head."

"Rick treated you like a queen. What about the jewelry he gave you? He doesn't want anything back?"

My fingers toyed with his most recent gift—a gold pendant with diamonds forming two entwined hearts—one of a kind, according to the jeweler. "How could such a sweet prince turn into such a royal prick?"

"You know what your problem is?" She studied me as though I was a piece of flawed jewelry. "You don't take life seriously. You see it as scenes from a movie."

"I deal with reality at work. My personal life should be a fairy tale—peasant reporter rises from covering high speed chases and brush fires to anchor queen. It's like a royal court adventure, where I destroy the young pretenders to my throne trying to stab me in the back. Paula's gone, but now there's Gwen, the latest Twinkie."

Delia bowed her head. "I'm certain you will vanquish her, Your Anchor Highness."

We laughed, but I *did* feel like a Queen. Royalty in designer suits with a three-story castle on the beach and a Mercedes convertible serving as my carriage. The Queen ruled from her anchor chair, bestowing millions of loyal viewing subjects with knowledge of the day's events.

I swiveled on my barstool-throne. Beyond the windows, the afternoon sun painted golden slivers of light on the empty patio courtyard and turned the ocean into a glimmering spread of undulating azure crown jewels. What a magnificent June afternoon—the sort that made me glad I ruled in Southern California. A perfect day for the Queen to lick her wounds by planning the murder of that traitorous backstabber, Count Rick the Weasel.

When he was Rick the Debonair, he fit perfectly into my court. I smiled at Duchess Delia the Trustworthy. "You have to admit the jerk looked good in a tuxedo. He was a great date for parties."

"He *throws* great parties. He should have planned events instead of buying that wine shop."

I'd miss Rick's parties. They provided the perfect opportunity to hold court—evenings filled with exotic fare and great wine from his personal stock.

"His final party for me was a doozy." It sounded like a weekend fit for a queen—luxury hotel suite with ocean view, dinner by candlelight, a hot night in bed followed by a leisurely breakfast on the balcony. Then the party came to a crashing finale with one last proclamation: *"I've found someone younger."*

Frustration washed through me as I drained my glass. How did these things disappear so quickly?

"You need fresh tuxedo material." Delia tapped a nail on the bar to get Toby's attention before turning to me. "When was the last time you were without a guy?"

I couldn't remember. I'd been dating since I became a teenager and my older sister's boyfriends flirted with me.

"What about that guy you co-anchored with last month?" Delia asked. "Didn't he send flowers?"

"Brad Singer? He sent them because I was helpful and professional." I batted my eyes for effect but shook my head. "I don't like the gossip that goes with dating coworkers."

"What about that cop you were dating when you met Rick? Isn't he still single?"

"I don't know who you mean." My pulse quickened but I hated that thoughts of him still made me react. Now *there* was a worthy king—except he preferred being a commoner.

"Don't give me that! Suave as George Clooney, sexy as Brad Pitt. Built like a superhero. Want me to call and invite him to a party?"

"You're going on your South American adventure next week. There's no time for a party. Besides, I dumped him for Rick. I'm sure he'd love to hear the Weasel has now tossed *me* over."

"Hank Patterson!" Delia waved her bejeweled fist in triumph. "Cute as hell in uniform. I bet he'd look fine in a tuxedo."

"You wouldn't catch Hank in a tuxedo, and he's beyond uniforms. He's chief of police in Mira Loma." I ignored the warm surge that his name sent through me and changed the subject. "I'd rather see Rick in a tux stained with blood. Maybe I should spring for a hit man. Where do you find one? Hire-a-thug-dot-com, 1-800-killers?"

"I'm sure Walt knows shady characters. You should see the guys he brings to the house."

Before I could pursue her comment about her husband's friends, Toby arrived with fresh drinks. "I hope this is okay, Miss delaGarza."

"I'm certain it is, Toby."

He watched as I took a sip, eyes anxious.

"Perfect." I winked at him.

Toby grinned and blushed like a thirteen-year-old

page boy.

"Say, Toby, do you own a tuxedo?" Delia nudged my knee under the bar.

I shot her a fierce look. She'd been setting me up since we met as college freshmen. I'd never liked it.

"I know a rental place. I had to get one for a performance. I'm studying drama." Toby's eager eyes sought me out. "I make recordings of announcers and study them, like your newscasts. Maybe you could listen to my practice recordings and tell me what you think?" He pulled a black iPhone from his pocket.

"Sure," Delia agreed. "Give him a card or your email address."

I took a silver card holder from my Prada handbag, removed a card and handed it to him.

He studied it as though it contained a hidden treasure map. "Thank you, Miss delaGarza."

Delia picked up the holder. "Nice. With your initials outlined in diamonds?"

"Birthday present from Rick, the soon-to-be-dead prick."

"I promise not to tell police how he died." Toby grinned as he pocketed my card along with his phone.

Delia's laugh rang out and I glanced around to make certain we weren't disturbing anyone. An older man at a nearby table frowned at us. He cleared his throat loud enough to draw Toby's attention. Excusing himself, Toby walked toward the table.

"He'd look cute in a tuxedo." Delia eyed him as though contemplating a chocolate sundae. "Don't you have an event coming up? Wouldn't it be great to have a young stud escort?"

"If I return to dating I'm setting two rules—no

coworkers and no young guys. I'm not a cougar!"

Her eyes grew wide as she pointed a red tipped finger at the door. "There's tuxedo material. Check the guy who just walked in. He's not wearing a wedding band..."

"You can see that from here?" I glanced into the mirror and my breath caught. The tall man carried himself with regal assurance and sported the patrician look of privilege. His peach polo shirt emphasized his tan as did white tennis shorts that displayed long, muscular legs. A man who wasn't afraid to wear peach was fit to be king, right? Or gay. This guy didn't look gay, despite the shirt, chiseled features and precisely trimmed silver hair.

Delia was right. Enough of this pity-party. A new king was preferable to thirsting for revenge. I swiveled toward the door.

His eyes zeroed in on me like blue lasers and I smiled my queenly best. He tipped his head, returning the smile. Definitely royal material!

"Maybe he wants to buy us a drink." Never one to let a good looking man get away, Delia slid off her stool as he disappeared through the glass door that led to the outdoor deck.

I held up my drink to her departing back. "To the conquest of new kingdoms."

Before I could contemplate where to find those kingdoms, the outer door swung open again. My martini-dazed mind cleared, and I whirled around and grabbed a menu from the bar to shield my face.

Rick's new girlfriend had just pranced through the door, blonde hair dancing around bony, golden shoulders.

Chapter Two

I hunched behind the menu until I heard approaching footsteps and caught sight of Delia's emerald skirt.

"He's meeting his sister." Disappointment dripped from her voice as she resumed her seat. "What's with the menu? I'm not hungry yet. I'm doing fine with the olives."

I jerked my thumb toward the door. "It's her!"

"Who? The bimbo?" Her voice rang out in the quiet room.

My barstool wobbled as I reached out to shush her, and I teetered back and forth. "Del, keep your voice down," I hissed. "What's she doing here? Is he with her? Can you see without being obvious?"

She craned her neck toward the door. "I don't see Rick. She's with an older guy who's wearing a toupee and a young blonde babe who's probably a trophy wife."

And she would know a trophy wife. Delia proclaimed in college her goal was to marry older, wealthy men. Walter was her third.

"You're safe," she said. "They're going to the patio. How do you know it's her?"

Warmth rushed to my cheeks, and I put the menu between us as I delivered a hated confession. "I checked Rick's phone. He had pictures of her, and her name was on top in his contact file—Bobbi. Not only that, but you know how he hates programming things? He had her address listed. She lives in a gated mansion in Bel Air."

Delia pushed the menu aside to confront me. "You went by her house?"

The memory still disturbed me. "Like a jealous teenager."

She erupted with a raucous giggle. "Why didn't you call me to go with you? I love that sort of shit."

That was why I hadn't called. I kept hoping to change my mind. I still couldn't believe I'd stooped low enough to stalk the Bimbo. "Enough. What happened with the silver-haired god?"

Her brows danced up and down above a sly smile. "I gave him your number."

"What did you tell him? That I'm dumped and desperate? I hope you didn't give him my real name." Giving false names to guys was one of the first tricks we'd played together in school.

Delia rolled her eyes. "He knew who you were, of course. He wants to meet you. His name is Miles S. Brookings."

The name was vaguely familiar.

She leaned toward me. "As in *Miles Standish* Brookings?"

"Like the pilgrim? You're lining me up with pilgrims?"

She flicked her hand at me. "Dummy! Pilgrim Development. Surely you've seen that name plastered on building sites from here to Riverside. His name constantly pops up in the society columns. He's between wives so maybe he'll call."

"Whatever." I slapped back at her and my hand hit my drink, tipping it over. The glass shattered as it hit the bar, and the sound reverberated like the crack of a rifle shot. Cold liquor splashed me.

"Oh, shit!" As I jerked away, I wobbled and the olive rolled toward me. I stabbed at it to keep it from falling and toppled off the stool. Somehow I managed to land on my feet, but the vision of me tottering on my stiletto sandals to save the damned olive was so ludicrous, I burst into giggles. The olive bounced harmlessly to the floor and Delia joined in until our wild laughter echoed through the bar.

Good thing the group had gone outside. I didn't know if the girl knew me, but it would be quite a story to tell Rick about the drunk and disorderly Ex.

"Are you all right, Miss delaGarza?" Toby rushed to our aid, concern etched on his face. He handed me a wad of napkins and began cleaning up the broken glass.

"My olive attacked me," I said, setting off another round of hysterical laughter.

Using her cocktail napkin, Delia picked up the stem of my broken glass—a wicked looking object with a sharp point at one end. "May I keep this? I might be able to use it."

Toby flicked her a look of uncertainty but didn't protest. Delia wrapped it in a napkin and stuffed it into her purse.

Soaked with gin, I excused myself. "Order me a fresh drink and watch for Rick. I don't want to run into him."

Delia pointed a finger at me, similar to aiming a pistol. "I'll shoot the sucker on sight."

****

Walking into the cool quiet of the restroom was like entering church. I paused, letting silence envelop me, fighting to clear my fuzzy head. Of all the places with trappings of wealth that I frequented, bathrooms in upscale restaurants never failed to amaze me. Marble walls and floors. Stalls with wood-shuttered doors. Vases filled with fresh flowers on the vanity beside piles of cloth towels and baskets of toiletries and hair sprays. A hair dryer was hooked into one edge of the basket. Did people use this stuff?

Water pooled at the edge of one of the marble sinks. Making a face, I reached over and plucked a towel from the basket and wiped it. I glanced at my reflection in the mirror. For an instant I wasn't the number one anchor in the number two television market in the country, wearing Chanel casual wear. I was young Kimmie D, in faded jeans and sneakers, scrubbing toilets in fancy restaurants to earn money to get through college.

With a shake of my head, Kimmie D vanished and I stopped wiping. I focused on cleaning the liquor off my knit shell with a damp cloth. Behind me, movement caught my eye. The woman from the Bimbo's group stepped through the door. Beyond her, Rick's young fiancée came into view. Bobbi. From her wild blonde hair to the blue eye shadow to the pink-and-green extra-tight, extra-short dress to her bright extra-high yellow stiletto sandals she resembled a real-life Barbie doll.

She drew back when she saw me. For an instant we stood frozen like a snapshot. The girl moved first, tossing back her head, like a defiant rearing horse. Her blonde mane flew in all directions before settling back around her narrow skull. She stepped into one of the stalls and closed the wooden door.

I stood my ground. I wasn't going to let these two chase me out. I focused on drying my top with a soft towel.

Bobbi's petite friend approached the vanity. She was in her mid-thirties, with a pixie haircut and gold hoop earrings that were too large for her small face. Her tanned face looked untouched by makeup, except a hint of blue eye shadow. She wore a sleeveless white cotton blouse with beige trim that showed off small, freckled shoulders. Matching capris clung to short, muscular legs. I'd seen the outfit at Neiman's carrying a two-thousand-dollar price tag. Thick gold and gem-studded jewelry dripped from her wrists and fingers. Delia was wrong. This woman was no trophy wife. She'd been born to money and wore it like a gilded cloak. Pixie and Barbie were pure California thoroughbreds.

The woman nodded at me with a nasty thin-lipped smile. "Looks like you're having a good time."

My anchor smile came forth, though my lips were numb. I was tempted to tell the joke about being attacked by my olive, but instead I turned to gather my purse from the counter. It hung open and a lipstick tube spilled out. I reached for it but my visual acuity had grown impaired and I missed.

The woman caught it as it rolled off the counter. With a throaty laugh, she handed back the golden tube. "Had a few too many?"

"I'm fine," I lied. I took the lipstick and turned to the mirror to prove it. The hazel eyes that stared back looked glazed and the high cheekbones Delia admired were flushed. For a moment I feared the woman could see through my perfectly made-up face to the unwaxed brows of Kimmie D.

I took my time reapplying lipstick and powdering my nose in deliberate motions. I wasn't Kimmie. I was the Queen of L.A. TV.

Ask Toby.

The door flew open, revealing Delia. She looked from me to the Pixie, sizing up the woman like a rival gunfighter.

Here it was. Showdown in the Geneva John.

Delia, whom I considered the Doc Holliday of bathroom brawls, fired first.

"I hate women who go to the bathroom in pairs, but I couldn't wait any longer." She took cover behind the door of a stall, leaving me on the open battlefield armed only with my lipstick.

Pixie fussed with her hair, ignoring me, but she shot back, aiming her voice toward the Bimbo's stall. "Bobbi, is the wedding announcement in this week's paper or the next?"

Aha! Aiming at the heart. I ignored her to let her know she'd missed her intended target.

"Next week, I think." Bobbi the Bimbo's voice was small, an uncertain potshot.

"I'm so pleased Rick talked you into registering at David Orgell. It is *the* place for brides." The Pixie was determined to wound. She faced me point blank. "Don't you agree?"

The Beverly Hills jewelry store with its array of china and silver, plus an exquisite jewelry collection, was one of Rick's favorite places. My gaze fell on the platinum diamond-studded bracelet on my wrist and the diamond and sapphire ring on my right hand.

Wait. I had weapons and some pretty damn lethal

16

ammo. I held up my hand to let the light catch the glitter of diamonds, like an explosion from a firing gun. "Absolutely. My old boyfriend bought both of these there."

A barrage of dual flushing drowned the Pixie's response, but she appraised my jewelry with glittering eyes. She knew who the boyfriend was.

Direct hit.

Delia's grin was pure malice as she stepped from her stall and discharged a rapid-fire round. "Didn't you tell me he bought you something there last week?"

"This?" I touched the delicate pendant at my throat in reflex. All eyes traveled there. It was like dropping a cache of dynamite. We all knew who bought it and Delia's words made it clear he'd given it to me since becoming engaged.

The Pixie's catty smile froze, and her tanned face blanched as Bobbi stepped out of her stall. The girl's wide eyes rested on the diamond pendant. The confident confection who'd tossed her blonde hair vanished. She crossed her arms and hugged herself, as though taking a direct hit to the mid-section. Her eyes wore a wounded look that penetrated my insides worse than a bullet.

What was I doing? This kid had probably never done battle like this. Delia and I were old hands at bathroom shootouts. This was Billy the Kid facing a farm boy experimenting with his first set of pistols.

I closed my purse and marched out of the restroom without waiting for Delia to go in for the kill.

She stomped out behind me. "Damn bitches! Maybe we should bomb the wedding and wipe them all out."

Del believed in big-time revenge, having once spray-painted a lover's Rolls Royce. She'd destroyed another boyfriend's marriage out of spite and socially demolished her first husband's ex-wife. Vengeance soothed her, but I didn't have the stomach for issuing pain, despite my loud proclamations against Rick. I'd wounded that girl but I felt like I was the one bleeding as I struggled to walk a straight line back to the bar.

Chapter Three

Sunday, 4:30 a.m.

A rocking woke me, setting off a throbbing inside my skull, which threatened to explode.

What the hell?

For an instant, confusion clouded my brain, and fear clutched at my chest. The bed shook as though I was having great sex with an athletic guy. But I was in no condition for anything like that. My head pounded like a bass drum. No, a Chinese gong.

As faint tinkling drifted into my groggy consciousness and the agitation intensified, I realized what it was—earthquake. I waited for the shaking to stop as my heart began to thump in rhythm with the throb in my head.

Fingers of fear edged into my muscles. How long was this sucker going to last? Was this the Big One that brought the house crashing down on me? The ten-point-zero that cut California in half?

The shuddering slowed, but the pulsating rhythm in my head intensified from one gong player to a symphony. My dry mouth resembled a basket of cotton balls, but my stomach threatened a violent revolt if I tried to drink anything.

I forced myself to my feet. Beside the bed, the green numbers on the clock read 4:32.

Rebecca Grace

Four in the friggin' morning. Why didn't earthquakes ever hit in the afternoon? I wanted to crawl back into bed, but when the earth trembled, TV Queen Kimberly delaGarza had to act. Time to go on the air and calm the Southland subjects.

I didn't bother checking in. Showing up for work on a big story was automatic. "Preferred procedure," the boss called it. I considered it a "pain in the ass," but my agent Evan Flynn labeled it a "profitable inconvenience," useful at contract time.

I tried a quick, cold shower to numb my skull. That's how I felt—like a total numbskull for drinking so much on Saturday. To make matters worse, my stomach roiled like a storm swept sea. Dressing was agony—what do you wear to an earthquake? I grabbed the first suit in the closet and matched it to a pair of Jimmy Choo sandals.

My stomach and head competed for a gold medal in misery as I drove to the station, searching in vain for open coffee shops. My cell phone buzzed and I checked the number before hitting the talk button for Reba Mackenzie, our executive producer.

"On my way." My voice had the timbre of a frog after a busy night at the bog.

"Superb! Probably not much damage, but you never know." How could anyone sound so awake at this time of the morning?

I cleared my throat. "Do you know where it was?"

Her response was staccato, Reba's normal cadence. She could make a vending machine selection sound critical. "Near Baker. The satellite truck and a crew are on the way, another van is headed to Cal Tech and another is searching for local damage. If they're not on

20

the air when you arrive, get 'em going. Lindy is a new producer."

Baker was a desert town on Interstate 15 between Las Vegas and Los Angeles. A crack in the road or downed bridges that closed the freeway could wreak havoc on Sunday afternoon when California gamblers came home.

Delia, you evil witch! I recalled only fuzzy bits and pieces of the day after our battle with the Bimbo. We turned from discussing murder to Delia's upcoming four-week trip to the Amazon. Her husband eventually sent a car for her and a driver to take me and my car home.

Now I felt like a throbbing piece of crap. I gulped back rising waves of nausea, sipping directly from a Pepto Bismol bottle like a wino as I turned into the station lot. The parking space painted with my name was taken, so I parked in my co-anchor's slot. I'd beaten James to work, let him walk the few extra steps.

Peter Murphy, a weekend reporter, lounged by the door. "Wow, the big guns. I get to be part of the 'Jim and Kim Show' on Sunday."

I was tempted to yank the cup of coffee from his hand as I caught a whiff of the aroma. His sarcasm annoyed me but wasn't surprising. I'd embarrassed him with on-air questions he should have been able to answer. He probably blamed me for being stuck on weekends.

"Don't let the promo people hear you say that," I replied. Our management loved people to think of us as "Jim and Kim," but they used our formal names to keep away from that silly rhyme. "Shouldn't you be on your way to a live shot?"

"Grumpy to be up so early? I'm waiting for the van to pick me up."

"Uh-huh." I yanked open the door and it brushed him as I walked past.

Behind me, he cursed. "You hit my coffee. Shit, that's hot!"

I suppressed a smile as I marched into the building to the newsroom. Weekend anchor Gwen Cardinal sat at the flash-camera desk, fidgeting with a microphone, cheeks flushed. "Someone needs to write up information." She stared at the computer in front of her and gestured wildly around the room. "I can't go on the air without written copy."

A young woman in a baggy T-shirt and worn jeans that hung from nonexistent hips hunched over the desk, sorting through papers. This must be the new producer. Mousy hair the color of a dirty spider web hung in an uneven curtain around a pale, hawkish face. She looked two years out of high school.

"All I know is what I wrote down. Can't you say that?" Her apologetic tone was lost on Gwen.

"Then what? What do I do after that?"

"I don't know!" The girl lifted thin shoulders, looking ready to burst into tears. Bright red spots dotted sunken cheeks. "We could get on first. No one else is on the air."

I jerked my gaze to banks of monitors that ringed the upper newsroom walls. Sure enough, stations were broadcasting infomercials. Only our station had a red stripe with a news crawl along the bottom of the screen, mentioning the earthquake.

Adrenaline surged through me, erasing my cobwebs. Quake size might be the number that mattered at the moment, but tomorrow the ratings' numbers would reign, along with who got on the air first.

"I'll do it," I said, and they whirled toward me. Gwen's eyes narrowed to brown pinpoints of anger, and a startled look flashed across the young producer's face.

I sensed confrontation in the making. Gwen was early weekend anchor, but I knew Alan, our news director, would want me on the air.

Gwen's gaze shot daggers my way. "You're not ready. You look..."

She paused, but I knew how bad I must look. I'd seen the bags under my eyes that resembled steamer trunks when I got dressed. In my current condition I knew I was unrecognizable without makeup.

"Give me two minutes." My voice rang with more confidence than I felt. It would take longer than that to fix what ailed me, but I couldn't back down. Gwen had made it clear that she'd love to claim my job.

"Why should you go on? I'm the morning weekend anchor." Gwen appealed to the producer to make the decision.

I tried to keep from sounding catty. "I know what to say. Are we getting any calls? What about on our website? Any people sending in comments on what they felt or if they have damage? Fire up the camera. Let's go!"

The girl blinked at my orders, caramel eyes darting to Gwen for permission.

My pounding head was like a snare drum. Tired of hesitation, I snapped my fingers. "Come on, Laurie."

"Lindy," she corrected, not moving.

Gwen started to argue, but Reba marched into the newsroom. Her curly red hair tumbled around padded shoulders and she teetered on three-inch mules that made her nearly six feet tall. Her oversized sweater was a jumble of red and orange streaks over neon pink tights and her fuzzy mules were crimson. She began firing orders in a sharp tone that would make a drill sergeant proud.

"Gwen, get on the air until Kimberly is ready. James is in Las Vegas, but Brad Singer's on his way." Brad was her evening co-anchor, and she bristled again.

I ignored her and smiled at Reba. "How did you manage to put on makeup so early in the morning?"

She never wore foundation over her perfect white skin, but her emerald eye shadow and thick black liner that made her green eyes resemble a cat's were in place.

"I do it in the car at red lights." She winked, and without missing a beat, turned to the producer. "Lindy, we need information. Surely people are tweeting what they felt."

I snapped my fingers as a sudden thought hit me. "Call James on his cell. He should have felt the quake in Vegas. We'll do a phone report. Also, call Earl's Diner in Baker. It's open 24-7. See if anyone will talk."

"Is there anything else you need?" The girl's voice was no longer questioning.

"Coffee, Laurie. Lots of coffee."

I started to turn toward the makeup room, but caught a look of dismay on her face. I could hear the story now—I marched in like a diva, demanded to be put on the air and ordered her about like a waitress. And her name wasn't Laurie.

A sudden jolt sent everyone scrambling. The girl stared at me with wide, terrified eyes.

I smiled, voicing bravado I didn't feel in my shaken

insides. "It'll be okay, Lindy. Feed me info, and we'll get through this."

****

Four hours later the crisis had passed and the floor director counted me down.

"Thank you for tuning in. We'll update today's quake throughout the day, and join Brad and Gwen at five for the latest." I nodded at Brad beside me and presented a wide smile until the red light on the studio camera went dark.

He removed his microphone and held out both hands. "You are phenomenal."

Brad was a new anchor who had come over from the network, but he resembled an L.A. boy. Tall, photogenic, and oozing charm. His sandy hair sported a style that would fall into place no matter how the wind blew and his suit was Armani, though he'd arrived in a T-shirt and jeans and still wore his Nikes.

I nodded and winced as my head resumed its earlier pounding. At least aspirin and coffee had slowed the tympanic symphony in my head to an occasional bongo solo. Lifting my shoulders, I stretched and rolled my aching head around.

"Feeling better?" he asked.

"It shows?"

"Only the red eyes." His grin was playful as he reached over to brush his fingers over my temple.

Closing my eyes, I concentrated on the soft circular motions of his moving fingers. "All I need is a good massage."

His hands dropped to the shoulder of my Escada suit. "I've been told I have great hands."

My eyes flew open. Was he flirting? I might be a

free agent, but there was my rule about dating coworkers. I eased away.

Reba appeared at the edge of the set and clapped. "My heroes! We beat everyone in town. Paula Gardner and Joe Harte didn't show till an hour ago. Wanna be my permanent team?"

"Keep paying me what I'm getting and I'll work weekends." I moved toward her, farther from Brad's tempting hands.

"Pay me half of what you pay her, and I'll do anything you want."

Ouch. My salary was a major sore point. Every time Jim or I signed a new contract, our salaries were open topics of discussion. I'd been told reporters once counted up words in an hour-long script to determine how much I was paid for each word.

"I'm buying mimosas," Reba announced.

My stomach revolted at the idea. I'd barely made it through the morning. I patted her arm as I left the set. "Next time."

Escaping the bright studio felt good, but the searing lights of the makeup room were nearly as bad. After dimming them, I sank onto one of the padded chairs. Seeing my reflection in the wall of mirrors was painful. My eyes were bloodshot and I'd applied so much makeup even Picasso might be proud. I felt like one of his paintings filled with rich, distorted color.

My cell phone buzzed on the counter, informing me I had messages. I reached over and checked the numbers—my mother, my sister Nancy, Delia, and Rick.

Rick the Weasel? What did he want? We hadn't talked since "The Great Break Up" one week ago today.

The prick could rot in hell.

I punched "call" and said, "Mom." She answered so quickly she must have been sitting on her phone.

"You looked wonderful, *Mija,*" she cooed. "*Que bonita.*"

Four hours on the air, calming the city, and all Mom could say was that I looked pretty? At least she hadn't spotted my hangover. If I looked haggard on the air, she would tell me.

"I don't think that shade of orange is a good color in the morning. It's too bright. You should have worn your green suit. It brings out the green in your eyes."

"I'll remember next time." It was pointless to say I didn't have time to think about clothes. Ever since I took her with me to shop before my first reporting job, she had appointed herself my style expert. She considered it her duty to keep me looking good.

"What time will you be here for dinner?" she asked.

"I've been up since five..." I sighed. Normally I scheduled Delia's martini lunches around Mom's Sunday dinners, but this weekend had been our only opportunity to discuss Rick's betrayal before Del left town. Now I faced driving to Pomona with a raging hangover and Mom wouldn't accept an earthquake as an excuse. As the orchestra tuned up in my head, I agreed to arrive by three.

"*Bueno.* Next time remember the green suit."

My phone beeped as I was about to tap off. I feared the sound of my sister's strident voice as I hit the talk button, but it was worse.

"Good morning, you were great today," Rick said as though we were still friends.

The throbbing returned in the form of a persistent thump, like an unwanted guest at the door. "What do you want?"

"You're certainly in a mood." His voice grew teasing.

"Goodbye, Rick."

"Wait! We need to discuss things..."

I started to click off, but caught the words "clothes" as he continued to talk.

"I must return your belongings," he was saying. "And I left things at your place."

Oh, hell. Some of my clothes and shoes remained at his house. "Pack them up and I'll get them. I may dump your crap in the alley behind your store."

"Not my silver bat."

"Your *silver-plated* bat. You left it at my house."

Trust Rick the baseball fan to focus on that stupid bat. He claimed it once belonged to Duke Snider when the Dodgers were still in Brooklyn.

"For your protection, but then I got you a gun. You can keep that, and we talked about not returning gifts like jewelry..."

"Good," I snapped, glancing at the Rolex he'd given me.

"One thing..." Why did the man never finish a thought? How had I put up with that for so long? "That diamond pendant I sent you last week..."

The one I'd used to subdue the Bimbo and her pal? "Yes?"

"You realize I bought it out of guilt. You wore it today and it upset Bobbi."

I was on the verge of yanking it off, but his comment stopped me. "So?"

"Why did you tell her about it?"

So Rick had been lurking as Delia and I suspected. We spotted his car as we left Geneva. We'd even tossed a nasty note onto the front seat.

"I need it back, Kimberly, and please don't make any more scenes."

"Scenes?" What was he talking about? Had he seen me fall off the barstool?

"You need to find better ways to spend weekends than getting drunk, becoming disorderly, and tormenting girls."

I'd had enough. "Wells, you low-life fucking piece of crap! You really want to know how I spent the day? Planning the best way to kill your lousy, lying ass!"

I threw the phone on the counter with such force that it shattered on the tile, sending plastic shards bouncing in all directions.

A gasp came from behind me, and I swung around. Gwen and Lindy stood in the doorway, mouths open, eyes filled with shock. Behind them, Brad stared at me as though he was looking at a deranged stranger.

Chapter Four

Friday, midnight

"Screw you, miserable prick," I muttered as I guided my car along Pacific Coast Highway toward Rick's wine shop.

The last thing I wanted to do on a Friday after work was see the Weasel and return his shit. But he'd been calling all week, pestering. I should simply toss it on the doorstep.

My cell phone vibrated. Probably Rick checking to see if I was coming. I knew it couldn't be Delia. She'd be boarding her flight for South America. When Brad's name appeared, I picked up the phone and answered.

"Thanks for giving me background information for my story tonight," he said. "Feel like dancing? The night crew is headed over to that retro place, Azure."

"Unfortunately I'm on my way to see my ex-boyfriend."

"Ex?" Was that surprise in his voice?

I hadn't told anyone at work about Rick, nor had I explained my outburst the previous Sunday. I'd been looking for a reason to let Brad know. "Extremely ex. At least he will be, once I return his shit."

Rick's belongings were heaped into three boxes in my trunk. Everything except that diamond pendant. I'd sent it to him by courier earlier in the week.

"Come by after you're done. If not, may I buy you dinner this weekend and help you make a fresh start?"

Should I take a chance with a coworker? Delia had been right about one thing—it had been ages since I'd been without male companionship. A Queen without a consort? I didn't like the idea. "Call me tomorrow."

"It's late to be driving alone. Where are you?"

"Just entering the business district in Mira Loma." I rounded a bend into a familiar sweeping boulevard with its welcome sign surrounded by palm trees.

"Isn't that a dangerous area? Maybe I should come help."

"Thanks a lot. I live not too far from here. It's safe enough. Besides, I'm armed with a baseball bat and a gun."

"I didn't know you could shoot."

"Rick bought it for me, and I took one class. I never liked it, so I'm giving it back. He's lucky I'm a lousy shot. I'd be tempted to shoot him."

"Now, be cool."

"I'll be cool as a cucumber in a chilled salad." Easy to say, but I didn't feel cool. Despite the chilly breeze that swept in from the beach, sweat dampened my skin, sticking to me like a clammy veil. "I'm here. I'll carry the bat for protection, though he'd scream if I used it. You'd think it was the Holy Grail."

"Stay calm. Talk to you later."

****

My attempt at calm lasted until I stood at Rick's front door. My stomach wiggled like it contained a bowl of nervous goldfish as I pushed the after-hours buzzer. The RW Fine Wines logo caught my gaze. I helped design the stylized script graphic.

Prick!

My hands shook and I felt as though I grasped a greased rope, dangling over a cauldron of seething emotion. I gripped the bat. My palm was wet against the metal. I felt like a major league hitter coming to bat in a World Series. Score tied, bases loaded and two out in bottom of the ninth.

"Keep cool," I whispered. "You're Kimberly delaGarza, Queen of TV. This is the last time you ever have to face him." Like Robert Redford in *The Natural*, I'd end this game in a victorious shower of fireworks.

Seeing no movement inside, I jabbed the buzzer again. Maybe I should toss the bat into the ocean across the street. Let him spend the rest of his life combing the beach for it. I should dump his crap here so homeless scavengers could scramble like fans in the bleachers after a home run ball, taking their pick of Ralph Lauren shirts, Tommy Hilfiger sportswear, and Armani suits. Someone might use the gun to hold up the store. Even as I imagined the event, light enveloped me and the door slid open.

Rick greeted me with a smile. Handsome enough to be a male model, he maintained a year-round tan that emphasized salt-and-pepper hair and soft brown eyes. His well-defined cheeks and cleft chin might have been sculpted by a GQ photographer.

I refused to say hello as I stepped inside, tapping the bat on the tiled floor.

"Good show tonight," he said.

I froze and studied him like a batter sizing up an opposing pitcher. For once Mr. Impeccable was a mess. His hair was mussed as though he'd run his hands through it. Wrinkles creased his blue shirt and the sleeves were rolled up on his arms. His eyes were bloodshot. I stifled the urge to ask if the Bimbo was wearing him out.

"Your crap is in the car." I pointed the bat toward the door.

He offered an easy pitch in a soft voice. "You want a glass of wine? I've opened a new red." He gestured toward the area where he hosted wine tasting parties.

I spotted a bottle and two glasses. Trying to strike me out with a seasoned Pinot Noir?

I stood my ground, the batter digging into the box. "I'd rather go home. Get your stuff."

As I started to hand him my keys he pulled a key ring out of his pocket, held up a duplicate, and walked out the door.

Ouch! He'd delivered a nasty pitch that brushed me back. I stared at my key ring, realizing not only did he have my keys, but his house and car key remained on my ring. Like the commitment we'd made when keys were exchanged, this was the ultimate moment in the other direction. The Return of the Keys.

My grip on the composure rope slipped. Maybe I no longer loved him, but did all those years count for nothing? What about loyalty? I shook my head. We were on opposite sides. Wearing uniforms of different teams.

Huffing with exertion, he returned with a box. "There's a lot there."

I nodded, a knot forming in my throat. "I'm leaving your keys on the counter."

He blinked in surprise, as though The Key Exchange just hit him too. "Okay."

While he made two more trips, I paced the shop.

Together we designed the layout when he expanded. Delia and I labored for hours over handwritten labels above wine bins.

Taking a deep breath, I fought nostalgia. The last couple of years hadn't been hot on the romance scale, but they were fun—chatty evenings at favorite restaurants, getaways to Mexico, weekends of Saturday parties and Sunday brunches, baseball games and movie premieres.

He returned with the final box. "Sure you don't want wine? We should talk."

"We have nothing to discuss." I had to get away before I broke down. Crying was a certain strike out. I still held the bat. Tapping it against the floor helped me keep a grip on my emotions.

"What about our business plans?" His eyes darted sideways. "We should...uh...discuss money..."

We had money invested together through our shared accountant—his buddy, Carl. Rick had even given me a partnership in the shop as repayment for money I'd loaned him. "I'll have Adrienne call Carl."

He drew back and hurt flashed in his eyes. Foul ball. "Your lawyer? That's cold. These are personal deals."

"We no longer have a personal connection."

"Someday you'll understand. Maybe if you got to know Bobbi—"

"No!"

His hands flipped up. "Maybe that was the wrong thing to say."

"Damn right it was." I snapped my fingers. "Give me my keys. Where are my clothes?"

He took out his key ring and gestured. "Your

things are in those suitcases and clothes bag. The shoes are in the tote bag."

I looked toward the bags. We bought the matching set of Gucci luggage for a trip to Alaska and used them when we traveled together.

Putting down the bat, I reached for the keys. This had become a standoff, a tie, game called on account of pain. I just wanted it over. I walked toward the bags.

"Let me know if anything is missing. I was surprised she managed to get all your things into those bags."

Anger pricked me like a sharp needle and I whirled toward him. "She packed my stuff?"

His response to my rising voice was a shrug. He approached the bottle of wine and glasses, oblivious to the anger that zoomed through my veins. "Yes..."

"You let Bobbi touch my clothes?"

His nod was a high, fat pitch over the middle of the plate. "Let's have a glass of wine and I'll take your bags to the car."

My hold on the greasy emotional rope released, and I gripped the bat. As I slid into a hot boiling pot of anger, I swung for the fences.

Chapter Five

Saturday, 7:30 a.m.

The chiming doorbell jerked me from deep sleep. I blinked at the clock beside my bed. This wasn't how I wanted to start the beginning of a new life. The Week from Hell that began with an earthquake and concluded with a midnight baseball battle was over.

The melodious chimes rang again. Who dared show up at my doorstep this early? I started to bury my head under my pillow, but...

I shot to a sitting position. Bad news came from early visits.

Mom! She lived alone in a townhouse in a retirement community in Pomona. It was supposed to be safe, but...

Delia? She'd boarded a plane for South America last night. What if it crashed?

Coldness seeped into my bones as I stumbled out of bed. I rubbed bare arms to shake the chill. Grabbing my terrycloth robe, I groped my way down two flights of stairs to the bottom floor entry.

The bell became persistent. *Urgent, urgent, urgent*, it called. Tightening the belt on my robe, I peered through the peephole and blinked.

What the hell? My mind refused to register what I was seeing.

Hank Patterson.

I dropped my head, breath catching as I grasped the truth. "Del, you evil witch," I muttered. Her parting shot as she left town was to call my old boyfriend.

Brushing back my hair, I glanced down at my faded yellow robe. How could she do this to me? Checking the peephole again, I studied him. His full, pouty lips wore a scowl, serious blue eyes intent on the bell. He shifted, leaned toward the door and pounded on it. The quick move and loud noise startled me and I emitted a cry.

"Kimberly?"

Had he heard me? I clapped my hand over my mouth and held my breath.

"Kimberly? I need to see you."

Delia must have come up with a tall tale to get him here, but he didn't look pleased. Maybe she told him I was suicidal after my breakup with Rick.

Fine, let him see me without makeup, with my hair a ratty mess. In an act of defiance toward Delia, I yanked open the door. Let him see I was okay, even if I was a disheveled disaster.

"What are you doing here? Is this some kind of sick joke?"

For a second my harsh greeting knocked him off balance. "Are you okay?"

"Of course I am. Why wouldn't I be?"

I stared up at all six-foot-two of him. Oh, hell, I'd made a stupid mistake. Here I was, looking my worst. And he looked good. Oh, so damn good. As crisp and clean as a summer morning. Ebony hair neatly combed. Eyes as clear as a deepwater lake. A leather bomber jacket emphasized wide shoulders, while his clinging polo shirt outlined the flat lines of his midsection. I'll bet he was as hard as ever, a six pack of abs before the term grew stylish. Black jeans showcased his long legs. A strange heat fired up my lower inner regions. This guy could still ignite my female hormones.

He cleared his throat and attempted a smile that only made me more aware of his masculine appeal. "May I come inside? I need to talk to you."

I brushed aside a stray strand of hair. I didn't like anyone to see me without makeup. Especially Hank. I should greet him in full female armor—clingy dress with a low cut neckline and my face in flattering war paint.

"Do you know what time it is?" I turned my irritation on him. I didn't know if I was angry at myself for answering the door or at Delia for instigating the awkward meeting. "It's seven in the freaking morning."

"Sorry to disturb you, but this is important." Was that a hint of softness in his voice? He'd often teased me for my bitchiness before noon. Mr. Macho seldom spoke in this gentle tone. He was all hard police jargon or manly swagger. "Official business."

Official business? Why would the Mira Loma police chief pay an official visit to me on Saturday morning? I stepped back and opened the door. Looking beyond him as he crossed the threshold, I expected Delia to leap out and wink before running off on her trip. But the driveway held only Hank's black police sedan.

I turned to lead him upstairs, but still wobbly from sleep, I nearly tripped on the shoes I'd removed when I arrived home the previous night. I frowned at the dark dots staining my hot pink satin pumps. The latest from

Dior and I'd never be able to wear them again.

From behind me came the sound of Hank's quick intake of breath.

I whipped around. "What?"

His gaze was pointed at the ground, but he jerked up, eyes narrowed. Their blue depths bored into me as though searching for something. "Maybe this isn't a good idea."

"Too late, cop." I adopted the sarcastic tone I'd used when he got that grave look. "You woke me, and I'm curious about this 'official business.' Come up, and I'll buy you a cup of coffee."

I was aware of him behind me as we climbed the stairs. I could sense tense energy emanating from him. I wished I had eyes on my backside. Was he noticing the way I moved? He once claimed that watching me from behind was mesmerizing. Could my wiggling tush still tantalize him?

Hank had never been in my current home and he paused at the top of the stairs. I could imagine what he was thinking. The beachside townhouse once belonged to a TV star who had it custom built when he was on top of the ratings world. I got it for a song when he had to pay taxes on income he neglected to report.

The house was three stories of glass in front. Its top two stories offered a glorious view of the ocean a stretch of beach away. The bottom floor housed my office, a private, walled-in patio and a two-car garage. This middle level kept me above a walking/biking path and the prying eyes of strolling beach goers. It consisted of a large open room with the living area taking up the full width of the house. The dining space and kitchen were grouped along the back wall with a wide granite counter providing separation.

"Nice place," Hank said, looking toward the windows. "Much better view than the back of a mall, which is what I see from my front window."

I could imagine how much better the view must be. An anchorwoman made more money than a police chief. Excessive salaries paid to broadcasters versus the low pay of public servants had been the source of one of many arguments near the end of our relationship.

With a wave toward the kitchen, I started toward the flight of stairs that led up to my third-floor bedroom. No way could I continue our discussion in this horrible condition. I hadn't even brushed my teeth.

"Make yourself at home. The coffee pot is ready to go with the flip of a switch. Mugs are in the cabinet, and the TV remote is on the counter in case you need company. I'll be right back."

In my bedroom, I removed my robe and started to pull on a silk lounging robe. I stopped—too suggestive. I needed something stylish but simple. Feminine, but not forward. I chose a long multi-patterned jersey skirt and cashmere sweater, the perfect outfit for lounging at home. Clingy enough to show curves, but informal enough to say, so what?

I smiled at the mirror and twisted my hair into a thick dark knot and tied it at the back. What waited below was a dance with an old partner. Would it be a waltz—lyrical and lilting? Or a jitterbug—frenetic and lively? With the old Hank, it would be a tango—sensual, seductive. This time it would start slow, each of us gauging the moves of the other, like new partners.

I brushed my teeth, washed my face, and touched it up with foundation to hide wrinkles—where had they all come from overnight? I applied a hint of shadow to bring out the hazel in my eyes and finished with a delicate hint of mascara.

Hank stood ramrod straight beside the wall of windows, staring toward the ocean, coffee mug in hand as I walked down the stairs. He gave no indication that he heard my approach.

My cell phone on the kitchen counter beeped as I reached the bottom. I picked it up but he held up his hand.

"Wait. You have a number of messages, but I think I know what they're about."

I glanced at the phone. It blinked with the number 24. Had Delia tried to let me know what she was doing? I turned off the phone after leaving her a message on my way home. As I watched, the message number popped to 25. I tapped a button and caller ID identified TV8 as the source.

I put down the phone and poured a mug of steaming, dark coffee. When we were together, Hank taught me to like it strong.

"What can I do for you, Chief?" Out of habit, as I came around the counter, I flipped on the small TV and muted Gwen's nasal voice.

"Let's sit down." He pulled out one of my molded dining chairs.

I followed his lead and seated myself at the glass table. My furniture was Swedish and ultra modern— glass tables, black leather chairs and sofa, blond wood accents. Very clean lines, very rigid. Delia convinced me to buy it, but I regretted the purchase. It might be chic, but it was also damned uncomfortable.

Hank showed no sign of discomfort as he settled at

the head of the table. My home phone rang sharply, and he reached across the table and put his fingers on mine, a delicate touch. "Wait."

His fingers were warm and I responded with a gentle smile to let him know I'd forgiven him for waking me so early.

"That's the station ring, and I'm only taking calls from Alan, my news director, since I worked last Sunday. What brings you here so early?" I lifted the mug to my mouth, meeting his eyes across the top.

He drew a deep breath, withdrawing his hand. "Kimberly, I'm sorry to tell you, but Rick Wells was found dead at his wine shop this morning."

Huh?

My brain was fuzzy so the words took a minute to register. I placed my mug carefully on the table so coffee didn't slosh, though my fingers quivered.

"Say that again." I sought to regain my equilibrium, which burst around me like a popping bubble. As an anchor, I was used to receiving bad news and masking any reaction as I repeated it on air. I prided myself on never losing my cool, but looking at Hank's serious eyes, I found myself on the edge of an implosion—of laughter.

I'd compared this meeting to a dance and music soared in my head. So that's what this was! A dance full of surprises and wild movements. I should have kept my hair down, because I felt like tossing it wildly.

Who was he kidding? Rick, dead? Delia had done this. What was she thinking—cheer up Kimberly by sending Hank the Hunk as messenger to tell me the Weasel was dead? Toooo delicious. A giggle burbled from my throat. I clapped my hand over my mouth.

Hank played his role perfectly. Totally deadpan. I didn't know he was this good an actor.

"Are you all right?" His eyes were filled with what? False concern?

I swallowed the laughter that threatened to erupt. "This is Delia's doing, isn't it?"

His gaze never wavered and his brow furrowed. His look appeared too serious for a joke, and yet... Delia had probably reacted to the babbling message I'd left about Rick's final treachery.

"Kimberly, I can see this is a shock, but he *is* dead."

What if it wasn't a joke?

"Heart attack?" I thought of Rick's disheveled appearance the previous night. It would serve him right if screwing the Bimbo had killed him.

"We think he was murdered."

That did it. All trace of doubt was gone, and a laugh burst forth, bordering on hysterical. "I should have known! Men don't die of natural causes when they're marrying young chicks. Naturally he was murdered."

Delia had thought of everything—except the timing. She should have let Hank wait a couple of hours instead of having him show up when I looked like crap.

"Are you all right?" A startled look shot across his face. Hank wasn't the sort to lose his equanimity, but he looked perplexed.

"Wait!" I waved my hand. "Was he shot? Body washed up on the shore?" My motions grew more frantic as I fought to jerk him out of his serious mode. "Or was he beaten to death? Pounded to a pulp with a bottle of Dom Perignon? Or maybe his prized possession, that damn bat? It's only silver-plated, you know. And wow, you're the person bringing me the news?" I chortled at Delia's thoroughness. Sooner or later, he would drop this act. I was dancing now. Freestyle, bold, theatric!

Delia had done me a favor. I wouldn't have called him, and he looked sooo good with those thin wisps of silver feathering the edges of his dark hair. His chiseled face was leaner than it had been ten years ago, but it suited him. And those pouty lips—god, what he could do with those lips besides fake murder announcements.

The lips moved. "I know this is a shock."

"Not at all. Are you here to help me dispose of the body? Or do I need to find a reasonably priced thug?"

He shot to his feet so violently the dining table shifted and coffee sloshed onto the polished top. His blue eyes transformed to a glacial glare. "I don't think you should say any more. You need to call a lawyer."

My next bout of laughter caught in my throat as Gwen's muted picture flashed to a shot of Rick on the TV screen. The snapshot was familiar—until yesterday it had been tacked to the bulletin board in my office. My skin prickled, and my cheeks grew hot. Below the picture, a caption read, "Wine Shop Murder."

Black spots dotted the backs of my eyelids. My mouth moved, but the words lodged in my windpipe. As I jerked around to see Hank's startled face, the dance music faded, and the world around me dissolved into blackness.

Chapter Six

"Kimberly?"

I blinked, my eyes unfocused, as the room swam about crazily, forming spinning geometric figures. Slowly, the chalky ceiling and a row of gray skylights, two floors above me, settled into clarity.

"Kimmie?"

How long had it been since someone beside my family or Delia called me that?

Hank's face floated into view. Curious? Concerned? At least his eyes no longer carried that hint of accusation I'd seen before darkness claimed me. I must have fainted. When was the last time that happened?

Never. I was stretched out on the hard leather sofa. Had he carried me here?

Hank kneeled on the rug beside me. A gentle hand stroked my hair. "Are you okay?"

I swallowed hard, trying to remember what caused me to faint. A joke about Rick. No, no joke. He said Rick was dead. So had the TV. Confusion fluttered inside me as fear gripped my middle in a tight vise.

Not simply dead.

Murdered.

Had I heard that right? I brushed my hand across my face to clear mental cobwebs. This was no movie shootout, no baseball game, no dance sequence.

This was real.

I struggled to sit up and gentle hands assisted me. His palms rested on either side of my ribcage, holding me upright. My gaze focused on Hank. His mouth was moving, but all I heard was a vicious buzzing in my ears.

Pay attention.

"We don't have a cause of death. Perhaps beaten."

My hands shook. *Rick was dead. Murdered.*

Licking my parched lips with a cotton ball of a tongue, I tried to speak, but nothing emerged. An inner blizzard took possession of my body, freezing my insides all the way to my bones. I shivered, folding my arms together across my chest.

"Here." He pulled off his leather jacket and wrapped it around me.

His warmth remained, and I burrowed into the jacket, hoping for transference of its heat. The familiar scent of sandalwood soap wafted up to me, a disturbing reminder of the past, but it didn't bring pleasure. My world spun at a topsy-turvy angle as my vision blurred and sharpened, expanded in length and reduced in shape, like I meandered in a crazed funhouse faced with distorted mirrors.

He squeezed my shoulder. "Would you like a glass of water? Or I could put something into your coffee."

I cleared my throat and words pushed out in a hoarse whisper. "Something strong. The bar's at the end of the counter."

Hank left my line of vision. Words blazed in front of me, giant red letters scrawled across the windows.

Murder!

I shook my head to clear the ghastly view. This

couldn't be true. I'd seen Rick...when? Hours ago. I didn't want to think about the messy scene I'd left in the wine shop. We had a horrible argument and I emerged feeling like I'd been through an emotional meat grinder.

At that moment I wanted him dead. I wanted to bash him with the baseball bat he nagged me about or strangle him with that damned diamond pendant he wanted back. Instead I got into my car and drove away, driving through a rainstorm of tears.

My silent wish had been granted by some genie with a wicked sense of humor. Joking about about killing him during a drunken binge was one thing. The actual occurrence, well, that was something else. Something scary.

"Do you want me to call someone? Delia?" Hank returned and held out my mug.

The scent of liquor rose along with the strong smell of coffee. He sat on the sofa beside me, not relinquishing the mug. Together we lifted it to my lips and I sipped gratefully, letting the warm, potent liquid open my parched throat. The liquor blazed a hot trail through my icy insides, but it didn't thaw me much.

"Delia left last night. You know how she always wanted to see the Amazon? Her husband arranged a river cruise..." I stopped. He probably didn't remember that much about Delia.

"You mentioned Delia." Hank had always been a difficult man to decipher and that could make me crazy. Like now. What was he thinking?

I chewed on my lower lip, remembering the craziness before my collapse. What must he think about my reaction?

The chiming of the doorbell startled me, and I nearly dropped the mug. Luckily, he still held it. What could that be? More bad news? No, I knew the alternative. It would be much worse.

"Let me get that." He rose, setting the mug on a glass coffee table. I could read him now. He was relieved at the interruption.

"Thank you." My voice sounded hoarse, unfamiliar. "I'm not home, okay? To anyone."

"I understand." He squared his shoulders as though he was a warrior headed to battle. That was exactly what I feared he faced—a media battle.

The phone buzzed, but I ignored it. The mystery of the numerous messages was solved. I knew my newsroom had called, but other stations were probably calling too, wanting my reaction to Rick's death. Voices drifted up from below, but I couldn't make out words. Hopefully Hank was playing bodyguard.

Footsteps came up the steps and I turned, prepared to thank him. I didn't want to resume the conversation, but I should explain why I reacted in such a bizarre manner. But instead of Hank, Reba's frizzy red hair popped up the stairs.

"You okay, girlfriend? We've been worried." She loped into the room with a look of concern on her pale face, making the flashes of green at her eyes and the red slash of mouth stand out. As usual she wore skin tight black leggings. Her baggy sweater was an unnatural shade of lime and her mules resembled pink stilts.

"I'm fine." I drew a deep breath, looking beyond her. "Where's Hank?"

"The Chief? He had to return to the crime scene. You know cops. Wham, bam, I gotta go arrest people, ma'am."

My fingers caressed his leather jacket as disappointment surged through me. I'd wanted him to stay.

Reba surveyed the room. "Anything I can do? Make coffee or tea?"

I lifted my mug. "Hank made coffee."

She dropped onto the black chair across from me and leaned forward as though prepared to grab me if I toppled. I must look like hell. Maybe the warm coffee and strong liquor would help.

"Do you know what happened?" I asked.

"The story is that a security guard on patrol noticed an open door. When he checked, he saw blood on the floor so he went inside and..." She lifted her shoulders and spread her hands wide.

"He'd been beaten?"

A brow twitched. "I hadn't heard that."

Hadn't Hank mentioned it? "They're sure it's Rick?"

"The guard identified him. That's why I came over. You didn't answer your phone. I was worried you might..." She shrugged again. "It's a good thing Chief Patterson came by. He seemed worried. He wanted to make certain I stayed with you. Our media vulture culture is in hot pursuit of the story."

"How long do you think it'll be before they turn up? Every station in town knows we dated but ironically, we broke up two weeks ago."

Reba jerked back, shock widening her eyes. "You did?"

Guilt sliced through me and I turned away. "I haven't told anyone except Mom and Delia. It wasn't going to be secret much longer since he's getting...I mean...*was* getting married in a couple of weeks."

Reba leaned over and rubbed my hand. "Babe, I'm sorry. The two of you were inseparable."

"I'm fine." Even as I spoke, I knew that wasn't true. I'd talked about killing the guy. I drew a deep breath and blew it out slowly, practicing the exercises I used when I needed to calm down.

"Well, no one's going to bother you. I'm here to run interference."

As she spoke, my home phone rang again, followed quickly by the buzz of my cell. This would go on all day. I ignored them, but she hopped to her feet and marched to the counter.

I put down the mug and wiped my palm across my face. Who would want to kill Rick? Besides me, of course. Was it robbery? Probably. He'd never liked the beach bums that sometimes turned up at his door begging handouts.

Rising, I walked on wobbly legs to the wall of windows. The morning fog had receded and beyond the tinted windows, the Pacific was a boiling mass of waves, crashing on the sand sending foam, spraying in every direction.

Reba appeared next to me. "I called the assignment desk and ordered them to get our PR person to release a statement saying that you have no comment and asking to give you privacy. Uh...you wouldn't know the name of his...new fiancée?"

"Bobbi something...with a B." I stifled the urge to say Barbie or Bimbo. "I think the wedding announcement is supposed to be in tomorrow's paper."

She patted my arm. "Thanks, babe. I'll get the desk

on that." She pulled a cell from her pocket and walked away.

Perhaps that would turn news crews in another direction. I bit back a smile as I thought of them chasing Bobbi the Bimbo instead of me. Had I told Hank about her? Oh, hell...what did he think of my weird reaction? No wonder he ran.

"Did Hank say anything?" I asked when Reba returned.

"Like what?"

"I didn't believe him when he told me. I thought it was a joke." I trusted Reba enough to know she'd accept my comments in their proper context so I explained my drunken conversation with Delia. "We also talked about finding me a new guy and she suggested Hank since I dated him before Rick. I thought she'd sent him so when he told me about Rick, I figured it was her doing and laughed like a lunatic."

"Oh, fuck!" Reba slapped a hand to her face.

"I should have known Delia would never send a guy early in the morning. What if I'd answered the door in a ratty T-shirt?"

She rolled her eyes as she surveyed my clothes. "I doubt you own ratty T-shirts."

The phone rang and I jerked around, frowning at the offending monster. "Maybe we should turn off the ringer or move it downstairs."

"Good idea." Reba tottered to the phone. She glanced at the caller ID and a quizzical look came over her face. "Paula Dominguez-Gardner? I didn't know you were still in touch."

Paula had been a pretender to my anchor throne. She'd thrown a fit because Alan and general manager

Vincent Adams refused to promise her a weekly anchor spot and stormed out shortly before a newscast. She never returned. No one knew whether it was her choice to quit or she'd been fired. Two weeks later she turned up on another station using her married name, Paula Gardner.

"We haven't spoken in ages. You know why she's calling. Probably convinced her boss she could get me to talk. As if."

Reba's laugh was loud and contagious. We both knew Paula's tactics. Chimes sounded and we exchanged startled looks. The media vultures had arrived.

"That's probably her," I said.

"It'll be my pleasure to get rid of the bitch." Reba unplugged the phone.

I returned to the sofa and huddled on the extra-firm seat, wondering if I would ever feel warm again. Despite the coffee with its strong mate, I still felt chilled. I listened for Paula's whiny tone, but male voices floated up from below.

What a mess and no Delia to help, she'd be in South America by now. I couldn't recall any crisis I'd faced since college when she wasn't nearby to lend support.

Reba reappeared at the top of the stairs, followed by two men. Short haircuts, square jaws, ill-fitting suits with cheap ties, eyes that darted around the room like I might have stashed a body somewhere.

Police.

Chapter Seven

"Miss delaGarza?" An olive-skinned, balding man stepped forward. He was smaller and shorter than the other, but I sensed muscle beneath his baggy jacket.

"Yes?"

The other man, younger, with a buzz cut, moved toward me as well. He was tall and big shouldered with hard brown eyes that stabbed me like he could see right through me. "We're with the Mira Loma Police Department. We understand you're a friend of Rick Wells. We need to ask you a few questions."

Reba made a face and lifted a shoulder. "I tried to tell them you couldn't talk right now."

Drawing a deep breath, I waved them forward. I might as well get this over with. "It'll be better to talk before the media camps outside my door. I can see the story already. Video of you leaving with the reporter saying that I was questioned. It's a good thing no one was around when your police chief was here."

The men traded surprised glances.

"He came to tell me about Rick's death. I take it this is more like questioning?" I rearranged myself on the sofa, sitting straight. I felt like my body was contained in a block of ice.

"Not really questioning," Buzz Cut said. "Just a talk."

I put down my coffee mug. No sense letting them

catch a whiff of that and making them think I was half loaded at eight in the morning. The men introduced themselves as they settled on the stiff leather chairs facing me. The older man was Lt. Jose Torres, the younger Detective Steve Callahan. I hoped they were as uncomfortable on those tortuous chairs as I was on the hard sofa. Maybe I'd replace the set while Delia was out of town. I blinked, forcing my brain back to the scene at hand. How stupid to think of something so inane at such an important moment.

Focus! I summoned the anchor face I pulled on every night to begin the news. It was supposed to convey composure, calmness and an "everything is right with our world" attitude, according to my first talent coach.

"Would you like coffee?" I asked, ever the good hostess.

The men nodded and Reba stepped forward. "Got it covered, babe."

"When was the last time you saw Rick Wells?" Torres asked, taking out a small notebook and pen.

These guys didn't beat around the bush. I debated how to answer, but there was no reason to lie. My final visit had been innocent. "Last night, around midnight."

Neither registered surprise. They'd already known that.

Callahan leaned toward me, gaze intent as though watching for something. "What time did you leave?"

"Around one. When I got into my car, the one o'clock news was starting on the radio. I usually listen to news on my way to and from work. I like to keep informed."

"Did you notice anyone outside when you left?"

Torres asked.

I strained to recall, but I'd been too upset. "No."

"Why were you there so late?" he continued.

"I worked until 11:35 anchoring the news. I stopped on my way home."

"Where did you park?" Torres showed little interest in my answers though he scribbled in his notebook.

My gaze bounced to Callahan. He watched me with unwavering eyes.

"I park in front. It's well lit with no place for anyone to hide. What time...do you know when he was...killed?"

"We don't have an exact time of death," Callahan said.

"Well, I can tell you it had to be after one."

"Really?" Callahan said.

My mouth went dry, and I licked my lips. Neither had registered any change in demeanor, but I suddenly sensed an electric charge in the atmosphere. I looked from one to the other. "I left at one. Don't you think I might have noticed or called 9-1-1 if he'd been dead before then?"

Callahan didn't flinch, voice hard. "Maybe, maybe not. Not if you wanted him dead."

"Wanted him dead? What kind of a comment is that?" I started to protest but stopped. I'd been planning Rick's demise last week. Did these guys know that? I forced myself to look calm, sat forward and picked up my mug. I took a long, deliberate gulp of coffee.

Reba stepped from the kitchen, carrying a tray of mugs. Concerned blue-green eyes focused on me as she set the tray on the coffee table. "Maybe you should call a lawyer before you say any more."

"Why?"

"You're probably one of the last people to see him alive. You could become a suspect."

An alarm bell clanged in my head.

Hello?!

Me, a suspect?

I blinked, trying to clear my fuzzy head. What the hell had I been thinking? I whirled to the police officers, but their demeanor remained stoic.

"He was fine when I left him."

"Did you argue with him?" Torres asked in a staccato voice.

"Argue? Well..." I bit my lip. What if someone had been passing and heard my tirade? "How was he killed? The chief said he was...beaten?"

"We're waiting for an autopsy to determine cause of death," Torres said.

A shiver ran through me as I recalled the stunned look on Hank's face when I was ranting about the murder. "Was it the bat?"

The men shifted before exchanging a glance. A definite reaction. *Damn!* I should have kept my mouth shut.

"Did you see a baseball bat while you were there?" Torres asked, eyes never leaving his notebook.

"Um...yes..." Should I say more? What would clear me and what would get me in more hot water? Reba was right. I needed a lawyer.

"Something wrong?" Callahan inquired.

"I didn't kill him."

Neither man moved, their faces impassive.

I gestured at Torres and his notebook. "I want that

written down. On the record."

Callahan nodded, but Torres didn't write anything down.

"If I heard this story in the newsroom, the first person I'd suspect is...well, me." I tapped my finger against my chest. "I am his ex-girlfriend."

"Mind if we look around?" Callahan's gaze shifted around the room.

"Like a search?" Reba's voice was sharp. "Don't you need a warrant?"

"Not if she gives us permission," Torres replied.

I had nothing to hide, but as I rose on shaky knees, I knew I was in over my head. "Let me get in touch with my lawyer. Then I'll be happy to answer any other questions. You can tell the press I've agreed to be questioned."

Both men rose. Torres nodded at Callahan who pulled a phone from his pocket. "This shouldn't take long."

They were going after a warrant. What did they hope to find? Reba had taken my home phone downstairs, so I excused myself and headed down to make my call in private. This was a bad joke, but how far would they take it? At the bottom of the stairs, I tripped over my shoes again. I started to pick them up and toss them in the closet, but Callahan's bark froze me. He'd been watching from above.

"Don't move anything."

I stared at the shoes in dismay. Small red flecks stood out against the pale pink satin. It was wine, wasn't it? Or could it be blood?

Oh, hell. It could be either.

I recalled Hank's surprised look when he saw the

shoes before we went upstairs. Was that why he left so quickly? Hell, was that why these guys had shown up, ready to search the place?

"We'll need to get into your garage and the keys to your car." Callahan hurried down the stairs as though he didn't want to let me out of his sight.

"Rick wasn't in my car."

His dark granite eyes bored into me. "It could hold evidence."

Oh, shit! The romantic comedy that was my life's movie was taking a sinister twist. It was becoming a police drama, and I had no script prepared.

****

Saturday, noon

"This sucks!" I squirmed and tried to straighten my leg that cramped from its unnatural curled up position. Huddling under a wool blanket that smelled of dust and rubber in the luggage compartment of an SUV was not my idea of a good time.

"Did you say something?" Reba called from the front seat.

"Let me out. Any longer under this blanket and I'll suffocate."

Three hours had passed since police showed up at my door. It hadn't taken much time to get a search warrant and for crime tech types to swarm my house and transform it into a CSI episode. From the moment I watched an officer bag my stained pumps, I knew I couldn't watch. The thought of someone touching my belongings was bad enough. But total strangers?

Even worse, the media horde arrived en masse, led by my old nemesis, Paula Gardner.

"When was the last time you saw Rick Wells?" she

shouted as I peeked from an upper window. I withdrew like a turtle into its shell. I didn't know which was worse—the plague of media locusts swarming outside or the mass of crime tech bees buzzing inside.

"I have to get out of here," I pleaded to Reba.

The ever-resourceful EP lifted a red-tipped index finger. "Lindy's on her way in a station van to oversee the search. I'll have her drive into your garage and we'll stash you in the back. I did that once to get a crew into a restricted area."

It sounded like a good idea, but now I'd had enough. I was no female action star in a black leather jump suit. I was the Queen in cashmere!

The vehicle jerked to a stop and Reba lifted the cover. I unwound my stiff body and blinked like I hadn't seen sunlight in days.

"What did your lawyer say?" she asked as I buckled myself into the front seat.

"Adrienne's firm doesn't handle criminal cases, so she's finding someone. Her advice was to funnel interview requests to my agent and stay out of sight."

"Evan Flynn, right? I'll tell the station. Got a game plan?"

I chewed on my lower lip. "No. I wish Delia was here. Her father was a criminal lawyer."

"You can't call him?"

"Mr. Burnett has been dead for years." The deaths of our fathers our freshman year had bonded us. We shared every good and bad event in our lives until now.

"Damn, this story will lead every newscast tonight." Nervous tension vibrated in Reba's voice. "Murder among the rich and famous is a big draw."

"Rick wasn't rich or famous."

"You're well known, and we looked up the engagement announcement. His fiancée's family is big money. What about going to your mom's?"

I'd called her while we waited for the search warrant, but she had seen the news.

"Poor man. He could be so nice sometimes." Her lukewarm reaction was no surprise. She'd labeled Rick self-centered and fake from the first. "*Como* them Ken dolls, pretty but plastic."

I shook my head. "I'd rather not put her in the line of media fire. She'd invite them in for cookies."

"And the rest of your family?"

"My brother has a house full of kids and my sister and I have never been on good terms." Nancy would think I deserved any bad thing that came my way. We'd been competitors from the moment her first boyfriend flirted with me.

"So where to?" Reba asked.

"Rodeo Drive. Those cops didn't let me take anything but the clothes on my back and my wallet. I need makeup and clothes. I have no idea when I can get into my house or if I want to, given those TV trucks lined up outside. I refuse to be smuggled in and out."

"Unfortunately, I have to get to work."

"Then take me to the Four Seasons Hotel in Beverly Hills. I can stay there, and they'll get me a rental car."

Reba threw me a startled glance, but I met it squarely.

"If I'm going to end up in the Big House, I'm living it up in the meantime."

Chapter Eight

Sunday, 5:30 a.m.

Waking up at dawn is unusual for me. Years of getting off work at midnight have made me a night owl. Maybe it was Rick's untimely death.

Or the thought of police prowling through my home, touching my things.

Or the fact someone else was under my roof while I tossed and turned in a strange bed at the Four Seasons Hotel.

Whatever the cause, I was awake. With a sigh, I rose and paced my suite like a caged tiger until the walls closed in. Jerking on the capris and sweater I'd bought at Neiman Marcus the previous day, I took an elevator to the lobby. A sleepy valet jerked to attention as I approached the door and made short work of getting my rental Jaguar.

I had no idea where I was going, but the instant I turned onto Santa Monica Boulevard, I wanted to be at the beach. Rose-tinted clouds feathered the western sky above the dark gray of the ocean as I parked near Venice Beach. The area was deserted except for seagulls and I stepped onto the sand, letting morning mist envelop me.

The scent of the sea and the cry of seagulls hit me like a slap. And reminded me.

Rick Wells was gone. *Forever.*

Suddenly, he wasn't the Weasel.

He was Friend, Lover, Romantic Fool, Steady Companion for ten years. I ran across the sand, fighting the drag on my pumping legs, forcing myself to move until I reached the damp edge of the water. A sob clogged my throat.

Rick was gone. Rick, who made up names for me like Gorgeous Goddess, TV Diva, Princess K or Pumpkin. Rick, the Charmer, who showered me with flowers, trips, and jewelry. Removing my shoes, I walked along the ocean's edge. Tears streamed down my face as time blurred my vision.

I was Kimmie D, sitting at a rickety table in a beachside café that smelled of fried shrimp and beer. Scribbling furiously in a reporter's notebook, I crafted the beginning of a story. As a man walked by, the wobbly table tilted. My cup of Diet Coke sloshed over its rim, and a quick hand grabbed it. I looked up into a pair of laughing brown eyes.

"Whoops. Wouldn't want to ruin that beautiful suit. St. John?"

I glanced at my navy suit. I paid a bundle for it, but considered my wardrobe an investment in my future. It shocked me that a man would know the label, and I examined him. He was tall with a face carved for the big screen and a tan that beach boys would envy. I pegged him for a wannabe actor in his black polo shirt and khaki shorts.

"My name is Rick Wells. Where have I been all your life?"

I reached for the cup and accidentally knocked it out of his hand. Liquid splashed over me. He turned wonderfully efficient, producing a handful of napkins. Unfortunately, the drink drenched my notebook and left me with a soggy page of unreadable notes for the story about to air live.

From the door, my videographer called, "Five minutes, Kimberly. They need you for a tease."

With dripping notes in hand, I approached the lighted area outside the shack. "What am I going to say?"

"Wing it," my new acquaintance said. "You know the story, right? Tell it instead of reading it."

I wanted to throw the notebook at him, but the cameraman handed me an earpiece so I could hear the anchors. I lifted the microphone and the words for the tease slid out of my mouth. As the station went to commercial, the sound of clapping hands rang out.

I whirled around. "What the hell do you know about live television?"

"Only what you're going to teach me." With a sly grin, he sauntered over and dabbed at my jacket with a napkin. "Still a few smudges there."

I knocked his hand away, dropping the notebook, and he kicked it away.

"What the hell are you doing?"

His reply was a wink. "Show me your stuff, beautiful."

"Stand by," the cameraman warned.

I lifted my shoulders and took a deep breath, knowing I couldn't use an expletive with a live microphone in my hand.

"If you pull this off, I'll buy you dinner at the restaurant of your choice," he added.

Pointing the mike at him, I smiled. "You're on,

buddy."

James was anchoring, and his deep voice came through my earpiece. "...small storefront businesses could be wiped out by the decision. Kimberly delaGarza is in Santa Monica with the story. Kimberly?"

Damned if the guy wasn't right. The absence of the notebook freed me. I knew the story and it poured from my lips. I would never read directly from a notebook again.

As I removed the earpiece, he approached. "Where am I buying you dinner?"

"The most expensive place in town," I retorted.

"My type of place. I'll call you."

I didn't expect to hear from him, but the next day when I arrived at work, a bouquet of roses sat on my desk. The card held another surprise.

"Here's the name of my cleaner. I'll pay the bill. If it won't clean properly, we'll go shopping and I'll buy a new one. Loves ya, RW."

While I was still reeling, my phone rang.

"Kimberly?"

I knew the voice immediately. "Mr. Wells, are you rich?"

"Nope, but I will be. Where am I taking you to dinner?"

I named the most expensive restaurant I'd uncovered and he didn't flinch.

"Eight o'clock. I'll pick you up in a limo."

"You're a certifiable nut."

"Absolutely. And getting more deranged at the thought of seeing you again."

That was how it started. All fun and promise.

"Damn you, Rick," I whispered into the soft beach breeze. "What the hell happened?"

As I looked inland I realized I stood a block from where we met. This was almost the same spot where we ended our first date, picking seashells in the glow of a full moon.

Spying a shell, I picked it up. The tide was out, and I walked across the damp blanket of sand to the edge of oncoming, rippling waves. What a magical time those first days had been. Small gifts or flowers appeared on my desk. Rick's treatment was in direct contrast to my souring relationship with Hank. Our dates ended in arguments. Rick sought only to please me.

Even Delia couldn't believe my good fortune. "Hang onto this guy. I wish I'd met him first. He makes me tempted to forget our bargain."

The bargain was that we'd never poach on each other and whoever met a guy first had unconditional rights to him. Del was between husbands, and I was plenty glad I'd seen Rick first.

He wasn't rich. His liquor stores did okay financially, but he had a bigger dream—a specialty wine shop. Together we set out to pursue the future. My reporting gig evolved into a midday anchor job while Rick sold his stores to buy a wine shop. His increasing contacts and my growing popularity resulted in invitations to more prestigious parties. Rick was a major hit on the cocktail circuit, offering special bottles of wine or using his expertise to get good deals.

Delia's second husband helped Rick move his shop to a location near the beach, where he catered to wealthy clientele while I took over on the main anchor desk. We were a dream couple, but content to keep single, separate lifestyles.

What changed? Why had he chosen to leave me for that anorexic girl?

The ending had been a surreal disaster movie. I played the role of happy vacationer, relaxing over breakfast on the veranda of a resort in the fictional shadow of a dormant volcano. Rick was the meek scientist who knew danger lurked.

He calmly announced the initial warning. "I'm thinking of getting married."

"You have someone picked out?" I barely looked up from my newspaper. Marriage had died as a subject years ago.

"I think so."

I emitted a forced laugh, the tourist ignoring rumblings in the distance. "I hope it's not soon. We have a ratings period in July and Delia's leaving town for a month."

He cleared his throat. "Not us. I mean, not me and you."

My stomach took a sudden drop, a shudder from the volcano or a boulder plunging down the side. "You're thinking of...*you* getting married?"

He submitted the first scientific fact. "I'm over fifty. If I want a family, I can't wait and she wants children."

"She..." The volcano began to steam. "Does this mean you've been seeing someone else?"

The scientist revealed his research in a soft voice. "Well, yes."

The steam began to flow, pouring out. "And you're serious? Enough that you want to marry her?"

And then came the undeniable truth, uttered in a

matter-of-fact way. "We set the date..."

Eruption!

"You son of a bitch!" I flung the paper at him. It fluttered like falling ash. My stomach boiled with inner fire.

"I didn't know how to tell you..."

Flames shot up. "Was that what this weekend was? An expensive Dear John?"

"This has been our spot when we need to talk."

He was lucky the ensuing blast didn't sending him plummeting from the balcony.

I didn't want to recall the fiery argument that burst as I dressed. Or the grief that spilled like magma as I packed. Or the cold fury that congealed like hardening lava as I drove off.

For the past few weeks I still burned with anger, but now as I gazed out at the ocean, I realized I felt hollow inside—cleaned out as a volcano left with an empty crater. I squeezed the shell in my hand until sharp edges bit into my fingers just so I could feel something.

Then I reared back and flung the shell toward the ocean.

"Goodbye, Rick," I shouted into the mist.

Chapter Nine

Monday, 8:00 a.m.

Who killed Rick Wells?
I'd been trying *not* to think about that question, but as I sat in the dining room at the Four Seasons, prepared to meet my new criminal attorney, I forced it to the front of my consciousness. What happened after I left?

The theory I'd developed was that one of the street people from the beach had come in. Had he locked the door? Had I left it open? That led to troubling questions. Could I have saved him if I'd stayed? Would I have ended up a victim too? I shuddered. I didn't want to think about that.

Movement at the door drew my attention. Oliver Nichols marched through the room with the force of a sledge hammer. Even the eyes of those at nearby tables who normally ignored fame turned. From press conferences I knew he stood 5'4 but the sureness of his stride elevated his stature. His narrow, refined face carried a pleasant smile as he glanced around, nodding from time to time.

Elegant and fastidious, he wore a charcoal Armani suit with a red silk tie and matching pocket kerchief. His white shirt looked like it could stand on its own. Thinning brown hair was tinged with gray at the sides and looked so natural, he probably had it done that way.

I'd heard his speeches in court, laced with southern witticisms, watched his blunt news conferences on numerous courthouse steps, but I wasn't prepared for the high-powered aura he displayed in a one-on-one setting. As he grew closer and his eyes fastened on me, I felt like I'd been skewered by twin high voltage brown lasers.

He took my hand into both of his as he sat across from me. "Miss delaGarza, it's good to meet you. May I call you Kimberly?" He spoke with a drawl, squeezing my fingers with a firm grip.

"Certainly, Mr. Nichols." No invitation to call him Oliver.

A waiter arrived out of nowhere, filling our cups from a silver coffee pot. Nichols ordered a bowl of fresh fruit without opening the menu.

He removed a legal pad and Mont Blanc fountain pen from his briefcase and leaned toward me. "Tell me what you need. I'm at your service." His tone was pure southern gentility, like he was performing a favor, though I knew his bill would be hefty.

I explained my predicament and as he asked questions, the drawl transformed into a buzz saw of words. He scribbled on the pad, his pinky ring—with a diamond the size of a small marble—flashing as it caught a ray of sun. As we finished, it occurred to me he'd made one omission.

"You didn't ask if I did it."

"Darlin', that isn't important." He smiled, though it didn't reach his eyes. If snakes could smile, that would be how they did it.

"It is to me. I didn't do it." I tried to keep my voice from becoming huffy.

His tone dripped honey and he gripped my upper arm and squeezed it. "Well, that's fine. You keep saying that."

Wow, he didn't care if I was guilty. I could have beaten Rick to a bloody pulp and it wouldn't matter. As long as I paid, Oliver Nichols would fight to keep me out of jail.

I didn't know if that was good.

****

Monday, 10:00 a.m.

I didn't want to be at the Mira Loma Police Department, sitting on a hard metal chair inside a drab cubicle of a room. Were they trying to kill people with the chairs? Too much time on this backbreaker and people would confess to anything.

To my right, Oliver opened his briefcase and removed a fresh legal pad. "This is all a formality. You're here to give a statement, but if they ask anything I don't want you answerin', I'll interrupt. If there's anything you don't want to say, look my way and I'll stop 'em." He put his pad on a gray metal table and sat back.

The small, sterile room closed around me. Was this what a jail cell was like? I stood and began pacing. To our left was a horizontal mirror. Was it a two-way mirror? Were people behind it watching?

"I didn't do anything wrong," I said, in case someone was back there. "I was returning his belongings. If that bat was the murder weapon, it would have my finger prints. It had been at my house for months. I'd hardly wear gloves to return it. If I had used it, I would have wiped it clean, right?"

He held up a hand. "Perhaps we should postpone

this until you're in a calmer frame of mind."

"Can you blame me for being agitated? I don't like to be kept waiting, and my maid says police made a mess of my house."

His responding glare was like being pinpointed by a searchlight during a prison getaway. Not good to make the lawyer angry. I resumed my place on the torture chair and smoothed my pale yellow suit. The slim-fitting ensemble hugged my figure and the pencil skirt was slit halfway up the front of my thighs. I tweaked the pink-and-yellow silk scarf at my throat and tapped at my hair. I might be seething inside, but I wanted to present a perfect picture, from my pinned up hair to my purple pumps and matching Prada purse. P for Poise.

The door clicked and Callahan entered. He nodded at me and introduced himself to Nichols.

"This is a formality," he began. "I hope you understand that we may repeat some questions we asked earlier. Please bear with us."

"Is Lieutenant Torres joining us?" I asked.

"Not this morning." He settled his large frame onto a metal chair, scraping it across the tiled floor. Glancing at the mirror/possible window, I wondered if Torres watched us behind it, preferring to gauge my reactions in private.

In a monotone, Callahan explained the session was being taped and began with simple questions like name and address. I felt like I was already under arrest—a prisoner being grilled by the hardened cop in a film noir whodunit. I was ready for the overhead fluorescent lights to transform into a harsh spotlight pointed at my eyes.

I imagined Torres and a squad of detectives behind the mirror. Were they hoping I'd fall apart? Did they expect me to be coy, ala Sharon Stone in *Basic Instinct*? Were they waiting for my legs to cross? Sorry, I was wearing underwear. No one could see anything anyway. My legs were under the table.

Could Hank be behind the mirror? Maybe I should sit sideways and provide a good view of the legs I'd bragged about to Delia.

"Tell me why you were at the wine shop so late," Callahan began.

Swept up in my thoughts about Hank, the question caught me off guard. I stammered before repeating the original answer I'd given him and Torres.

"Why didn't you do it the next day?"

"He'd been calling me every day, demanding I return his crap. I wanted to get rid of it."

Beside me, Oliver shifted. I glanced at him and saw his knitted brows. He gave a small shake of his head. I winced, realizing how hard I'd sounded. This guy had been late on purpose. He was trying to rattle me.

"Were you angry about having to come by that late?" Callahan asked.

Enough letting this guy get to me. I was dressed to play "cool customer," and that's what I was going to do.

Summoning my best anchor smile, I lowered my voice, the one I used to soothe viewers. "It was no big deal. I often stopped by after work."

The questioning progressed in a boring pattern of earlier questions mixed in with a more detailed explanation of Friday night. How long was this going to continue? The detective was repeating questions. Then he asked something new.

"Did you ever threaten Wells?"

"Why would I threaten him?"

Oliver cleared his throat, and when I glanced at him, he shook his head.

Callahan leaned toward me with a smug smile and picked up his notebook. He flipped a few pages. "Didn't you tell him you were quote, planning to kill your lying ass, unquote?"

A chill ran through me, and I gasped. "What the fuck..." Whoops! That wasn't cool. I blinked, batting my eyelashes, fighting to sound confused. "Who would say that?"

Except I knew. Four people heard me make that statement, but I doubted Brad and Reba would say anything. I didn't know about Lindy, but I'd bet Gwen couldn't wait to spill her guts.

Nichols put his hand out toward me, shaking his head. His voice turned deep and commanding without a trace of southern gentility. "My client won't answer that."

Callahan and I whirled toward Oliver. He pierced me with probing dark orbs. Uh-oh, I hadn't told him about that stupid threat.

The interruption didn't disturb Callahan. He leaned back in his chair, crossing his legs, ankle resting on his knee, as though the tension he'd brought on didn't exist. He again flipped through the notebook. "Tell me about the bat. You touched it?"

I sat up, determined to be more alert. This was the first time the subject of the bat had come up. "I was returning it. I carried it inside."

"Never touched it again?"

My mouth grew dry and my head buzzed. I swallowed, trying to get saliva into my mouth so I could lick my lips. "I picked it up and...sort of swung it..."

"Swung it? At him?" His tone grew sharp as a razor.

"Don't answer," Oliver directed.

Too late—I was already speaking. "I swung at the air. A practice swing. Rick did that all the time." I stood and demonstrated, rolling my shoulders as I completed my action. "I'm not very coordinated. I hit a wine bottle and it broke. You know that. You took my shoes with the stains."

"Was that what all those stains were? Wine?"

I squeezed my eyes shut. I didn't know. That crazy Friday night scene played out in slow motion in my brain. I saw myself swinging the bat at that damn wine bottle. I connected as Rick reached for it. Blood erupted on his finger as he grabbed at the broken bottle before it toppled to the floor and exploded. I jerked back when wine hit my shoes, but his finger dripped blood too.

"He cut his finger on the broken bottle."

Nichols slapped his hand on the desk, making me jump. His voice boomed in the tiny room. "Detective, my client has nothing more to say. We've been very cooperative. When she left the store, Wells was still alive. End of story."

Callahan didn't appear threatened. He never took his eyes off me. "Do you know of anyone else with a grudge against Wells?"

"No." Then I realized what he'd asked. "What do you mean anyone *else?*"

"Isn't it true that *he* broke up with you because he

was marrying another woman?"

"Well, yes..."

"What about pictures of him? Did you rip them up and throw them in your office wastebasket the night he was killed?"

"We're finished." Nichols opened his briefcase and shoved the pad inside. "She's given you the details of that final visit."

"Did you argue with him?" Callahan persisted.

I knew Oliver didn't want me to say any more, but I didn't want to leave the wrong impression. "A few cross words."

"Kimberly, stop." He turned to Callahan. "I understand you are finished with her car and she can retrieve it."

"It's parked out front, but we need her fingerprints."

My fists clenched in a reflexive gesture. "I don't mind answering questions about Rick, but I refuse to talk about our personal life so it ends up in the media. They're making it sound like I did it because he dumped me!"

"Kimberly!" Oliver's voice boomed in the room as he rose to his feet.

Callahan stood too, but he refused to back down. "It'll take a few minutes to get this statement printed for her to sign. I'll be back."

I could sense Oliver's displeasure as Callahan left, but when I opened my mouth to speak he shook his head as his gaze slid toward the mirror. We waited in silence until Callahan returned. He directed me to the second floor for fingerprinting and to pick up my keys.

Oliver caught my arm as I walked toward the

stairs. "I must go. Don't talk to anyone, and next time, follow my instructions." His icy voice rippled with anger as he took out his cell phone. He whirled and marched away, phone to his ear, off to save his next client.

Picking up my keys was easy, but the finger print experience made me feel like a criminal. I scrubbed at the black ink that they said would come off with tissue. Like hell. This crap was going to ruin my new suit if I wasn't careful.

As I turned toward the stairs to go in search of my car, Hank stepped into the hall directly in front of me.

Chapter Ten

My heart did a tap dance against my chest as a rush of warm embarrassment surged through my veins. My first inclination was to ignore him, but I couldn't. I needed to explain my silly behavior. Besides, he might help convince his officers that I was innocent.

"Well, Chief Patterson. Were you coming to see me?" As the words left my mouth, I glanced beyond him. The door had a sign with his name. Damn, I hadn't noticed I was walking by his office.

"Kimberly." His nod was noncommittal, blue eyes watchful but wary. He appeared as uncomfortable as I felt. "I heard you were coming in to give a statement and be fingerprinted."

I held up my blackened fingers, pleased they weren't shaking like my insides. "Like a common criminal."

Hank glanced at my fingers, and his lips turned up in a half smile, but his voice remained flat. "Normal procedure. You were at the wine shop. We need to eliminate extraneous prints."

"Were you watching while they gave me the third degree?" I asked, gesturing with my head down the stairs toward the interrogation room.

He shifted, displaying discomfort. Behind us, an open office area buzzed with activity. "I knew you were giving a statement. I don't normally take part in active investigations."

With Hank looking uncomfortable, I couldn't help putting a flirtatious note in my voice, producing a smile and batting my mascara laden lashes. "Even for me?"

His lips drew into a straight, narrow line and he stood like a military officer ready to march off. He wasn't going to play games. And this was no time for frivolity. I lowered my 100-watt smile.

"Actually, I would like to talk with you."

A quick glance at his watch produced a slight grimace. "I have a meeting..."

"I need to return your jacket."

He glanced at the open area. Checking for eavesdroppers, perhaps? His hand gestured toward his office and I walked by him, inhaling the warm pleasant scent of sandalwood soap. He towered over me, even in my three-inch stiletto heels. In a well cut navy suit that emphasized his muscular shoulders, he looked more like a successful Hollywood player than police chief.

Part of me tingled—the very feminine part—and I wasn't certain that pleased me. Here I was panting like a teenager, while he hadn't indicated any interest in me. On the contrary, he appeared ill at ease.

He closed the door behind me. The room was small but pure Hank. The furniture was standard issue maple, like a department store layout displaying office décor. His desk was neat and orderly except for a stack of papers in one corner. Plaques and pictures dominated one wall while file cabinets and shelves filled with books—probably all law enforcement related—lined another. The third wall contained a long sweep of windows that provided a view of the short stretch of trendy galleries, boutiques, and restaurants that made up downtown Mira Loma. Strung out along a stretch of the Pacific Coast Highway, our city was known for surfing and beaches. In reality, it consisted of strip malls, intertwined with aging apartments, beach townhomes, and vintage 1940's cottages.

"I suppose you're wondering why the police chief doesn't rate an office on the ocean side." He gestured me to a chair in front of his desk.

I offered a smile as I sat. "I figure you requested this side. The Hank Patterson I know wouldn't want the distraction of an ocean view to keep him from work."

His laugh was quick, and my stomach did a minor leap at the sudden appearance of dimples. Hell, how could I have ever forgotten those dimples? And damn, did he look good in that suit! It brought out the vibrant color of his eyes, as pure blue as the Pacific on the other side of the building.

He perched in front of me on the edge of his desk, long legs stretched in front. "I was thinking about calling you."

"About the jacket or business?" I tried not to study him closely, but I couldn't help noticing the taut skin of his lean cheeks. His tanned face and neck provided sharp contrasts to the white shirt. His tie was slightly crooked and while tempted to straighten it, I knew better. Why had he never married?

His gaze lowered to the papers on his desk and he rearranged them. "Partly business."

A shred of disappointment laced through me. I stifled the urged to ask what the other part was. "My attorney is gone. I can't speak without him."

"This isn't about the murder."

What could he want? Something personal? I put

my purse on the floor and crossed my legs. The slit in the front of my skirt slid open. Tanning at the pool had given them a golden hue. I hoped he noticed.

He did. For an instant, his gaze fastened on my legs. Hell, he looked damn near hypnotized. I started to smile as I pulled the flap closed, but he shot to his feet and walked toward the window, as though he couldn't turn his back to me soon enough. He looked outside. "Lots of press gathered down there."

I didn't want to think about that mess. I was more interested in what was happening inside this office, which was growing smaller by the minute. I could sense an electric buzz in the air. Was I imagining it? No, I'd seen a surge of heat flame in his eyes when he looked at my legs.

"They know you're here," he continued.

"Wonderful." I knew they were hanging around hoping to catch someone coming in for questioning—like me. I'd expected them to leave me alone once Rick's connection to Bobbi the Bimbo emerged, but according to Lindy, who was playing house sitter, photographers remained staked out near my driveway. Hopefully Oliver provided a statement when he departed, but I didn't want to take chances. "Is there another way out? Maybe an officer can take me home and you can send over my car later?"

He stiffened and turned away from the window, lifting a finger, as though making a point. "That is why I wanted to talk to you."

"The press?"

Hank returned to his desk, sitting behind it. He stared at me across the wide expanse of oak. I was good at reading body language. He wanted to put distance between us. He leaned back in his chair and clasped his hands across his midsection.

"This is rough. How are you holding up?"

The change in subject surprised me. I lifted my shoulders in a shrug. "Iron lady. Isn't that what you called me when we were working the Bates murders?"

His lips twitched into a smile. "I could have gotten fired for showing you those crime scene pictures."

I'd insisted on seeing the disgusting photos, though they couldn't be used on the air. While he expected them to make me sick—and they had—I wanted to see how brutal the killings were.

"I showed you those pictures as a favor," he continued.

We became close during that murder case. Very close. "That was a long time ago."

He spread his hands wide and shook them like he was shaking a Christmas present. "That is why I wanted to talk to you. We were once friends."

I uncrossed my legs and leaned forward. "It was a little more than that." For an instant I recalled those gesturing hands on my cheek, stroking it. I remembered the tension inside me as I waited to find out if Mr. Straight and Narrow meant to kiss me for the first time.

His hard voice broke the spell like a bursting bubble. "I don't want to seem like I'm playing favorites. We had an actor arrested on DUI two years ago, and his parents thought they could buy him out of it."

"They must have. I don't remember that story." I was upset over his comment about "once" being friends. The irritation made me perverse. "And we weren't friends, we were lovers."

"Now that you've gotten that out in the open, *that* is my point." He leaned forward, looking directly at me, all traces of good humor gone, blue eyes so razor sharp they could cut. "I will not give you preferential treatment. I came to this position with the promise to be fair. The mayor will hold me to it. She's already upset I visited you before seeing Wells' sister."

Despite the fierceness in his eyes, pleasure swelled inside me. His first thought on hearing of Rick's death was to see me? I knew the reaction I was having to him. Given his look a few minutes ago, could it be possible he had the same thoughts about me?

"Should you be talking to me?" I pressed my tongue to my upper lip to keep from smiling. Poor Hank, caught in a crisis of conscience. I leaned back and crossed my legs, letting the slit fall open purposely, but his eyes remained glued to my face. He wasn't going to get caught in that trap again.

"You're here on business." His tone was hard as granite and one brow arched. Yep, he meant business. "Don't expect special treatment from me or my department."

"All I want is fair treatment. Have your officers searched the Bimbo's house? Messed it up like they messed up mine?"

His face transformed into a rigid, frowning mask. "You were one of the last people to see Wells alive. Your breakup was acrimonious, and you don't seem distraught over his death."

"How the hell would you know that?"

"People overheard arguments, and you were seen shopping on Rodeo Drive Saturday. That doesn't sound like someone who's upset."

He was managing to upset me. A tremor of anger rippled through me, but I kept my voice steady. "How would you know I was shopping unless your guys are following me? Did they tell you what I bought? Toothpaste and underwear because your officers wouldn't let me take anything from my house. Why did you call me in here? To interrogate me without my attorney?"

"You said you wanted to talk to me."

I drew a deep breath. That was true. But what I'd wanted was...well, to get his people to leave me alone...

He waved his hand at the door. "In your typical manner, you sashay in here and ask me to hide you from the press or have my officers do a favor for you."

Damn! I hated when someone successfully one-upped me.

"Screw you! The bottom line is I didn't kill him. Put that on the record." I bent over to pick up my purse to leave.

There was a tap at the door, and I heard Torres' voice. "Hey, boss, I hear our anchor lady was here with her high powered attorney. Did the bitch confess..."

I jerked up. His gulp was audible when he saw me. Clutching my purse so I didn't throw it, I glowered at Hank. "Maybe you should give your officers the 'Favored Treatment' speech, Chief."

Torres turned so red, even his bald head flamed with color. "Miss delaGarza, I didn't... "

"Don't say another word to me," I muttered as I stomped by him. "Or I may punch out *your* lights with a baseball bat." Let the pricks think what they wanted about my outburst.

****

I was ready to step outside before I realized my predicament. Through the glass front doors I could see my car, but between it and the door was a row of microphones. Several reporters, including Paula Gardner and Peter Murphy, lounged on a wall nearby.

Why was Paula, a weekday anchor, covering regular news? Wasn't Peter off today? Why were two of my biggest enemies out there? Hell, they'd probably begged to cover the story.

I searched for another exit and spotted a side door, but reporters would see me when I ran for my car. Callahan probably had it placed in front on purpose.

Footsteps sounded behind me and I whipped around, surprised to see a familiar, but out of place, face—the silver-haired guy Delia accosted at Geneva. What was his name? Something to do with a pilgrim?

"Mr...Miles?"

He nodded and his smile displayed very white, very straight teeth. He was more striking up close than seen through the haze of martinis. His face might have been sculpted by a master geneticist—deep set eyes, strong jaw, and nicely formed lips. His gunmetal gray suit was perfectly tailored for his broad-shouldered physique and the light blue of his shirt turned his eyes blue-gray.

"Ms. delaGarza, how good to see you."

The voice was like thick honey. I didn't want to answer why I was at the station, so I didn't ask why he was there. He cast a glance toward the front door.

"I'm not with that bunch," I began in case he got the wrong idea. Whatever he was doing, he probably didn't want to talk to the press either. "I'm trying to elude them."

"But they're your friends." A hint of sarcasm laced his voice.

"Not today. They're media vultures, ready to devour me for the evening news. I'm trying to figure out how to get my car without facing them."

His quick chuckle eased my wariness. He gestured toward the side door. "My chauffeur is outside. Would you like me to have him bring it around?"

What luck! I thrust my keys at him before he could change his mind. "It's a black Mercedes convertible with the license plate, Newsat11."

"Be right back." He stepped outside and talked to a uniformed man lounging on the steps. What had Delia said about this guy besides he was rich and unmarried?

He turned toward me, then stopped and pulled out a cell phone. He frowned at the display but remained outside to answer the call. I took advantage of the time to call Adrienne and let her know how things had gone with Oliver. It felt good to know that two of the best lawyers in the city were on my side.

When my car pulled up to the door, I signed off and peered outside. The side of the building was empty so I rushed through the door and down the steps to my car. The man put away his phone and held the car door for me.

I rewarded him with a smile as I slid into the seat. "Thanks. I owe you one."

He closed the door and leaned forward, speaking in a low intimate voice. "I like to have beautiful women in my debt."

Delia had been right. Definite tuxedo material. Hell, a possible King!

"Send me the bill anytime." My laugh rang with flirtation. "You have my number."

As I started to put the car in gear, something stopped me. I glanced up and realized that Hank stood at his window. Watching.

****

I was still reeling from the King's warm smile and Hank's frosty glare as I drove toward the street.

"Hey, Kimberly," came a shout from my left, setting off a scramble of photographers.

I stepped on the gas and made a hard right onto the street, nearly colliding with a passing car. It honked and jerked around me. My heart thumped as I sped away. Luckily, no one in the media followed. The only car I glimpsed in my rearview mirror was a gray sedan that pulled away from the curb down the block.

I turned onto the wide strip of busy traffic that flowed along Sepulveda Boulevard to drive home. I needed fresh clothes and I wanted to pick up my jewelry, which was locked in my safe. I didn't like leaving it there, even with Lindy's presence. At the next red light, I pulled out my phone to let her know I was coming.

"I think there's someone from Hollywood Happening and one of the cable networks outside," she cautioned.

The jewelry could wait. I didn't feel like another game of cat and mouse. No one would stake out the house twenty-four hours a day. I could go by later.

"Brad Singer called," she continued. "I guess he doesn't have your new phone number."

"I'll call him." I had gotten a new cell number that morning. Even my mother didn't have it yet. "No calls from Delia? She's the only one you can give it to, understand?"

"She hasn't called. What about the station? Like Mr. Adams?"

I doubted the general manager would call, but I assured her I would call him. I clicked off. Damn, that girl sounded timid.

A sign ahead pointed to an entrance to the 405 freeway. I gunned my car to pull right across two lanes to get to the onramp. Cars behind me honked as tires screeched. One came around me on the left with the driver holding up a middle finger.

Behind me, more cars honked and I heard a crunch. I glanced in my rearview mirror. The gray car that left the police station behind me, or one that looked like it, had attempted the same maneuver. Its front fender was smashed into the back of a car while a third was attached to its hind end.

Had that car been following me?

Chapter Eleven

Tuesday, 12:30 p.m.

"You shouldn't have to stay much longer." Reba sank onto a lounge chair at the edge of the Four Seasons pool. "Everyone is camped outside the girlfriend's house. A gated compound in Bel Air is a better backdrop since her family comes and goes."

The thought of the Bimbo facing the determined media while I remained anonymous made me smile. I rubbed another layer of suntan lotion over my shoulders. Under a big hat, hidden by sunglasses, I could pass for a tourist relaxing by the pool.

"Thanks for coming by."

Reba tossed up her hands in a dramatic wave. "I took the afternoon off and told Alan he's paying for us to go to lunch. How are you doing?"

"Evan, Adrienne, and Oliver are handling everything. I got my car back, but after I had to drive like a maniac to escape the media, I'm keeping the rental for now."

"How did things go with the cops? They won't say shit, except they don't have suspects."

I made a face. "I'm glad Oliver's on my side. Southern charm wrapped around a pit bull."

"That was quite a news conference he held at the police station." She adopted a soft southern drawl.

"'My client's only interest is to help police find the killer.' He'll make them toe the line."

I believed her. After I'd told him about Torres' comment, he promised to send a letter to Hank demanding a formal apology.

"I've given up watching TV or getting on the Internet. Everyone makes me sound like a jealous, jilted bitch. Relax. This is like vacation."

She signaled a poolside waiter and ordered a mimosa before removing her bright blue mules and putting up her feet. "I could handle hanging out a few days in a swanky hotel."

"I thought about going to Delia's since I have her keys, but I won't do that until I ask permission. Her snooty neighbors probably wouldn't like having media camped out. I wish I could reach her. I get no answer on her cell and she hasn't answered my texts or email."

"Can't you call her hotel?"

I made a face. "Dummy here forgot to get the name. I think they're taking a cruise along the Amazon after a couple of days in Rio. This is fine. I've got a suite and room service."

"Suite?" Her face jerked toward me. "Isn't that pricey? I know Alan agreed to pay your rental car and hotel room, but…"

"It's only a couple of days."

The waiter returned with the mimosa, and she lifted her glass. "Here's to Alan's checkbook."

I had no illusions about Alan. The station was getting something from me too. I provided personal pictures of Rick and a video taken inside the wine shop when it opened. That gave TV8 an exclusive until everyone pirated it. Alan would probably expect me to give them an interview eventually. Sometimes I hated my profession.

Reba's cell rang and she turned to me as she read the caller ID. "It's Brad. I told him I was coming to see you. Want to talk to him?"

I reached for the phone. I'd forgotten to call him back.

"How are you, Kimberly?" His voice rang with concern. "I've been worried about you."

"I'm doing okay."

"I'm here if you need me." He sent flowers the previous afternoon with a card offering to buy dinner. After my terrible morning, I opted for room service.

"I could use an alibi," I joked.

Brad didn't laugh. "If people hadn't seen me dancing that night, I might lie. You should have joined us."

"Given how things turned out, I wish I had. But it'll be okay. Oliver keeps his clients out of jail. I've heard the threat of tangling with him can keep the DA from going to court."

"I have friends in the DA's office, if you want me to ask around."

Warmth spread through my insides, much like the sun that glided over my shoulders. I turned away, lowering my voice so that Reba couldn't hear me. "Brad, you're being very kind."

"Just trying to help. Call me if you get bored, since I don't have your new number."

I gave it to him and hung up.

"Something going on between you and anchor stud?" Reba asked as I handed back her phone.

"Anchor stud?" I couldn't restrain a laugh. "No,

but tell me about him."

Reba clapped her hands together like an eager teenager. "You *are* interested."

"He's been nice." Maybe I didn't need a man around, but I liked having one available.

"You're blushing."

Normally I might have protested, but gossiping about a hunky guy was preferable to thinking about photographers camped outside my house. Or that stranger inside. Was Lindy trying on my clothes and shoes? I hadn't seen any telltale signs when I picked up my jewelry at midnight, but I noticed she was my size. At least my jewelry was safe. It now rested in a Louis Vuitton train case in a hotel safe. If only I could have a man stashed in a safe somewhere! I could pull him out whenever I needed him.

"Delia says I need to get back into dating, but think about it. That first-time sex thing? At my age?" I shuddered.

Reba looked me over in my bikini. "I should look so good."

The compliment didn't help. Men my age preferred younger women—ask Rick. And while men might want to take me out, I didn't kid myself about why. Dating the Queen of L.A. TV counted for something in this fame-driven city. Maybe I would hear from the would-be King who helped with my car. In the meantime...

"Do you know if Brad is seeing anyone?"

Her nose wrinkled in distaste. "He and Gwen had a thing for a while, but it's over. Haven't you noticed how tense they are on the air?"

This was the reason I didn't date coworkers—gossip or on-air rivalries. "What did he see in Gwen?"

"May I ask something?" she asked instead of answering. Her tone had grown serious. "Are you really okay? I know we've been joking, but, well...Rick was your guy."

"Ex-guy." Was I okay? I didn't know. I said my goodbye at the beach, but part of me still felt raw. I drained my mimosa. "The sun is getting hot. Let me grab a shower and we'll do lunch in Beverly Hills and go shopping."

"Didn't you pick up clothes last night?"

"I need something new. Something fun." And I wanted to make Hank's officers work if they were following me. The more I thought about the previous day, the more convinced I was that gray car belonged to a police officer. Non-descript sedan equaled police tail. Let them report to Hank that I was shopping again. I should let Brad take me to dinner. Let them tell him that!

"I don't think you're taking this seriously," she grumbled, sliding into her shoes.

"Are you kidding? I take shopping very seriously."

****

Reba tried to look interested while I wandered from store to store. Since she seldom wore anything besides oversized sweaters and leggings, I knew this was not her idea of fun. I needed Delia. Shopping was our antidote for depression or frustration.

"This is my last stop," I promised hours later when we entered Genie's House of Fashion. "What about this?" I picked out a silk wrap around dress and placed it in front of me. "Great for summer and Mom approves of anything green. She'll love this lime color."

I pranced in front of a mirror, but a sudden shifting

nearby caught my eye. I whirled, fearing a reporter, but saw no one. Had someone been watching? Sensing further movement, I whipped around in time to see the shop's door closing. Uneasiness swept through me.

"Did you see anyone leave?" I asked, approaching Reba.

Her neck arched as she surveyed the shop. "I haven't been paying attention."

A sudden chilliness set off goose bumps on my bare arms. "I felt like someone was watching and took off."

"News guys?" She scanned the row of windows that faced Rodeo Drive.

"They'd have confronted me. This was someone who didn't want me to see him." Discomfort blossomed inside me. Would a police officer follow me *into* a store?

Reba rolled her eyes. She posed with one hand on her hip. "People watch you all the time. We pay you to be watched. Are you going to try that on?"

I put the dress back. Shopping had lost its appeal.

As we stepped onto the sidewalk, I gave our surroundings extra attention. Weekday shoppers ignored us, but the uneasy sensation crawled along my skin again.

"Shit!" Reba clattered down the sidewalk toward an electronics store. She stopped outside a window filled with TV screens.

I glanced at my watch. Just after five. "Look at all these people, out and about," I said with a laugh as I joined her. "I've discovered in the past couple of days there are thousands who are not concerned with news."

"Fuck!" was her reply.

I looked at the sets. Peter Murphy stood in front of a stone wall. The other sets carried a picture of a silver-haired man above strips carrying various titles of Wine Merchant Murder.

"Hey!" I waved at the video of my would-be King as he hurried along a sidewalk. "Need an interview? I can…"

My words caught in my throat as his name flashed on the screen.

"Miles S. Brookings, Fiancée's Father."

Chapter Twelve

Friday, 2:30 p.m.

My office at TV8 had the look and feel of desertion as I stood in the doorway. I didn't want to be here, but Alan's secretary had summoned me for a meeting. I didn't know why he wanted to see me today. Maybe he wanted to set the ground rules for my return to work on Monday. At least I could pick up my mail and check for messages. My first glance told me I faced a daunting task.

The light on my phone blinked, showing voicemail waiting. A stack of message notes was tacked to my bulletin board where the pictures of Rick had been before I ripped them off in a fit of anger before my last visit to him. A plastic post office bin piled with mail sat on top of my desk along with several unopened newspapers.

I'd been avoiding news for the past week, but I knew the story of Rick's murder had exploded into gargantuan proportions. Reba and Brad kept me informed, while my mother kept calling, fearing the worst. Police had no suspects so far, but that didn't stop lots of speculation. People of interest—mainly me ! Tabloids, cable programs, and Internet bloggers turned it into national headlines. A murder triangle involving the *"Anchorwoman's Slain Ex"* and *"Debutante's*

Murdered Beau" begged for coverage.

Evan was earning his ten percent as my agent, turning down interview requests, while Oliver and Adrienne issued statements that there was no reason to suspect me.

Tell that to Torres and Callahan. And Hank. His response to Oliver's letter had been basically, "Go to hell." His coolness bothered me. I didn't expect favoritism, but how could he forget our past so easily?

If Delia had been around, we might have plotted *his* death. I still hadn't heard from her. How could anyone be so out of touch in this digital age?

I unfolded one of the papers. *"No Leads in Wine Shop Murder,"* the headline read over a picture of Torres holding a news conference. Another headlined, *"Who did it and Why?"* below pictures of me and Rick, like I was the only suspect. A tabloid screamed *"The Anchorwoman's Secret,"* over a terrible shot of me at the anchor desk. I didn't normally receive that paper. Someone left it on my desk on purpose. I shoved the papers into the empty wastebasket, though I was tempted to find out what my "secret" was.

My phone buzzed. I'd skirted the newsroom, but I should have known my entrance would be noticed. The caller ID showed Alan's number. He must have alerted the desk to let him know as soon as I showed up.

"Hey, Kimberly, want to come in?"

"Be there in two minutes." I hung up as a light knock sounded.

Lindy peeked in, her face lighting up when she saw me. "Someone said you were here."

I didn't feel like company, but if I had to see anyone, she was best. She was too shy to ask personal questions. I beckoned her inside. "I have to go see Alan. How's the house?"

Her mousy hair bounced up and down as she nodded. "Fine. Do you know when you're coming home?"

I shook my head as I searched her for traces of my makeup or clothes. She wore a thin shell under a white cotton blouse and jeans. I'd never seen her dress up. Maybe I was wrong to worry about her going through my things.

My feelings softened into gratitude. It couldn't be easy for her staying away from her own home. "I appreciate what you're doing. Maybe we can have lunch one of these days."

Her face turned bright red and she nodded so vigorously she resembled a bobble head doll. "That would be awesome. When?"

"Soon." Maybe I could pump her for info on the Brad-Gwen thing. He was still calling me every night.

Her response was another eager nod.

"I'd better go before Alan has a fit. Do you have time to go through this mail? Toss news releases and open the personal stuff?" I couldn't imagine anything important in the pile. Who wrote letters these days?

"Sure!" She did her bobble head imitation again and I left her at my desk with a letter opener.

Alan's secretary greeted me with a hug. A plump and middle-aged woman, Susana alternately played watchdog for Alan and mother to the newsroom. "How are you, Kimberly? I've been worried."

"I'm fine." I wanted to tell her to pass that on, but I knew she would anyway. Susana was a major pipeline for gossip.

"He's waiting for you." She gestured toward Alan's office.

I entered the cramped office, smiling at the mess. It wouldn't have been cramped, except he had it filled with...well, stuff. Memorabilia, piles of resumes, stacks of reporter tapes and DVD's. Did reporters looking for work still send tapes? They were probably years old. He hefted his large body from behind his cluttered desk and waved me inside.

Allan filled the room with his bulky presence and when he spoke, his gravelly voice could drown out a fog horn. His acne-scarred, jowly face was made for radio, where he'd earned his journalistic stripes before rising through the TV ranks, and he always seemed to wear part of his last meal on his polyester ties.

"How goes it? Heard anything from police?" he growled.

I settled into a chair across from him. "I gave a statement. They searched my house and car. I can't imagine what more they need."

"The sooner we put this shit behind us, the better." He wasn't the sort to play Mr. Sensitive, so I expected no sympathy. "Do you know if they have any leads?"

"You probably hear more than I do." I didn't want to talk about the murder case. "Listen, Alan, I'm still at the hotel. I'd go home, but if something happens, reporters will be back at my door. Lindy is doing a good job turning people away and keeping the curious from hopping the wall into my yard. Thanks for sending her."

He waved a hand of dismissal. "No problem. But do you mind doing an interview while you're here? Maybe a statement about bringing the killer to justice?"

I should have seen that coming. My head began shaking until it was going back and forth like a sideways version of Lindy's bobble head. "I'm sorry. I can't."

His gaze zeroed in on me. "We're getting slammed on this story. Four and Seven were first to interview the new girl and everyone in town got her dad. We're honoring your request not to bother your family, but we need something. This is your chance to let people know how you feel."

I'd used that "opportunity to tell your story" ruse too many times to fall for it. "I'd like to, but Oliver won't let me."

His large shoulder lifted in a half shrug. "I can't force you, of course, and we're trying to be here for you." Now he was turning to a guilt trip.

I wouldn't give in to that either. "I appreciate it. Did Reba tell you I still have the rental car?"

"I thought you got your car back."

"Yes, but people keep following me."

Before he could answer, his phone buzzed and he reached for it, looking relieved. I started to rise, but he gestured for me to remain seated. He didn't speak more than a couple of words before putting down the phone. "Vincent wants to see you."

I made a face. The general manager had seldom spoken to me since he made a drunken pass at me at a party. I let Evan perform all negotiations with him. The two were golfing buddies who worked out contracts between tee shots.

"Shouldn't we discuss when I can come back to work?" I asked. "I'm ready to go back on the air after Rick's memorial next week."

He held up a large hand. "Talk to Vince."

My stomach muscles tightened. I was picking up strange vibrations. "What's going on?"

He shook his head, a small strip of hair on his comb-over wriggling like a silver snake on his balding head. He reached for his phone in a gesture of dismissal. "Call me if you decide to do an interview."

****

The executive offices on the fourth floor resembled a hushed cave as I got off the elevator. The entire floor was decorated in shades of gray. Light gray walls with reprints of Ansel Adams photos, smoke-colored carpet, slate drapes.

I was ushered immediately into Vincent's corner office. Its sweeping views of the Capitol Records Building and Hollywood sign resembled a wrap around poster. He greeted me at the door, gesturing me toward a gray leather chair opposite his enormous glass and chrome desk.

"Kimberly, thanks for coming. Would you like something to drink?" He waved a manicured hand toward a built-in wet bar, but I shook my head.

Vincent was the opposite of Alan. Tall, slender, and sleek with black hair carrying an appropriate touch of silver, he portrayed elegance but with a lethal twist. His face bordered on gaunt, with most of the flesh on his protruding nose and jaw. He favored designer suits, silk ties and custom shirts. Mr. GQ in his sartorial best, a charcoal suit and blue-gray tie.

"This murder investigation is an ugly thing," he began with a benign smile as he unfastened his suit jacket and settled into his custom-made executive chair. Unlike Alan's desk, Vincent's contained only a pile of

100

papers in the center and an Emmy statue in one corner.

"Tell me about it," I replied. Adrienne and I considered Vincent cold as a fish, more like the Shark King swimming upstairs in his gray walled aquarium, looking for fresh victims to devour from his black leather throne.

"I can imagine how you must feel," he said, shaking his head and displaying a sharp-toothed smile. "To lose a friend and be looked upon as a possible suspect."

I fought to hide my grimace at his words. "It's not quite that bad."

He leaned forward, hands folded. "It's drawing a good amount of negative national attention about you."

I nodded, sensing something disturbing in the air—or the tank. Like a shark passing by so close it brushed against you.

His dark emotionless eyes zeroed in on me. "It must be difficult to stay away from work, but I want you to know you're not to worry. You are on leave until this is settled. I have made arrangements to have Gwen Cardinal fill in for you until further notice."

Chapter Thirteen

Ouch! The Shark King had just taken a big bite out of my midsection.

"Gwen? Not Miranda?" Our weekday morning anchor had been filling in and was my normal replacement.

"Since we don't know how long you will be gone, we need a regular replacement. This is the best alternative."

The words hit me like a crashing wave of cold water. I struggled to catch my breath. "What do you mean 'replacement?' I'm prepared to go back on the air *now*. I know James would have to read the murder stories, but other than that, I'm ready."

"Perhaps, but it's not necessary." His face showed little emotion beyond the bland smile that contained no humor. His flat black eyes betrayed nothing. Adrienne and I were right about his being a shark. Here I was in the middle of a *Jaws* moment, and I hadn't even sensed him circling. Hell, I hadn't even realized Alan had tossed me overboard! Vincent struck with a swoosh so sudden I'd barely had time to register pain.

"What's the bottom line here? I'm fired?" My throat constricted.

"Not at all. I simply think it would be best if you remain off the air for now."

My mouth had grown incredibly dry and I fought

to keep my tongue from sticking to the roof of my mouth. "I could work behind the scenes on pieces for July sweeps."

"I admire your courage, but again, it's not necessary." The Shark King circled again, looking to take a fresh bite. "Actually, it would be best if you sever your connections to the station for the present."

"Wh..." This time I did sputter, as I treaded water in a battle to save my life. *"Sever?"*

"Perhaps that's the wrong terminology. I simply mean you should devote your time to getting this misunderstanding cleared up." He offered the toothy grin he gave clients before he shoved their shows into midnight time slots next to the infomercials.

"How can you yank me off the air? That is what you're saying, right? May I remind you I have a contract to anchor the news? Have you talked to Evan about this?"

"Of course." He lifted the papers on his desk, and I recognized my contract. He dropped it and tapped it with a manicured finger. "He knows I'm right. We always include a clause about causing embarrassment or bringing negative publicity to the station."

The tightness in my throat released long enough to allow a hoarse whisper of protest. "Embarrassment?"

His sharp nose wrinkled. "All the news stories say the same thing. Channel 8 Anchor Kimberly delaGarza. We're mentioned like *we've* done something wrong."

"I haven't done anything wrong either."

He inhaled sharply. "Accept this and don't complain, okay?"

I jerked to my feet, refusing to let this damn shark catch me again. "I'm not going to accept anything until

I've talked to Evan and Adrienne."

He remained calm, tapping his nails on his desk. "Evan understands our dilemma. He knows that fighting this could only be detrimental to your career. As for Adrienne, I hope that you don't bring her fire-breathing act into this. It could only make matters worse. I'm certain she'll want to do battle, but any steps she takes in the short term could only make things more difficult in the long run."

"Meaning?"

"Don't fight this, Kimberly." His expressionless eyes tracked me like prey. "Don't make the guys upstairs unhappy."

The "guys upstairs" were actually in New York, but they were meaner than Vincent and ten times more lethal. He might take a big bite out of your leg. Those guys chomped you in whole chunks and left your skeleton for the plankton to finish.

I drew a deep breath. Maybe the wisest plan was to simply get out of this pool. "You're saying that I'm taking time off to deal with personal difficulties?"

"Exactly," he agreed with a tight smile. "You've elected to take time off."

"*I've* elected?" Another bite, and I hadn't seen that one coming either. Damn, this guy was lethal.

"Yes. I'm suggesting this be your choice."

Now I fully understood. He'd cut me in half. Now there was only the battle to keep from drowning. If I made the decision, it appeared that the station was being the good guy—letting me take time off to deal with my problem. But it also made me seem like I was guilty, as though I expected to be charged.

"This sucks!" I protested, but I sank back onto the

chair. "I'll take the time off but I get paid, right?"

As he lifted his flat eyes to me, I felt my arm being torn off. "Do you think that would be fair? We contracted you to be an anchor and you won't be fulfilling those terms. Your contract calls for six weeks of vacation a year and you've earned three. According to our records, you've taken off two weeks, and we've given you this week for bereavement, so I would say that you are out of leave and all our payment obligations are at an end."

Unbelievable. I was bleeding all over the place, and he'd done it in such slick motions. And then it hit me. He thought I was guilty. He was cutting our ties before things got worse.

"I'm off the air and I'm not getting paid?"

He returned my challenging glance for a minute and then his eyes slid away, studying the papers on his desk as though they might be the most exciting things in the world. "Correct."

"For how long?"

He flipped through the pages, shrugging. "That depends. Once there is an arrest in the case..."

"If I am arrested, what then?" I didn't think that could happen, but I wanted to toss anything I could into his smug face.

He drew back, black eyes glittering in shock. Finally a reaction from that slippery shark. I could see the wheels turning in his narrow head, probably thinking about what other stations would say. Not to mention millions of dollars in promotion that would go down the tubes. There were all those buses with my picture.

"Do you think that's possible?" he asked, a hint of

concern in his tone.

I feigned a Mona Lisa smile, hoping to make him nervous. "Who knows? It's a ghastly business." My voice dripped sarcasm.

"May I ask you a favor?"

This should be good. Vincent didn't ask for favors. "What?"

"If it does happen, will you call me first?"

I stifled a laugh. "You mean, like before I call my attorney?"

Putting his elbows on his desk, he leaned forward, hands together. "Kimberly, we're like family. I can call him for you."

This time I did laugh, though it came out as more of a bark. "Family? You're kicking me out the damn door like used garbage, and you have the fucking nerve to talk about family? The way I see it, you're on your own. Hell, I may walk out of here and call Paula Gardner for an interview. I don't see that I owe TV8 any favors."

The black eyes never wavered, though his lowered lip twitched—the shark was irritated. "You're being childish."

Maybe so, but it hurt to learn that people I thought I could count on were leaving me to drown. Damn Alan! Why hadn't he hinted the sharks were circling? Why hadn't Evan called me?

"I might do an interview, if you keep paying my salary until this is over."

His face grew hard. "We don't pay for interviews."

I couldn't stay any longer. If I did, I was liable to reach across the desk and pick up the damned Emmy and throw it through the window at the Hollywood sign.

No. With my current string of lousy luck, he'd be found dead later, sprawled across the desk with dried blood on his temple and my fingerprints on the statue.

"Call Evan when I can go back on the air." I stomped through the door and tried not to slam it. As I punched the elevator button to get out of that gray, underwater world, it hit me that I didn't know when I might get another paycheck.

Maybe it was better if I did drown.

****

I walked to my office trying to retain my composure, even though my hands shook with anger and frustration boiled inside. Did people know what was happening? I doubted Gwen would keep quiet about getting an opportunity to anchor "until further notice."

I remained stoic until I was inside and closed the door to my office. Tears threatened, but I refused to let them fall. I was Queen of L.A. TV!

My phone rang, making me jump. I started to let it go to voice mail, but saw Reba's extension. I swallowed hard and kept my voice calm as I answered. "I can't talk."

"You okay?" Reba's voice was filled with sympathy.

"Iron maiden." I felt more like glass at the moment, ready to shatter.

"The whole thing sucks."

"You knew?" Shock sliced through me.

"The pricks put out a release when you went upstairs."

"Alan and Vincent?"

"Vincent and Evan. Didn't you know Evan is also

107

Gwen's agent?"

No wonder Vincent had been so confident. But why would Evan push Gwen at my expense? I made more money...oh, hell. Unless he thought I was guilty.

"Are you still at the Four Seasons?" Reba asked.

"I'll have to leave. I don't think Alan will continue paying."

"He may not pay at all." Her voice lowered. "He's pissed you're in a suite and kept the rental car. I can't fight him after Tuesday's debacle. I took time off while everyone in town got Miles Brookings. Like I'm the only one who can get a tip. Did Alan mention an interview?"

"Can you believe that? One minute they're asking for an interview and the next they're tossing me under the bus."

"Hey, Anchor Stud is headed your way. Want me to head him off?"

I didn't want to see anyone, but I refused to hide. "I'll talk to him."

Pushing aside neat piles of mail left by Lindy, I took my compact from my purse. I checked my face, but it showed no sign of inner turmoil.

I pretended to be looking at mail when Brad knocked and peered inside.

"Hi, Kimberly. I'm sorry," he began.

"I'm just taking time off." I raised my voice, hoping people in the newsroom heard me. "Let me grab my mail and you can buy lunch and explain this interview thing."

I scooped up the pile marked "personal," shoved it in my oversized bag, and linked my arm with his. I marched through the newsroom with a smile firmly fixed in place. I might be bleeding, but the Queen wasn't leaving like a body washing up on the shore.

Chapter Fourteen

Brad turned to me with a smile as we reached the sidewalk. "Are you serious about the interview?"

I felt bad because Brad was one of my supporters, but I had to shake my head. "Oliver won't let me."

"Then why the game?" he asked, irritation hardening his voice, waving back at the building.

I couldn't say I wanted word to get back to Gwen that we left together, so I used another excuse. "So Alan would let you take me to lunch."

He checked his watch and his lips tightened in annoyance. "Unfortunately, all I have time for is coffee. Let's go to the Starbucks across the street."

While he ordered lattes, I claimed a table in a corner. A few people from the station waited in line, including Susana. Good! Let them know I wasn't running away. Word of our meeting would be back in the newsroom in time for the afternoon meeting.

I sat back and took a deep breath, fighting frustration. Work had been a steady part of my life since high school when I took my first job helping my mother as a maid. Days off were fine if you had something to do. This past week I had lounged at the pool one day, visited a spa before dinner with Brad the next day, and gone shopping in Newport Beach. I couldn't spend more time doing things like that—especially if I didn't have a salary.

Feeling bored, I lifted out several of the pieces of mail from my bag. I only read the top line of the first letter. "You murderous bitch…"

Holy shit!

The next piece was only slightly better. "I am praying for you. You need to confess. Jesus says…"

I flipped to the next letter, a repeat of the first. "I know you did it."

Were they all that way?

Shivering with disbelief, I put down the offending letters. My phone buzzed and I saw my mother's number. Brad remained in line so I clicked the "talk" button.

"*Mija,* I was so worried. My neighbor, Ida, said you might get arrested. Those reporters keep talking like you did it."

I sighed heavily. "Stop worrying, Mom. It'll be okay once they arrest the killer."

"But who coulda done it?"

Yet one more person asking that question. "I don't know."

"Ida says it's probably someone who knew him. Didn't you know the same people?" Her voice was tense, worried.

"Mom, I don't believe it's anyone we knew. I think someone broke into the shop. I returned some jewelry and he probably saw Rick unloading my car and waited until I left. You know what that area is like at night. Police will arrest the guy when he tries to sell the stuff and the case will be solved."

"*Mija*, you should go on the news," she urged. "Tell them about that robber and that you didn't do it. Your brother agrees."

"Tell Stevie my lawyer won't let me say anything."

"Your friend called to ask if I could talk to her."

"Reba?" She wouldn't do that, would she? She knew I didn't want Mom involved.

"Not Reba, *Mija*. Paula Dominguez. That friend who used to work with you."

That damn rat! She hadn't gone by Dominguez in years. But I could see her using the name and pretending we were friends. Anger streaked through me, but I clenched my teeth and tried to sound normal.

"Tell her I won't let you talk. Mom, maybe you should go to San Diego and visit Stevie."

"I don't like the train and it's too far to drive. Unless you want to drive me down tomorrow."

I'd walked right into that trap, but getting her out of town again might be a good idea. And I could scare Hank's cops if they followed me. Let them think I was headed for Mexico. "I'll pick you up at nine."

Brad approached carrying two cups as I hung up. He handed me one and sank onto the oversized chair across from me. I sipped my latte and made a circle with my index finger and thumb. He'd ordered it with an extra shot, the way I liked it.

"That press release was crap," he said.

"I'm not worried about it," I lied. "I just wish police would find the culprit and end this."

He swiveled to scan the coffee shop. The only seated customer was a scruffy youth at a corner table tapping keys on his laptop with rapid motions, eyes fixed on the screen. Brad leaned toward me, speaking in a low voice as though someone might be listening. "I talked to my friends in the DA's office. They say their boss wants to move slowly. He considers this case high profile."

Rick's murder wouldn't be a major case unless... Images of the newspapers returned. "Meaning they think I did it?"

"No one will say it like that."

"Damn right, they won't. Not when it means tangling with Oliver." I gave him a smug smile. "The DA may run for mayor in two years and his office lost their last two big murder cases. They aren't about to rush into a big case and lose before the election."

"You sound confident."

"Confident, hell! I'm innocent!" But that didn't seem to matter. Because of innuendo, I no longer had a job, and there was that weird sensation of being watched. "Do you think police are following me?"

He was the only person who knew about my fear of being watched. "Have you seen that gray car anymore?"

"No. I thought a black SUV followed me around Newport Beach." I peered through the window. No gray car or black SUV in sight.

"Cops wouldn't waste time or money unless they had good reason. If they thought they could find incriminating evidence, perhaps."

"They can't find evidence that doesn't exist. I can't imagine what they're looking for, unless they think I paid to have him killed and need to meet the killer for the pay off." I laughed at the idea Delia and I had tossed around.

Brad's stern expression indicated he didn't appreciate the joke. "Has it occurred to you that if someone is following you, it might be sinister?" He bent close, touching my hand with warm fingers, and his voice dropped to a dramatic whisper. "What if you saw something, or the killer thinks you saw something? Hasn't that occurred to you?"

"The..." I couldn't repeat his words. I shook my head, a shuddering breath escaping me. I'd been convinced if anyone was following me, it was police or a determined member of the media. This was...well...scary. "What could I have seen?"

"I don't know, but he might be worried so he's keeping an eye on you."

A chill skittered down my spine. I looked out the window, studying the street. I didn't like this frightening new premise.

"It could be paparazzi. Or a stalker. I've had people do that every so often."

Brad put down his cup with a plop, looking exasperated. "How can you sound so blasé? Stalkers can be dangerous. Not everyone is a fan."

I glanced at my bag with its nasty letters. Could one of those "fans" be angry enough to pursue me to punish me?

"You need to be more careful," Brad continued. "Do you have an alarm system?"

I tilted my head in a "get real" fashion. "I come home at midnight. Of course."

"Maybe you should stay with me for a few days."

He was being sweet, but that wouldn't work. "The press would jump all over that, even if you're just a friend. Can't you see the headline? 'Killer Anchor Moves into Love Nest.' Hell, you could become a suspect too."

Brad's eyes widened and he grimaced. "You're right. But I'm not joking, Kimberly. Someone killed

Rick, and that person is still out there."

Tiny fingers of fear rippled over my skin. What could that person gain by keeping an eye on me? Had I seen something and not realized it?

Glancing at his watch, Brad drained his cup. "I have to go. Call me this weekend. Maybe we can get together."

I put my hand on his as he got to his feet. "Thanks for being a good friend. I appreciate it."

His smile was quick and playful, earlier traces of tension gone. He caught my fingers and squeezed them. "I like being your friend."

My fingers burned as I watched him jog across the street with athletic grace. It felt good to have a man watch me the way he did, to have him worry about me. Did he have more in mind? The thought set off a warm tingle inside. It wasn't that hot sensation Hank ignited, but it made me feel womanly.

My phone buzzed. I hit the "talk" button without thinking.

"Miss delaGarza?"

The male voice was unfamiliar, and I started to say he had the wrong number. It sounded too tentative to be a reporter, but who had this new number? I looked through the glass window as though my caller might be watching from the street.

"I have no comment if you're a reporter."

"This is Toby, the bartender at Geneva."

It had been so long I'd forgotten about him. I forced a civility to my voice that I didn't feel. Had he talked to police? *Oh shit!*

"I remember you, Toby. It's good to hear from you. How are you?" How had he gotten this number?

The card I'd given him had my work number.

"I'm…uh…fine. But…I need to talk with you…in private."

Uneasiness gnawed at me. I drew a shallow breath. "I don't have time right now."

"I need to tell you something. You see…I have a recording."

"Recording?" Apprehension dissolved into fear.

"I recorded you and Mrs. Lindsey talking about your dead boyfriend."

Fuzzy memories pricked me like a pesky mosquito. "Is this a joke?"

"I told you that I record people for voice classes."

It was bad enough he might tell police about our crazy conversation, but to have a recording? The coffee in my stomach turned to acid as the table in front of me blurred. "What's going on, Toby?"

"I'm sorry." The young idiot did sound apologetic. "I liked the way you pronounced things. When I listened to it later…it occurred to me you might want it."

There it was. The bottom line. The acid in my stomach stopped sloshing. At least I knew where I stood. A strange calmness settled over me. "I suppose it wouldn't do any good to tell you to erase it. That isn't why you called is it?"

"I can erase it, but it occurred to me…"

I knew damn well what occurred to him. "Just tell me how much you want, Toby."

He hesitated. Was he talking to someone? Was this a conspiracy? Suddenly he blurted, "Two hundred and fifty thousand dollars."

Was he kidding? "What makes you think I have

that kind of money?"

"I read in the paper today that you make a million dollars a year."

Anger replaced my fear. The blackmailing prick! "Have you talked to police?"

"No, but Chief Patterson has dinner at Geneva every Sunday night. If we can't come to an agreement, I may give it to him when he comes in."

Hank ate there every week? Delia and I had never seen him.

"I am not paying you a red cent until I hear the recording."

"I can't play it now," he said in an agitated tone. "I'm at work."

"Can you wait until next week? I'll need to talk to my accountant about…uh…financing." That was partially true, but mainly I needed to stall him so I could think it through.

"I'll call you Monday," he said.

I clicked off without answering and realized I gripped the phone so hard my wrist hurt.

What was going on?

The Queen had been yanked from the throne. Subjects were sending hate mail. And now a blackmailer had entered the picture.

What happened to the romantic comedy of my life?

I shook my head. This was no comedy. This was the darkest film noir I could imagine.

No, worse.

A killer might be watching me.

Chapter Fifteen

Sunday, 9:00 p.m.

Hank sat in a booth in the main dining area of Geneva, sipping coffee, his posture one of relaxation. He bore no hint of the uptight police chief I'd visited in his office. In a pale blue sport shirt with tanned arms showing, he looked more like a movie producer who lived up the beach in Malibu. His neat black hair gleamed under the overhead lights.

I'd looked for Toby when I arrived. I wanted him to see me, to realize that his threat to tell Hank about the recording was hollow at best. Should I tell Hank about it? I'd been debating that since Friday's phone call. I edged closer to the table, knowing he might not like my presence, but he wasn't going to make a scene in public.

His head jerked toward me as I approached, deep blue eyes widening when he saw me.

"May I join you?" I offered a bright smile, the one I practiced to convince recalcitrant interview subjects to spill all.

He inhaled sharply, and I waited for a smile but his face remained set. "Do I have a choice?" His voice carried a distinct bite. He glanced around as he gestured toward the seat across from him. "Don't try to tell me this is a coincidence."

"I needed to return your jacket and I knew you wouldn't want me doing it at the station, so I decided on neutral surroundings." I placed the garment on the seat beside him before sliding into the booth. "I'll only stay a few minutes. I won't compromise your damn principles. I'll buy you a drink."

"You'll be my guest, but only for coffee."

I knew why he was looking around. Even as a reporter, I'd been recognized when we went out and it irritated him. At the time, I'd been caught up in the excitement of newfound celebrity. Every time someone noticed me or knew my name, it was like winning a prize. Tonight the restaurant buzzed with activity, but no one looked our way. This was a crowd used to famous faces, even possible killers.

He studied me, but I saw none of the fleeting desire I witnessed on Monday. I'd pulled my hair back and swept it up out of my face and dressed in a simple, sleeveless Donna Karan dress that clung to my curves in all the right places. The light beige hue gave luster to my golden arms and the low cut front displayed a hint of cleavage—hopefully to give his male senses a jolt.

If he felt anything, it didn't register on his stony face. He disliked being manipulated and that was exactly what I was doing. My motives were two-fold. I wanted Toby to think I wasn't afraid of his threat, and I was curious about being followed.

After my discussion with Brad, I started checking my rearview mirror more often and being aware of cars and people around me. As I drove my mother to San Diego, I kept an eye out. Several times in different places, I could have sworn I saw the same green car.

Hank signaled for the waitress and after ordering

coffee for me and a refill for himself, a tense silence settled between us. I tried not to look at him, but it was impossible. I kept glancing at his strong folded hands and the muscular forearms covered with a fine coat of black hair. I wanted to touch him, run my hand along his arm, but I knew I couldn't.

For a few minutes he kept his gaze fixed on the door as though he wanted to escape, his face a sculpture chiseled in granite. "What was so important that you had to follow me?" he finally asked.

"I didn't follow you," I protested, but his question was so direct, I had to look away. He knew me well enough to know when I was lying.

"Uh-huh. How did you know where I was?"

"A little birdie told me you normally have dinner here on Sunday."

He grunted. "What's on your mind?"

I licked my dry lips before continuing. I should have asked for a glass of water. "I wanted to return your jacket, but there is something else..."

"Naturally." His smile was hard, fixed.

"I'm not asking for a favor. I want to know if you have people following me."

"What?" He drew up so quickly, I knew the question was a surprise. "Why would we follow you?"

"To make certain I don't skip off to Mexico? Meet a hit man for a payoff? I don't know."

Before he could reply, the waitress returned with a silver coffee pot and white china cup for me. She filled both our cups and left a tray with cream and sugar. I sipped at the strong, hot brew, watching him ladle sugar into his. I suppressed the urge to tease him about it.

After stirring it thoroughly he took a sip and

glanced at me, shaking his head. "You know I don't feel right discussing the case, Kimberly. I have officers handling the investigation if that's why you wanted to talk to me. Maybe you should ask them."

"Would they be honest?" Too late, I realized what I'd done. I'd made it seem like I came to him because I knew he might tell me. As a favor. "Hank, don't take that wrong."

His gaze over the top of his cup was accusing. "Of course not. You just happened to *follow me* here to find out if my men are *following you.* Sounds like you want information."

I sighed unhappily. "Can you blame me? Hank, this whole thing is surreal. Being followed seems like part of the procedure."

Hank lifted his shoulder in a half shrug. "You've reported on murder cases. You know the process."

My eyes flicked around the restaurant and I spotted Toby in the bar. He looked in our direction. He knew I was here! With Hank. Even if Mr. Hard Ass wouldn't tell me about the tail, knowing Toby had seen us made it worth the effort.

I turned back to Hank. "If he was killed with the bat, my fingerprints were on it, but..."

He put down his cup and shot me an angry look. "Please, Kimberly. This is not a topic I can discuss. Tell me the real reason for your visit. Do you think we have someone following you? Why? It doesn't make sense. If we had evidence, we'd pick you up. You'd never get bail on a murder charge."

The reality of what he was saying chilled me. If I was arrested, I was going to jail and staying there. My gaze slid around the familiar restaurant as though it might be the last time I was free to enjoy such luxuries.

"Hank, you must know my arguments with Rick didn't mean anything. We'd broken up and he kept bothering me about getting his stuff back." I stopped. That didn't sound good.

"I know how you are when you get angry," he said in a tight voice. "Breaking things."

"I've never broken anything of yours."

"You broke a plate once. For a second I thought you were going to toss it at my head."

I started to protest, but he grinned, bringing a touch of softness to his blue eyes. I smiled back, pleased at his change in direction.

"It was my plate." I pounded it on a counter in frustration during an argument, though I did consider launching it at his head. The past swirled around me. For an instant our eyes locked, and a crazy knot of awareness tugged at my midsection.

His eyes pierced me with a blue-flamed gaze that warmed me all over. We made up that fierce quarrel right there in the kitchen, making feverish love on the counter with the broken plate on the floor beside us. Part of me wanted to reach for his hand, to squeeze it, to see if he remembered.

The moment passed as quickly as it surfaced. He broke the connection, lowering his glance as though he wanted to forget our past. An uncomfortable silence enveloped us, smothering any fire that might have blazed.

The waitress reappeared, carrying a check in one hand and the coffee pot in the other. She put the check on the table. "More coffee, Chief Patterson? Miss delaGarza?"

Hank winced at her use of my name. I could imagine what he was thinking. What would his mayor say about our having coffee? He put a credit card on the plate with the check.

"You should go," he urged after she retreated.

I balled my hands into fists and pressed them together on the table. "You're making this very difficult."

"If you have something to say, come to the office tomorrow. It doesn't seem right for me to socialize with a murder suspect."

Murder suspect.

The words echoed between us. Would he care if the killer was following me? Maybe, but he'd turn the matter over to his men who wouldn't believe me. They would think I was using it as an excuse to get suspicion transferred away from me.

And what about Toby's recording? Would Hank listen to charges of blackmail or demand to hear it or give it to Torres—the final chink in the chain that would march me directly to jail?

"Murder suspect," I repeated through gritted teeth. "Do you have any other suspects, Chief?"

He stared down at his coffee as though he wanted to climb into it.

I leaned toward him, not wanting to trigger the sort of scene he loathed. "You know, I've been waiting for you to arrest the thief who killed Rick when he tried to sell the jewelry that was probably the motive. Then yesterday as I explained this to my brother, I realized, how could you, when your crack detectives didn't even ask me about the jewelry?"

Hank's head jerked up and his shocked eyes met

mine. "Jewelry?"

For the first time since the whole debacle started, I felt like I had the upper hand. "Rolex watch? Gold chains? Diamond cuff links? There was close to a hundred thousand dollars' worth of jewelry and a gun inside those boxes I returned to Rick. I have no idea how you're going to track down the contents when I'm the one who packed them, so I'm the only person who knows if anything is missing. Neither detective has asked me to list what was in the boxes even though I told them that was why I visited Rick that night."

He sat very still, staring straight ahead as he digested the information. His jaw clenched and I could see a muscle snapping on one side.

I rose, feeling every bit the Queen. "Don't forget your jacket. The list is in the pocket." I stomped out of the dining area, shooting an angry glance at Toby on my way through the bar.

Ignoring customers, he hurried toward me. We reached the front door at the same time. With a pleasant smile, he held it open. "I didn't know you knew the police chief."

"We're old friends."

He drew a deep breath. "I wasn't giving him anything tonight. I want..."

I knew what he wanted. Money. The room behind us was noisy and I shifted toward him. "Meet me at the end of Mira Loma pier Tuesday evening and we'll talk about it."

"I work until six."

"Seven then. I want to hear the damn thing."

"Sure, it's on my phone." He tapped his pocket.

"There better not be copies."

"No, and we can erase it after..." His smile was hesitant. He was still playing the adoring fan.

"Damn right we will." I turned and marched away.

Outside the restaurant I handed my ticket to the valet. I had given him a twenty earlier to keep my car nearby. I climbed into it and turned south on the Pacific Coast Highway. Despite Hank's coolness, the trip had been useful. Police now had a list of jewelry so they could search for it, and I knew Hank's officers weren't following me. So who was?

Damn, I hadn't checked my rearview mirror. Two cars were directly behind me, and another was on my left. Farther back, a car turned onto PCH. Had someone been waiting for me to leave?

I slowed, allowing the car beside me to move ahead. The others behind me became frustrated with my pace and also passed. The car I'd seen pull into traffic remained in the mirror. That driver must have slowed because he was no closer to me than when I first saw him.

Stepping on the gas pedal, I tried to put distance between us, but the car matched my speed. I remained in the right lane until we approached Sunset Boulevard. With only the suspicious car behind me, I yanked the steering wheel hard to make a sudden left across two lanes. I didn't think it was legal to make a left turn against the turn light, but I did. I swung onto Sunset and watched as the other car made the same illegal turn.

"What's a good crime movie without a car chase," I whispered and stepped on the gas. My heart thudded, but I kept my mind clear. This far west, Sunset was a winding ribbon through residential areas, rising and plunging through a series of canyons.

I checked the mirror. Only one set of headlights shone behind me. If I was in my Mercedes I'd have more confidence, but I drove the rental Jaguar. Approaching a twisting stretch, I slowed, waiting for the car to pass. It hung back, remaining behind me. On the next hill, as I came down onto a straightaway, I gunned the car, zooming up the next hill. Steve McQueen at his *Bullitt* best.

The persistent lights stayed on my tail.

Fear clawed at me and my fingers gripped the steering wheel so hard they began to hurt. I whizzed around a sharp turn at a fast clip and the other car stayed with me. We climbed another hill, gaining speed and at the top I maneuvered through a quick set of turns, surprised at my own skill.

I blew through a yellow light and he followed through the red. *What the hell?*

Maybe it was time to lose him. I leaned over the wheel like Mario Andretti in an Indy 500. The car fishtailed and tires shrieked as I jerked left onto the next side street. The tail car made the same turn. *Damn!*

I was taking a major chance since I had no idea where this street led. It climbed a canyon and narrowed to two lanes, flanked on either side by gravel strips. As I whipped around a turn, my wheels hit gravel and the car swerved. Trees and bushes filled my vision.

"Oh, shit!"

I fought to get the wheel under control and then I was back on pavement. This was crazy. I couldn't even grab my cell and call for help. Another bad move and I'd go over the side and end up submerged in someone's swimming pool.

My lights flashed on a sign showing a hair pin turn

coming. I gripped the wheel, bracing myself. Leaning into the turn as though my body controlled the car, I waited until it slid easily around the bend before pressing my foot on the gas pedal. I pushed forward enough so that the other car would have to do the same as it neared the curve. Behind me it spun crazily on the road, headlights wobbling.

I held my breath, hoping…

Then it came up the road, engine roaring. As it passed under a street light, I could make out its shape— a dark SUV, not a gray or green sedan.

Buzzing around another turn, I spotted a dead-end sign straight ahead while the road itself swung down to the left. Twin sets of lights struck me at once, one coming from the dead end street, the other from the street on the left. Inspiration hit me and I flipped off my lights and proceeded up the dead end street. The car from that street turned down the hill while the other car drove straight in the direction of my pursuer.

Driving into the dead end street far enough to get out of view, I made a U-turn and turned off my car. My breath came in shallow gasps while I waited, hoping he would follow the tail lights of the other car. Seconds passed and then the lights of the SUV approached. What if he saw me? Even as I considered confronting him, the car swung by and turned left, going down the hill.

A big whoosh of air escaped me and I squeezed my trembling fingers. I'd lost him.

****

I didn't feel safe until I double bolted the door in my hotel room and gave the place a quick search. I debated calling Brad to come stay with me, but I feared he might overreact to the chase or my invitation.

Police needed to know, so I called Callahan.

"Detective, this is Kimberly delaGarza. Someone's following me."

"Really?" His voice dripped with skepticism.

"I was at Geneva on PCH and a car followed me onto Sunset. I tried to get away, but it stayed with me."

"You don't think it was a coincidence?"

My words spilled out—like my speedy driving. "I made several illegal turns, went through a yellow light and it went through the red. I know you're not following me...I mean, Hank told me..." *Oops.*

"Hank? As in Chief Patterson?"

"I ran into him. I told him I thought I was being followed..."

"Do you think he'd give away how we're conducting our investigation?"

"You *are* following me?" A tiny sliver of relief surged through my veins.

"Miss delaGarza, what do you want me to do? Follow *you* to see *who* is following you?"

"Could you? I mean, what if it's the killer?" I found myself repeating Brad's theory, but as I spoke, I realized how silly it seemed. Hell, I sounded lame even to myself. I'd let myself get caught up in Brad's fears, watching for non-existent pursuit cars. Gray sedans? Green cars? Dark SUVs?

"Miss delaGarza, is someone overtly threatening you?"

"Overtly?" I thought of the hate mail I'd received, but I didn't know if it contained threats. I put the whole pile of letters through the shredder in the hotel business center without reading them. "I don't know."

"This sounds like a coincidence."

"Do you think I'm making this up?"

He paused. "I think you may be overwrought. Wells' girlfriend says she thinks she's in danger..."

I gulped. "The Bimbo is being followed?"

"That's not what I said, and that's not what I called her."

His casual tone was getting to me. "I'm not an overwrought teenybopper, and I'm not making this up. You know what? Forget I called." I hung up.

No way was I going to be placed in the same category as Barbie the Bimbo.

Chapter Sixteen

Monday, 1:00 p.m.

"Say that again." My voice was weak, my ears unbelieving.

"You don't have any spare cash, Kimberly. Your house, car, your mom's house and car, bills, expenditures. Your money is tied up." Carl Edwards, my accountant, licked thin lips as he slouched forward. "Investments."

"Like stocks? Can't I sell them and get immediate cash?"

"It will take a few days and you'll lose money. Early withdrawal penalties, taxes." He spread long fingers wide and lifted his narrow shoulders in a weak shrug.

Carl resembled a human tumbleweed, skeletal and ready to blow away—unless his scrawny frame got gobbled up first by his taupe leather executive chair. Thinning ash hair covered a white skull and his tawny eyes were almost devoid of color. His white shirt and beige sports coat draped like curtains on a lanky body that was probably the color of dirty chalk. I'd never liked him, but Rick assured me he was a genius with money. The corner office with its teak furniture in a Santa Monica high rise indicated that he made money somehow.

"How much do I have?" I asked, fighting irritation.

He tapped a manila folder on his desk with a yellow-nailed finger. "Right now you have approximately seven thousand in your cash account, but that won't begin to cover your bills. If you don't get another paycheck…" Another shrug.

My throat turned parched as a desert and I could barely croak out words. "You're saying I'm in the hole? I make more than a million dollars a year and I'm in the fucking hole? How can that be possible?"

Carl had controlled my money since I'd signed my first anchor contract. Rick told me I needed someone to oversee my assets so I didn't end up owing my life to Uncle Sam. He claimed his accountant could make us rich and provided glowing reports of the man's abilities.

Was this what Rick meant about going through our money situation? But Rick was gone, and I was faced with a bank account shrinking as fast as the emaciated figure across from me.

"I want an explanation, Carl."

"I keep several liquid accounts for you. One covers fixed payments like your cars, houses, employees. You live on credit cards for personal expenses so I maintain two cash accounts to pay them, plus cover unexpected extras." He steepled bony fingers with a pen between them, rolling it back and forth, skinny neck twisting his head from side to side as he explained. "Every time the first account accumulates more than twenty-five thousand dollars, I remove the excess and put it into the second account in case you need it later. If I see a good financial deal, I use that money for investments."

This sounded better. "Can I use that account to live

on until I get a regular check again?"

His thin face wrinkled like a prune. "No, you can't. You see Rick and I..."

I wanted to jerk the pen from his hands and fling it at him. Instead I waved my hand to stop him. "Rick has nothing to do with this."

"Of course he does. Have you forgotten? You opened that second account in both your names. He used it more than you ever did."

Fear inched under my skin, sending a prickling sensation through me. "You mean to tell me you put my money into a cash account every month, and he spends it?"

"No, like I said, we'd invest it. Funds, stocks..."

"Then sell the stocks and give me the fucking money! I don't care if I pay penalties. I need it now!"

Carl sagged like a collapsing skeleton. "He took it all out."

I felt like I'd been slapped. Hard. "What?"

At least the prick had the decency to look away, face ashen. "The week before his death, he asked me to move it all into his account to pay debts on the shop."

"What do I have to do with his debts? Get the money back!"

Regret filled his pale eyes as he turned back to face me. "I can't. His sister has power of attorney and all his assets are frozen. "

"But it's my money!"

"I know, but it's in his personal account."

"You never thought to ask me before you gave it to him?"

"We consistently moved money back and forth. I understood that he had your permission. I send you statements each month. You've never disputed them."

While wild anger pinched my side, I didn't protest. The statements sat unopened somewhere on my desk at home. Carl paid my bills and provided cash whenever I needed it. Nothing was ever late and if I made sudden purchases, I had unlimited credit cards.

"We'll sell stocks to cover the bills from the Four Seasons plus other expenses this month. You said you needed a lot of money right away. How much?"

I hesitated, but there was no way around it. I fastened my gaze on the edge of the desk. "Two hundred and fifty thousand dollars."

"An investment? I can look into—"

I jerked up and skewered him with my eyes. "It's personal."

He began to blink rapidly, face growing more chalky if that was possible. "You and Rick live too close to the edge..."

"Forget Rick! This is *my* money. What you're saying is he stole it and you let him. That's fraud."

It was as though a puppeteer had jerked up a skeleton figure straight in the chair. "Oh, no! You and Rick shared that account. It was a private agreement. As far as I'm concerned, both of you had legal rights to that money."

"I should sue your fucking ass."

He cleared his throat. "It isn't like he tried to cheat you. Whenever he removed money he responded with shares in his shop. You own half of it."

"Does that mean I have profits coming?"

"It's barely solvent. You know how he is, I mean, was. He spent anything it ever made. And now..." He spread his hands wide, shaking his head.

I knew how Rick loved to spend. I used credit cards, but Rick kept a wad of cash in a diamond encrusted money clip that I'd given to him for his birthday. He tipped lavishly and never skimped on anything. Had I helped finance that?

"I never asked what he did with his money," Carl continued. "I know he spent fifty thousand dollars on jewelry in the last two weeks. I just paid that bill."

"Fifty..." I shot to my feet and leaned forward across the desk as a horrible thought choked me. "If you tell me *he* spent *my* money on jewelry for that rich bimbo, I'll pound you to smithereens."

He gulped, blanching—if he could grow whiter—and reached for the phone, fumbling it and dropping it on the desk. "Don't threaten me. I'll tell the police. They already think you..." he stopped and I could feel the mood in the office shift. Color returned to Carl's sunken cheeks and he replaced the phone.

"You're threatening to sue me for fraud, but do you realize what this means?" He lifted the folder and rapped it sharply on the desk. "If police discover you think he ripped you off, it provides a perfect motive for killing him."

His final words were issued in a hoarse tone, and for an instant I saw delight creep into those amber eyes. *Oh, shit.*

It was my turn to clear my throat, seeking to wipe the slate clean. "So now what?"

His smile reminded me of a grinning skull. "No one needs to know your financial arrangement with Rick. That was between the two of you." His bland tone made his words more sinister. "My advice is to let me go through your finances and see how much money we have once current bills are paid. If I were you, I'd go home and return the rental car. You can't afford this lifestyle until you return to work."

I knew he was right, but I refused to agree with him, so I rose. "Let me know what you figure out. I'll call later."

I left Carl's office furious with him and Rick. What had the Weasel been doing with my money? How had he expected to pay me back? Did he think I was never going to discover his theft? Or was he hoping his new girlfriend might help?

Fuck Rick, who was going to help *me*? How was I supposed to come up with two hundred and fifty thousand dollars for Toby?

****

Tuesday, 2:00 p.m.

Returning home should have been such a joyous occasion. Beyond the windows, the ocean sparkled in the sunlight, but my mood was as gloomy as a foggy June morning.

"Kimberly?" Lindy's voice floated down from above.

"I'm here." I dropped my purse on the kitchen counter.

She came to the edge of the stairs to peer down from the top landing. "I didn't expect you until later. I'm packing my things."

I started to sit on the hard sofa, but rejected the pain. Maybe I could sell the ridiculous thing for a good price on eBay and replace it with something cheap and cushy. I walked upstairs where Lindy was frantically changing out of a jogging suit. Unless I was wrong, it was mine.

Anger roared through me. "Have you been wearing my stuff?"

Her pale face turned bright red. "I ran out of clothes and this is the only thing that fit."

"How would you know that if you didn't try on my stuff?"

She winced. "I didn't. I...I looked in your closet...well, maybe I tried on a jacket, but it was too big."

Too big? Just because the woman was a stick! "Versace gowns and all you tried on was a jacket?"

Her eyes shot toward the closet as though it might tell me the truth. "I couldn't touch them. They're so...fancy..." She sounded so frightened I believed her.

As I looked at her anxious face, her comments hit home. Yes, she was close to my height, but her shoulders and waist were smaller.

"Don't worry about it, Lindy. Keep the jogging outfit. It looks better on you." I couldn't remember the last time I'd worn it anyway. "I have some bags in my car. Can you help bring them in?"

"No problem!" She did her nodding thing before hopping down the stairs.

I began shoving through hangers in my closet, seeking evidence that she'd tried on other things. While the elegant designer gowns might intimidate, the designer suits provided a huge temptation. Perhaps she'd been afraid to remove the plastic cleaning bags.

A sudden thought hit me. Spotting an Anne Klein suit that I hadn't worn for a while, I pulled it out. My mother didn't like the navy color and it was tight. I selected a pale champagne silk shell and a scarf I'd never liked, plus a pair of black Bally pumps that I considered frumpy.

That completed, I went downstairs and checked the refrigerator. It was stocked with fresh fruit and yogurt. I took out grapes, rinsed them and went back to the sofa, munching and plotting while Lindy made three trips upstairs with my bags.

"I'm sorry about this..." She waved her hand at the jogging suit after completing her task.

"Don't worry," I reassured her. "What are you doing this evening? Working?"

"I'm off tonight." She glanced around as though searching for something. Maybe she was making certain she didn't leave anything or had replaced everything she'd touched.

"No hot date on your night off?"

Lindy turned bright red. She sank onto the chair across from me and pressed her hands between her knees. "This guy asked me to dinner tonight, but I don't have anything to wear unless I go home. Do you need me to stay? Are you going out? I saw the suit on your bed..."

"I got that out for you, actually. Do you want it? It's two years old, but it's classic. You could wear it to meet that guy."

Her eyes widened as they lit up. "You would give me that? It's beautiful."

I feigned indifference. "It's too small for me, and I wanted to give you something for helping me. I'd like you to do something else in return."

"Anything!" Her eyes were vibrant and thankful.

"I want you to pretend to be me when you leave. I think we can pull it off if you put on the suit and wear one of my dark wigs. Hell, I'll even throw in a Fendi bag. What do you say?"

Her face crumpled into uncertainty. "The press will know it's not you when I get in my car."

It wasn't the press that concerned me. "You can borrow mine and we can swap cars tomorrow afternoon. Reba's taking me to Rick's memorial, so I have to go to the station."

She tried to keep from smiling, but I could see her excitement. By the time she left in my car, wearing my suit and wig, I felt good about my efforts at subterfuge. I donned a blonde wig and dressed in jeans and a bomber jacket. Pulling a baseball cap low over my eyes, I went out to her Toyota. If anyone was following me, they should have gone after my Mercedes. The street was empty.

This was one trip I needed to make alone. Keeping a careful watch on the rearview mirror, I turned her car in the direction of the ocean and my meeting with Toby, the Blackmailing Bartender.

****

Mira Loma Pier, 7:00 p.m.

Toby waited at the end of the pier, staring at the ocean, a light breeze ruffling his blond hair. I surveyed the people near him before approaching. An elderly fisherman in a gold cap fidgeted with his line. A portly Hispanic man and pregnant woman huddled around three poles while a child danced around them. Farther down the pier two lone fishermen leaned over poles in the water. My footsteps thumped on the wooden planks as I walked toward Toby.

His head jerked up and he stared at me in confusion before recognition dawned. He moved forward, shoulders hunched, hands in pockets. "Hello,

Ms. delaGarza."

I put my finger to my lips and approached with caution, looking from one direction to the next, trying to see if anyone turned when he called my name. Could I be recognized? I was taking no chances. I wore dark glasses, even though the sun was sinking low at the edge of the ocean. The cap hid a portion of my face and I pulled the collar of the jacket up around my neck.

Toby's smile switched from pleased to crestfallen as I snapped my fingers.

"Let's hear the recording," I demanded. I didn't like this situation. I should have let Hank handle it. But if the police heard that audio…

Toby glanced around, as though he feared someone might overhear. "It's on my phone. I left it in the car."

"You were supposed to bring it."

He leaned toward me, voice lowering. "Did you bring the money?"

This time it was my turn to waffle. "I wasn't going to bring it out here. Let's walk back to the parking lot." What would he say when he found out I didn't have the money? Hopefully I could stall for a few days. Mainly I wanted to hear how much of our conversation he'd recorded.

"Are you certain we can't resolve this some other way?" I asked as our footsteps thumped on the wooden pier.

He shoved his hands deeper in his pockets. "Like what?"

"Didn't you say you wanted to be a sportscaster? I might be able to help."

He stopped walking. "You would do that? Even after what I did?"

"You haven't done anything yet." I made the offer out of sarcasm, but I sensed interest. Removing my sunglasses, I faced him, forcing false sincerity into my smile. "Maybe we need to talk this over."

"I would do anything to be a sportscaster..." His eyes were intense. Definite interest.

I rushed on, punctuating my words by putting my hand on his arm. "Think of it, Toby. I pay this money and it's over. Do you know how much our sports guy made last year? Twice that much. Not to mention network deals. All you need is an introduction to a top agent and someone who believes in you. Do you know who Evan Flynn is?"

His eager nod was no surprise. People pursuing broadcast careers knew Evan's name.

"He's *my* agent." I squeezed his arm. "I could get you an introduction."

His grin reminded me of an eager puppy. Even his mouth hung open and I expected him to pant. Would he go for such a simple solution? Maybe I wouldn't have to spend a cent.

"The studio crew at the station can make an audition video. I'll take it to Evan and recommend you. He trusts my judgment."

"That would be awesome."

This was almost too easy, and momentarily I regretted taking advantage of him. I leaned forward. "Just give me your phone. I'll get you a new one—the latest model—and take care of everything else."

His lips twitched and his nose wrinkled. "I don't know. I need..."

"You need what? To think about the opportunity of a lifetime?" Somehow I knew if I didn't get a commitment from him, he would change his mind.

He looked away, kicking his toe at the pier. "I need to think. I'll call you later."

Before I could react, he turned and ran, full speed as though I was chasing him.

Chapter Seventeen

Wednesday, 3:00 p.m.

Rick's memorial service. Ugh. Why had his sister chosen to hold it so soon? In a graveyard chapel, no less. His body hadn't even been released by the coroner.

I sat at the end of the third row, trying to convince myself people weren't staring at me. No matter where I looked, I found eyes focused in my direction. They quickly shifted when I caught them watching. I lifted my chin high, though my muscles were tense as rubber bands. Thanks to my damn colleagues in the media, people knew police considered me a "person of interest". That silly phrase translated in big red letters to SUSPECT.

What were they thinking?

"There's the black widow"?

Were they watching for emotion? Hoping I'd break down? I should have worn a dark veil, something long and flowing from a stiff brimmed black hat. Something very 60s-ish. I had chosen an elegant charcoal Prada suit with a light blue scarf around my neck. I'd skipped going to my regular hairdresser to save money and swept up my hair into a fancy knot that I feared could fall apart at any second. I kept touching it, hoping it remained in place.

Maybe coming was a mistake. No, I belonged here as much as anyone. Maybe I hadn't loved him at the end, but I was closest to Rick in his final years. I belonged as much as that skinny Bobbi the Barbie doll in her frilly pink dress and oversized hat in the front row between the silver-haired Pilgrim—her father—and the Pixie from Geneva.

Who wore neon pink to a memorial service?

And what was the deal with her father? He helped me at the police station, though he knew knew who I was. Weren't we figuratively in opposite camps? He told Delia at Geneva that he was meeting his sister, probably the Pixie. Today her petite figure dripped black from her tiny pillbox hat to her giant onyx jewelry.

Rick's older sister, Jennifer Roberts, was also dressed in black. She sat in the front row on the other side of the aisle, leaning stiffly against her husband, a grim look on her narrow face. No love was lost between us, though I'd never understood why.

In the row behind them sat that financial rat, Carl Edwards, and while I recognized the petite, curly-headed woman beside him, I didn't recall her name. Didn't she work for Rick from time to time? Several of Rick's employees filled out the row. The only person I knew by name was Darryl Young, the assistant manager.

Who were all these people? The chapel was filled to overflowing. Some faces seemed familiar though names escaped me. I wished Delia was here. She would have known everyone. I still hadn't heard from her and I missed her like crazy, especially today.

Reba fidgeted next to me, craning her neck to see

whoever came in the door. At least she dressed for the occasion in a black tunic over her leggings. Even her mules were muted—a fuzzy mix of black and brown feathers.

I almost decided not to come, but that would have fostered questions about why I hadn't shown. Could it mean I was guilty? I knew people said that because I was avoiding the press. Somehow I managed to remain stoic as Jennifer, Carl, and Darryl gave memories of Rick, and the minister conducted a solemn ceremony.

Reba pressed her fingers against my arm as the service concluded and the crowd began filing toward the front door. "You okay, babe?"

I offered a small smile. "Iron lady. Thanks for coming with me."

"I wouldn't have missed it." Reba tilted her head. "Look at Vincent and Evan chumming it up over there."

"They're probably betting on whether I did it."

"Of course you did it." Peter sauntered up beside us, flashing a wide grin. The gangly reporter embraced me like we were buddies.

I accepted the disgusting hug and pasted on a false smile. "You're a real pal, Peter."

"The reporters have a pool going on how long it takes the cops to arrest you," he added with a wink.

Reba punched his arm. "Aren't you here to do a story?"

"I can only paint a verbal picture, since they didn't allow cameras inside. Besides, Kimberly knows I took 'no' in the pool."

"Right." I didn't believe him. He would cheer if I got arrested.

He scanned the crowd, face turning serious. "Quite

a turnout. Movers and shakers, couple of stars, athletes. Even shady characters."

"Shady?" I twisted my head, feeling the knot on top of my head shift. The instant we got into Reba's car I was taking the damn thing down, even if I'd sprayed it to high heaven to get it to stay. I should never have attempted this on my own.

Peter tilted his head to his left, his eyes sliding in that direction. "*El Patron.*"

"Who?"

He repeated the gesture. "Nice old mob guy. Mexican Mafia. Retired to an estate in Malibu years ago, one step ahead of an indictment. He's become respectable, a philanthropist. But I hear *El Patron* still takes bets and can get you anything you want—if you know what I mean."

I couldn't imagine Rick knowing anyone like that, but most of these people were regular customers. I followed Peter's gesture until I located an older man, short, slight and dark with graying hair. He wore a black blazer over an open sport shirt.

The muscles bunched in my stomach. I was horrible with names, but I was good at remembering faces. He and the short blonde woman with him had been at Geneva the afternoon Delia and I got drunk. He'd frowned at me when we laughed loudly over breaking the martini glass.

Patron meant boss in Spanish, but this guy didn't look dangerous. Did he recognize me? As if on cue, he looked my way. He nodded, hawk-like eyes performing the same cool appraisal they had at Geneva.

Peter shifted, tapping my arm. "Hey, Kimberly, let's do a quick interview. I'd love to get your reaction."

"Leave her alone," Reba ordered.

"Can't fault a guy for trying." Peter whirled and disappeared into the crowd.

"Don't let him get to you," Reba said. "Ready to go?"

Through the front door I saw cameras lined up at the edge of the sidewalk. I knew what they wanted—a shot of me leaving. Even Reba wanted me to make that journey so our camera could catch it. My legs refused to move and I looked around for a way out.

"I need to give my regards to Jennifer, Rick's sister, swing by the ladies' room and then I'll be ready to go, okay?"

Reba studied me and glanced at her watch. Impatience vibrated from her. "Do whatever you need to do. I'll meet you outside."

Drawing a deep breath, I approached Jennifer, who stood near the door accepting condolences.

She stiffened when she saw me. "If you say one word or try to touch me, I'll slap you." She turned away and folded her arms, closing up like an armadillo.

A knot formed in my stomach. This was no time to bring up past battles, but perhaps this was her way of dealing with grief. I moved to her husband, Ian, and held out my hand.

He took it with a sad smile. "Thanks for coming, Kimberly."

"I'm so sorry."

"Like hell!" Jennifer's voice shook as she swung toward me. Red spots formed on her cheeks.

"Jennifer, please." Ian took his wife's arm.

"You don't belong here. Not after what you did to

him." Her voice was rising and several people turned in our direction. Ian stepped between us, and I hurried away. This was not the time to protest my innocence.

Determined not to let on that her vitriolic remarks disturbed me, I pulled my face into a pleasant expression, the one I wore when listening to my co-anchor ramble. I needed to get away before the mask fell. I searched for an alternate exit and froze. Hank stood along the back wall, scanning the crowd.

His glance met mine and I started to wave. Too many people lingered. What would they think of me waving at the police chief? That I was seeking preferential treatment? My hand dropped.

I spotted a sign for the ladies room and stepped toward it. As the door clicked shut behind me, I drew a deep breath and realized I wasn't alone. One of the stall doors was closed and whoever was inside blew her nose. Well, at least I'd managed a partial escape.

A quick glance in the mirror over the sink reflected a composed Queen. Only misty eyes betrayed emotion, even if my insides shook. I drew a deep breath, fighting to get a firmer grip on my feelings, then the door behind me opened.

Bobbi the Bimbo stepped out, eyes widening when she spotted me. She flipped back the wild mane of blonde hair. Her big hat was gone, and the pink dress glowed in the garish light. Her eyes were red-rimmed and a surprising surge of sympathy ran through me. So young to be left at the altar.

Better to be civil, I decided. No need for Showdown: The Sequel.

"How are you?" I wanted to say I was sorry, but weren't we both sorry for losing Rick? The girl had lost him to death. I had lost him to her.

She approached the vanity counter, slender face rigid, pointed chin jutting forward. "You're pathetic," she said in a shrill voice.

"Excuse me?"

Her eyes were hard blue spots. "You think no one knows about you? That you're nothing but a frigid bitch?"

I wasn't often caught off guard, but this threw me. This was Rick's memorial service, not the proper venue for a renewed bathroom brawl. With no Duchess Delia and Bitchy Pixie reprising their co-star roles, this would be a horrible sequel. I resolved to keep calm.

"You think Rick didn't tell me about you?" she spat. "He said you're cold as ice."

Had Rick discussed our sex life? Or was she looking for a reaction? He hadn't considered me frigid the last weekend we spent together. It sickened me to recall how loving he'd been until the final morning. And he'd been engaged to her!

I drew up my shoulders, playing controlled Queen in Charge to her Bad Mannered Debutante. "This isn't the time. Besides, he wouldn't discuss our personal life..."

"He told me exactly how demanding you are."

Hot sparks of anger ignited my blood, and my fingers curled into claws. Maybe I should tell Bobbi the Bimbo that Rick called me "Hot Latin Mama" that last weekend.

Drawing a deep breath, I shook off the temptation. Rick the Weasel had lied to the girl as he lied to me. Let this sad sequel fizzle instead of sizzle. I turned away and flung my new Valentino bag on my shoulder in a sweeping motion. The Queen would make a grand exit.

"You bitch!" the girl screamed behind me.

I whirled around. The girl had been repairing her lipstick and my large bag accidentally made her hand slip, carving a long red slash across her cheek.

Stifling a laugh, I started to apologize but she responded by flinging a tiny red lambskin bag at me. It hit my fancy hairdo with a soft thud and fell to the floor. Was this the plot for The Sequel? Memorial Service Smackdown?

A basket filled with cotton swabs and wrapped tampons flew at me, catching the side of my head. Luckily it was light but the stainless steel tissue holder that followed looked dangerous. I deflected it with a forearm. That damn thing hurt!

"You're nuts," I cried as it flew back toward the girl like a returning tennis ball, catching her on the other cheek.

She recoiled and lifted a hand to her face. When she pulled it away, we both stared in horror at a smear of blood. A small trickle appeared below a thin slit on her cheekbone.

"I'm sorry." I was, though I wanted to laugh at the result of her tantrum.

The girl's face contorted and she shrieked.

I reached for tissues that floated to the counter to hand her but she grabbed a ceramic vase and heaved it toward me. It missed my head, though cold water splashed me as it flew over my shoulder. The crash behind me was loud as gunshot, and an explosion of broken glass showered me. She'd busted the damn mirror! Talk about bad luck!

Before either of us could react, the door flew open.

Shocked faces stared in.

"She hit me!" she screeched, waving her bloody hand toward me.

Chapter Eighteen

The outright lie stunned me but only momentarily. The wave of gasps beyond the door stirred me into action.

"Get real, Bobbi." I drew myself up and enunciated my words slowly in my most controlled anchor voice, gesturing at the mess around me. "Since everything came in my direction, it's obvious that *you* threw the childish tantrum along with this debris. I merely defended myself."

I could imagine what the onlookers were thinking. She was the more sympathetic figure with lipstick smeared across her blotchy face on one side and a purple welt forming on her other tear-stained cheek above the cut.

This didn't look good and it would look worse on the evening news—Queen Downs Debutante in Bathroom Brawl. Outside the chapel, TV cameras waited for my exit, but in minutes the crush of photographers would rush the door—the minute word of our skirmish reached the street. I couldn't walk out that front door now, not with my fancy hairdo feeling like a leaning tower and water drops staining my suit.

With attention focused on Bobbi, I pushed through the gathering crowd and hurried around the corner. Spying a door, I jerked it open. It led outside to the side of the chapel. A single figure stood on the sidewalk talking into his cell phone.

Hank glanced up as I stepped through the door. I was so focused on him I didn't see the step and stumbled.

"Are you all right?" He was beside me in an instant, taking hold of my elbow to steady me.

I drew a shaky breath. At least I saw no accusation in his eyes, or maybe he saw the stark terror in mine. "Can you get me out of here?"

He released my arm like I was hot.

"Look, Hank, in a minute that door is going to burst open and a horde of photographers is going to rush out looking for me. You'll have to give the press conference to explain—"

He reached up and touched my hair. This time I jerked back, but he smiled as he held up a wrapped tampon.

"Some hairdo," he said, but he took my arm and guided me down a narrow brick walkway along the side of the chapel. We skirted the building until we reached the back of the stone structure. "Wait here and I'll bring my car around."

I drew deep breaths to calm my anxious nerves as he disappeared around the side of the chapel. Shouts reverberated from somewhere in the distance and my phone vibrated at my waist. I jumped and fumbled with it, seeing Reba's number appear on the ID screen.

"Where are you?" Her voice rang with agitation. "Someone said there was a catfight in the john, and I was afraid you might be in it."

I forced my voice to a calm level. "I ran into an old friend. Where are you?"

"Headed for the john, of course. Are you over that

way?"

My watch read quarter to five. This was not the time to test Reba's loyalties.

"No, but don't worry about me. Do what you gotta do. I'll get a ride." I clicked off.

The purr of a car engine sounded around the corner, and I held my breath until a black car with tinted windows slid into view. The front window lowered so I could see Hank in the driver's seat. I slid into the passenger seat and slumped back against soft leather. He hit the door locks and raised the window. Sanctuary! I doubted anyone could see inside the smoky windows.

The car wound down a drive behind the chapel and along a wide avenue surrounded by elm and fir trees. Forest Lawn Cemetery in suburban Glendale was a maze of roadways along grassy rolling hills and before long the chapel was behind us.

Only then did I begin to breathe normally. I tugged at my hair, which felt like it had been hanging around my head since my tiff with Bobbi. I found a brush in my purse and began shaking out the knot. Two more tampons fell into my lap.

I glanced at Hank, whose eyes were fixed on the road. "Thanks for the lift. I know you're trying to keep away from me."

A muscle in the side of his lean cheek jumped. "I know I was tough on you the other night. I almost called you to explain."

He couldn't say he was sorry, not Hank the Hard Ass, but his attitude bordered on apologetic. I wasn't about to make remarks that might anger him, so I didn't reply. I concentrated on my stiff hair.

Two police cars whizzed at us from the opposite direction, followed by two TV trucks heading toward the chapel.

"I hope I'm not getting you into any trouble," I said.

He glanced at his rearview mirror. "This is Glendale's circus."

I twisted in my seat to see what was happening. Above us, near the chapel, people moved in frenzied motion. Police cars and TV trucks jockeyed for position.

"I didn't hit her. She threw things and I knocked them away. Some flew back and socked her. Clearly a case of self defense."

"Self... Damn!" He hit his palm against the steering wheel and fixed me with fierce blue eyes. It was like being in the headlights of an oncoming vehicle. "I didn't realize anything had occurred. This isn't right. I shouldn't have removed you. We should go to the Glendale Police Department so you can give a statement."

I should have known better. Reba was a better person to trust. Hank believed in being a cop before being a friend. "Can't I give it to you?"

The tension in his jaw didn't waver. "No, and ducking out like that won't look good."

"But nothing happened!"

An ambulance with sirens flashing came around a corner, going up the hill. Despite Hank's harsh demeanor, I suppressed a laugh at the thought they were there to fix Bobbi's lipstick-ravaged, tear-stained face.

"All that for a flying tissue cover? She should have ducked or deflected it like I did. The kid may be young but her reflexes aren't as quick as mine."

"Is that what happened to Rick Wells?" he asked, voice deadly serious.

I clenched my hands into fists but held them to my side. "You are such a royal prick."

He exhaled sharply. "You're right. That was uncalled for. Where shall I drop you? There's a coffee shop ahead. You can call a cab and return to pick up your car or better yet, call Glendale police."

"I came with Reba and told her I had a ride. You can drop me off on your way home." I'd left Lindy's car at the station as we planned. Maybe if I offered to buy Lindy dinner she would return my car when she took her evening break.

"I'm not going home," Hank said. "I have to pick up my dad at Glendale Hospital. He's taking medical tests, which is why I went to the service." He tipped his wrist to check his watch. "I'm twenty minutes late."

The tower of the hospital loomed straight ahead. "Let's go get him." I liked Sam Patterson and I hated to think of him waiting. "What kind of tests?"

"Just a check up. He had a heart attack two years ago."

"Fine. Drop me at the hospital. I can grab a cab home from there."

"*You're* offering to make a sacrifice?" He feigned surprise.

Fighting the urge to snap at him, I summoned a smile instead. "I like your dad. He's a nice guy, unlike his son."

"I didn't have to help you."

"I suppose not. Why is everyone so eager to come down on me?" I sounded like a petulant child, but that's how I felt.

He cast a quick glance at me. "Haven't you heard the saying, 'the bigger they are, the harder they fall?' People love you when you're up, but they pile on if you slide."

"It's not fair."

A quick laugh erupted from him, but I saw no trace of humor in his eyes. "I'm not used to you feeling sorry for yourself."

Neither was I. The Queen didn't grovel. Straightening my shoulders, I sat up straight and peered out the window in defiance. "You're right. Screw them all!"

Hank didn't reply and we remained silent until he pulled up near the side entrance of the main structure beside a tall, lanky man.

It took a minute to recognize Sam. Though he was at least six feet tall, he looked shorter, or maybe it was the hunched shoulders. He shuffled toward the car in small steps. He was thinner than I remembered and his face was gaunt and lined, his wavy hair a shocking white.

With a grunting effort, he crawled into the back seat. His light blue eyes came to life when he saw me. He reached over the seat and squeezed my shoulder with surprisingly strong fingers. "Kimmie! What a great surprise. I'd hug you if I could."

"And I'd hug you, Grandpa. You're looking sexy as hell."

Unlike his wasting body, his robust laugh hadn't diminished. "Don't feed me that crap. I look like hell, girl. I've lost so damn much weight, eating all this good shit, I might as well be dead. No whiskey, cigars, no T-bone steaks. Who the fuck wants to live like that?"

I laughed, but as I looked into his alert eyes, I realized that his mental faculties had not faded one bit. The new lifestyle was probably better for him, but he wouldn't admit it. He'd been big before, his midsection forming a paunchy barrel. Now he looked lean but wiry.

"Life is hard, Gramps."

"Are you coming to dinner with us?" He leaned forward, sounding like a kid begging to make a stop at the candy store.

"I'm taking her around the corner to get a cab," Hank said.

"Oh, hell no. I've been fasting all day. You gotta feed me, and I want good company. Female company! If you don't want to join us, go to hell, but I'm having dinner with Kimmie."

The idea of food appealed to my growling stomach. I hadn't been able to eat before the service, and I was ravenous.

"I'd love to have dinner with you," I said, watching Hank's knuckles on the steering wheel turn white with tension.

Sam tapped Hank on the shoulder. "There's a coffee shop around the block. I'll see she gets home safely if you don't want to come."

"It's not that I don't want to..." He shot me a venomous look, probably wishing he'd left me at the chapel. "Do you promise to call Glendale Police?"

I offered up a playful salute. "Aye, aye, *mi capitan.*"

Sam was one of the few people I'd ever seen overpower Hank and he dropped further protests.

Following Sam's orders, he turned onto a tree lined street. His cell phone buzzed as he parked.

Sam and I left Hank speaking in low tones on the phone and entered the low slung building. Bright to the point of garish, the coffee shop was a page out of the 1950's. Orange vinyl booths with speckled Formica table tops lined one windowed wall alongside a long counter with orange stools. It might be considered retro, except everything was probably installed when the style was fashionable.

A plump young woman in an orange uniform greeted us and waved us toward a booth after a personal hello to Sam.

We settled in and ordered iced tea.

Sam glanced outside where Hank paced the sidewalk, phone to his ear. "Hank won't stay. Something will come up. He does that every time we get together. But I'm glad you're here. How ya been?" he asked, tapping my hand.

"I've been better. You've heard about Rick Wells' death?"

"Sure. I didn't know you broke up with the guy. You and Hank going together again?"

I avoided his eyes, settling my gaze on the plastic menu. "No, he's helping me."

"Uh-huh." His comment rang with disbelief, and when I hazarded a glance up at him he was studying me thoughtfully. "Tell me about this nonsense. Who do you think did it?"

Strangely enough, Rick's death was an easier subject than Hank's life. "Someone after his money or jewelry."

"Hank told me all the cash was locked up and there

was a box of expensive jewelry near the body but nothing was missing. They didn't even take his expensive watch."

His comment jolted me as a shiver of unease flickered down my spine. Nothing was missing? Had they checked the boxes against my list?

The waitress appeared with tea and water and asked if we were ready to order. I hadn't picked up the menu yet, so I waved Sam to go ahead.

"I'll take the diet plate," he said and tapped the top of my menu. "It's not too bad. Comes with cottage cheese and rubbery hamburger that's edible if you douse it in ketchup. The vegetables ain't overcooked and the fruit is fresh."

"Sounds good," I agreed, closing the menu. "Should we wait for Hank?"

"He can order when he comes in." The waitress walked away and Sam leaned back, rubbing his palms together. "Let's get back to the killing. I haven't discussed a good murder case in ages."

I started to beg off, but something hit me, like being doused with a bucket of water. Sam might make a perfect sounding board. He'd spent forty years with the LAPD, including thirty as a homicide investigator. Maybe he could calm my concerns about being followed and give me ideas on what to do about Toby's blackmail scheme.

Before I could reply, Hank approached the table. He touched his dad's shoulder. "Sorry, Dad, but I have to go back to work."

His father met my eyes across the table. "Told ya."

Ignoring the contrary comment, Hank turned to me, speaking like he was issuing orders. "I'll give you a ride to Mira Loma and an officer will take you home."

Sarcasm took possession of my voice. "I wouldn't want you to perform any special favors. I'll stay and have dinner with Sam. We've already ordered."

Hank shifted, impatience radiating from his stiff body. "That's not a good idea."

"Who the hell cares?" Sam said. "I don't feel like eating alone. I feel like keeping company with a pretty girl, so go do your damn business."

"I thought you needed a ride," Hank insisted, leaning toward me, long fingers dancing on the table top as he peered down at me.

I could hear the warning in his icy tone, but like Sam, I didn't want to be alone.

"I can get a cab," I said, punctuating my words with my sweet anchor smile.

Hank started to protest, but his phone beeped and he muttered a curse as he grabbed at it. His grimace as he read the number said it all. He had no time to argue.

"I don't like this," he intoned before turning and marching toward the front door.

"Hank's too damn protective," Sam said with a laugh. "He knows I can take care of myself, but he volunteered to play cab driver to make sure I took those damn tests. I think he's worried about you too." A long bony finger pointed at me.

That might be nice, but I knew differently. "He spent the past week letting me know I can't expect special treatment."

He took a gulp of iced tea and his face wrinkled into a scowl. He reached over and picked up a packet of sugar, sighed and put it back before selecting a packet of artificial sweetener. He mixed the sweetener into his tea before taking another sip and nodding in approval. "Hank's an uptight guy, everything by the fucking rules."

"I bet you were that way too when you were a cop. It's probably where he learned it."

A wide grin splashed across Sam's face. "Hell no. Every so often you gotta bend rules. Don't get me wrong, some things are right and some are wrong, no matter what, but if you can take a few short cuts or grease a few skids, what's wrong with that?"

I'd never heard such a thing from Hank, but I nodded in agreement. I recalled why I enjoyed Sam so much. He was no-nonsense, calling things as he saw them.

The waitress placed two oval platters in front of us. The hamburger looked overdone, though its grilled aroma was enticing. The steamed broccoli and carrots were bright and firm, and the strawberries, melon chunks, and blueberries in a small bowl looked fresh.

Sam grabbed the bottle of ketchup and dumped it on the naked burger while I began to cut my vegetables.

"Sam, I have a question for you."

"Shoot," he urged, cutting into his crimson burger.

"Police consider me a suspect."

"Of course," he said around a mouthful of burger. "Ex-girlfriend. Last known visitor. Only makes sense."

"I didn't do it," I said quickly.

Sam stared at me as though I'd confessed. Then his smile returned and he winked. "Of course you didn't. I know that."

Except for my mother, he was the first person to sound so positive of my innocence. "What makes you so certain?"

"The person clubbed him to death. That's not your style. I'll bet there was blood all over the damn place." He pointed at the small red pools of ketchup on his plate and then flicked his finger to my plate. My broccoli and carrots were sliced into tiny even bits. "You're a neat girl, Kimmie. I can't see you getting blood on your fancy clothes."

I threw my hands up in the air. "Hallelujah! Why can't anyone else see that?"

He stopped chewing. "Does Hank?"

Meeting his direct gaze, I shrugged. "Hell, I don't know. He won't discuss the case." I held up both hands, crooking my fingers in quote signs. "Department regulations."

"I'll bet he thinks the same way. You aren't the bludgeoning type. A gun, a nice safe distance, maybe."

"Or a hit man," I volunteered with a shaky laugh. "If I wanted anyone dead, I'd pay someone else to do it."

He pointed his finger at me again. "Exactly."

Oh, hell, big mistake. "But I didn't do that either."

He waved his hand. "I know. You're not the evil type, even if his sister thinks so."

She'd said that at the memorial, but how did he know? "Has she said that publicly?"

"Almost. Channel 2 interviewed her last night. She said she didn't understand why police hadn't arrested you." A shrewd smile crossed his face. "She called you the Dragon Lady."

"Dragon Lady?" From Queen to Dragon Lady? I didn't like the demotion. Dragons lived in caves, not castles.

"Yeah, but I say if you were a real Dragon Lady,

you'd be manipulating all the stupid TV people. You're dodging the press. Besides, what kind of motive would you have?"

Chapter Nineteen

For long moments I didn't answer. I had so many motives I couldn't risk admitting them. I offered the one everyone knew. "He broke up with me to marry that girl..."

"No go. That's a heat of passion thing. If you were going to kill him for that, you would have used the bat when he told you."

"I wanted to push him off the balcony when he told me. And…" If I was going to be honest with anyone, Sam was the best guy to tell. I wiped a slow tongue across my lips, hesitating before letting the truth slip out. "He may have stolen money from me."

He stopped chewing and put down his fork. Confusion laced with concern wrinkled his brow. "Tell me about it."

"We shared a bank account and an accountant, who never bothered to ask if it was okay for Rick to take out money whenever he wanted. I guess his wine shop was in trouble."

His gaze skewered me and he wiped his lips with his napkin. "That changes things. Did he owe anyone else?"

"I didn't even know he had a money problem. Rick always had plenty of cash. Now it appears I was funding him and didn't realize it."

"Who owns the wine shop now? Did he have a

partner?"

"Me."

"Shit." He exhaled and put down his napkin, shaking his head. "That's not good. Money. That's the sort of thing that makes you want to hire a hit man. Did he have insurance?"

"I don't know."

"Hmm. The insurance is probably in both your names if you're part owner. So if the shop's in financial trouble, why wouldn't you have the hit man torch the shop so you could get insurance money? Do you have a good alibi?"

"No. See?" I laughed, but it sounded as nervous as I felt. "I haven't thought of any of these things. I am not a good criminal."

He resumed his attack on the cottage cheese. "I'll bet you couldn't even plan a murder."

My breath quickened audibly and I put down my fork. "What if I did plan it. For fun? And someone overheard me?"

He drew back, a frown slashing across his lean face. "That's not good either."

"What if they have audio of me making such a plan?"

His quick shake of his head made me feel a little better. "I wouldn't worry about a recording. These days anything can be doctored so police might not even listen to it. I'd worry more about whoever made the recording if they heard you. That's a witness to a threat."

So I might not have to pay for the audio? Would Toby want the same amount not to talk to police? I debated telling Sam about Toby but decided against it. I didn't want to compromise him. He might bend rules, but I doubted that extended to withholding evidence.

"Are you trying to solve it yourself?" he asked, waving a bony hand at me. "I know you reporter types. You think 'cause you can look up information and hang around crime scenes, you know everything."

"I hadn't thought about it. Like you said, I don't know anything about planning a murder or digging up evidence. Thanks to Rick helping himself to my money, I can't even afford to hire a private investigator."

He stared hard across the table at me and I could sense his displeasure, though he didn't say anything. He wiped his hands on his napkin and dropped it on the table.

"What?" I finally asked.

Impatience laced his voice. "Come on, girl. You've been a reporter. You could do it if you had to."

"But why? They'll find the person. I didn't do it, so I'm not worried."

His blue eyes blazed across at me. "You know how many crimes go unsolved? How many innocent people are in jail?"

I had done a series the previous year on an innocent man who spent years in jail. I gulped. What if they didn't find the killer? If my name became tarnished, my career as Queen of L.A. TV was over. I'd forever be known as the woman who got away with murder. Memories of the shredded letters I received ran across my brain. *"You murderous bitch…"*

"You think I should try to find out the truth myself?" I asked.

"Not a bad idea. Who's your attorney? Maybe he has a PI."

At the mention of Oliver Nichols, he grunted. "That guy won't try to solve anything. He'd rather use a clever way to get you off so he gets plenty of press. I can find you someone who works cheap."

Sam was right. I needed to make something happen myself. No one else was going to prove my innocence. Torres considered me the main suspect. Did that mean he was ignoring other leads? Could the real culprit escape while I ended up on trial due to circumstantial evidence and Oliver's desire to hold press conferences?

"What should I do?"

"Find a way to turn the investigation in another direction."

"How?" Damn, I missed Delia. She'd always been the more devious . She would have come up with a plan immediately and provided money to hire someone. "I'm not sure I'm able to handle this on my own."

His hand slapped the table. "What the hell's happened to you, girl? Fourteen years ago I remember you sneaking into a murder scene to get a story. Now you're afraid to dig to save your own skin? I expected you to already be looking into it. I was gonna give you my 'damn you reporters' lecture and then say go for it!"

The Kimmie D he'd known had been a determined young reporter, a tough Warrior-ess ready to battle everyone and everything to succeed. When I ascended my anchor throne and transformed into Queen Kimberly, things changed. People wanted to please me so everything was done *for* me. All I had to do was point from my pedestal and people ran off to do my bidding. Now my pedestal had collapsed like a falling elevator. No one was going to do what I demanded, much less listen to a request. I was on my own. A

Queen without her army. And my battleground skills were long gone.

Cue movie music here—a sad orchestra swell as the camera closed in on a tear at the edge of my eye. I wasn't going to cry, but I could feel the camera pulling back on me, a sad pathetic figure in a stained suit with her stiff hair in disarray, huddled in a bright orange booth.

"You've become soft," Sam chided, making me feel smaller. "Like a damn marshmallow. Where's the gumption of that girl I used to know?"

Feeling uncharacteristically low, I didn't know how to answer, and we finished eating on a low key level. While Sam stopped to pay, I walked outside to call Lindy to make arrangements to get my car. Our normally unflappable assignment editor Kent sounded frantic when he answered.

"Is Lindy around?" I asked.

"Lindy?" he shouted into the phone. "Didn't you hear what happened?"

A tiny flicker of dread ignited inside me. "No."

"Someone ran her off the road last night. She's in the hospital."

Nausea threatened to overwhelm me, bringing back up the cottage cheese and strawberries. My fingers trembled. "What happened?"

"When she didn't show up for work today, we started calling around and found out no one knew where she was. Apparently her roommates didn't think anything about her not coming home because she's staying at your house. We tracked her down at the Mira Loma Hospital. Hit and run, they say."

"What about the car?" I asked, feeling cold all

over. My Mercedes!

"I don't know."

Then I realized how callous I sounded. "Is she going to be all right?"

"I think so. Gotta go. Hey, do you know anything about that fiasco at the chapel?"

"Uh, no. Thanks for the information."

I clicked off the phone. My already topsy-turvy world was going around again, like a ball rolling down a hill. My knees began to shake and my ankles felt wobbly. I spotted a metal bench outside the door and slumped onto it.

Was Lindy's close call an accident? Or a deliberate attempt on her? Chills slithered up and down my spine. She'd been driving my car, wearing my clothes, purposely dressed to look like me. Had someone tried to kill me and ended up hurting that innocent girl instead?

Footsteps sounded behind me and I jerked my head up. Seeing Sam saunter toward me was a relief.

"You look as though you've seen a ghost," he said.

I attempted to stand but found myself tottering and he took a firm hold on my arm.

"You're trembling. What's wrong?"

I tried to lick my parched lips though my tongue felt dry. "Someone ran one of our producers off the road last night. She was driving my car...pretending to be me."

Shock stiffened his face and he pulled me back down onto the bench. "Maybe you better tell me about this."

In halting sentences, I explained having Lindy disguise herself as me. I didn't reveal exactly why I'd done it, providing instead details of my fear that I was being followed. I even told him about my Sunday night chase. Stream after stream of guilt washed through me as I spoke. Finally I put my hand to my face as a final shudder snaked through me. "Oh, God, I don't want to go home."

He squeezed my shoulder in a comforting touch. "Then don't. Come to my place. They can't know where you are now, right?"

"I don't think anyone saw me leave with Hank." We looked up and down the peaceful street. A few were cars parked along the curb, but none were black SUVs or gray sedans.

He gestured with his head and I followed obediently, though my feet protested in my stiletto heels. The Jimmy Choos looked great but they weren't made for walking long distances.

"Where are we going to find a cab?" I looked around desperately, wanting to get under cover. What if the person was cruising the streets looking for me?

"No cab." He stopped near the corner—a bus stop. Huh? When was the last time I'd taken a bus? Back in the days when Kimmie D could only afford public transportation?

Before I could protest, a bus lumbered to the curb.

"I don't have change."

"I got passes," Sam announced.

As I waited to step onto the bus I caught a glimpse of the side. A familiar logo winked at me. *Catch up on the events of the day. Join us at 5, 6, and 11 on TV8, the news team you trust.* Slogan only, no anchor pictures or names. Damn. They hadn't wasted any time.

Feeling empty as a deflated balloon, I followed

Sam aboard and grabbed hold of the hand rail as the bus lurched onto the street. He found a seat and I slid in next to him. This was like a nightmare. Surely I'd wake up and Rick wouldn't be dead. I wouldn't be a suspect. My public wouldn't hate me. People wouldn't be following me.

And I sure as hell wouldn't be riding a friggin' bus!

The interior smelled of sweat mixed with a faint scent of urine. Or maybe that was the guy in the dirty plaid jacket in front of us. I met Sam's gaze and he winked.

"This isn't you, is it?" he said in a teasing tone, tugging at the lapel of my suit.

"Well…"

He chuckled. I could imagine him telling the story to his son and how much Hank would enjoy knowing I'd had to take a bus.

Sam lived in a hilly Glendale neighborhood north of the 134 Freeway with palm trees lining the neatly kept streets. His home was a Moorish style bungalow with a large arching window in front. I followed him inside to a pleasant, bright interior. White walls, high-beamed ceilings, and tiled floors gave the living and dining rooms a spacious feel. The furniture looked chosen for comfort and had seen lots of wear. He led me into a small family room that bordered a tiny kitchen with a cramped breakfast nook in one corner. Despite its gentile shabbiness, everything was neat and orderly.

"Maybe I should go home. I don't have any clothes. "

He waved an impatient hand. "Don't worry.

Besides, I need company. Let's talk about this case some more. I want to know who might be following you, besides police."

We hadn't said a word as we rode over on the bus. Now I could see concern etched on his weathered face. I sighed heavily. "One of the guys at work said it might be the killer. You know, maybe I saw something that night and didn't realize it."

He pointed a finger at me. "Bingo. Haven't you thought of that?"

"Well, sort of."

He made a disgusted sound and pointed at a chair. "Sit down. I'm going to get a notebook. I want to write this down."

I took off my jacket and sank onto a plush overstuffed chair. Heavenly. Yes, I was definitely replacing my stiff, uncomfortable furniture. I shook my head. I needed to stop thinking about comfort. Someone injured Lindy. Someone who thought it was me. Maybe she tried to get away from him as I had done on Sunday or maybe I'd angered him with my silly car chase?

Fear clenched my fists into tight round balls. Drawing several deep breaths, I practiced my yoga breathing. Somebody was making my life dramatic. *And scary.*

Sam marched into the room, carrying two notebooks and a jar of pens, face flushed with determination. He handed me a notebook and kept the other for himself.

"Let's go through this." His tone was all business as he settled into the chair opposite me and pulled a pen from the jar. "I want to hear everything about the night Wells was killed and everything that's happened since."

"You're going to help me?" This was better than hiring a private investigator who would cost money I didn't have. As an ex-cop Sam would be a great asset. He could think in terms of cops and robbers. Good guy versus killer.

"If I have the info, I can help the PI."

I held up my notebook. "What shall I take down?"

"You keep that. After we finish, if you think of anything else, write it down."

As I watched him talk, I found myself smiling. He looked nothing like the haggard man Hank picked up outside the hospital. Color tinged his gaunt cheeks and a sparkle lit up his blue eyes. He was excited. Did Hank know how much his father needed company and a purpose in life?

"Did you see anything strange when you arrived?" he asked. He made sporadic notes in the notebook while I recited my story. Unlike Callahan and Torres, he insisted I keeping going through it, over and over, making me describe everything more than once.

Finally, the monotony and repetition made me protest. "Why do you keep asking the same damn questions? You're not even taking anything down anymore."

He tapped the side of his head. "I want to see if you remember anything else. Sometimes when you go through a story again, you'll remember more details. I'll print this and you can read it. Maybe it'll spur more memories. Now tell me what's happened since that night. Everything."

I went through my steps for the past week, omitting my trip to meet Toby. I even told him about my clash with Bobbi in the bathroom.

As we concluded, he tapped the pen to his chin. "This is a good start. After I print this, I'll call around to see about an inexpensive PI. I want you to think about Wells' enemies and write 'em down in that notebook. We'll come up with our own suspects. Maybe you'd like to get settled. You can stay out in the little house. You'll be more comfortable there."

He pointed through a sliding glass door to a small building behind a tiled patio. "It's an old garage I turned into a playroom for the grandkids. Got a couch, daybed, TV, bathroom, even microwave and fridge. They stay out there when they visit so they don't get on my nerves. It'll give you privacy. If you need food or anything, there's plenty of fresh fruit in the kitchen. No booze except wine because they say it's good for the heart."

I was thankful for the offer of a place to stay. As I walked out to the little house, I thought about how far down I'd come in the past week—from driving a Jaguar and staying in a deluxe suite at the Four Seasons to riding the bus and sleeping in a converted garage in Glendale.

How far the Queen had fallen!

Chapter Twenty

I paced around the guest house, nerves on edge. I started to gnaw on a nail and stopped. How long had it been since I'd vanquished that habit? I couldn't start again. I couldn't afford a manicure to fix it.

What the hell was I going to do? I couldn't stay here long. The place was smaller than my hotel suite. It was basically one big room, containing a sitting area with a TV and electronics console, built in shelves with books and games and a long counter with a small refrigerator and microwave. The bathroom had a miniscule shower and the bed was a twin pull-down from the wall.

I dropped onto a chair and picked up the notebook and pen. Sam wanted a list of Rick's enemies.

Me, but I knew I was innocent.

Delia, but she had an alibi since she'd left the country that night.

Who else might want to kill him?

Unknown burglar? I wrote that down.

I stared at the sheet, but nothing more came. Did Rick have enemies? What did I know of his business? I'd never paid attention to that part of his life. I'd been interested only in "us".

I turned the page. Before night arrived, I was going to need night clothes, fresh underwear, pajamas, maybe a robe, slacks and a top, and probably sandals. That list flowed from my fingers into the notebook. I made another list for toiletries before I took out my phone and called a boutique I frequented in Pasadena. I trusted the manager to pick out things in my style if I gave her the items I needed. She agreed to get a courier to bring over my order and offered to send him by a nearby department store for cosmetics and a drugstore for other items. I added on a tote bag and winced when she announced the total price. Oh, well, Carl, that lowlife accountant, would have to figure out a way to pay my bills. It was my money, right?

With all my orders in, I went back to the main house to see how Sam was doing and get his address for the courier delivery. He sat with a laptop on his knees in the family room. He set the computer aside as I entered and reached for my notebook.

"Whatcha got?" He stared at the list of clothes and fixed me with a puzzled frown. "What the hell is this?"

His hard, accusing glare reminded me of my freshman college English professor who called me in to tell me that my paper and Delia's obviously had been written by the same person. After a half-hour meeting with Delia he agreed to give us C's.

If only she was here to explain my list. I shrugged. "I need some things if I'm staying. I called a boutique in Pasadena, but I have to call back with your address."

He slapped the notebook on his thigh so hard I jumped. "Missy, you better stop screwing around! This ain't no fuckin' garden party! This is serious!"

As chastised as a six-year-old, I chewed my lower lip. "I did start a list."

He turned the page. "Burglar? It would have been robbery since he was present. You should know that."

I wrinkled my nose. Journalism 101 and now I'd flunked that too. "Sorry. But I don't have any other ideas. I don't know if he had enemies."

He scribbled something in the notebook and handed it to me. "Here's the address. Call your damn dress lady. I'll pour us a glass of wine and then we'll read through these notes again and see if there's anything else you remember."

I made the phone call as he went into the kitchen. When he returned, he carried two glasses of wine. He handed me one.

"I don't think you've grasped what is at stake."

"Of course I have. My reputation—"

"No!" His face grew taut and his blue eyes grew hard and sharp as icicles. "Your life. You could end up on death row or someone might want you dead for seein' somethin' and you don't even know what it is."

****

Thursday, 11:00 a.m.

Sam and I started out the next day with a simple plan. First, we needed a car since mine remained in the shop for body work. My insurance paid for a rental, so I ordered a black Volvo from a nearby agency. Next, we drove to Mira Loma Hospital to learn more about Lindy's close call. Feeling guilty, I bought a bouquet and pink teddy bear in the hospital gift shop.

She resembled a lost child, sitting up in bed and staring out the window. Her right arm was in a cast and the right side of her face was bandaged. Long scratches extended beyond the bandage. She turned at the click of my heels and tears filled her eyes. I walked over to hug her, and she gripped me and the bear like a ten-year-old.

"I'm sorry about your car," she sobbed.

"It'll be fine," I assured her and introduced Sam who placed the flowers on the bedside table. It already held a huge bouquet—probably from the station.

Sam didn't waste a minute, going from grandfatherly to lead detective in the blink of an eye.

"How did it happen?" he asked, pulling out his notebook.

Lindy hugged the pink bear. "I was getting used to the steering but I kept overreacting. Suddenly this car came up beside me. Real close."

"Did you get a good look at it?"

"Not really. Black or green, I think. Big."

"An SUV?" I volunteered.

"Let her tell it," Sam instructed, eyes remaining on the notebook.

The untouched side of her face scrunched like a wrinkled pink ribbon. "It was an SUV. I couldn't see any driver. I didn't know if it was his fault or mine, but it was like he wanted to push me off the road. I swerved away."

"Had the car been following you?" he asked.

"I wasn't paying attention. It came up so quickly. I was worried he would hit the car. Kimberly, I'm so sorry." A tear rolled down her cheek.

I caught her hand and squeezed it, guilt mixing with my concern. "I am too."

"I'll pay..." she began.

"Don't worry about the car, sweetie. That's what insurance is for. But if there's anything you need, let me know."

Her young face filled with gratitude as tears flooded her eyes. "Thank you."

As we walked out the door, I turned to Sam. "Someone went after her, didn't they?"

He shook his head. "No. They went after you. Let's go over to your place. I know you said you have a security system, but let's beef it up so you feel totally safe."

****

Several photographers lounged across the street from my townhouse as we turned onto my block. They didn't react to the unknown Volvo, and by the time they realized our destination, I'd managed to turn into the driveway.

The phone was ringing when we entered the house and I rushed upstairs to grab it.

"Kimberly, where the hell have you been?" Brad demanded. "I've been calling you all night. I was worried. Reba said you disappeared after the service yesterday. I had no idea where you went."

"I went to visit a friend," I said, not certain if I was pleased or perturbed that he was being so protective. I smiled at Sam who was walking around, studying the interior.

"I've been calling your cell all night and all day," Brad said.

"I turned it off. Someone leaked my new number. Did you hear about Lindy?"

"She's fine. I was worried about you. Do you need me to come over?"

The idea was tempting. I didn't like the idea of being alone once I took Sam back to Glendale. My phone beeped. "Someone else is calling. It might be my mother. Call me later, okay?" I clicked off to the other line.

"Kimmie!" Hank sounded as apprehensive as Brad. "Are you okay? I heard about the accident with your car."

Unlike the last call, his words sent a rush of warm pleasure surging through me. "I'm fine, Hank. I let someone borrow it." Sam jerked toward me and I lowered my face, knowing I was blushing.

"Good." His voice filled with relief. "I mean, not good, because I understand the driver's in the hospital. When I saw the report indicating your car, I thought...well, as long as you're okay. How did you get home? I've been trying to call Dad, but I can't find him."

"I rented another car and your dad's fine. He's right here."

"At your house? What the hell is he doing there?" Relief flipped to annoyance as quickly as turning on a light switch.

"He's helping me..."

"*No*! How did he get there? Did you go get him?"

I knew I was only going to anger him more, but I saw no reason to avoid the truth. "The rental company brought the car to his house."

"Don't tell me. You stayed with him last night?"

My phone had converted into a block of ice. "I didn't want to come home after what happened to Lindy."

Sam approached me and wiggled his fingers. "Let me talk to him."

I handed the phone to Sam, making a face. "He's not happy."

"Fuck him," he said, taking the phone. "She needed a place to stay, son. Someone's been following her.

Yeah, well, go to hell. She needs help."

He paused, and I could hear Hank's loud voice though I couldn't understand what he was saying. Sam chuckled. "Yeah? Well, fuck you. I'm looking over her security system. If you want me to leave, you can pick me up, but I'm not agreeing I'll go." He clicked off the phone and laughed as he handed it to me. "He's pissed. He may come over."

"Now what?" The gloomy room felt cold, and I walked over to open the drapes and let in the afternoon sun. Light flooded the room and Sam let out a whistle as the magnificence of the Pacific Ocean filled the view.

"What does a place like this go for?" he asked, voice filling with awe.

Suddenly I felt self-conscious, thinking of his tidy little bungalow in Glendale. He'd spent years saving lives and probably sacrificed to buy that home. I'd spent my life giving details of Hollywood gossip and had this handed to me.

"I have no idea. My accountant says it's a good investment, but I'm no longer certain about his advice since he and Rick were playing fast and loose with my money."

"Could he have played with Rick's money too? Could he be a suspect?"

The possibility smacked me like getting hit by a football in the head. What if Carl lost Rick's money too? What if Rick threatened to reveal it to authorities? Why hadn't I considered that? "He sure as hell could be."

Sam rubbed his hands together. "Okay, Kimmie, I'm gonna get busy. You take your notebook and start making lists. Forget thinking in terms of enemies. Make one list with the guy's friends and relatives, one with business associates like that accountant fella and one with people around him—neighbors, anyone. Hell, write down everyone you remember from that service yesterday."

I watched him stride around the room with determination, jotting things in his notebook. Despite Hank's anger, I liked providing Sam with a purpose. Leaving him to work, I retreated to my office with my notebook. I dug out colored pens from my desk—blue for friends and relatives, green for business associates and employees, purple for people at the service, and hot pink for mere acquaintances. The list hadn't gotten very long before a pounding on the front door interrupted me. It didn't take a genius to know who it was.

"Let me deal with him," Sam said, hopping down the stairs.

Hank barged in, blue eyes blazing. "This is the craziest thing I've ever heard!" He looked from me to Sam. "What the hell do you think you're doing?"

"Helping her out. Someone has to."

Hank's gaze swiveled to me, face hard, voice accusing. "This was your idea, wasn't it? You need someone to do your dirty work. I bet he's doing it out of the goodness of his heart."

We hadn't talked about a financial arrangement, though Sam knew I couldn't afford a PI, so how could I pay him?

Sam cleared his throat. "I volunteered. I'm capable of providing assistance so why the hell shouldn't I?"

"Because it's in my jurisdiction! How is that going to look?"

"I'm advising her on a security system," Sam replied with an unconcerned shrug.

"It looks like I'm playing favorites..." Hank walked away, shaking his head.

I didn't like coming between the pair, but Sam was smiling. The old cop was enjoying the confrontation.

"Families help others all the time. Look, son, I need to finish going over this system. Maybe you can give me ideas for what she needs, since you know the area. If you don't want to help, then go about your business and come back for me later." He stomped upstairs.

Hank remained, glaring at me, his face a dull shade of red. "Crazy idiot! He's enjoying this."

"What's wrong with that? Maybe he needs something more in his life." I thought of the neat house that yawned with emptiness. My mother's home was cluttered with toys in case anyone needed a babysitter, cloth remnants from her sewing club and piles of books for her reading group. She kept a pot of coffee warm and cookies laid out for anyone who might stop in and she made regular bus trips with friends to Las Vegas.

"You had to do this, didn't you?" Hank accused.

"He might have health problems, but he's not an invalid. He likes having a purpose. Hank, my life is at stake here. Did you know that Torres and Callahan didn't talk to Lindy? I told you I was being followed. Have you had them check that?"

He turned away and ran his hand through his hair. "That's my fault. I wasn't certain..."

Anger pierced me, but I fought it down. "Someone followed me that night I left Geneva. They chased me up Sunset Boulevard."

Rebecca Grace

His head jerked toward me, and alarm leaped into his eyes. "You never told me that. Why the hell didn't you call Torres or Callahan?"

I folded my arms, trying not to sound haughty. "I called Callahan. He said it was a coincidence. I don't want to tell tales out of school here, but your crack detectives are for shit! Your dad was much more thorough when we talked last night."

"Was Oliver Nichols present?" His voice dripped sarcasm.

"Fuck you and fuck them! They don't want to talk to me until they can read me my rights and slap on the cuffs. Can't you see what's happening here?"

Hank walked away, shaking his head. When he spoke, frustration replaced his earlier sarcasm. "I'll deal with them." His unyielding face told me he hadn't totally forgiven me, but he knew I was right. Hank seldom backed down. Tension crackled between us. Finally, after one final, fierce glare, he marched to the door.

"I'll pick you up in an hour, Dad," he shouted up the stairs.

"Fuck you, I'll call *you* when I'm ready to go."

The minute Hank slammed the door, Sam appeared at the top of the stairs and hopped down toward me. "Sometimes I worry I raised that boy to be a real asshole," he said with a chuckle.

He followed me into the office and wandered around the room, looking at my wall of framed awards and pictures with famous people, including three presidents. He fingered one of the Emmy trophies and lingered at the wet bar with its selection of liquor bottles.

184

"Pour me a drink," he said, lifting one of Rick's expensive scotch selections. "Let's sit on your fancy deck upstairs and talk."

I wasn't certain he should be drinking, but who was I to ask? I poured two glasses, handed one to him and followed him upstairs. The afternoon sun bathed the deck, but a cool ocean breeze kept us from being uncomfortable.

"Feeling better?" he asked.

Closing my eyes, I let the gentle air rush over me. The scent of the ocean filled my nostrils. Sitting in the sun normally soothed me, but nothing had been ordinary for the past week. Sam's presence helped. So did the scotch that burned a path down to my stomach.

"Yes. I'm sorry about Hank."

"He's too uptight. He figured this job would be a stepping stone to a position in a big department, but he's no desk jockey. He prefers working cases. Police chief means politics, pleasin' the fucking bureaucrats."

"He's worried about you."

"Thanks, Kimmie, but you're the one who needs concern. I'm beginning to see what you're up against. Torres and Callahan are working to nail your ass. I've seen it happen. Even good cops can head in the wrong direction. They get blind to facts. But it could get you hurt."

I shivered and not from the ocean breeze. Sitting up to face him directly, I launched a topic I'd been trying to avoid. "Do you think I'll be safe once I get the alarm system fixed?"

"Probably. Whoever hurt that girl wasn't out to kill you. The crash wasn't serious. If he wanted you dead, he would've finished the job. He wanted to scare you."

"He succeeded."

His blue eyes flashed. "Enough to take the rap for what *he* did? Enough to let those cops drive you into the ground?"

"Hell, no. That makes me want to fight back."

"Damn straight! This guy out there don't know the old Kimmie. That's the gal I remember, the gal Hank loved so much."

Sam's comment was like a punch in the gut. Or maybe it was the scotch hitting home. Had Hank loved me? He never said it. He never tried to hold on to me when I dropped him for Rick. Tears threatened and I picked up our empty glasses and got to my feet. I didn't want to think about the wasted years.

"Tell me what I need to do next," I said, fighting the constriction in my throat.

"We need his records. As part-owner of the wine shop you should be able to get them. If he was taking your money, could be there's a reason. Hell, we oughta make up a big board." He stroked his chin thoughtfully. "I used to keep a board where I'd write everything down. Then I could sit and study it. After a while, things would fall into place. Make a note—get a big board."

"I have a dry erase board in my office. Let's go down and see what else we need."

As I led Sam down the stairs, my step carried a spring that I hadn't felt since the day I learned of Rick's death. I had purpose again. I was going to figure this out. The Queen had found herself a General. She was marshaling her forces to go to war!

Chapter Twenty-One

Who killed Rick Wells?

I studied the dry erase board Sam and I had nailed to the wall of my office before Hank returned to pick up his father. It listed time, location, and method of Rick's murder. Below it Sam delineated columns for suspects and motives. He assigned me to post the list I started and begin assigning possible motives to each name. His instructions were to allow my imagination to run wild.

Digging out a fresh supply of colored dry erase pens, I began with my favorite possible culprit: Bobbi the Bimbo. Under motive I wrote with a fiendish smile, "Rick decided to come back to me and she went ballistic." A nice thought, but was that stick figure strong enough to swing a bat with much force? I recalled her heaving the heavy ceramic vase at me. "Sure as hell could," I muttered.

What about a motive for her father, the silver-haired Pilgrim? He helped me at the police station, but why had he been there? I put a question mark under motive. I'd come back to him.

Next came the golden Pixie. I'd seen that woman in a sleeveless dress. She had the defined muscle tone of someone who could swing a mean bat. But why? Another question mark.

I began to copy down Jennifer's name and stopped. No motive. Unless there was something I didn't know.

Hey, she was trying to pin it on me. Did that mean anything? I finished her name and assigned another question mark. I did the same with her husband, Ian.

In big letters and with much glee, I wrote down Carl. Motive was easy. "Stolen money?"

I hesitated before transcribing the next names from my list. Delia and Walter. How could they be suspects? A pang of guilt pinched me. They might not even know about Rick. I'd left messages on her cell, but maybe I should try Walter's office. Maybe they had a number where he could be reached. Grabbing my notebook, I made a note to call his office. I liked the idea of action steps. So would Sam.

Moving back to suspects, I entered the sales clerk, Darryl. While Rick employed a series of clerks who drifted in and out, Darryl had been a constant presence. He worked as a movie extra and kept hoping for the big show biz break. At times he exasperated Rick with tardiness and sick calls. Maybe he was on drugs. Maybe he'd been stealing. All good motives.

Per Sam's instructions I listed people from the memorial service, like the old man from Geneva. Peter called him *El Patron,* a mob figure. Was he a customer? Did Rick owe him money?

I made another note on my new Action Steps page: check mob guy. That was probably too obvious, but it was someone besides me I could point out to police. "Mob Guy" with a question mark went on my board.

Other people who were at the service didn't make sense as suspects so I didn't list them. There was the curly haired woman whose name I couldn't recall, much less assign a motive. Ken Gardner, an actor, was one of Rick's customers. Vincent and Evan? I would like to assign motives but they had played golf with Rick. Joe Flaherty was a football player who threw big champagne parties; Doreen Graham was a socialite who liked Rick's ability to find rare wines. I didn't recognize anyone else. Rick's records might help with this list.

Another entry on the Action Steps page: get Rick's books.

My phone rang and I checked the number before answering. Mira Loma Police.

"Miss delaGarza?"

"Well, Detective Callahan. Did you hear about Lindy Nolan? She was driving my car and someone ran her off the road. She says they were following her."

He ignored my sarcasm, speaking in a monotone. "Can you come by the station tomorrow? I'd like to talk to you."

"I'll check with my attorney."

"No need to bring Nichols. This is a statement on the possible attack."

"Possible? She's in the damn hospital. Even as a journalist I wouldn't call it an alleged attack."

"Have you had threats made against you?"

The question jarred me and my pulse quickened. "Threats? Like what?"

"Notes, letters?"

Coldness washed over me as I thought of the letters I'd picked up at the station the previous week. "Only about a hundred letters. Maybe more."

"Why don't you bring them with you. I'd like to see them."

"Why? I don't have them. I...shredded them."

"Shredded them?" He sounded incredulous.

"I can get more."

Damn, that sounded wrong. I rushed to explain. "I got dozens of nasty letters last week. More probably came in to the station this week. I'll have someone pack them up and send them to you. They were so vicious I couldn't stand to read them. That's why I shredded them."

"I see. As a public figure you would receive a lot of mail."

"Has it occurred to you geniuses that while you're so busy suspecting this public figure, you're letting the real private guy off the hook? Maybe he was trying to kill me because he thinks I saw something and that's why he ran Lindy off the road."

A pause lingered between us, but when he spoke, it was with the old crisp note of barely controlled civility. "I think you've seen too many movies. What time can you come by?"

"I'll check with Oliver and get back to you. And yes, I want Oliver there. Torres is liable to chain me to a chair until I confess."

"We're not that bad." His chuckle was a surprise.

"Right." I was about to make another sarcastic comment, but then I remembered something. "Did you know I own half the wine shop?"

"Yes."

Had they discovered he stole my money? "We were business partners and intended to continue even though our personal relationship was over."

Who could argue that? The only person who knew the truth was dead. I adopted a business-like voice.

"Can I get into the shop or is it still a crime scene? I need to check his books and see if there are any

190

customers expecting special shipments."

"We have his books but we're finished with them. You can pick them up tomorrow."

I hung up with a smile and turned my attention back to the list. I marked off "get books" on the Action Steps page. The next time Professor Sam Patterson studied my homework, I was going to get an "A".

****

"This is a bad idea." Brad frowned at my board before flipping through my notebook.

We sat in my office after dinner. He had come over at my request since I still felt uncomfortable about being home alone. The security company wouldn't reinforce my system until the next day. I showed him my board, thinking he would approve, but he agreed with Hank.

"Police should handle this."

"You said the killer could be watching me."

"Then hire a bodyguard or PI. Do you want me to find someone for you?" His voice was eager and he watched me like a puppy waiting for a treat.

"That's sweet, but I have professional help—a retired LAPD homicide detective named Sam Patterson. The board and notebook were his ideas."

"Good. Let him do the dirty work." He closed the notebook and the subject. "Let's go back upstairs and I'll make you a drink. You need to relax."

No argument there. It was nice to have someone who wanted to pamper me. He'd picked up dinner and made a salad while I showered and changed into a new silk lounging gown. For the first time in days, I felt human.

Settling onto the hard sofa, I grimaced. "Do you

like shopping? I've decided to get new furniture. Normally I'd take Delia, but since she's not here..." I gestured toward him as he approached holding two martini glasses. He held one out to me and sat beside me.

I sipped it, swishing the cold liquid in my mouth and savoring the taste. "Perfect."

"This is more like it. You should be shopping, not worrying about this killing." He leaned toward me and I was aware of his arm on the back of the sofa and the whisper of his breath on my bare skin.

"I know shopping. I haven't done much investigating since I was a reporter and that was years ago." Taking another drink, I leaned my head back and let the liquor do its relaxing work. Maybe he was right. I'd provided Sam a good start. Now he could take over.

"I'll go shopping with you, especially if it keeps you out of trouble."

I shot him a teasing grin. "Being with you won't get me in trouble?"

His fingers pushed a lock of hair back on my forehead. "Could it?"

A quick breath escaped me as memories shot through my brain—and body—of the day his gentle fingers massaged my shoulders.

His eyes were warm as his handsome face lowered until it was a few inches from me. I could see the light stubble of a late afternoon growth on his sculpted chin. I brushed his chin with the palm of my hand, letting the rough layer tickle my hand.

"You might be more deadly than the killer."

His lips curved into a smile and he caught my hand. He squeezed it and touched it to his lips in a gentle kiss that made my insides tingle.

"I hope so." Keeping hold of my hand, he put his glass on the coffee table and took my glass from me. Our eyes held as he leaned toward me again.

My stomach tensed, and a tiny spark of awareness swept through me. I sensed that the moment had come—the tantalizing pause between awareness and action. The next step would be the first kiss.

His face moved toward me and I closed my eyes and waited, ready to accept whatever was coming. Suddenly, it was as though something jerked my head back, like an invisible rubber band attached to the rear of my skull. I pulled my hand from his. "Wait!"

He jerked back as though I'd slapped him. "I'm sorry. I didn't mean to rush you."

I touched his chin with my fingertips. "It's okay. I...wanted..."

I didn't know what to say, but I knew sex was not the answer. I'd never shared Delia's "if it feels good, why not?" motto.

"It's too soon, I guess... Rick's only been gone...well...." It sounded like the excuse it was. Rick had been gone from my life for weeks.

Brad's smile filled with sympathy as he stroked my hair. "I understand, Kimberly. But you know I find you incredibly sexy."

"Because of who I am? I might not have that role much longer."

He took my hand again and his voice rang with boyish hurt. "How can you think that?"

"Would you would find me sexy if I was a maid changing the sheets in your hotel room?" I asked, thinking of Kimmie D's old life.

He lifted my fingers and brushed them across his lips. "We'd be wearing out those sheets."

I leaned forward and kissed his cheek. "Thank you."

He caught my chin and turned my face toward him and kissed me quickly on the lips. "I'm in no rush. Whatever happens, it'll be worth the wait."

Chapter Twenty-Two

Mira Loma PD, Friday 10:00 a.m.

Dressed in a pale lime pantsuit with my hair tied back, I projected cool-as-a-cucumber style as I arrived to meet Callahan. Oliver had been delayed on a case, but he provided me with strict instructions on what I could say. Instead of the interview room, Callahan led me to his cluttered desk in the open squad area.

"Did you talk to Lindy?" I asked.

"Detective Torres is interviewing her. Tell me why you think you're being followed."

I repeated the information from the first moment I felt uneasy. Callahan jotted notes on a tablet, nodding every so often, but he never asked a question.

When I concluded, I reached into my purse. "I've come up with a list of people who might want to kill Rick." I pulled out a duplicate of my suspect list.

He put it on the desk, not checking it as he flipped through pages of the notebook. "Let's talk about Wells for a minute. Tell me about his gambling."

Of all the things he could ask, that surprised me. "What do you mean?"

"Did he do a lot of gambling?"

Where had this come from? "Super Bowl, World Series, March Madness. Football pools."

He nodded, his eyes cool, giving nothing away.

"No Lakers, no boxing, no Vegas?"

With his financial problems? I almost asked. "We used to go to Las Vegas quite a bit. For a while we went every month."

"Uh-huh?" His eyes flickered to me, scrutinizing me. I sensed he was searching for something. "Did he enjoy it?"

"Rick could have developed a serious gambling problem. A couple of weekends he lost thirty thousand dollars. One weekend it was creeping toward sixty, before he started winning it back. At that point I put my foot down. I wasn't going to lose thousands just to stay in a gaudy hotel room and get free meals. We stopped going."

Callahan stroked the side of his face as though he had a beard. What did he know? Was this something to tell Sam?

"Was he gambling?" I asked, thinking about my lost money.

"Possibly," he said and turned back to a folder on his desk.

Gambling made sense. We had a lavish lifestyle, but this might answer how he managed to spend so much of my money.

"I worried he could become compulsive about it," I continued, hoping for a response. "His eyes would glaze over at the slot machine or he'd sit at the blackjack table for hours, convinced he had a system. Every roll of the dice was going to bring a fortune. I could watch when he was winning, but when he lost, he became morose and mean."

"Mean?" That grabbed his attention and he sat forward. "In what way?"

"He'd get verbally abusive. Not to me. He knew better, but to others. Waitresses, dealers."

"What do you mean he knew better than to be abusive to you?"

That sounded like a question Oliver wouldn't want me to answer, but I sensed Callahan might read more into it if I didn't. Besides, the reason was simple. "I'd leave him there and come home. Several times I took his car so he had to fly back."

Callahan stared at me for a moment, and he started to say something and then stopped. Could Rick have been going to Las Vegas without me? We never questioned each other if we made separate weekend plans. There were weekends he had business meetings or I might go to a spa. We kept in constant touch by cell, texts, and email. It would have been easy to say he was in San Francisco and be in Vegas instead.

I glanced around the room, digesting what I'd learned, and spied Hank. As though he knew I was there, his eyes flashed across the expanse of desks and met mine. I turned away, but I could sense him moving toward us.

He stopped by the desk, not acknowledging me, addressing Callahan. "I'll send you notes on what Brookings said about the threat against his daughter."

Callahan leaned back on his chair and nodded. "Thanks for going over, Chief. Brookings is a prick. Where does he get off saying he'll only speak to the chief? Like we're nothing but errand boys. What the fuck was so important?"

Brookings? As in Bobbi the Bimbo? As in the Pilgrim—Miles Standish Brookings? Callahan's frustration amused me. Finally! Someone he couldn't push around!

Hank handed him a manila envelope. "See what you think. You might send that glass to the lab, but they passed it around, so if it had viable fingerprints, they're gone. Might be something on the note, though."

Hank fierce blue eyes flickered to me for the first time. "Miss delaGarza, can you come by my office before you leave? I need to discuss the security work my father was doing on your behalf." His voice was loud enough to carry beyond me and Callahan. He was attempting to get my connection to Sam out in the open.

I started to say no, but Callahan emptied the contents of the manila envelope onto his desk. Inside were two plastic bags. One held a lethal looking sliver of glass, the other a note written in large red block letters.

I gasped and both Hank and Callahan jerked toward me.

"Has anyone sent you anything like this?" Callahan asked.

I stared at it, shaking my head and realized that Hank had become very still. My eyes met his, and I could see he was starting to catch the significance.

"Are we finished here?" I asked Callahan, my hand beginning to shake.

"Yeah, sure," he said, distracted by the glass.

I sensed Hank watching me, but I couldn't meet his eyes. Because I knew the origin of the glass and the note.

****

Hank stood by his desk, absently rummaging through a folder when I tapped on the open door. He waved me inside without looking up.

"Hank, I need to talk to you. About that note..."

He held up a hand. "Let the lab handle it."

"But..."

His eyes avoided mine, eyes focused on the folder. "I mean it, Kimberly. If you have anything to say, you'd better have your attorney with you. I don't want to hear..."—he held up his fingers in a quote sign— "anything 'off the record,' that might get it disallowed in court."

He was right. I needed to discuss this with Oliver. It had been a joke. A terrible joke.

Even though my afternoon at Geneva with Delia was a boozy fog, I recalled that part with the clarity of yesterday. We'd stumbled along the cobbled walkway as we waited for her driver to take us home. We stopped when we saw Rick's Jaguar convertible.

"I thought you said he wasn't with her," I told Delia.

"I'll bet the lousy Weasel went up the back walkway to avoid us. He probably saw our cars and knew we were in the bar." She paused beside the open convertible. "We should smash his windshield. There's a rock garden over there and the valets are all busy."

"We'd get busted for vandalism." At least I hadn't been drunk enough to do that.

"Then let's leave a note saying we're after him. Remember what we did to the creep who dumped me senior year? We'd leave notes on his car and it made him crazy. I've got a notepad and pen. Think of something obnoxious to say." She opened her purse and reached inside and shrieked.

"What?"

She lifted out a napkin and unrolled it to show the

sharp glass stem from my broken martini glass. "Let's leave this. I'll get a key envelope from the valet. You write the note."

While she was gone, I searched in her purse for a pen. Not finding one, I opted for a red lip liner pencil and scribbled on the napkin. I couldn't remember the exact words—something about death. I figured Rick would know my handwriting and write it off as the nasty joke it was supposed to be.

When Delia returned with the envelope, we put the glass and note into it and tossed it onto the passenger seat of the car. As Delia's limo pulled into the drive, we rushed toward it, giggling like school girls.

How Bobbi ended up with the broken stem was a mystery, but it could be another nail in my coffin. I let the memory fade back into its drunken fogbank and turned to Hank.

"Why did you want to see me? Thanks for bringing Sam to oversee the security installation. He said he stayed with you last night."

"Sam made it sound like the two of you are investigating." He looked at me, eyes sharp as darts.

"Someone needs to find the killer. What if he's after me too? Think about Lindy. She was driving my car. The hit and run driver might have been after me."

Hank waved an impatient hand. "Torres is talking to her, but from what I've heard, she was driving too fast and may have been racing the other car."

"She told me she was careful."

"You think she'd tell the truth if she was racing? Look, I would appreciate it if you hired a PI and left my dad out of this."

"All you're worried about is looking bad for your

mayor and people like the Brookings family. I'm sure they'll give you a nice contribution to your next campaign for providing personal attention."

"I am not elected," he said through gritted teeth.

"But you are worried about your job and appearances. Isn't that why you were making such a big deal out of my 'security arrangement' with your dad?" It was my turn to hold up the quote fingers.

The coldness that grew in his eyes was like an approaching glacier. "Look, I know what's happening. You're doing your normal Kimberly crap."

His harsh words smacked into me like a slap of hard wind to my face. "My what?"

He unloaded on me with the force of a blizzard. "You're a pampered princess who is so damned used to getting your own way that you can't handle it when the real world invades your private fantasy life! Well, it's here, lady, and it's real. But I won't stand by and let you hurt my father by getting him involved."

****

Friday, 3:00 p.m.

I wasn't certain how much to tell Sam about my confrontation with Hank. He had remained at the house working with the security company while I drove to the police station. Now he wanted to go through my list of suspects. He sat in my office, leaning back on his chair, reading glasses perched on the end of his nose as he examined my notes. A bony finger tapped the page. "Girly colors, but this is good."

His comment was the equivalent of a good grade from a teacher and it improved my dismal mood. My nerves had been on edge since I left the police station. Thank goodness for Sam and the glass of scotch at my fingertips.

"I have Rick's books," I said, patting the pile on my desk. "I don't know if they'll be much help." Callahan had them waiting when I left Hank's office.

Sam leaned over and opened one, frowning at the lines of neat little figures. "Why isn't all this on a computer?"

"Rick was a techni-phobe. He did most things, like take orders, by hand. I fought to get him to switch from a Filofax planner to a Blackberry and he only recently got a smartphone."

"What we need to do is to go through the wine shop. Do you have a key to the place?"

"No, and now that Jennifer controls things I doubt she'll give me one."

He peered at me over the top of his glasses. "You're part owner. That counts for something whether she likes it or not."

"Wouldn't the police have taken anything of interest?"

"They might have missed something that only you could peg as important. They're looking for the obvious. We need to look beyond that. How are your skills of observation?"

The question made me smile. "I can tell you the exact way to pick out a copy of a designer dress."

The fierce frown that washed over his face reminded me of Hank, though it was an older version. "You better take this more seriously, missy."

His displeasure had an equal effect as his earlier praise, but in the opposite direction. Lurching to my feet, I walked to the sliding glass door and yanked it open. As I stepped onto the patio, I took a deep breath, pressing my lips together.

Hank's granite expression at the police station haunted me. I once described his blue eyes as dreamy warm pools I'd like to dive into. But they were hard as polar ice today. I'd have cracked my skull if I had tried to jump into them.

Why did his words hurt so much? Was that how he saw me? Sam said that Hank had loved me, but I doubted anything was left of those feelings. Maybe they were dead when we broke up and that was why he let me go so easily.

"Do you think I'm a pampered princess?" I asked, turning to Sam.

He was staring at a notebook, deep in thought. As my question floated through the door, his head jerked up like a deer startled by a sudden sound. "What?"

Not revealing the cause of the argument, I related portions of my battle with Hank. "He called me a pampered princess who lived in a fantasy world." The words stung as I repeated them and Sam seemed to recognize my pain.

He stood and walked over to me, placing a gentle hand on my arm. His smile was as warm as Hank's glare had been cold. "Why shouldn't you be a princess?"

"That's how I've always felt—special. The bartender at Geneva called me a Queen."

His chuckle was as soothing as scotch. "Okay, a promotion."

"Good things happen to me. Even Delia teases me about my good luck. I'm like a star in my own private movie. Is that so bad?"

Sam's lined face grew thoughtful. "It can be,

especially since your luck is for shit right now. From here on, if you come up with a movie scene, think crime dramas. This ain't no romantic comedy."

A gavel rapped sharply in my head. I could see myself standing at the defense table in a nicely cut blue suit. Vera Wang, maybe. No! Enough about the clothes! I thought of a judge in a severe black robe with eyes as hard as Hank's facing me from the bench, reading the verdict:

"Regarding the count of murder in the first degree, we the jury find the defendant, Kimberly Rose delaGarza, guilty."

The gavel rapped.

Was that how it happened?

I shivered, blinking away the offending image. I didn't like the thought of a courtroom thriller. Not if I was the person standing at that defense table. It didn't matter what designer suit I chose to wear. My next outfit would be an orange prison jumpsuit. I hated jumpsuits. And my mother said I looked horrible in orange. What kind of shoes would I wear? Nikes? Keds? Certainly no Manolo Blahnik.

Maybe I should forget movies. I turned to Sam as the sidekick to his Sherlock Holmes. Except I wasn't even a good Dr. Watson. "What's next, boss?"

He waved at the board and held out a dry erase pen. "Let's go through these names. Maybe we can come up with more on why they should be suspects."

Chapter Twenty-Three

Tackling Rick's books after Sam left was tedious. I had no idea what I needed to find. Most of the clients were initials and the writing wasn't Rick's.

Wait! He had a bookkeeper who handled store accounts. I found the name in tiny script at the bottom of a page—Betty Arguello. How could I have forgotten her? I needed to put her name on my list.

Across the room, the board now listed more motives next to suspects. I grabbed my black marker and added "Betty A" to the suspect list. Under motive I wrote, "embezzling?" It was as good as anything else.

Like my notebook, the board was appropriately color-coded, but was also geared toward suspect level. Names in red denoted strong suspects, like Carl. I'd originally written the Brookings in red, but Sam insisted I change them to black—a second tier of suspects—since we had no motives beyond speculation.

He had been confused by "mob guy," until I explained *El Patron*. As a former LAPD officer, he knew the name but agreed with Peter that the old guy was no longer in business. At least he provided a name—Benito Dominguez.

Delia and Walter's blue names pulsated on the board. I felt guilty even listing them. I pasted neon stickers beside their names with their alibi: "On a plane to South America." Once we verified they were on the flight, we would erase them.

My gaze swept back to Betty's name as I recalled what she looked like and the last time I'd seen her—the woman sitting beside Carl at the service. A suspect? Probably not. I'd seen her at the store a few times. Her clothes were out of an Ivy League boutique—sweater sets and pleated skirts. Her coffee-colored hair was styled in short, permed curls. She wore low-heeled pumps and no make-up except for burgundy lipstick.

Maybe I should call her. She could answer questions about Rick's finances. Why was the shop in trouble? Or was it? I had only Carl's word. She would have information on day-to-day operations. I found her phone number written on the inside of one book. I got no answer and didn't leave a message.

Was there another way to decode the names in the books? I should have kept Rick's Filofax. All his clients were listed in that fat black notebook. It sat on my desk for months after we transferred the information to his Blackberry. I'd had the Blackberry too. He'd thrown them aside as easily as he replaced me with his new bimbo. Both had been packed into one of the boxes I returned. Jennifer would have his new phone with current contacts. Would she care if I took the old phone or notebook from the shop?

****

Saturday, 10:00 a.m.

My visit to Betty set into motion a terrible day. The small, tidy woman greeted me with a glum expression. She wore a fitted floral vest over a white cotton blouse and tailored slacks. Her only jewelry was a thin gold bracelet with diamonds dotting every few links and a gold chain that peeked from the inside of her blouse.

Her short hair curled tightly around her round face.

I made the drive to Burbank keeping a close watch on my rearview mirror. No one appeared to follow me as I drove up the 405 and crossed into the San Fernando Valley. I offered to pick up Sam, but Hank wanted to play golf. Sensing Sam's excitement at the unusual invitation, I assured him I'd be fine on my own.

"I'm not sure why you wanted to see me," she said in a clipped tone, sitting very straight behind a wood veneer desk. Her office was in a converted garage that extended from a neatly tended bungalow in western Burbank. Despite being half a foot taller, I felt like she was looking down her wide nose at me.

I ran my tongue over my strawberry lip gloss, uncertain where to start. This was a different kind of interview than I was used to. I needed information, but wasn't certain what I needed to know.

"You worked for Rick a long time." I used my anchor smile, hoping to relax her. "You knew his business dealings better than anyone except Carl."

She seemed to weigh each word as she spoke. "I kept track of transactions for the store. Carl saw to Rick's personal finances."

"You know how the store is doing, if it's in financial trouble."

Her eye lids fluttered and a tiny crease formed at the center of her brow. "The store turns a profit every month, if that's what you're asking."

I kept my expression blank, not wanting to show surprise. "Carl says the business is having problems. How can that be true if it's profitable?"

She fixed me with a pointed dark-eyed stare. "Maybe you need to ask Carl."

Indeed. The scrawny accountant was looking more suspicious. I had only his word that Rick took my money. What if *he* took it along with Rick's profits? It could add up to a motive for murder.

"Why would you care about the business anyway?" Her voice rang with sudden impatience. "His sister assured me she wants me to remain working."

It was my turn to stare her down. "She isn't sole owner. I own half."

Surprise flared in her eyes. "Who said that?"

"Carl. Why would he lie?"

Her enigmatic demeanor returned and she flashed a polite smile, but I sensed something sinister. "Why would *anyone* lie to you?"

I drew a quick breath. Definitely sinister! "Is there something you know?"

"Rick was my friend, thoughtful, sweet."

Her tone alerted me to a deeper current to this stream. The woman never liked me, but this was more calculated. She never socialized with me and Rick. At store functions she seldom came near us. Her gaze ventured to a picture on her desk. The framed snapshot was of Rick and her at a Christmas party. His arm was slung around her as he grinned at the camera. Her eyes were on him and the look was anything but that of a good employee. *Holy shit!* Had she been secretly in love with him?

"Rick liked you," I offered in a soft voice.

Her placid face swiveled back to me. "I know."

How had Rick shown friendship to her? Had she demanded more and he refused to provide it? I could hardly wait to scribble "spurned lover" on my suspect board. Her name might even turn red.

"I'm not sure why you wanted to talk to me."

"I'm visiting people who knew him, whether or not they were important." Okay, so I was being catty. "I need to find out who killed him."

Her brows arched in accusation. "Really?"

This inscrutable act began to perturb me. "You think I did it? Why would I?"

"We both know why." Her voice filled with sarcasm. "Are you visiting all his women? What do you hope to gain?"

His women? Hello! I leaped to my feet as her words crashed over me like the cracking of a vase on my skull. "What are you saying? You were his bookkeeper. That was all."

Her steady stare refuted that. "You spent years with Rick, but you never knew him."

My heart thudded and rage threatened to crush my chest. "Rick was loyal to me."

Again, that disturbing flatness filled her black eyes. "If you question all his women, you're going to learn a lot more than you want to find out." She leaned forward and a pendant that had been on the end of her gold chain slipped out of her blouse.

My gasp was audible. "Where did you get that?"

Her fingers flew to the pendant with the entwined diamond hearts, much as mine had that first time I battled the Bimbo. The store clerk claimed it was one of a kind. Rick demanded I return it and now it was around her neck.

Her dark eyes flashed with triumph. "I think you know. He gave it to me the day before he died. Do you want to read the card that came with it?"

I whirled away and stomped out, gasping for

breath.

Oh, hell, oh bloody fucking hell!

Had Rick been more than a liar and thief? Had he also been a cheat? How many women were there in his life and were they all laughing at me?

Or was one of them the killer?

Chapter Twenty-Four

Betty's nasty charge that Rick was seeing others reverberated like a banging gong as I drove back across the city.

How long had he been fooling around?
When had the damn prick had the time?
Were they one night stands?

If he'd been with his bookkeeper the week before he died, that had nothing to do with me. If anything, it improved motives for Bobbi and her father. Had the Pilgrim discovered Rick's infidelity and killed him?

I pulled into the parking lot of Margo's, a trendy restaurant, with my mind buzzing. I didn't want to take Lindy to lunch, but I hated to cancel because of the yucky sensation in my stomach.

She sat hunched on a bench in the waiting area, dejected eyes on the floor when I entered. One arm protectively covered her other arm that remained wrapped. She sprang up like a jack-in-the-box when I entered. "I was afraid you weren't coming."

"Sorry I'm late." I tried to smile but my face refused to cooperate.

The hostess greeted me with polite recognition, then picked up menus and led us to a table with a view of the Sunset Strip. Margo's nestled on a hill overlooking West Hollywood. I recognized well-known faces at other tables, but this was the sort of establishment where you didn't acknowledge them. At least no one would acknowledge me either.

"You need to wear brighter colors," I told Lindy after we ordered iced tea. I needed to think about something other than what had happened in Burbank. "You have beautiful skin, but that color makes it drab."

She wore a pale yellow sundress that was too light for her fair complexion. She didn't look like the fearless race driver Hank labeled her. "Thanks for the advice. I'll keep it in mind."

"Maybe we can go shopping someday." Maybe when Delia returned, we could take Lindy on a shopping expedition as a reward for watching my house.

The waitress delivered our tea and leaned toward me, speaking in a low voice. "I'm so sorry about Mr. Wells. He was such a wonderful man."

The words sliced through me, reopening my wounds. I studied the woman. "Vicki" was stenciled on her black plastic badge. She'd waited on me and Rick several times. In fact, thinking back, we normally sat in her area. How well did *she* know Rick? As she retreated, I yanked open my napkin with barely disguised violence, making the thick material snap.

Lindy bent across the table. "Are you all right?"

My anger spilled over and I slammed my fist on the table, making the silverware jump. "I'm fine. It's Rick the Weasel! I found out the prick was fucking around. And not just with Bobbi the Bimbo. There were others."

Her small mouth formed into an O. "What a fucking bastard!" She clamped her hand over her mouth and looked around hastily, but I laughed.

"My mom says I cuss too much," she admitted.

"Mine too." I took a gulp of tea, put it down and signaled the waitress. "I've decided I'd rather have a martini? What about you, Lindy?"

"Sure," she replied with her bobble-head nod.

For the next two hours and over several martinis, I told Lindy about Rick the Weasel.

"I should have figured it out when he told me about Bobbi. That should have been a warning. How could he be so damn sneaky? How could I be so fucking clueless?"

Lindy shook her head, hair swinging like a limp brown curtain. "Men are fucking rats!"

Was I so isolated? I knew what Delia would say. I ignored anything that didn't directly affect me. We were both self-centered. That was why we meshed so well from the first moments of friendship. We focused on our own immediate needs, whether it was getting a boyfriend, dumping one, or buying an outfit for an upcoming occasion. In many ways, I was a Pampered Princess, just as Hank said.

****

My home phone was ringing as I walked in the door, but it stopped before I reached it. I hit the return call button, but the number came up as "private". No message, but that had been happening a lot, even though I'd changed my number. My phone showed three calls and similar hang ups. All had "private" as the call back number.

I was still mildly buzzed, but I wanted to get back to my investigation. I had downed cup after cup of coffee while waiting for a cab for Lindy. The caffeine jolted me awake as I drove home and sparked a sudden realization. While Betty's claims hurt, they opened up a new line of suspects.

Retreating to the office, I wrote her name in bold red letters on my board. Maybe he gave her the pendant as a goodbye present. When he broke off with her, she went bonkers with the bat. She looked mean enough to do it.

I perused names of women on the list with a new purpose—Rick's cheating heart. I turned Bobbi's name red and wrote "caught him cheating" under motive. I did the same with the Pixie and the Pilgrim. Either might murder the bastard to save Bobbi from marrying a philandering bum.

What other women could I add? Thalia, his big-breasted masseuse? She hadn't been on the list, but I added her, along with Vicki, his favorite waitress from Margo's. Who else did Rick flirt with? Well, everyone. He played the role of Mr. Charm wherever we went. He'd even taken Reba and Gwen to lunch when I'd been unable to get away.

I shuddered as I thought of Gwen. She would rub an affair in my face, but to admit even a one-night stand might make her a suspect. She told police about my threat against Rick, probably even about my ripping up his pictures. Did that mean anything?

What about Paula Gardner? She flirted with him so much Rick and I argued over his attention to her. I scribbled down both names. Damn Rick. I never questioned his devotion, not when he showered me with gifts. What was he giving everyone else?

****

Sunday, 7:00 p.m.

The sight of Hank Patterson standing outside my

door was a complete shock. Given his vicious words the last time we spoke, he was the last person I expected to visit me.

He shifted when I opened the door. "We need to talk."

I was as off guard as the first time he'd come, but I opened the door wider, beckoning him inside. "Please come in."

Following him up the stairs, I steeled myself for whatever might be ahead. I was in no mood for a confrontation, though I feared one might be possible. I was meeting Sam in the morning to give him a report on my session with Betty. Hopefully Hank hadn't come to put an end to that endeavor.

"Have a seat. May I get you something to drink? Beer?"

"This isn't a social call."

"Iced tea? Coffee? What do cops drink on the job?" My attempt at humor went unanswered.

He faced me with eyes as cool as the ocean in February. "It's not an official call either."

Now I was confused. "Okay, tell me what's on your mind."

Hank sat on the sofa with one leg crossed over his knee. He wore his leather jacket over a pale blue polo shirt and black jeans that fit like a glove on his long legs. I perched on a chair beside him, wary since his frown indicated this was not going to be any more pleasant than our last encounter.

He pulled a slip of paper from his jacket pocket, unfolded it, and handed it to me. "Is that your handwriting?"

I studied the paper, my cheeks growing hot. It was

a copy of that damned note we'd thrown into Rick's car. I should have known the truth would come out. They must have gotten my fingerprints off it. Was he here to arrest me? Where were Torres and Callahan? They wouldn't want to miss this treat.

Drawing a deep breath, I attempted a smile. It froze on my lips. "I think you know it is."

Maybe he didn't. Perhaps he didn't recall the foolish notes I left for him when we were together. I'd slide them under his door, slip them through the cracked window of his car, tuck them into his jacket pocket. They were cute notes with happy faces when he pleased me or sad faces when he broke a date because of work.

No happy face tonight. This was more like a frowning face in black eyebrow pencil instead of the cheery cherry lip liner I once used.

His chiseled face solidified into a sculpture captured in granite. Well, granite except for the nerve that twitched in his clenched jaw.

"Bobbi Brookings thinks you—or whoever left the note—is out to get her. She's afraid that Rick's killer might have targeted her too."

"It wasn't meant in that sense," I protested, attempting a shrug. "Yes, Delia and I did it, but it was a joke."

"Uh-huh. And it was left with a sharp object? That was a joke too?"

His best interrogator voice. Coming at me like a striking whip. I had watched him use it on people when questioning them. My body stiffened. "Yes, it was supposed to be funny."

"Not a good idea, wouldn't you say?"

Not a good idea at all if the Bimbo thought the note was meant for her. Given our confrontations, she might have a reason to think I was after her.

"I didn't mean it." I lifted the piece of paper and re-read it.

"The Grim Reaper is chasing you," it said. It had seemed like such a fun joke, and the words still tempted me to smile.

I bit my lower lip to keep a straight face. "It was meant as a harmless prank."

"You understand that some people might see it as a death threat."

I jerked my gaze up to his. The glacial look in his eyes made me shiver. I might be caught in the middle of a snowstorm for all the warmth I saw there.

"Threatening a life is hardly harmless." His monotone voice was cold, frigid vibrations emanating from it. Jack Webb on *Dragnet,* lecturing a suspect.

"We'd been drinking all afternoon. Rick obviously didn't think it was a big deal."

Surprise flared in his eyes. "He knew about this?"

"Of course! We threw it in his car. It was meant for him..." The instant I made the statement, I recognized my error.

Hank snatched the note from my hand. "It was meant for *him?* Not her?"

Realization hit us both at the same instant. The note as a threat against the girl was one thing. That damn note was a direct threat I'd made a week before Rick died. It was evidence. Or it could have been. His visit might get it tossed out in court and we both knew it.

He slapped his forehead, muttering obscenities.

"I'm sorry, Hank."

"You knew what this and that glass meant the other day, didn't you?" he said through clenched teeth, waving the note at me.

"Did you get fingerprints?"

"Of course not. If we had, I wouldn't have come. I wanted to make you stop this silly nonsense before you got into trouble. You fought with her in the church, didn't you?"

"She threw things at me! That note was a joke that had nothing to do with her. And it doesn't prove I killed Rick."

Before I could protest further, the phone rang. We both started, and I let out a little laugh. He was as jumpy as I was. I made no move to answer and waved a hand of dismissal.

"I screen all my calls so if you ever need to reach me, talk so I know it's you. Whoever it is won't leave a message. They never do. It happens all the time." The phone stopped ringing and as predicted, there was no message.

Hank blew out a deep breath. He'd been watching me, but I couldn't read what was in those indecipherable eyes. "You're in a lot of trouble."

"Is that why you came?"

He crumbled the note and jammed it into his pocket. His fingers balled into fists, but I had the feeling his anger was not aimed at me. "To be honest, I'm not certain why I'm here. This is such a fucked up mess and it keeps getting worse."

"I won't tell anyone you were here."

"Doesn't matter. I'm probably on my way out anyway." His voice sounded sad, almost defeated, very unlike Hank. He rubbed the back of his neck, a gesture I'd once found endearing. "I screwed it up from the beginning."

Sympathy softened my voice to a near whisper. "I'm sorry."

The hardness in his eyes had thawed. "I should have gone to his sister first. I shouldn't have talked to you at Geneva. I shouldn't be here now, and I've destroyed a possible piece of evidence." With a deep sigh, he shoved himself up from the sofa.

I approached him and put my hand on his arm. "You're only in trouble if I did it. But you haven't screwed up anything, because I didn't do it."

He looked down at me and I sensed something behind his steady gaze. His eyes drifted to my fingers and he reached over to touch them. "The note wasn't the only reason I came tonight."

My breath caught. If there was any remaining ice within him, it melted with the electric shot of heat that surged between us.

His finger played over my hand, heating my skin. "I wanted to apologize for what I said the other day. That was cruel."

An apology from Hank? My heart fluttered like a bird taking flight.

"Do you hate me?" I asked, squeezing his arm, hoping that what I saw in his eyes was the truth, not the bitter words he'd spouted two days ago.

His head tilted toward me, his voice low and intimate. "I think you know the answer to that. You don't fuck up an investigation for someone you hate, Kimmie."

The nickname said it all. My insides felt like it was

Fourth of July—a virtual fireworks shower! A smile slid across my face, threatening to grow so large, my whole face might burst.

"Unless you're trying to railroad them," I teased. I flipped my hand over and caught his fingers, clutching them. He squeezed back, and heat shot through me. Our entwined fingers dropped to the side, linked together like teenagers. I tried to slow my quickened breath to no avail.

"I should get going," he said, but he made no attempt to drop my hand.

I ventured another squeeze of his hand. "Are you still angry about Sam?"

"That's another reason I came by. I wanted to let you know you were right. I haven't seen him this excited in a long time. I'm not sure the two of you will come up with anything, but it's given him new purpose. I didn't know he could still move so fast. Even my sister thinks it's good for him, and she's never been one of your fans."

I rolled my eyes. Did anyone's sister like me? "So now what?"

"Talk to your attorney about the note and tell Torres and Callahan. Sooner or later, they're going to find out the truth."

"You knew I wrote it?"

"I had a hunch about the handwriting. It seemed like something you two might do. But I thought it was meant for the girl."

Relief swept through me. He knew how Delia and I could behave at times. Or misbehave. Perhaps I should tell him about the joking conversation and Toby's threats. Before I could proceed, he released my hand.

"How are you holding up?" he asked.

"Iron lady."

"How about the family?"

I wrinkled my nose. That was another story. I'd spent the day with them. "The press is making things difficult. Paula keeps calling. My sister and brother had to change phone numbers."

"Damn media," he said with a knowing smile.

"Tell me about it. I took Lindy to lunch at Margo's yesterday and today there's a picture of me on the Internet. Like I'm not allowed to live a regular life."

"It has to be rough on your mom."

Hank adored my mother, and the feeling was mutual. "They're going on vacation. Stevie owns a time share in Puerto Vallarta, so he's getting them booked in starting Wednesday. Mom's threatening to post a blog online protesting my innocence. Hopefully, being away from the steady barrage of press will calm her down. Plus she won't have easy access to the Internet."

He chuckled and shook his head. "She's always been your biggest fan. I better go."

I followed him down the stairs and caught his arm as he reached for the doorknob. "Hank, when this is over, can I make you dinner?"

His pouty lips drew into a smile, and his cheeks dimpled, sending a raging buzz through me. "You learned to cook?"

My lips felt dry and I licked them, fighting to keep my breathing even. "No, but since I'm not working, I could learn. I can't afford to take anyone out."

He chuckled and a long finger stroked my cheek. "Play your cards right, Kimmie, and I might be convinced to take you out."

Chapter Twenty-Five

Monday, 10:00 a.m.

Sam met me as I came up the parking garage escalator at Walter's Century City office building. I needed a phone number to reach Walter so we could track down Delia. Sam waited in the lobby to make phone calls while I took the elevator to the top floor.

Walter's tall, elegant secretary greeted me at the door. She was in her early 50s and radiated efficiency—June Cleaver in a DKNY suit. She hugged me like an old friend, though I didn't know her well. I seldom visited Walter's office and we socialized only once at a Christmas party. Delia and I spent a champagne-fueled evening advising her about a cheating husband.

Now I knew how she felt. "It's good to see you, Bertie."

"Bernie," she corrected, but her smile didn't lessen.

"Sorry. My mind is shot these days," I said with a self-deprecating laugh.

"I understand." She patted me on the arm. "What can I do for you?"

"I need to get in touch with Walter and Delia."

A startled look crossed her face. "I have Mr. Lindsay's information, but I'm not sure about Mrs. Lindsay. She's not with him."

A queasiness pricked my stomach. "What do you

mean? They went to South America."

She nodded in acquiescence. "I made the arrangements, but she refused to go on the jungle expedition at the last minute. I've never heard Mr. Lindsay so angry."

Delia's change of mind surprised me, though I never pictured her in the jungle. She had called it a cruise. She would spend days on deck, sipping champagne served by sexy stewards while Walter hunted in the jungle.

"Where are they?"

"He's hunting. I'm not certain where she went. She wanted to make her own arrangements. I may have a phone number."

She led me toward an inner door into Walter's corner office. The view took my breath away, offering an unobstructed vision of the Pacific Ocean. Walter's desk was bare on top except for a crystal clock and two picture frames. One was of me and Delia at their wedding, the other of Delia, Walter, and me at the Christmas party where we discussed Bernie's husband.

I picked up the first picture. "Boy, did I look young."

"You always look young, Miss delaGarza. Mr. Lindsay says that all the time."

I felt like I had aged ten years in the past month.

The woman clucked in disappointment. "I can't find her number. Let me give you a number for Mr. Lindsay. He can tell you how to reach her."

"But they both left two weeks ago on Friday, right?"

"At midnight. I booked the seats myself."

Alibi confirmed. I could take them off my suspect

list. Knowing Delia, she arrived in Brazil, decided against the jungle trip and booked a spa or her own cruise.

We returned to the outer office where Bernie scribbled on a note pad, ripped off a sheet and handed it to me. "That's his number along with the codes, too, for the long distance operator. His cell phone isn't working down there."

No wonder I hadn't heard from Delia. Perhaps she hadn't received my messages.

****

The door at Well's Fine Wines carried a closed sign, but I led Sam around back. A beer truck stood in the alley outside an open door. I stepped through the door into the dim back hall. An eerie silence overwhelmed me as I walked along the familiar slate tile to the front.

My heart began to thump as I glimpsed the tasting area where I had last seen Rick. If it was the location of a violent, bloody scene, all traces were gone. A burly man in green overalls stacked beer along one wall, while Darryl watched. Rick's clerk was a slender man of about thirty with thinning light brown hair. In his acting roles he played the best friend or neighbor, the sort of nondescript character no one ever noticed.

A look of surprise crossed his face when he saw me, but he walked over to clasp my hand. "Kimberly, I wanted to talk to you at the service, but people kept getting between us."

"How have you been, Darryl? This is Sam Patterson. He's doing investigative work on Rick's death."

Darryl pumped Sam's hand with enthusiasm.

"Someone needs to do something. Those cops barely questioned me. All they wanted to know about was..." He stopped, eyes sliding to me, and his face blanched.

"Me?" I asked.

His thin shoulders lifted in a half shrug. "Sure seemed that way."

"Is there some place we can talk?" Sam asked.

"Rick's...I mean, the office."

We followed him into Rick's cramped office. I could sense things were out of place, although the room was cleaner than I'd ever seen it. Rick's papers were in a neat stack on his oak desk, but the phone and pen holder were not in their normal positions. The silver framed picture of me was gone, replaced by a picture of Bobbi in a crystal frame.

Sam's questions were simple, but I sensed from the moment we sat down that Darryl was uncomfortable. When the beer delivery man came in to get paperwork signed, Sam tapped my arm and tilted his head toward the door.

"Didn't you have some personal things you needed to pick up?"

This would provide my opportunity to search for Rick's Filofax and old Blackberry. I excused myself and closed the office door. I shivered as I returned to the tasting area, thinking of Rick living his last few minutes there. How much time passed between when I left and the killer attacked him?

My eyes scanned the room and I drew a quick, pleased breath. The boxes I returned rested beside a work table. I located the one with his belongings from my office and dug through it. The contents were a jumbled mess of pictures, books and clothing, but I didn't know if that was my doing or the police search. I hadn't packed it, mainly tossing in stuff. I moved carefully, knowing this was the box where I put the gun. Was it loaded? I was liable to shoot myself if I wasn't careful. I spied his black Filofax planner as I neared the bottom. I reached for it, but a voice startled me.

"What do you think you're doing?" Jennifer stood in the archway, eyes hostile, hand on her narrow hip. She wore jeans, a cotton shirt, and leather vest. Color flamed in her thin cheeks and her blues eyes were icy as January in the Rockies. She was like fire and ice. Fiery hatred and icy anger. "You have no business being here."

I jerked up but held my ground. "I own a portion of the store. According to Carl—"

"I wouldn't trust that sneak." Her voice dripped with venom. "Now get out of that box and get the hell out of here."

"I need his Filofax to contact our old friends."

"I've contacted everyone."

The store phone rang, startling us both and she turned away to answer it. "Don't touch anything."

I glanced at the box, trying to figure out how to get the planner, and spied the Blackberry. When Jennifer turned to check something for the caller, I leaned over, slid my fingers into the box and grasped the old cell phone. I slipped it into a pocket and was reaching for the planner when she hung up.

"I told you to get out of there."

I held up empty hands. "I'm out. What happened to the gun?"

"Gun?" She blinked with surprise and stretched

forward to peer into the box.

"I put his gun in there, but I didn't see it. Did the police keep it?"

Her hard gaze swung to me. "Rick never owned a gun."

"He bought it for me. For protection."

"You're the only person he needed protection from."

Footsteps came from behind her and Sam and Darryl stepped into view.

Jennifer pounced on the unsuspecting clerk. "Why the hell did you let her in?"

Sam gestured with his head for me to leave and I didn't argue. Jennifer would soon learn if she wanted to be involved with the shop, she would have to deal with me. And my attorney, Adrienne, loved property battles.

As we left the premises with her angry rants still falling on Darryl's ears, I turned to Sam. "I swiped his Blackberry, but she stopped me before I could take his planner. Did Darryl give you a client list?"

Sam's grimace said it all. What had they been discussing for so long? "You own half the place, right?"

"Yes, but Jennifer won't give me a key without a fight and I doubt Darryl will let us in. Poor guy. I'll call him later and apologize. I hope she doesn't fire him."

Sam grunted. "She can't fire him. And that security system is for shit. I can get in anytime I want. We'll go back when we won't be interrupted."

****

"How well did you know Wells?"

Sam's question caught me off guard. We were back at my house, sitting outside on the lower patio sipping scotch. I sensed he had something on his mind as we drove home, but he remained silent, scribbling in his notebook.

I studied his gaunt face, but his sharp eyes were unreadable. "We were together ten years. What did Darryl say?"

"Did you know Wells had a serious gambling problem?"

"Callahan mentioned that. I thought that was why the shop might be in trouble, but Betty said it was making a profit."

"That doesn't mean he wasn't personally in money trouble. The guy was visiting Vegas several times a month and had a bookie he regularly called."

"He was gambling the profits? Is that what Darryl said? I got the impression he didn't want to speak in front of me. Was that why?"

Sam downed the rest of his scotch and faced me squarely. "Wells didn't go alone."

A chill ran through me despite the afternoon sun. I inhaled a quick breath through dry lips. "What do you mean?"

His direct gaze unnerved me. "He took a friend. Or friends. All female."

Pain sliced through me and I dropped my head. I concentrated on breathing, slow and easy. It shouldn't hurt, but it did. "Do police know?"

"Probably."

"Doesn't that help? It creates a case against the Bimbo. Why would I care?"

"Maybe you just found out. And there's still the matter of the money. Darryl mentioned Rick was in danger of losing the shop until six weeks ago. Then he came into a chunk of cash and paid up. Darryl thought he won the money."

"Why would Betty say the shop wasn't in trouble?"

"She might not know. The books probably don't show it. All she saw was what came and went out through the store. Maybe he used the profits. Edwards would know since he was paying the bills."

"Couldn't that strengthen Carl's motive? What if Rick needed money so he didn't lose the shop and found out Carl was stealing his money and mine? Maybe they got into a fight."

Sam didn't reply. He walked into the office and poured himself another drink. Hank probably wouldn't approve of the drinking, but Sam seldom had more than one.

"What next?" I asked when he returned.

"Let's follow the money trail. Darryl said Wells was worried about losing the shop. Records indicate the mortgage was never late, nor was his business loan. That tells me he was borrowing on the sly, using the store as collateral, and someone was threatening to take the shop. Somehow he managed to make the payment. He could have won the money, but Edwards told you that Wells took your money the last week. That sounds like he either lost big again or borrowed money for the first payment and needed your dough to square the second debt."

"This is all over my head," I admitted.

"Did you get anything out of the Blackberry? Any names we hadn't come across? We need to match names with the initials in the ledgers."

I frowned at the black device on my desk, sitting next to a charger. "It totally lost its charge and everything was wiped out. We need to get that Filofax.

One thing I did notice was that his gun was not in the box where I put it. Do you suppose the police kept it? Or maybe it's in another box?"

Sam put down his glass without finishing the drink. He stroked his chin in a thoughtful manner. "Maybe. How are you feeling these days? Safer?"

"With the new alarm system working and since we haven't spotted any cars following us, I'm feeling better." I felt physically safer, but I wasn't certain about my emotional steadiness.

"Good. I'm gonna grab a bus to Mira Loma PD and make my son take me to dinner. Those guys consider me a nosy old codger who barely remembers which way is up. Maybe I can learn a few things."

****

Once Sam was gone I went back to the board. The female names jumped out at me. Had Rick taken them to Las Vegas? He loved to have someone cheering him on at the gambling tables. He hated when I drifted away.

Betty? No. I had trouble thinking that a roll of the dice might cost me a new handbag or shoes. Would the careful accountant allow him to spend like that?

Bobbi the Bimbo? Maybe I needed to look more closely at the Brookings family. Real estate development? What if Rick promised Miles Brookings that corner where his store was located? Property near the beach was a valuable commodity. Jennifer and I were squabbling about the shop, but what if *neither* owned it? I made a note on my Action Steps page to research Pilgrim Development.

Next I called Las Vegas. When Rick and I visited, we stayed at a luxury hotel off the Strip where an old reporter friend was in charge of publicity. Rick's steady gambling always got us a free room.

Fred Jenkins greeted me with a happy laugh, reminiscent of when we worked the late shift together at TV8. We traded gossip for a few minutes as I tried to come up with a way to turn our talk toward the reason I had called.

"When are you coming to visit?" he asked, providing a perfect opening.

"Soon. Right now if I try to leave the state, I'll probably get a police escort back."

Fred chuckled. "I heard about your old boyfriend. Crazy shit, huh?"

"Totally crazy, and…" Suddenly I couldn't ask him what I wanted. I paused and cleared my throat. "We broke up, you know."

"I figured that when I saw him a couple of months ago. That woman he was with didn't compare to you."

Shoving away a pang of jealous pain, I adopted a light voice. "He still stayed there? Running up big gambling tabs? That bothered me."

His quick laugh was harsh. "Bothered us too. We finally cut him off. Too many unpaid markers. I hear he got engaged to some rich chick?"

"Bobbi Brookings. Her father is Miles Brookings."

He let out a whistle. "That guy's buying up half the desert outside of town to build a big resort. No wonder Rick was marrying her. He could have his own gambling palace."

We hung up moments later and I digested what I'd learned. Had Rick gotten involved with Bobbi hoping to become part of the family business plan? Had he taken money from the Pilgrim and lost it? What about the woman who was with him in Las Vegas? I'd have to run the information by Sam.

My cell phone beeped, making me jump. I felt safer, but sudden noises still startled me. The number was unfamiliar, but I answered. Maybe it was Delia.

"Miss delaGarza?"

Damn, I knew the voice. "Yes, Toby."

"I'm tired of waiting. If you can't get my money by tomorrow, I'm going to the police."

"I thought we talked about other ideas."

He sighed. "I need the money."

Sam had said audio could be doctored, but I also knew Toby would be a credible witness. Torres would love Toby's account of how I plotted Rick's murder. Maybe it was time to tell Sam about this problem.

"I need time to get cash."

He hesitated, his breathing growing heavy. "I'll give you until Friday."

Chapter Twenty-Six

Tuesday, 8:00 a.m.

I intended to tell Sam about Toby the next time I saw him. He called to say he was spending the night with Hank, who would drop him off on the way to work. I got up early to prepare decaf coffee and chop fresh fruit for a salad. I even drove to a nearby bakery for low-fat muffins. I laid out a spread on the lower patio, but he barely gave it a second look.

"Why are you keeping things from me?" he demanded, striding in like an unleashed tiger.

My stomach knotted. Had he discovered the truth about Toby? "What?"

"Why the hell didn't you tell me about the glass? The threat you made against that girl?"

I blew out a breath of relief. "Did Hank tell you?"

"Why didn't you?" He whirled on me, blue eyes blazing with fury.

"It was a stupid joke and I didn't want to get Hank in trouble."

He stopped pacing. "Why would he be in trouble?"

"For coming to see me about it. It could have become evidence."

Sam sagged like a wilting rose bush. He flopped onto his normal chair, shaking his head. "We're supposed to be partners," he grumbled.

How angry would he be about his partner hiding a blackmailer? Maybe I should break it to him after he calmed down. "I'm sorry."

"Here I am lecturing him about you being in danger because of the note and he tells me you wrote it. You threatened that girl?"

Hank had not been totally honest. He hadn't told him it was meant for Rick. He had not told Torres or Callahan either. Which meant... I found a smile stealing across my face. That meant he believed me. Hank wasn't the sort to shirk his duty. If he thought I killed Rick, he wouldn't protect me.

I summoned my brightest smile to battle the fierce scowl that hardened Sam's face. "It was a joke."

The granite features refused to yield. "I don't like that sort of joke. I'm sure her family didn't either."

I stopped being apologetic. "Her family may have gotten Rick killed."

"What do you mean?"

"Did you know that the Brookings family is buying property outside Las Vegas? Maybe that's why Rick got involved with her. Maybe he found out something about their dealings, that they're crooked. Maybe they're involved with mobsters, like *El Patron*. You know Vegas—"

He waved an impatient hand to cut me off. "You need to stop with these wild theories. This is going to be something simple."

"How do you know?"

He tapped the side of his head. "Intuition. What about your friend, Delia? Did you get hold of her?"

"No, why?"

"Apparently he owed her husband money. His

company holds the mortgage on the shop."

The comment surprised me. "Who told you that?"

"It's in the case file. It was in the statement from his accountant."

"They let you look at the case file?"

For the first time since he arrived, a sparkle lit his eyes. "Nah. I was shooting the breeze with Callahan and he got called away. The file was sitting there, so…" He shrugged, his face creasing in a wide smile.

"Did you come up with anything else?"

Sam leaned forward, rubbing his hands together, a motion I'd learned to interpret as enthusiasm. "We knew he was in money trouble. The guy apparently couldn't hold onto a cent. As soon as he made anything, he spent it or bet it."

"Or as soon as I made it." I didn't attempt to hide my bitterness.

"That wasn't in the statement Edwards gave. He didn't tell them the guy was stealing. He said Wells borrowed from you and repaid it through stock in the shop."

"That makes sense. Carl could be charged with fraud for what he was doing."

"He told police the two of you shared an account and you were both lavish spenders. Neither paid attention to what you spent. Is that true?"

There was no escaping his damning gaze and I felt uncomfortable making the admission. "I don't lose thousands gambling." The results of my spending were visible in my closet and my safe.

"Gambling losses didn't show up in Edwards' statement, but Wells had lots of people he was paying back, like Lindsay and Brookings, plus a couple of other names I didn't recognize." He pulled out a little stub of paper and checked it. "Phillips, someone named B. D., and Blankenship. Any of those ring a bell?"

I shook my head and turned to the board. "B. D.? Benito Domingez." I jerked my finger at it. "The mob guy from the funeral. Maybe he's Rick's bookie."

Sam joined me at the board and studied the list. "I doubt he would have his accountant paying off a bookie. This was a payment he made every so often."

"Why would he owe so much money if he was taking my cash? Were these personal loans?"

"Apparently. According to Edwards' statement, he was constantly behind. When there was a lean month, he'd take out a new loan. When he made a profit he'd pay back old debts and spend whatever was left. Edwards didn't say a word about gambling. It was Darryl who spilled that can of worms."

I should have told him about Toby right then. But he hadn't liked the glass joke. He certainly wouldn't appreciate my conversation about killing Rick.

Sam picked up a marker and tapped on the board. "We need to visit Edwards."

Much as I longed to confront him, I wasn't sure he would tell me anything. "Do you think he'll be honest in front of me? He didn't tell police the truth."

A bony finger pointed in my direction. "Good point. I'll go alone. I can stop on my way across town. Surprise visits are easier."

"Don't you want breakfast first?" I pointed toward the table where the white table cloth flickered in the morning breeze.

"Sure. Let me tell you what else I found out." Sam was beaming. He enjoyed his moments of subterfuge and he went on to disclose the investigation was at a dead end. Fingerprints at the shop were no help since they could belong to delivery people or customers. Carl's statement did not provide a hint of financial problems that would make anyone a murder suspect. Darryl's comments about gambling mentioned a bookie, but he had no name and most of the losses had come in Las Vegas.

"Is the Bimbo frightened?" I asked.

"She's afraid of you. She thinks you're out to get her. Have you called her? Hung up on her?"

"Of course not."

"Someone did, the week before he died."

I pressed my lips together and looked away. *Oh, hell...*

"Kimberly?"

"I called her once. Maybe twice. To talk..."

He clucked his tongue in disgust, gray head shaking in disapproval. "They're going through her phone records. That's going to show up."

I felt like the chastised teen caught smoking in the girls' restroom. The childish idea went back to my college days. If a guy dumped us for someone else, Delia and I would call the new girlfriend, make nasty remarks and hang up. It was a vicious game, but we were young.

"No wonder the cops don't take threats against you seriously."

"Someone chased Lindy. They were following me," I insisted.

"I haven't spotted anyone while we're driving around."

I could hear skepticism in his voice. "Maybe they

stopped after hurting Lindy, or they don't know what my rental looks like. As for hang-ups, I get them all the time."

Sam pushed himself to his feet. "I'm going to see Edwards. How long has he been working for you and Rick?"

"Eight or nine years. Carl and Rick were friends from college. Rick believed that Carl would make us rich, but it looks like he was a crook."

"If I were you, I'd get the account audited and hire a new accountant."

"Should I do anything while you're gone?" I looked down at my chipped fingernails. I knew what I wanted to do. "Maybe I'll take a quick break and get a manicure."

He whirled on me, eyes blazing again. "Fine. Take the damn day off. Go shopping, do lunch. Catch a movie! This is only your fucking life at stake."

Why could he and Hank make me feel like such a failure? I held up my hands. "Okay, okay, I'll chop off my nails."

As I picked up the remnants of breakfast after he left, my cell phone beeped.

Reba's voice was a pleasant surprise. "How are you?"

"Wonderful." I knew she could decipher my sarcasm. "How's the looney bin?"

"Gwen moved into your office. She brought in her maid to clean it. Do you want me to pack your stuff and bring it by? I hate to see anything get damaged. You have some nice jackets in the closet."

I fumed at the thought of Gwen touching my clothes. "Do you mind?"

"No. Lindy can help. She's become your biggest defender since she got back."

"We sort of bonded." An afternoon of martinis could do that.

Reba cleared her throat. "I hate to ask you this, but..."

My stomach tensed. I knew what was coming. "I won't do an interview."

"Kimberly, it could help. Brad volunteered to do it."

I hadn't seen Brad since the evening he nearly kissed me, though we talked every day. He hadn't mentioned an interview.

"I know Alan wishes he'd stood up for you," Reba continued. "Vincent used this as an excuse to get his girlfriend a shot at anchoring."

"Girlfriend!"

Reba's exasperation floated across the line. "They're suddenly an item."

A quick rush of anger heated my face. "All the talk about me being a prima donna, and she's fucking her way up the ladder?"

"I'm sorry. Consider the interview, okay? Ask Oliver."

Angry with Vincent and Alan, and with silent apologies to Reba, I called my agent as soon as we hung up. "If Oliver approves, I'll do an interview with anyone but TV8. I'll even talk to Paula."

Evan Flynn, the man with a cash register for a heart that rang fifteen percent, cleared his throat. "Kimberly, you could be burning your bridges with TV8."

"You and your pal Gwen already did that," I said and hung up.

The cell rang immediately and I picked it up, prepared to fire Evan. The crackling dismayed me until I heard a voice.

"Hey, baby, what's up?"

"Delia," I screeched. "Where the hell have you been?"

Chapter Twenty-Seven

"You sound happy to hear from me." Her laugh sent my spirits spiraling upward.

Static crackled and I grasped the phone as though that might hold on to her. "Where are you? I called Walter's hotel and they said he was gone and you'd never been there."

Her voice was like a cool glass of water on a hot day. "I'm visiting friends. I refused to go on his stupid, primitive jungle trip. Can you imagine camping out with no indoor facilities? Does a bear shit in the woods? Sure. Me? Never! Wouldn't you think the man would know me by now? I may dump him and take all his money when he gets back."

"Have you heard the news?" I wanted to hear about her trip, but I needed to discuss Rick, and the crackling phone carried no promise the connection would last.

"About Rick? Yeah, are you okay?"

"Yes, well, no! Del, they think I did it."

"Son of a bitch!" Her hoot was long and raucous.

"That's not funny. You wouldn't believe what I'm going through. They think I hit him with that damn bat."

"Oh, babe. Do you need me to come home?"

Something in her voice sounded hesitant, but I knew what I wanted. "Can you?"

I could hear her sigh all the way from South

America. "Harry and Nita have been so kind, I hate to run off. They're planning a party for me and you know how I always wanted to see South America..."

I swallowed my disappointment. "Sweetie, don't interrupt your trip. I'll get through this."

"Are you sure?"

"Sam Patterson is helping me."

"You've already got a new guy?" she shrieked.

"No. Remember Hank Patterson? His father. He's a retired cop, a real go-getter."

"Oooh, spending time with the handsome police chief? No wonder you don't need me."

"It's not like you think, and I'll have to tell you about that. Your suggestion to call him got me in a lot of trouble when he came to tell me about Rick."

"Sounds like a great martini story."

"Speaking of martinis, remember that kid, Toby? He recorded us at the bar. He's threatening to tell the police unless I pay him."

Her laugh was so loud she might have been next door. "Oh, hon, are you in a hell of a spot! Did you tell the cops?"

"How can I? That thing could land me in a jail cell. The cops don't even believe I'm being followed."

"What does that mean?"

"I keep noticing the same cars behind me. There's a lot going on here. Did you know Rick was having money problems?"

"Who didn't? He borrowed from everyone. Don't tell me he never put the touch on you. He was a fucking deadbeat. Walt lent him a ton."

"Did you know he was gambling?"

"Everyone knew that. What planet have you been

living on?"

I drew a deep breath. I had one more question and she was the only person I could trust to tell me the truth. "One more thing… Del, be honest…did you know he was seeing other women?"

The phone line crackled and to my horror, it went dead.

Frantically I called her cell, but there was no answer. For the next half hour, I sat by the phone, alternately waiting and calling her—all to no avail.

Finally, I gave up. At least I'd talked to Delia. With a new spring in my step, I approached my board to study the list of names. What should I do next? Who should I question? The answer was simple, considering Rick's gambling. *El Patron.*

****

Tuesday, 2:00 p.m.

After several hours on the Internet researching Benito Dominguez, I climbed into my rental car and headed up Pacific Coast Highway toward Malibu. Sam claimed it was easier to show up than call. Luckily, I saw no suspicious cars following me.

Thanks to my research, I knew where he lived. He had purchased the old Castelman Estate on a hilltop in Malibu and I knew the location. As a reporter I joined a press entourage camped outside the gate for a week, waiting for the death of film star Ike Castelman.

Getting into the compound posed a problem, but I could park and wait where we had once done live shots. When he came out, I could tail him until he stopped and talk to him then. The area had changed since Castelman owned the property. Rockslides had sheared away the lower part of the hill, destroying the wide road. What had been rebuilt was nothing more than a narrow strip of pavement. A "private" sign warned away trespassers. I ignored it and turned off PCH.

The road wound around the back side of the hill through orange and avocado orchards and a grassy meadow before swinging back around toward the ocean to start its steep climb upward. Glancing down the rocky inclines that tumbled to PCH and the beach made me dizzy, so I concentrated on the road.

When I reached the grilled gate with a big C carved into two stone pillars I discovered a major mistake. Stone walls, which had not existed when I was staked out with the reporters, ran along the upper hill. There was no place to park. Or hide.

I swung the car around to go back down, but a wiry man in a gray guard uniform approached me, a scowl on his swarthy face.

"This is a private road, ma'am," he said. "Didn't you see the sign at the bottom?"

A quick apology fluttered to my lips as I slid open the window, but he did a sudden double take. He touched the bill of his hat. "Miss delaGarza. Are they expecting you?"

Feigning comfort I didn't feel, I smiled. "I'm sorry. I got lost." I started to put the car into reverse, but he put a hand on the window and tapped it.

"No problem. I'll call." He spoke into a microphone he'd lifted from his belt.

This was far from what I expected, but before I could say anything, he waved toward the gate. "They said to go on up. *Senor Zapato* will meet you in front."

Why I was being allowed to enter and who was *Senor Zapato*? Literally translated it meant Mr. Shoe.

The gate swung open, and I swallowed my fear and subsequent jubilation and drove through the gates. The compound reminded me of *The Godfather* as the theme played in my head. I shook it off. No movies!

Sweeping lawns and double rows of swaying palm trees lined the driveway that led to a series of large houses at the end. Unlike the bumpy lower road, this was a wide, well-maintained street. I followed it until it swung in front of a three-story Georgian mansion that stood regally at the center of a wide circular drive. Lots of windows, lots of red brick. A veranda at one end came complete with columns and creeping ivy. If *El Patron* wasn't a bookie, he was doing something else illegal.

Senor Zapato was a barrel chested man in a black suit with a thick black mustache, slick ebony hair tinged with gray, and an air of danger about him. If I ever needed a bodyguard he'd be the guy to hire. That was probably who he was. If someone was going to put a bleeding horse head in a bed, this was the guy to do it. Mr. Shoe. He probably stomped out people for *El Patron*. Like people who weren't paying gambling debts?

Drawing a deep breath as I stepped from the car, I smoothed down my narrow skirt. I'd chosen a tawny silk blouse to go with my peach suit for my visit. I wanted to look good, but I didn't want them to think I was weak. Forgoing sandals, I'd opted for a pair of champagne colored pumps.

Senor Zapato greeted me with a gap-toothed smile and performed an elegant bow as he held open my door and spoke in a polite tone. "*Bien venidos, senorita.* Please come in."

"I don't have an appointment."

"*Senor* Dominguez does not need appointments with friends." His voice carried a thick accent.

Since when was I a friend? I'd only seen the old man at Geneva and the memorial service. Neither time had he displayed friendship.

Senor Shoe gestured toward a set of French doors on the right side of the massive structure. The doors led into a very nicely tended garden with white wicker patio furniture. At the far end of the garden I spied the old man. Sitting next to him was the thin blonde woman who had been with him at Geneva. I'd pegged the two as rich socialites, and while they were undoubtedly wealthy, I doubted they got many invitations to society soirees.

She stood as I approached and flashed a wide smile. "What a wonderful surprise. Thank you for coming to see us." Her voice was pleasant, slightly accented. She leaned toward the old man who looked up at me with that same scowl.

"See, *viejo?* Here's one of your favorite newscasters to see you," she said in a loud voice. "He had a stroke last year that partly paralyzed his face and he's grown hard of hearing, but he never misses your newscasts."

He nodded, and I could see light in his tawny eyes, but though his lips twitched, the scowl never shifted. He lifted a gaunt hand that trembled and I shook it, regretting my mistake. Whatever illegal endeavors this man had once committed, he was no longer *El Patron,* feared crime leader. She called him *"viejo"* or old man, and that was exactly what he was.

What was Rick's connection with this family? Had

he placed bets with them? Before I could contemplate further, a major distraction appeared. Paula Gardner swept onto the patio like she owned it, dark hair tossing around her shoulders.

"Paula..." At first I thought she'd followed me, but then the tumblers in my brain lined up like the combination for a safe. Duh! Paula Gardner—the former Paula Dominguez. I'd never known her family.

She was as surprised to see me as I was to see her. "What are you doing here?"

"I thought she came to see you, *mija*?" the blonde said, tilting her head toward Paula. The resemblance confirmed the origins of Paula's last name.

"You're ready to do an interview?" Paula asked, never missing a beat.

The thought gagged me since she sounded so positive. I'd considered it earlier when I was angry over Gwen, but faced with the prospect, I knew I couldn't do it. Still, the possibility could mask my real intention.

"I'm talking to my attorney about it," I offered, faking my best smile.

"You drove out here to tell me it's possible?" Her voice rose a nasty notch. Perfectly groomed eyebrows arched over cold black eyes.

"Don't start with your bad manners," her mother admonished with a slap of her daughter's hand. I nearly laughed. Here was an aggressive reporter trying to score a major scoop, and her mother was dressing her down as mine might.

Did Mrs. Dominguez give her daughter fashion advice too? I couldn't imagine what she thought about her daughter's turquoise tank top that left three inches of tanned skin visible between its bottom and the top of skin tight jeans. I let my gaze float back and forth between the pair. *El Patron* seemed to lose interest in the conversation as mother and daughter battled. Paula rolled her eyes at her mother and turned her hard gaze on me.

"I'm off today, but shall we set it up for tomorrow morning?"

"Like I said, I'm waiting to hear back from my attorney. I'll let you know."

The corner of her mouth twitched. "Are there any new leads in Rick's death?"

Rick's death? Not the Wells murder investigation? "You'll need to ask Mira Loma Police."

"Someone said you might offer a reward."

This woman was relentless. I stifled a laugh. I didn't have money to offer a reward. Still… A sudden thought flashed in my head. "I've thought about it, if it helps police…"

"How much?"

"I haven't come up with an amount…" I smiled and shrugged.

She didn't ask if she could quote me and I didn't say I was speaking off the record. I knew my comments would be at the top of her station's newscast that afternoon. Paula would probably insist on giving the report herself.

"I spoke to Kimberly delaGarza this afternoon and she says…"

This was as good as an interview. "I'll call you later, if you give me your private number." I pulled on my sweetest smile and nodded toward her mother. "Then I don't have to come looking for you and disturb your parents, though it was good to see you both."

Paula produced a card from her purse that was on a nearby chair. "Call me anytime."

I sensed she was in a rush—probably to call her station. I gave a quick farewell to her parents and she walked me to the door, probably hoping for further tidbits.

"I was sorry about Rick," she said. "He was sweet to Mom and Dad." The sun glittered on a diamond tennis bracelet, and a prick of annoyance pinched at me. How well had Paula known Rick? She was on my list of possible other women, but did I need to move her up?

As I drove away from the compound, I wondered how many women belonged on that damned list. If Rick wasn't already dead, I might have hired *Senor* Shoe.

****

I thought about her as I guided the rental Volvo down the steep, narrow drive. Rounding the first curve, the car fishtailed, threatening to spin off the road. Oops, too much of the old lead foot. Jamming on the brakes made the tires spin onto the gravel, and my heart leaped into my throat. I could see rocks and the ocean below me.

I better keep my mind on my driving. The car had touchy brakes and this road was too filled with curves to let my mind drift. As I approached the next turn, I tapped the brakes. It was easier at a slower speed and I made the next couple turns without incident. A sharper curve loomed and I eased my foot onto the brakes.

They went to the floor, but the Volvo didn't slow.

Chapter Twenty-Eight

Not another car adventure. I couldn't even watch if my life flashed before my eyes. I was too busy watching the road. I jerked the car hard toward the left, pointing toward the hillside, away from the cliff. The tires skidded, but the car carried me around the bend with a heart-stopping screech. Centering the wheel on the road, I let the car continue down without my foot on the gas.

It picked up speed and I pumped the brakes, waiting to get an indication they worked. Nothing. I swung around another curve and as I tried to remember how many turns lay ahead, I nearly blew the next one. Then something popped into my head from driving lessons with my dad.

If anything happens to your brakes, use the emergency brake.

I yanked it up and the Volvo slowed so quickly I had to fight for control. I kept a hold on the brake until the hill evened out to a straightaway. With shaking fingers, I glided the car to the edge of the pavement, let it crunch over the gravel and stop at the edge of a grassy field.

The scent of burning rubber overwhelmed me. My breath was coming in deep gasps and my heart pounded like a drum against my chest.

Fearing I might throw up, I opened the door and

stumbled out, falling to my hands and knees. Nausea invaded my stomach and fear sent shivers up my spine. Had the brakes been tampered with? Was someone after me?

Who? And why?

Did Jennifer want the shop all to herself?

Was Carl afraid I might go after him?

What about Bobbi the Bimbo?

A nameless, fuzzy face danced in a tantalizing ghostly outline.

Had Paula or someone back at the Dominguez house been responsible?

The pain of pebbles stinging my palms and scraping into my knees reached my brain with a crescendo about the time I caught my reflection in the chrome wheel wells. God, I looked ghastly.

A gasping laugh escaped me. Here I was, about to die and all I could think of was that my mascara was smudged and my hair hung like a limp black curtain. With a shaky effort, I pulled myself to my feet. The day was still, except for a gentle ocean breeze that stirred the grass. It felt good on my clammy skin. I inhaled a welcoming breath of fresh air. The odor of rubber was gone, and I could smell the faint scent of Eucalyptus trees that lined the road a few yards away.

My phone buzzed as I slid into the car. My unsteady hands fumbled with it before I could put it to my ear.

"Hey, gal, where are you?"

Sam's voice was such a relief I wanted to cry. I bit hard on my lip, unaccustomed to the emotion. "I'm fine..."

"That wasn't my question, but what's wrong?"

"Nothing," I said, fighting to erase panic from my voice. "Where are you?"

"Just finished with Edwards. Very interesting. How about if I buy you lunch to make up for being a jackass this morning? How's the shopping?"

Our argument seemed so long ago. A sob choked me and I held the phone away from me so he couldn't hear it. As I pulled the phone back toward me, I heard the sound of an engine and jerked my head toward the road. A black limousine rounded the curve, barely made it around my vehicle and slid to a stop.

Fear skittered up my spine and my fingers shook so violently I dropped the phone on the gravel. It bounced, hit the edge of the pavement and plastic flew in all directions.

The front door of the limo opened and *Senor Zapato* stepped out, huge and imposing as a boulder.

"You okay, lady?"

I stared at him in terror. Had he cut my brake lines and followed me to make certain the job was completed? Was that paralyzed old man thing of *El Patron's* a trick? Well, I wasn't going down without a fight. Without answering, I pulled off my shoes and looked around. My only escape route was to run across the field, through the orchard to Pacific Coast Highway.

Hiking up my skirt, I turned and ran. Maybe *Zapato's* bulk would slow him. I had a head start and stamina on my side. Not to mention the fear that propelled me. I might have escaped except I stepped into a hole and suddenly I was falling to the grass and tumbling like a gymnast.

Winded and scared, I lay on my back staring up at a clear blue sky. Was that the last thing I would see, or would it be a gun barrel? Footsteps approached and I stared up at *Senor Zapato's* dark round face.

His gap-toothed smile surprised me. "What's wrong? Why did you run?" He lifted me to my feet as easily as I might lift a piece of jewelry. When he touched my shoulder, I started to jerk away, but realized he was brushing the dust from my suit.

"You don't look hurt." He leaned down directly in front of my face. "Can you hear me?"

Drawing a deep breath I nodded and pushed away from him. "I'm fine. My car ran off the road." Despite my effort to be brave, my voice wavered. "I think someone tried to kill me."

"Que?" His head jerked back toward my car.

"My brakes went out." Suddenly the sob I'd been fighting exploded and I began to cry. Horrified I was doing it in front of this giant, I turned away.

His meaty hand rested my shoulder and he patted me gently. "You're okay. *Esta bien. No se preocupe. Estoy aqui.*"

Maybe I should tell him I worried *because* he was there. Slowly common sense took hold and I recognized the lack of threat in his gentle taps. He took hold of my arm and squeezed it as though he could transfer some of his immense strength into my own shaky frame. As I calmed, he handed me a handkerchief and I used it to dry my tears and wipe my face. I'd looked bad earlier. That ghastly appearance had probably increased tenfold.

"Can you walk?" he asked. "Let's look at your car."

I took a step, wincing as my bare foot hit a patch of rocks.

"I can carry you," he offered.

"I'm fine."

He put his arm around me and supported me as we walked back toward the cars, not releasing me until we were beside the Volvo. As I shifted to move away something hard near his chest rubbed against my side. He had a damn gun under that suit! I recoiled, but he moved away, leaning over to poke his head under my rear bumper.

"You say the brakes went out?"

"They went to the floor as I came down the hill. I was afraid I wouldn't make it to the bottom."

"You shoulda tried your emergency brake," he said, head emerging. His smile was wide, genuine, brown eyes soft and paternal.

"That was what I did."

"Smart girl," he said with an approving nod as he smacked his hands together to clean off the dust. "Did you call someone?"

"No."

"I saw you on the phone when I came around the corner. I thought you were calling for help. Do you need a ride down the hill? I can have someone tow your car to a garage. I got a friend who can tell you what's wrong."

"Thanks." I retrieved my purse and followed him to the limo.

He opened the back door for me, but I shook my head. "Can I ride in front with you?"

"Sure." He moved to the front door and opened it.

I slid into the luxurious car and breathed a sigh of relief, until I realized no one knew where I was. Noting a car phone as he slid in from the other side, I fingered it. I hadn't seen a car phone in ages. Did it work?

"Do you mind if I make a call? My cell phone broke."

"Go ahead." He handed it to me and I dialed Sam.

He answered on the first ring. "What the hell happened?"

"I dropped my phone and broke it. The offer for lunch sounds good. Do you know where Geneva is on the Pacific Coast Highway? I'll pay cab fare."

"I'm gonna have to take a rain check. My doctor just called and wants me to come in, so Hank insists on taking me today."

My stomach plunged like a falling elevator. Had something happened? He was looking so alert, so alive. Could our argument have triggered another attack? "Are you all right?"

His rich laugh soothed me. "Fit as a fucking fiddle. I'll call you later."

I hung up and realized I had not told him where I was or about my companion. If *Senor* Shoe wanted to kill me with his meaty hands and dump my body off a cliff, no one would know.

"Should I drop you at Geneva?" he asked.

Given my thoughts, I jumped at the sound of his soft voice. "Sure."

Geneva was nearby and it would take time to get my car checked. I eyed *Senor Zapato* across the interior of the car. Could I trust him?

"Were you going to call someone to get my car?"

He picked up the phone and conducted the call in rapid Spanish. He told the man where the car was and to take it to his garage to check.

"He'll find out what's wrong," he said when he

hung up. "I'll drop you at the restaurant and finish my errands. I can drive you to the shop when it's ready or take you home."

His smile was so benign I wondered why I'd been afraid. He was acting more like an older brother than a tough guy.

"Why do they call you *Senor Zapato?*"

He gave me his gap-toothed grin and lifted his foot off the gas. "I used to kick a lot."

"Kick?"

His smile faded into a grim look and he shook his head. "A pretty lady like you don't wanna hear about it. I don't kick no more. My sister takes care of the house for *La Senora* and I drive *El Patron* and run errands."

Errands, huh? If the old man still took bets, *Senor* Shoe probably picked them up and applied a little heavy footed pressure to those who didn't pay on time. Whatever his real job, he might be helpful.

"How long have you worked for Mr. Dominguez?"

"Twenty years. He's a good man." He pounded the left side of his chest. *"Un corazon muy grande."*

"I've heard he had mob ties."

The man's smile never lessened. "He grows wine now. Big vineyards up around Santa Barbara."

I'd been thinking bookie or customer. "That was how he knew Rick."

"Rick?"

"Wells Fine Wines?"

His thick, black hair danced as he nodded. "Ah, *Senor* Wells. He set up wine tasting parties for *El Patron.* Someone killed him, huh?"

How much could he tell me about the old man's connection to Rick? Before I could phrase a question, he continued.

"I don't know why they'd kill him. He was everyone's buddy at the parties."

"He and Paula were close..." It was a test, a hunch.

His brown face swung toward me, startled but troubled. "Who said that?"

The concerned reaction confirmed my theory. "I've heard rumors…"

His hair flew from side to side as he shook his head. "Uh-uh. She's married."

"I don't think that mattered to Rick."

He said nothing at first, wide mouth tightening. Finally, he lifted a massive shoulder in a shrug. "Who can blame her with that husband?"

"Wait, her husband is Ken Gardner, the actor."

"*Si*. A mean one. *Muy loco.*" He tapped the side of his head.

Damn, I was a lousy detective. Ken Gardner was on my list from the service. Another connection I hadn't made because I hadn't seen him with Paula. Wait a minute! Gardner had been in trouble with police because of his temper. Did that add up to something? Maybe he gave Rick a smack to the head for screwing his wife. I needed to continue this conversation.

"May I buy you lunch?" I asked. "Since you're helping with my car, it's the least I can do." Entering Geneva with this man as an escort might be helpful if that rat Toby was working.

His dark skin colored at my invitation. "I can't. *El Senor* expects me back soon."

Oh, well. The visit to the Dominguez house had paid off. It eliminated one suspect, but opened the door for two others. Paula and her husband were moving higher on my board when I got home. I might even put them in red!

He dropped me at Geneva and I walked into the bar. I didn't see Toby. Felipe, the regular bartender, was pouring liquor into an ice-filled glass. I claimed a seat near the windows.

Felipe, a slim man with a thin mustache that might have been the envy of Ronald Colman, came over immediately. "Is Delia joining you?"

"She's in South America, but I'll take a martini. I need one after the morning I've had."

While he mixed the drink, I pulled a notebook from my purse and wrote down everything I remembered about Paula and Ken Gardner. I was considering any ties to Rick when Felipe brought my drink.

I took a quick sip and smiled as the icy liquor zoomed down my throat. "Perfect. Toby's are good, but they'll never compare to yours."

"You won't be getting any more of Toby's. He's not workin' here no more."

My heart did a quick summersault. Was I off the hook? "What happened?"

"He quit the other night. No notice, nothing. He didn't show up. He called later to say he'd hit the jackpot and didn't need to work. Stupid kids."

Chapter Twenty-Nine

Wednesday, 10:00 a.m.

I stepped into the glacial chambers of Hall and Merrysmith, the offices of Rick's lawyers, and began shaking. This damn place was like an igloo. The walls were white, the shelves alabaster, and the thick carpets were creamy vanilla. Adrienne followed me and put her hand on my bare arm. Could she feel the goosebumps? I should have worn something other than a pale lime sleeveless silk sheath.

In a cream-colored suit with a flash of a gray scarf at her throat, and her platinum hair swept back into a chignon, her petite figure resembled a small white bird. Perhaps an Arctic bird of some sort.

We'd been summoned for the reading of Rick's will, though I had known that whatever he might leave me would never make up for what he stole.

"You okay, hon?" she asked.

I could feel the tension in her touch. She was still angry with me, just like Oliver. He had been furious about my talk with Paula. He left a caustic message on voicemail about her "Exclusive" report, especially my comment that I might offer a reward. "I won't be left out of the loop this way."

Her fingers gripped my arm and while I wanted to push them away, at least they were warm. "You're doing fine, hon. Just keep staying cool. And keep quiet about the money situation," Adrienne cautioned in a low tone, grasping my arm. "No one needs to know he defrauded you."

I nodded. "Mum's the word."

A pencil-thin secretary with a pinched face led us to the inner chamber.

If the outer office was an igloo, walking into the office of J.B. Merrysmith was like being forced into a snowstorm. Five pairs of frosty eyes zeroed in on us. Like the exterior, this room was all white. The leather chairs were white and any upholstery was pale gray.

J.B. was an overweight man in his sixties with a thick shock of hair too black to be real. In a black suit with a patterned yellow tie and white shirt, he resembled a penguin. Jennifer sat across from him in a pale suit that resembled a frozen peach margarita. I didn't know the thin, bloodless-looking man beside her. Carl slouched in a third chair, in an ill-fitting, rumpled beige suit. His brown tie looked so tight it appeared ready to cut off circulation.

I drew back at the sight of the fifth visitor. Bobbi the Bimbo, in a neon pink dress, summoned comparisons to a strawberry Popsicle. She huddled in a plush chair, looking like a doll in a child's seat. What was she doing here?

J.B. Merrysmith conducted introductions, but I was only aware of the final person in the room. The tall, distinguished man with thick silver hair and eyes as clear as ice cubes studied me as he walked forward, putting away his cell phone. He wore a gray wool suit that fit him so well it might have been poured over him. Miles Standish Brookings. The Pilgrim.

He nodded, displaying none of the warmth he exhibited at the Mira Loma Police Station. Had he discovered I was the culprit who left that sliver of glass in Rick's car? He turned to Adrienne and tipped his head. "Ms. Underhill."

"Mr. Brookings," she replied in a cool voice. How did she know him?

He settled into a seat beside Bobbi as the introductions concluded.

"Let's begin," Merrysmith said, picking up a sheaf of papers.

Carl fidgeted in his chair. Sam's description of his conversation with the jerk only increased my animosity. According to Sam, the louse saw no conflict in taking my money and replacing it with shares of the store.

Merrysmith droned on and my gaze wandered. Brookings was watching me. Rather his gray gaze had settled on my legs. I shifted slightly and the gaze never wavered. Well, well… Our eyes met and his eye twitched. Was that a wink?

The sound of my name caught my attention and I jerked into full alert.

"That gives her half ownership of the shop," Adrienne said.

"We'll go through the details later."

"That's outrageous." Jennifer's voice was high and anxious as she whipped toward Bobbi. "Didn't he tell you that he wanted that changed?"

The girl lifted a thin shoulder. "He never said anything about the store…"

Jennifer flashed me a glacial look. "I'm disputing anything that I feel is incorrect."

"So you've said," Merrysmith said, flipping a page.

He began reading off bequests of personal items, which went to Jennifer or Carl. By the time he reached the house I had tuned out. I didn't expect anything other than the shop. How solvent was it? Could it help my money crisis?

A sudden gasp caught my attention as Jennifer hopped to her feet, shouting. "The house goes to Carl? That doesn't make sense."

Carl didn't appear surprised. Why would Rick leave it to him? Did Rick owe him money? Shouldn't this make Carl a major suspect?

Jennifer's attorney calmed her as Merrysmith continued. The content of Rick's savings account was left to her, but she cried out when she heard the total: $1,900. It was probably my money, but I said nothing.

"I don't understand," Jennifer said. "He told me he made a great deal at the wine shop. She whirled toward Carl. "What about stocks and bonds?"

He looked down at his scuffed brown shoes. "He sold them last month to pay off debts."

Jennifer swiveled toward me. "He said he had joint ventures with you. You took his money when you found out he was getting married, didn't you?"

I started to reply, but Adrienne grabbed my wrist and squeezed to keep me from speaking.

"Actually, it was the other way around." Miles Brookings' calm voice drew our attention, and we turned toward him like a tennis audience. He proffered a smile, but his blue-gray eyes were cool. "Are we nearly finished?"

Why had he and Bobbi come? Nothing in the will mentioned her.

Merrysmith nodded. "There is only the matter of

his life insurance."

"We can deal with that when everyone's gone," Jennifer said through a tight smile.

The attorney's eyes shifted to me. "Except Miss delaGarza. She's primary beneficiary."

Another loud gulp erupted from Jennifer. She appealed to Bobbi. "You said he told you he was changing that."

The girl's face was devoid of color except for two bright red dots high on her cheeks. They looked painted on. "That's what he said."

"I'm certain that's *what he said.* But I doubt he meant it." Brookings put a hand on his daughter's shoulder. "Are you ready to go?"

With head down, she got to her feet and Brookings thanked Merrysmith, who walked with them to the door.

"Bet that was a rude awakening to her," Carl said with a bitter laugh, watching Bobbi shuffle out the door.

"Why was she here?" Adrienne asked.

"Bet her father brought her. He wants her to think Rick was a rat."

Adrienne shot him a fierce look. If her voice had been a knife, it could have cut Carl in half. "He did all right by you."

His thin lips twitched. "We'd been best friends since college."

I'd never witnessed much closeness. The spindly man in the rumpled suit was not the sort Rick sought for his social circle. But who was I to argue? I'd missed that Rick wasn't as close to me as I thought. Had he given Carl and Bobbi the same false messages?

As Merrysmith returned, Jennifer turned to me. "The police are going to find out the truth."

"I hope they do," I replied.

"I want his books back. You had no right to take them."

Adrienne cleared her throat. "On the contrary. Kimberly is half owner. She has every right to them and to have them audited." Her icy words were aimed at Jennifer, but her cold eyes were on Carl.

"I want a key and his client list," I said.

Her face was a mask of frustration, and Carl's pale eyes regarded me with stony bitterness. Jennifer might hate me for what she wasn't getting from Rick, but different vibrations emanated from Carl. He hated me too. How far would he take that hate?

****

To my surprise, Brookings remained in the outer vestibule, speaking on a cell phone when we exited Merrysmith's office. I saw no sign of Bobbi.

Adrienne's earlier frostiness thawed as she smiled and squeezed my fingers. "Kimberly, hon, you're in the wine business."

I blinked, not certain whether that pleased or panicked me. "I don't know anything about running a business."

She patted my arm. "We're going to find a business manager, someone who isn't a thief. Don't worry about his sister's claim about the insurance. I'll handle that and Carl too."

It hit me—my money problems were nearing an end. There was the insurance policy and I could sell my interest in the shop. No wonder Adrienne was smiling.

"I'll call you later," she said, turning toward the

door.

At that moment, Brookings put down his phone and approached us.

Adrienne stepped in front, whether to protect me from him or him from me, I wasn't sure. "Miles, we didn't get a chance to properly say hello, but it's good to see you."

He grasped her hand with a polite smile. "Always a pleasure."

When he turned to me, his smile widened. "Miss delaGarza, I'm pleased to see you again."

I nodded, not sure what to say. His handshake was firm, and he held my hand longer than necessary. When I looked in his gray eyes, the glint was enough to melt the frost I'd been feeling for the past hour.

Adrienne was talking about someone they knew, but he didn't appear to be paying attention. Our eyes kept meeting in a secret greeting. He scrutinized me in a way I knew well. Something was happening here, but Adrienne twittered on, oblivious to undercurrents.

Finally, she turned. "Do you have time for lunch, Kimberly?"

Apparently the conversation had progressed while I ogled the tall man. I could sense when a woman wanted to be left alone and even if I wanted to stay, I couldn't. Sam was downstairs.

"I have a friend waiting."

Brookings held out a business card to me. "I have your card, but that number no longer works. Please call. I have some business I'd like to discuss."

The look in his eyes as his fingers slid over mine to give me the card screamed he had more on his mind than business.

"Certainly." I walked away, adding a swish to my swing. When I glanced back through the glass doors of the igloo-office, he still watched. My temperature went from frigid to fiery.

Chapter Thirty

"Do you know where you're going?" I asked Sam as he drove east along Wilshire Boulevard. My car remained in the shop, and now the rental was there too, getting brake work done. I was going through cars faster than a demolition derby contestant. Sam had reclaimed his vintage blue Cadillac from storage after getting a clean bill of health from his doctor the previous day.

"Missy, I know this town like the back of my hand. And I need to put some miles on my baby," he growled, squeezing the steering wheel. "Tell me more about your damn meeting."

"Miles Brookings and the Bimbo were there. I'm curious about him. What if he wanted to keep her from marrying Rick? Carl said he was trying to show her Rick was a jerk." I chewed on the corner of a short, blunt nail. As soon as I got money, I was visiting Nanci's Nail Nook, no matter what Sam said. "Maybe he hired a hit man."

He grunted. "Why bother? Wells was in such financial trouble that Brookings could have bought him off and sent him away."

"What if he did? Remember Rick came up with money to get the shop out of the hole. What if Rick took money to cover the debt, then changed his mind? What if he needed my money to pay back Brookings and marry the Bimbo?"

Sam grinned at me. "Good questions. Let's post them on your girly board."

"And let's look closer at Carl. He made out like a bandit."

His mouth tightened. "The man is a crook, no doubt about that. You need to get your accounts with him audited along with the shop. That might prompt him to sell Wells' house and make your money reappear."

"That would fix my money problems. If only the murder could be solved so easily. What am I missing? Could Rick have been laundering money? What if he was losing money through his gambling and used that as a way out?"

"I thought of that too. However, I haven't spotted any evidence. That's why we need to figure out the initials in those books. We need to make certain those accounts belong to real people or businesses. Doing parties for the Dominguez family might bear examination. Could be the old man's paying for some fancy soiree that never happened. That gives Wells cash and then he pays it back, minus his laundering fee, by claiming it's for wine from the old man's vineyards."

I thought of the books I kept ignoring. Now I understood why Sam found them significant. "I don't know how money laundering works. Could they get away with that?"

"Probably. An audit would spot it." Sam checked the rearview mirror, the third time he'd checked it since we left Century City.

"Are we being followed?" I started to twist around.

"Don't look. There's a black GMC that's staying

with us. Is that what followed you?"

"I have no idea. It was a big-ass SUV."

He checked again as he changed lanes. "I spotted it earlier and caught part of the license tag. I'll have Hank run it."

"If Carl is the killer, why would he follow me?"

"Actually, following you doesn't make sense."

It didn't to me either, but someone ran Lindy off the road. "Now what?"

"We need to check the books to verify big customers and how much wine they bought and make certain Wells purchased what he claimed to buy. For all we know, his records indicate he paid money for stock he never got or sold wine that was non-existent or to people who were non-existent. That's how money laundering works. If he was doing that, checking those books against his inventory is the only way you're going to find it."

I groaned. "This sounds like busy work. He sold dozens of bottles every day to people. How can we check all that?"

"Never mind day-to-day sales. We're looking for people he might bill monthly or who spent a bundle for a party. On the other side we're looking for a company or distributor he regularly used. If he was laundering money, someone on either end is going to be a phantom."

I sighed at the enormity of what he proposed. "That sounds boring."

His head swiveled toward me, blue eyes hard and unforgiving. "Investigating can be dull, but it's little details that get the job done. I solved one case from days of going through a guy's phone records."

Rebecca Grace

"Can't the computer do that?"

"Maybe that's why he kept records by hand."

The thought sent fresh chills down my spine. "I might give Miles Brookings a call. I was getting weird vibes about his relationship to Rick." Pulling his card from my purse, I studied the embossed design.

"Do you think he'll talk to you?"

"If I visit him wearing a short skirt," I said with a quick smile.

Sam glanced at my bare legs and then up. "You would stoop to using feminine wiles?"

Thinking about Brookings' gaze, I nodded. "Whatever it takes. Well, almost whatever."

He turned away. "Have you thought more about other women?"

"Besides Betty and Paula? No, why?"

"When I was looking at the police file, I saw a note. 'Thanks for the weekend, love, P, or B or D.' Something like that."

My skin prickled. "Why didn't you tell me before?"

"I was too pissed and you were in the dumps. I might as well tell you. Edwards admitted Wells had someone the whole time you were together."

Was there no end to Rick's treachery? I could forgive a few months. But years? Nausea snaked up my esophagus.

"Betty?" My voice was a hoarse rasp.

"This woman had money. She helped when things got too bad." He seemed to realize my distress and he touched my arm. "She could have been from before he met you. Some rich old dame who considered him her boy toy."

The thought didn't help much.

"Think. Someone whose first names start with B, P or D?"

"Doreen Graham? She's rich and I saw her at the service. She's been a customer since before we met." My insides churned with disgust. "She's at least sixty years old."

"Rich? Maybe needy?" He rubbed his chin and winked at me. "Maybe I'll pay her a visit and use my own wiles."

"If Delia calls again, I'll ask her."

"What about her? I notice she's off the list."

"She's in South America, so her alibi checks out. Besides, we made a blood pledge years ago. No male poaching." It remained untested. Her older dates never appealed to me, and men I dated seldom provided enough financial enticement for her trophy wife ambitions.

My phone buzzed and I fumbled to check caller ID. I'd picked up a replacement the previous afternoon and still hadn't figured it out. I finally hit the right button.

"How's our favorite killer?" Delia chirped.

"Speak of the devil! We were talking about you. We got cut off last time."

"Shitty phone service. Tell me what's happening. You discovered that louse was fucking around? Worthless piece of shit!"

"We ought to kill him," I joked and her loud laughter rang through the ear piece, though I could see Sam's face tense.

"With who?" she asked.

"Betty, his accountant. He gave her my pendant, the one Bobbi wanted him to get back." That thought

271

still angered me. I clutched the phone tighter.

"Does the Bimbo know? Maybe you ought to tell her. Anyone else?"

"Paula Gardner?"

"I wondered about her. She always acted so fucking smug."

"What do you mean?" Leave it to Delia to pick up on little things I missed.

"I've seen her at the store. When I ran into Rick at a gallery opening in December, she showed up and they were sooo cozy. Then they disappeared."

The churning in my stomach increased. "You never told me!"

"Would you have believed it?"

I slumped in the seat, feeling spent. "No."

"Sometimes you're blind, Kimmie."

"Do you think her husband found out?"

Her laugh bubbled across the line. "He'd have killed Rick. He's been arrested for beating up people who flirted with Paula. You should tell the cops."

I smiled at Sam. "I'm going to shout it to them."

"Should I come home? Do you need me?"

"Enjoy yourself. Sam and I have this under control. We're going to visit the wine shop, which I own. Think of it—an endless supply of champagne."

"Naturally you'd land on your feet, lucky bitch! I better go." I clicked off and pounded on Sam's arm like a bongo drum as I told him about Ken Gardner.

He held up a cautionary hand. "Before we go to police, let's check it out."

"He's not going to tell us anything. It's time Torres and Callahan did some work." I got the number for Mira Loma PD and asked to be connected to Callahan.

"Kimberly," Sam protested, but I put a finger to my ear and turned away.

Callahan's response echoed Sam's skepticism. "That name hasn't come up."

"I'm giving it to you now. He was at the service."

"Okay." He didn't sound convinced.

Frustration gripped me. "Never mind. We'll do it ourselves."

I hit the off button before he could reply. When were these guys going to start looking beyond me?

"What did he say?" Sam asked.

"Nothing. Stupid jerk."

"You can't accuse people based on whim. That isn't the way cases are built. Which brings me to something else..." He shook his head in disapproval. "Do you realize how dangerous that trip to the Dominguez house could have been if the old man was to blame?"

My thoughts turned to *Senor Zapato*, who turned out to be more teddy bear than killer. "What am I supposed to do? Go through books that don't show anything? Gardner was at the service, but Callahan said his name hadn't come up. It should have been in the customer books."

"There are no names in the books, only initials. You don't know that his wife had a relationship with Wells. This is all supposition."

"Maybe Rick owed him money?"

"Can you prove that? Give me something concrete, not fuckin' conjecture."

I slumped in my seat, deflated as a used balloon, and studied my bare, blunt nails. "Maybe I should stick to shopping and getting my nails done."

Chapter Thirty-One

Wednesday, 2:45 p.m.

I stared at my board in dismay. What was it Sam had said—get the information together and you'll see it all? I didn't see a damn thing except colorful sticky notes. I wasn't any closer to solving this than police who had a bull's eye drawn around my face.

What about the police? Maybe I needed to spend an evening with Hank. Too bad it wasn't Sunday. I could show up at Geneva. Even if he didn't want to talk, he might inadvertently divulge something.

My phone buzzed and I grabbed it.

"Am I forgiven yet?"

My muscles tensed at the sound of Brad's voice. I'd hung up on him the previous night when he went ballistic over my conversation with Paula. Apparently her "exclusive" set off an explosion at Channel 8. I'd calmed down Reba after fibbing that I ran into Paula and she took my words out of context.

"Am I forgiven?" I asked. "I didn't know Paula would use that. You and I talk regularly and you could say the same type of stuff. You could mention my fear of being followed."

"It would betray your trust. I couldn't do that."

"That's the difference between you and Paula."

"You're forgiven," he said with a sigh. "Am I?"

"We-l-l-l..yes!"

"Good, how about relaxing tonight? Can I tempt you with hot dogs and beer? I've got seats in the company box at Dodger Stadium."

The box held twelve seats and I shuddered to think about who else might be there. Visions of Vincent and Gwen leaped into my head.

"I reserved the box as a treat for the weekend crew. Lindy will be there and that director kid. Peter, his wife, Cindy Jamison and her husband are coming." Cindy was co-anchoring with Brad.

"No Gwen?"

"She's beyond the weekend crew. Everyone knows you got a raw deal, so how about it?"

The idea appealed to me. I hated sitting at home alone. "I'm not answering any questions about the case, okay?"

"No problem."

****

I pulled the baseball cap down across my forehead as Brad guided me through the crowd at Dodger Stadium. He stopped to greet people who recognized him, but with large sunglasses covering my face, I hoped to remain anonymous. I knew I could be unrecognizable without makeup, so I kept it to a minimum.

The company box brought sanctuary. It hovered above the field, so I didn't worry about anyone spotting me. The interior consisted of two rows of seats with a wet bar along the back wall. Bags of chips, peanuts, and popcorn were laid out on the counter, along with a tub filled with ice, soft drinks, and beer.

Tension sizzled in the box like a hot dog on a grill.

The disbelief on familiar faces did not bode well and I hesitated. Suddenly Lindy let out a happy whoop and hopped to her feet.

"Kimberly!" She nimbly vaulted over the seats. "I'm so glad you came." She resembled an enthusiastic teenager in shorts and a T-shirt as she hugged me.

"How are you?" I asked, checking her face. She no longer wore a bandage on her cheek or the wrap on her wrist. The only visible reminder of her accident was a tiny scar along her lower jaw.

"I'm doing great." Her tone rang with exuberance.

"Holy shit, look who is being seen in public." Reba stood and tottered toward me. She wore skin tight leggings and an oversized Dodgers jersey and three-inch high sandals. She snapped her fingers. "Someone call a photographer quick."

For an instant I panicked, glancing around like a hunted animal. She let loose with her familiar cackle before hugging me and whispering, "I ought to punch you for speaking to Paula."

Peter Murphy watched the scene with a cynical smile but he caught my hand as I walked down the steps.

"They let you out of jail?"

I gave him a false smile. "They haven't built the cell that can hold me."

"Or her ego," Reba teased.

Peter watched me with a knowing grin. "When are you gonna give your station an inside scoop?"

Brad stepped between us. "She's here as my guest and you're off duty, Peter."

"And out of line," Lindy added, to my surprise. She stood with her arms crossed, staring him down like a mother protecting her young.

Peter held up his hands. "Sorry, folks."

The show of support sent a pang of regret through me. Reba, Brad, and Lindy had been there for me, helping when I needed support. Maybe I owed them something.

I turned to Peter. "Okay, on the record, and then we drop it okay? Let's say that I have confidence in the Mira Loma Police to uncover the truth. If a reward will help, I'll offer it. I have an investigator looking into the case because I want the killer caught. Rick was my…" I paused. I couldn't say he was my friend. I wanted to see his killer caught to spare me a murder rap.

"We can say that?" Reba asked in a hushed voice.

"Word for word," I said, hoping it didn't anger Oliver. I wanted to do this for my friends.

To my horror, Peter pulled his cell phone from his pocket and the sound of my voice filled the room. "Mind if I use this instead?"

Our collective gasp was audible. Leave it to Peter to be so crass. But as I looked at Reba's expectant eyes, I couldn't refuse.

"Sure. But no more."

He grabbed his jacket. "I hate to miss the game, but I better go." He hopped up the steps, leaving us in stunned silence.

"That fucking prick," Lindy said. "No wonder he wanted to come."

Brad put his hand on my shoulder. "Don't worry about it. Let's watch the game." The tension evaporated with Peter's exit. Lindy insisted on sitting beside me, and with Brad on my left, I felt insulated.

In the fifth inning, an usher appeared. "Miss

delaGarza?"

"Yes?"

He handed me a slip of paper. All eyes were on me as I unfolded the sheet. The writing was small and masculine.

May I buy you a drink? It was signed M. Brookings and listed a box number.

"One of my friends has invited me for a drink," I said with a nervous laugh.

"La-de-dah!" Reba waggled her brows at me. "You can't take her anywhere without being bothered by her adoring public."

"Are you going?" Brad asked, his brow furrowed.

I might have refused except that man knew things. This provided an opportunity to cultivate his company.

"Maybe a quick drink." I re-folded the note and tucked it into my purse.

Lindy scanned the open windows of nearby boxes through a pair of binoculars. "I see! It's Adrienne Underhill."

"Adrienne is a big baseball fan. I'll be right back." I wasn't certain if she was the reason for my invitation, but I needed to warn her about my comments for TV8. Maybe she could soothe potential problems with Oliver. I stood and started for the door, but Brad followed.

"I'll walk you over."

He took my elbow as we stepped into the outer walkway, but I slid out of his grasp. "You're very sweet, but I'm a big girl."

"Who has people following her." As though someone might be watching, he glanced around. "I'm sorry about Peter. I didn't know he'd do that."

"I did it for you, Reba, and Lindy. As for being

followed, no one's going to attack me in public."

He caught my hand and squeezed it. "But I worry about you."

Our eyes met and I read concern…and something more. I kept getting flashes of his interest, but I wasn't prepared for it and couldn't lead him on. Pulling away from his grasp, I smiled. "I'm fine. I'll be back in a few minutes."

As he walked away I wondered if I was ignoring a good thing. While he could spark my interest, he didn't ignite heat.

And speaking of heat…

Miles Brookings answered my knock with a wide smile. He looked damned fashionable for a ballgame. Unlike Brad in his faded jeans and Nikes, Miles wore a cashmere turtleneck and wool slacks with Bally loafers.

"Welcome," he said, beckoning me inside with a bow.

"Good evening." While I presented him with my best smile, I had to force down the butterflies that set flight in my stomach.

"I'm so pleased you came over."

I stepped into the hushed surroundings and felt like I'd exited the stadium for another world. Unlike our station accommodations with its two rows of padded seats and outdoor carpeting, this box was triple in size and offered three spacious rows of individual leather loungers. The Dodger-blue carpet was so soft and thick I wanted to shuck my shoes. Tinted windows shut out the outside world when they were closed—like now— leaving us in a private, hushed atmosphere. No odor of beer or brats in here! The place smelled of money.

As far as I could tell we were alone. "I thought

Adrienne was here."

"She's a typical Dodgers fan. Two innings and she needs to beat the traffic. May I offer you a drink? I mixed a pitcher of martinis."

"A good martini is always heavenly."

He walked to the back of the booth while I settled into a seat. We were alone, except for thousands of fans who could turn binoculars onto this booth at any moment. How much did those tinted windows hide? I knew of at least one audience member who might be checking.

Miles approached with two glasses and handed one to me. "To the Dodgers."

I joined in the toast. "Since they're down five to one, here's to a rally."

Miles sat beside me, his handsome face growing serious. "I've been hoping for an opportunity to talk with you."

My head seemed to nod of its own accord. "Me too. I never got a chance to thank you for helping me at the police station."

He tapped my knee with a light fingertip. "I wanted to thank you too, but circumstances kept interfering."

"Thank me?" That surprised me.

"Let me apologize for my daughter. I know Bobbi can be high-strung, but she didn't mean to hurt you at the memorial service. I wanted to thank you for not telling police about her outburst. That was a difficult day for her."

"For me too." I tried to sound meek, rather than sarcastic.

"This ordeal has been overwhelming, and as I said, she is high strung."

I recalled my glimpse of her in the john that day at Geneva. She'd reminded me of a temperamental thoroughbred.

When I didn't reply, he gestured at my glass. "How's the drink?"

"Very good." I tipped my head toward him in approval. "And I'm a martini connoisseur."

He chuckled, a low sound that sent strange vibrations through my middle. His blue-gray eyes held me. "So I noticed. You were enjoying yourself that first day I saw you."

Had he seen me fall off the barstool? I cringed at the thought.

As though he picked up my negative vibrations, he tapped my knee again. "Let's focus on something more pleasant."

"Such as?"

His bright eyes pinned me with a laser beam. "You. I want to get to know all about you."

Chapter Thirty-Two

Me? Was he serious?

"I want to know what you like to do when you're not bringing me the latest news. What do you do when you're off duty?"

"Besides drink?" I raised the martini that was starting to blur my vision.

His laugh rumbled through the room. "Were you and your friend celebrating? She said something about going to Rio?"

I explained Delia's trip and gave him a summary of the long years of friendship beginning with the days of Kimmie D and Delia Burnett. "We used to play games when we met new guys, giving them false names. Like I would be Kara, and she might be Debor-AH. Not Deborah, but Debor-AH."

"I should be happy I got your real name," he said with a chuckle.

"Only because you knew who I was," I admitted, thinking of that first day I saw him. Sudden melancholy gripped me and tears stung my eyes. "Damn…"

"What?"

"I miss Delia. I wish she'd come home." I drew a jagged breath and lurched to my feet. As I stumbled toward the steps, he caught me. He lifted me to my feet and for an instant he held me with powerful arms. He smelled of expensive, exotic cologne. His soft sweater brushed my cheek. He felt like…oh, hell…Rick.

I pulled away. "I better get back to my friends." The stairs swam before my eyes, but somehow I made it to the top step. He was right behind me.

He put his hand on my shoulder. "I'm sorry, I didn't mean to be forward. I thought you needed comforting."

I held my head down, afraid to look up and see pity. I didn't know why sadness had swamped me. "I'm being silly."

"No." His low voice was comforting. "You're being human. May I take you to dinner tomorrow night? Let's talk when we're not sitting in the middle of a fishbowl."

"Sure." I rattled off my new phone number and scooted out the door, fearing he might touch me again. Brad met me as I hurried through the milling crowd.

"I'm ready to go home," I said. "Do you mind telling the others? I'll wait at the car."

****

Thursday, 7:00 a.m.

The ringing of my cell jerked me out of a sound sleep. I fought to brush away grogginess. What made people think I was awake at this hour? I blinked my eyes open to check the number. Sam. He launched in without preamble.

"I guess I don't have to tell you how fuckin' stupid it was to make those comments to the news. I ain't answerin' questions from anyone and if you tell them I'm helpin' you, I won't do it anymore."

"What time is it?"

"I'll call you later, if you haven't been arrested."

His anger was understandable. I'd admitted

someone was helping and it could bring unwelcome attention if news people learned his name. Hank would be furious. Why hadn't I realized that before opening my big mouth? My phone rang again. Didn't anyone sleep in?

"Good morning, Kimberly," a gentle Southern voice said. "This is Oliver Nichols."

I pushed my hair back from my face. My head hurt as though someone was yanking on my hair. Had I had that much to drink? I felt horrible. And I had a bad feeling about why he was calling.

"Yes, Mr. Nichols?" I cleared my froggy throat.

"If you say one more word to anyone without my permission, you can find another attorney." All trace of Southern gentility vanished. His voice grew hard as a rapping gavel. "I am your attorney. Any statements come from me or through me. I don't care how many friends you have in the media. When I work for you, you do as I say. I won't put up with shenanigans. If you can't live by my rules, then let's cut the cord and you can go right to jail."

"I'm sorry, Mr. Nichols…"

The phone clicked. What a crappy way to start the day. I might as well face it. Crime drama wasn't my thing. Where was my historical romantic life?

A shower didn't help, and I couldn't face the thought of staring at that damn board. I couldn't even go out, since my repaired Mercedes wasn't being delivered until noon. I called the one person who might cheer me up, even though I had no idea what time it was in Brazil.

"Do you know what time it is?" Delia rasped.

I was too pleased to hear her voice to care if she

complained. "My life is falling apart. I needed to talk to you."

"Oh, baby, what is it?" Sympathy replaced irritation, soothing me like a warm bath.

In halting sentences I let her have it all, unloading everything, including Sam's anger and Oliver's tirade.

"You should have told me this from the beginning, you nut. You need my help. As usual. I'll see what kind of connections I can get and be home in a few days."

Pangs of guilt struck me immediately. "I don't want to interrupt your trip. I just needed to vent. I can get through this."

"You're horrible in a crisis when it's personal. Give you an earthquake or fire that affects others and you'll go on the air and calm the world. When it's your own mess, you fall to pieces without me."

Her lecture was as painful as Sam's because I feared she was right. "Things aren't all bad. I might have a date."

"What?" She squealed like a teenager. "With who?"

"Miles Brookings. The Pilgrim guy from the bar."

Her gulp was so loud I feared she might choke. "He actually called?"

"It's not that simple. He's the Bimbo's father. I've run into him a few times."

"Now you're going my route? Trophy wife? That's what I need—your sexy ass for competition."

I laughed. "I don't think so. Besides, you have Walter."

"I'm ditching that idiot. But he doesn't think much of your Pilgrim. When I mentioned I met him, Walter said the guy is known for shady deals."

Shady deals? That sounded promising. "Like what? Can you ask Walt?"

"He's hunting elephants somewhere. I can't reach him." Disgust rang in her voice.

"I don't think they have elephants down there."

"Whatever," she said with a laugh. "I don't care. I'm ready to go home."

"Don't do it just for me. I need to do things on my own sooner or later. I might as well start now. Give me your phone number so I can call if I need you."

"You just did."

"I mean the place where you're staying."

"Call my cell."

"What if it isn't working?" I persisted, not wanting to be left without a connection again.

She sighed. "I'll have to get it. I'll call you later. Will you be around?"

"I may have dinner with Miles, the Pilgrim."

"Don't forget condoms…just in case."

Recalling his gentle touches, I gulped. Would he put a move on me?

"You're thinking about it, aren't you?" Delia asked with a delicious giggle.

"He probably has his own supply. Custom made."

We hung up laughing. She could do so much to raise my spirits. I looked toward the stairs, but couldn't face my board or Rick's ledgers. I needed a day off. Slumping on the sofa, I turned on the television and tuned to a news channel.

A cool blonde in a sleeveless shell read headlines. She needed my mother's fashion advice. The fuchsia blouse and thin white arms did nothing for her. An unflattering photograph of me jumped out behind the woman's helmet hair.

"Did she do it?" the caption read. The screen split into two people—Joe Higgins, a former assistant district attorney, and Paula.

"Oliver Nichols won't discuss a reward or comment on Kimberly's latest interview," Paula said, "I understand he has threatened to quit."

Higgins glared into the camera, shaking his head. "She's her own worst enemy."

"Do police have any other suspects?" the anchor asked Paula.

"Not that I know of."

"This reward offer is her attempt to pretend she didn't do it. How many guilty people make that sort of offer?" Higgins added.

"She claims to have hired a private investigator, but we haven't been able to discover who it is." Paula's voice rang with skepticism.

"And you won't!" I shouted at the set and hit the off button. I might as well have a "guilty" sign pasted on my forehead. Could I get a fair trial if I was arrested?

My cell phone buzzed and I grabbed it. The caller ID showed "caller unknown," but I hit the talk button, hoping it was Delia. Wait until she heard about this lynch mob.

"Kimberly? I hope I didn't wake you."

I'd never heard the voice on the phone, but I knew it immediately. Miles! My heart skipped and I patted my hair into place, as though he could see me.

"I've been up for a while," I said, trying to sound awake.

"Good. I wanted to confirm dinner tonight."

Chapter Thirty-Three

Thursday, 7:00 p.m.

Miles picked me up in a black Jaguar convertible, opening my car door. He looked very handsome in a charcoal Armani suit with a crisp white shirt and pale blue Gucci tie.

I'd put my day to good use and visited Nanci's Nail Nook, my hairdresser, and my favorite boutique in Beverly Hills. I'd managed to find just the right dress in deep green to go with my favorite pair of gold stiletto Manolo Blahnik sandals. The day cost three thousand dollars, but I could make that up in profits from the wine store.

The dress was form fitting—I wouldn't be eating much in it—with a low cut top that outlined my cleavage. It ended above the knee and one side had a slit that ran halfway up my thigh, allowing me limited movement. As I slid into the car, I showed a flash of leg to get his attention.

Given the way his brows shot up, I knew he noticed.

"We have dinner reservations at Marcel's," he said as he climbed into the car.

I knew of Marcel's. Very swanky, very A-list with Hollywood power brokers, but I'd never been there. I smiled in delight. This was the life I knew.

The restaurant maitre'd greeted Miles as though they were old friends. We were guided through the dimly-lit, hushed room to a high-backed booth along the wall, a location that provided the ultimate in privacy. Martinis arrived as we were seated. Had Miles ordered in advance?

I took a sip. "Mmm, the way I like it."

"I got your special recipe from Geneva."

That surprised me. He had taken time to learn that little detail? Had he been talking to Toby? What else had he discovered?

"I thought Toby quit."

"Felipe," he said with a warm smile. "I've known him for years."

I breathed easier. That made sense. I'd known him a long time too. "Delia and I adore him." Such polite chitchat. Was that how we were going to spend the evening?

"And Rick Wells?" he asked.

I nearly choked on my olive. "Don't even ask."

His chuckle soothed me. "I have a feeling we share the same opinion of Mr. Wells."

I turned to him in surprise. "He was marrying your daughter."

He looked away, studying the room, handsome face growing grim. "Bobbi is old enough to make her own decisions, but that doesn't mean I approve of them."

"I thought you had business dealings with him."

Blinking rapidly, he turned to me. "Why would you think that?"

So much for conjecture. "I'd heard…"

He shook his head, gray eyes studying me. "There

are people you know from the get-go that you cannot trust. I had him figured the moment I met him."

I chewed on my lip, fighting to keep disappointment from my voice. "I guess I was the only one who couldn't figure him out."

He grunted and brushed my hand with his fingers. "No, you weren't. He was a charmer with the ladies. I watched him weave a spell around Bobbi that no one could penetrate. He even charmed Pamela."

"Pamela?" Was this someone else for my board?

"My sister. I think you met her at Geneva. Wells could make women believe anything he wanted."

Ah, the Pixie. "You didn't approve of the wedding?"

"There would never have been a wedding." His tone turned hard as brick.

I summoned my best poker face. How far would he go to stop the wedding? "Rick's death must have been a shock to your daughter."

"I was in Canada at the time and Bobbi fell to pieces. I wish police could understand she's high-strung, but she could never be violent enough to commit a physical attack."

A wave of shock surged through me. I was so focused on me I hadn't considered who else police might investigate. She was on my list out of spite. "Police consider her a suspect?"

"Seems that way, but I made certain they knew she could have been a victim herself."

Huh? Then it hit me. The broken glass! I kept quiet, not wanting to bring attention to it.

"It occurs to me we need to trust each other," he added.

"Why?" Could he hear my heartbeat quicken?

"I know Bobbi didn't do it, but I'm not certain about you."

I had to stifle an audible gulp. Prickles of fear ran along my skin. "You think I…"

His smile was steady, and those laser eyes zeroed in on me. "If you did, I won't find you less fascinating. You've done me a favor. You might say, I owe you, and as I've said before, I like being in debt to beautiful women."

My mouth was dry and I knew better than to moisten it with my martini. This man required I stay sharp. "I didn't…"

"You put a broken glass in his car." His voice was flat but his hard eyes defied denial.

Oh, hell! I grabbed my drink and took a sip before answering. "How…do you know?"

His head tilted forward and his lips twitched into a smile. The gray eyes suddenly sparkled with mischief. "I saw you and your friend. I heard you giggling about Wells. I figured you didn't know Bobbi was driving the car."

My forehead tingled, or maybe it was the martini.

"Your secret is safe. I used it to show police someone might be after Bobbi. I want them to think she's been threatened, so I took it directly to Patterson. Don't worry, I washed off any prints."

I avoided his eyes. I couldn't admit Hank knew the truth. "Why do we have to trust each other?"

"I need to trust that you won't do anything again, and you need to trust that I won't reveal the source of that glass. Now why don't we order dinner and drop the subject of Rick Wells? The man is gone, and I don't give a damn who killed him. The sooner he's forgotten, the better for both of us."

I don't think I tasted a bite. I ordered, chewed and swallowed, but my mind was a swirling mess. Our discussion topics were light and inconsequential. Who can think when they've been accused of being a killer and told it didn't matter?

I fell asleep on the drive home—too much good wine and those wonderful martinis. He opened my car door and took my house keys from me to unlock the door.

"Would you like me to come in and make certain everything is all right?" he asked, peering inside.

Normally I might have, but my burglar alarm had been working well and I was feeling too groggy. "No, it's fine. Maybe…"

"Another time?" he asked, straightening the collar of my jacket.

It was an intimate touch, and I could feel the heat of his fingers through the thin material even in my inebriated state. Suddenly, I was aware of our closeness and the warmth of his breath on my face.

"Certainly. Thanks for an enjoyable evening."

He leaned close to me and kissed me gently on the lips. I swayed toward him and he kissed me again, before taking my shoulders and standing me upright. "I'll call you tomorrow." He touched his lips to my forehead before he walked down the drive.

I stumbled inside, kicking off my new sandals. What a weird but interesting evening. I could hardly wait to call Delia. Did the man consider me the killer? Why would that excite him? Or maybe he knew I wasn't guilty, because he arranged it?

I started upstairs, feeling like I was floating, though I didn't know if it was from the liquor or him. A sudden thumping on the front door stopped me. My heart leaped into my throat. I didn't know him well, but Miles didn't strike me as the pounding type. It was nearly three . Who could it be? A media person with an interview request? Torres, arriving to arrest me? I made certain the alarm was on, tucked my cell into my hand and tiptoed to the door.

Through the peep hole, I saw Brad's angry face outlined in the exterior light. I opened the door with a sigh of relief. "Hi, what are you doing?"

"I could ask the same of you. What the fuck were you doing kissing that son of a bitch?"

Anger swelled inside me, tightening my hands into fists. "That's none of your business."

He grabbed my arm and pushed me inside. "You *are* my business!"

I yanked my arm out of his grasp and backed away. His breath reeked of alcohol and his blue eyes were bloodshot. He looked like hell. His hair spiked at weird angles, his loose tie was stained and the lapel of his jacket looked damp. "What are you talking about?"

He staggered forward, cornering me against the wall. "You know. You have to know."

I'd never been around physical violence, but I could sense his anger was ready to explode into physical force. I attempted a smile and appealed to reason. "Brad, you've been drinking. I think you should go home and sober up."

He leaned closer to me, his words slurring. "You mus' know that wha's happening iss not an accident."

"What is happening?" I turned my face away as he

tried to kiss me.

He caught it in a hard grip and jerked it up to him. "We're a team..."

I pushed my hands against his chest, attempting to put distance between us. "Go home and we'll talk later."

"We'll talk now." He leaned forward to kiss me, but I'd had enough. I tried to slap him, but despite being drunk, he moved quickly. He caught my arm and bent it behind my back, yanking me against the wall.

My head bounced hard, sending a shower of stars dancing behind my eyes.

"Damn you." I curled the fingers of my free hand into a fist and punched his side, but he caught that wrist and folded it behind my back. Why hadn't I taken self-defense classes recently? I tried to kick, but his body trapped me against the wall. One old lesson returned as he tried to kiss me again. I lifted my bare foot and came down hard on his toe. Too bad I wasn't still wearing those stilettos.

He howled and drew back, surprised. I pushed at him, elbowing him in the midsection and made it to the door and yanked it open. A hard wall blocked it—the bulky body of *Senor Zapato.* I started to scream, but he looked at me with a confused look.

"You okay?" he asked.

I shook my head and waved behind me. Brad had his head down and was coming after me, but *Senor Zapato* hefted a right hand, and I heard a loud pop! Brad crumbled to the ground like a dropped sack of potatoes.

My breath came in labored gasps and I bent over. What was the big man doing here? I lifted my eyes to see what he was going to do next, but he was kneeling beside Brad.

"He's okay. Knocked out."

I took another deep breath. "Thanks."

He nodded and hefted Brad over his bulky shoulder, like a longshoreman loading bags of bananas. *"Esta boracho."*

"Very drunk," I agreed.

"I'll take care of him and have someone get his car. *Buenas noches."* He walked down the driveway, Brad's limp body flopping against his broad back.

I closed the door and leaned back against it, waiting for my breathing to return to normal. What the hell was going on with Brad? But I knew. He'd been giving hints for a while and I'd ignored them.

What would have happened if *Senor Zapato* had not been around? I'd gotten in several good licks, but could I have held him off? Why the hell was the *Senor* outside my door at three in the morning anyway? I wasn't certain I wanted to know.

With trembling fingers, I locked the door and set the alarm. Should I call police? No, Brad had been drunk and jealous. I saw no reason to get him into trouble. As I started up to my bedroom, I noticed the light blinking on my answering machine. Two messages. Maybe Delia had called. What time was it in South America? I could use her counsel, if not her sense of humor. I walked to the phone and tapped the message button.

Toby's voice came across the line. "Miss delaGarza, I'm tired of waiting. You promised me the money by this weekend. If I don't get it, I'm taking my recording to police."

Before I could take another breath, a hoarse voice I didn't recognize came across the line. "You bitch! You're heading for a fall. If you don't stop making trouble, I'll see that you get what your boyfriend got."

Chapter Thirty-Four

I barely slept that night, sitting on my horrible hard sofa, watching old movies. I tried calling Delia to no avail. I wanted to call Sam, but I feared he might insist on coming over, and I hated the thought of his driving from Glendale in the middle of the night. I might have driven to his house except I feared someone lurking outside. Police would probably think this was another trick if I called them.

Was I in danger? That was the worst part. I didn't know.

At nine the next morning, my doorbell rang. I blinked awake, surprised to find I lived through the night. The bell sounded again, so I dragged my stiff body to a standing position.

Who would visit so early? I hoped for Sam, but instead a delivery man with a huge bouquet of roses stood outside.

Miles Brookings? It was the sort of thing he might do. The roses were a wild spray of colors, from vivid red to orange, pink and yellow. Wait until I told Delia! We'd always said that if a man sent flowers the next day, he was a keeper. And we hadn't even slept together.

With an expectant smile, I opened the card, thinking about how long to wait before I called to thank him. Maybe my luck was changing. My face froze as I read the card. *Please forgive me, Brad.*

It pained me to throw away anything so beautiful, but I didn't want the flowers. Forgive him? I never wanted to see him again. I carried the vase outside onto the lower patio. As I walked inside, my board came into view. It seemed to pulsate, accusing me of neglect. I needed to call Callahan about that threatening phone call. I decided to call Sam first.

"You should have called as soon as you got it," he said, showing no sign of his earlier anger.

"At three in the morning?"

"They called at three?"

"I got home at three." Anticipating his next question, I added, "I had a date."

"I don't like that Brad guy. There's something off about him..."

Sam might not understand about Miles, so I fudged. "I'm never seeing him again. I'm spending the day on my detective work."

"Great. I got plenty to tell you. Did you get the shorthand for those ledgers so we can check names?"

My nose wrinkled. He would go ballistic if I told him how I spent the previous day. How could I get those initials decoded? Perhaps I needed to see Betty. Had Jennifer told her that I could fire her?

"I have to run an errand in Burbank this morning, so why don't I pick you up and we can have lunch and catch up? I'll be there in two hours." The trip to Glendale would take an hour, which would allow time for a stop at Betty's office.

The phone beeped to let me know I had another call coming in and I rang off with Sam. The sound of Brad's throaty whisper sent a shiver through me.

"I'm sorry; I made a total ass of myself. That will never happen again."

Twice he had shown me an angry, volatile side. I'd never been in that sort of relationship, and I wasn't starting now. "Maybe we need to stop seeing each other."

"Because of Miles Brookings?" His voice rang with bitterness.

I fought the impulse to reply with anger. No sense riling him up again. I kept my tone calm. "No, because things are tense right now."

"When can I see you?"

"I don't know."

"I want to be there for you. I'll behave, I promise," he pleaded. "I went crazy, seeing you with that jerk. What do you see in him? Money?"

"It's nothing like that."

"You had a cozy dinner, let him kiss you." Accusation crept into his rising voice. "If I forced myself on you, would you would have reacted the same? Maybe I should have tried that."

This was getting us nowhere. "Enough, Brad! You tried last night. Let's drop things, okay?"

"Please give me another chance. I can talk to the cops and tell them to back off, or hire a PI. Whatever you want..." His plaintive voice had the opposite effect of what he wanted. No way would I allow myself to be indebted to him.

"It won't work, Brad."

"We belong together. I knew it from the first. I won't let him steal you." His voice had turned hard and frightening.

"I don't belong to anyone. Goodbye, and please

don't call again."

"You can't do this. I'll make you sorry. Real sorry." The line went dead.

Great! I had an anonymous guy making threats on voicemail, a blackmailer wanting money, and now Brad was going to make me sorry.

Better deal with the blackmailer.

"Give me my money," Toby said the instant I identified myself.

"What about—"

"I want the money," he shouted. "You've stalled long enough. I'll be at the Mira Loma pier tomorrow night at seven. Bring the money or else. You and your friend owe me."

His final comment startled me. "Delia? Have you talked to her?"

"I've left several messages."

"She's out of the country and her phone doesn't always work." It was strange that she hadn't mentioned them, but perhaps she hadn't gotten them.

"Tomorrow night or I'm going to the police." The phone clicked off.

I sank to a seat with a sigh. How was I supposed to get two hundred and fifty thousand dollars? Had Carl sold my stocks as I asked? Maybe he would provide me with an advance? I punched in his number.

"I need some cash," I said.

"You'll have to wait."

"I can't." I hated the desperate sound of my voice.

The bitterness in his reply was worse. "Your attorney informed me you're demanding an audit. What kinda shit is that? Rick ordered me to use the money. I wasn't cheating anyone."

Adrienne and I talked about the audit, but why had she pushed forward so soon? Was she worried about not getting paid?

"There's been a misunderstanding," I said.

"Your money is tied up until this is over. I won't be accused of trying to steal. You and Jennifer are trying to ruin me, but you're both gonna be sorry."

"Are you threatening me?"

"Maybe, maybe not."

"Did you call last night and leave a threat?"

The line went dead.

Great! Another guy on my case. Maybe I should borrow *Senor Zapato* for a few days. Toby wouldn't dare go to the cops if *Senor Z* hulked nearby, and a visit from him might calm down Brad and Carl.

Speaking of which, what was the *Senor* doing outside my house in the middle of the night?

****

Friday, 10:30 a.m.

Betty didn't answer my call, but I drove to Burbank anyway. The message on her voicemail assured callers she was in all week. She probably didn't want to take my call.

The door to her office stood slightly ajar, and I rapped lightly. The interior was dim, which surprised me. It had been light with morning sun the last time I visited. I knocked again.

"Betty?"

I pushed the door open to peek inside and gasped. The room was in shambles. Papers littered the floor and the green banker's light from her desk lay in pieces on the floor.

What was going on? And what was that funky

301

smell?

Except I knew. I'd been to enough accident scenes and murders to recognize that horrifying stench. The smell of death.

A narrow ribbon of burgundy ended in a dried pool at the side of her desk. I leaned down and saw only a hand holding a thin chain. The wrist had a thin gold and diamond bracelet. I stumbled backward, leaning against the doorknob as I struggled to keep from vomiting.

I hurled myself outside and collapsed to my knees on the grass.

Chapter Thirty-Five

I'd never been so happy to see anyone as I was to see Sam enter the interrogation room where I waited to give my statement at the Burbank Police Station.

"What's going on?" he asked, since all I told him when I called was where I was.

I grabbed his thin hand like a lifeline as my words spilled. "Betty's dead. At least I think it's her. I never saw the body. I saw her wrist, and I think that was her bracelet. I smelled and saw blood, so I called police. Sure enough, there's a dead woman in there, shot maybe. I wanted to leave so they brought me here."

His gaunt face wrinkled in concern as he stood over me, hands on narrow hips. "What were you doing there?"

"Trying to find the codes for those ledgers."

His head shook in disbelief. "You shoulda picked me up first. As angry as you've been with that woman..." he stopped. "Damn! Do you know how this is going to look?"

I gulped as what he said hit home. "No!"

"You better call Nichols before you talk to these people. I mean, like now!"

I reached for my phone, but my hand shook so badly I fumbled it. Nimbly, he caught it and followed my instructions to put in the call before handing me the phone.

"You're where?" Oliver shouted.

"Burbank Police Station. Someone…killed Rick's bookkeeper. I found her body."

"Don't say a damn word. I'm on my way."

I hung up as Sam got off his phone. He gestured toward the door with his head.

"What?" I asked.

"Let's go outside for a second. I need a drink of water."

In the hall he directed me to a plastic chair while he walked to a row of vending machines. I was no longer feeling as shaky, but I was pleased he was nearby.

"Tell me everything," he said when he returned with two cold bottles of water. "From beginning to end."

Sips of water kept my parched throat wet as I stumbled through the gruesome discovery, much as I'd told the story to the officers who first arrived on the scene.

Sam eyed me warily. "Whatever you do, don't tell them about your suspicion she was sleeping with Wells."

"Isn't that withholding information?"

"You don't know she slept with him. Maybe she wanted to make you jealous. Your only reason for being there was because you needed help with those books. Understand?"

I nodded. That was the truth. For once, I didn't have to fudge.

As I finished my talk with Sam, Paula came striding down the hall. Wonderful, the press had arrived. I started to protest I couldn't talk, but realized she had a police officer beside her, along with Richard

Williams—the Oliver Nichols of the north Valley.

Her angry eyes zeroed in on me like I was a target. "You set me up," she said, but her attorney gripped her arm and whisked her through a door next to where I'd waited for Sam.

As I turned away, I spotted Oliver coming through the main door.

"Tell me what's goin' on, darlin'," he demanded. I introduced him to Sam, but his attention stayed focused on me. "I want details before they question you. We have time since they'll wait until Mira Loma cops arrive."

Oh, hell. My shaking grew so violent, I splashed water on me. "They're coming to question me?"

"Burbank PD will conduct the interview, but I can guarantee Callahan and Torres will be listening. Remember that if anyone brings up details of the Mira Loma case, don't answer. You stick to this morning and that girl. Watch me for your cues. Do you understand?"

"Yes."

"Good. I don't want any freelancing."

He was treating me like a child, but I didn't argue. At his urging, I described my reason for seeing Betty and how I discovered her and called police. Then he threw me for a loop. "Where were you last night?"

"Last night? Why does that matter?"

"From what I heard on the radio, they haven't established a time of death yet."

I drew a deep breath. At least I had not been home alone. "I had a date."

"With who?" Oliver asked. "Will he vouch for you?"

Damn, would Miles mind being mentioned? Could

that bring him into this? How would that look?

"I got home around three this morning," I continued, not answering his question. "And then Brad Singer came by, but he wasn't there very long." Brad could attest to what time I got home, if he wasn't too angry.

"What about earlier yesterday?" Oliver asked.

I wet my lips, feeling like the kid who got caught playing hooky. I couldn't look at Sam as I admitted the folly of my afternoon. "I got my hair done at Andre's Salon, a manicure at Nanci's Nail Nook and spent the rest of the afternoon at Genie's Rodeo Fashions. They'll vouch for me."

"What about your date?" Oliver pressed. "Were you with Singer? We'll need to verify…"

"No, not Brad. What if he doesn't want his name given out?" I asked, making a face.

"Maybe we need to find out what time she was killed," Sam interrupted.

Oliver's attention jerked to Sam. "Let me handle this."

"She was with me," Sam said, not the least bit intimidated.

I didn't know why Sam made that claim, but it got me off the hook for the moment so I said nothing.

Oliver blew out a deep breath, playing a ping pong game with his eyes from me to Sam and back. I doubted he believed us.

The questioning itself was easy, after I waited several hours. Burbank Police had no reason to suspect me of anything. I knew Torres and Callahan were probably watching. Was Hank around too?

"Are you hungry?" Sam asked when we finally

departed. "There are a couple of coffee shops around here."

There were some nice restaurants too, but I knew I wouldn't taste anything. We ended up in a small café on the border between Glendale and Burbank. I toyed with my fruit salad while Sam dug into his cottage cheese.

"Where were you all afternoon?" I asked.

He'd disappeared for long stretches while I sat with Oliver. He waved his hand, lifting and lowering his eyebrows. "Snooping, of course. Listening in the background."

"Did you hear anything interesting?"

"Paula Gardner is in a deep world of hurt. Seems she dropped by to see the late Ms. Arguello last night and they got into a heated argument. The thing about these older neighborhoods is that many people have lived here for years. They know each other and watch what goes on. Anyway, people saw Miss G. arrive at the house around seven in a marked TV car. The two women argued and she left. Neighbors saw Betty go to her office later, but no one saw her come out. Light stayed on until around eleven when there was another big fight. No one saw anything after that. They figured she went into the house, though no one could tell cause she has automatic timers that turn off at midnight."

"So Paula could have killed her?"

"If she came back after the late news. Several people thought they heard gunshots, but no one is sure."

"Why would Paula or anyone want to kill Betty?"

His eyebrows did their dance again. "Makes you think she knew something, huh?"

My breath caught. What could she have known?

"Did they question Carl?"

"Did you suggest it?"

"I mentioned he was the other person working on Rick's finances. So now what? Where does that leave us?"

"The damn books," he said, putting down his glass of tea with a thud that made liquid slosh over the top. "What time does the wine shop close?"

"I don't know. Do you want me to call and check?"

"Yep. The sooner we get in there, the better."

The line went immediately to voicemail. "Wells Fine Wines is closed for inventory. If you have a special order, please leave a message…"

I clicked off and made a face. "Did Darryl say anything to you about inventory? The shop is closed."

He shook his head, scratching his chin. "Interesting. Maybe we should go look around."

"Jennifer still hasn't given me a key."

"Hmph!" He flicked a hand of dismissal. "I can get in. That security system is for shit. This way we won't have Mrs. Roberts interrupting or Darryl looking over our shoulders. Hell, it's your shop, right?"

"Yes." Another thought occurred to me. "Maybe we can find the gun."

"Gun?"

"It was missing from the box where I packed it. It was probably put into another box, but it might not hurt to take it back."

His grizzled face stiffened, and when he spoke, he was Mr. Cop. "You can't pick up guns whenever you feel like it. You gotta have a permit."

"It's registered to me. I can even shoot—sort of. Maybe I need another lesson." I'd never been big on guns, but given the last few days, perhaps I should learn how to use it.

His demeanor softened and he nodded enthusiastically. "I'll take you to the range." He wiped his mouth with his napkin and tossed it across his half eaten plate. Neither one of us had finished our diet meals. "Let's swing over to my house. I'll pick up clothes and stay with you tonight."

His suggestion was as welcome as the thought of the gun. Spending another night sitting on my couch didn't appeal to me, and I needed him to hear that threatening message on my phone.

****

We drove to his house and while he went inside to get clothes, I remained in my car. After my call to Darryl, I'd noticed three missed calls on my phone log. My cell had been turned off while I was talking to police. The log showed two calls from Delia's cell and one from Miles Brookings.

I checked voicemail, listening to Delia's chirpy voice. "Hey, babe, call me. What's the latest? Are you locked up yet?"

"Ha, ha." I forwarded to the next message. Miles baritone sent a shiver through me.

"Kimberly, this is Miles Brookings. I'm not certain what you hoped to gain with those pictures, but needless to say, I would appreciate no further contact with you."

Pictures? What the hell was he talking about?

My phone buzzed and I jumped, tossing up the instrument like a bouncing ball. I emitted a cry of delight when I saw Delia's number.

"Oh, Del, am I glad to hear from you!" My words

tumbled out like spilling milk. "You wouldn't believe what's happened. Someone killed Betty."

"What?" She shouted so loud Sam probably heard her in the house.

I gave her a brief rundown of my crazy day.

"They don't think you did it," she said breathlessly.

"I have an alibi. Remember? I had a date with Miles Brookings."

Another shout rang in my ear. "Yes! Did you do the nasty?"

Just like Delia to ask that first. "We went to dinner, concluding with a simple kiss."

"Oooh…you were supposed to call me," she grumbled.

"I did. Your phone was off. Anyway, unless she was killed early this morning, I'm off the hook. Except I don't know if he'll admit he was with me. He left a nasty message saying he doesn't want to talk to me anymore. I have no idea what that's about."

"I can hardly wait to get home. You'll never figure this out on your own."

"Sam's a big help. We're on our way to the wine shop to look for the gun Rick gave me."

"Sam might be great, but we've always been a team."

"You're right. You could probably talk that rat Toby out of his blackmail demand. Have you heard from him? He said he left messages for you."

"I ignored them. He can't touch me. I have an alibi."

"I'm supposed to pay him tomorrow night, though I don't know where I'm getting two hundred and fifty thousand dollars."

"You might as well face it. You gotta pay him."

"Maybe I should run it by Sam. He said a tape could be doctored."

"Uh-uh. Even if the tape is inadmissible in court, he heard everything. He's a witness. I wouldn't tell Sam. He'll go to the cops. I can get you the money. I'll call my bank and arrange for you to pick it up."

Relief rushed through me like a tidal wave. "Del, you're an angel. I don't know when I can pay you back."

"What are friends for? Men come and go, but best friends are forever. You know, BFF."

"Kimberly!" Sam called from the door, waving wildly.

"I have to go, hon. I'll call you later."

We hung up and I hurried up the walk to Sam. His face was etched with anger and he gestured me inside with an impatient motion. He waved at the TV in the family room.

"You mind explaining that?"

I stared in horror at the set. A photo of me and Miles taken the night before at the restaurant filled the screen.

"We're not certain who took the picture or sent it to Gossipcolumn.com," Peter intoned, "but it certainly raises new questions about the relationship between Kimberly delaGarza and Miles Brookings, especially given last night's murder of Wells' bookkeeper, Betty Arguello."

Chapter Thirty-Six

Sam was silent as we made the drive across town. I could feel his disapproval filling the car like a gathering rain cloud.

"Anything else you want to tell me?" he finally asked. "Like about Miles Brookings?"

"I told you I had a date last night. I ran into him at the ballgame the other night and he called me. Why did you tell Oliver you were with me?"

Sam grimaced and turned to look out the window. "I thought you were with Hank. You looked uncomfortable when he asked the question. Did you tell police the truth?"

I drew a deep breath. No wonder he volunteered an alibi. "I told them I'd need to check with the person before I mentioned his name. I guess the picture took care of that."

"Who took the picture?"

"I have no idea, but Miles is furious. He left nasty voicemail on my phone."

"He's the guy who threatened you?"

"No. That was someone else." Maybe I should let him hear the voicemail message before we got to the house. It might relieve the tension. At the next light I dialed my home voicemail and waited until I heard the frightening, hoarse voice before handing the phone to Sam.

"This doesn't sound good," he said when he finished. "Did you tell the police?"

"I wanted you to hear it first. I was afraid Callahan would think I was trying to take suspicion off me."

"You're right. I'm sure you know actors or TV people who could make the call, and it happened to come when you were gone? " He shook his head. "Too damn coincidental. We should call Hank."

"You think he'll believe me?"

Sam pounded a fist on his thigh. "I'll make him believe you. Who coulda left it?"

"Maybe Carl? He's furious that we're doing an audit. It doesn't sound like him, but maybe *he* had someone do it. He knows actors too. This guy sounds agitated, so agitated it borders on phony. Do you think we're on to something? Do you think it's related?"

"At this point everything's related."

I trusted Sam's hunches. "This morning you said you had things to tell me."

He pulled his notebook from his pocket and flipped through pages. "I checked on Ken Gardner. Wells owed him money."

"Couldn't that be a motive?"

"He has an alibi. He was in Vegas that weekend."

"He could have hired someone. Why was he in Vegas? Maybe he wanted an alibi…"

Sam held up his hand and tapped his head with his forefinger. "Think, Kimberly. Be logical."

"That's logical to me. Or maybe…" My breath caught and I whirled toward him. "What if…Betty told Ken that Paula was having an affair with Rick? Ken kills Rick and Paula finds out Betty is to blame and kills Betty. Or maybe Paula killed Rick and Betty?"

His gentle laugh rumbled through the car. "Well, you're thinking at least. That certainly does open up some interesting premises."

Something else flew into my mind. "Paula blamed me this morning. She said I set her up. Couldn't that mean something?"

"Sure as hell could. Even your invitation from Brookings last night might mean something."

"What?" That switch in direction was a surprise.

He reached over and tapped my arm. "Think about it. Did you know where you were going last night? Who knew where you were and took the picture? Who released it? Do you know?"

"But he's angry about it. He left a message blaming me. I wish I was as smart as all these people seem to think. Everyone accuses me of setting them up."

"Maybe it's the other way around," he said, stroking his chin. "Maybe he set *you* up. Maybe now that's he's rid of Betty and whatever she knew, he doesn't want you asking questions. Did you ever think of that?"

Huh? Had Miles taken me out to see what I knew? Was even his claim he thought I killed Rick a way to twist things around? I recalled his feelings toward Rick and his assertion that the marriage wouldn't take place. How did he plan to stop it? Was his Canadian alibi a set up? Like *El Patron*, there was probably someone, somewhere in his employment like *Senor* Shoe.

****

Sam surprised me with the ease he displayed getting into the store. A few flicks with a screwdriver and the door swung open. I knew the alarm code and switched it off. Unlike the last time, the store carried an aura of abandonment. Dust had formed on some of the bins and wine bottles. Open boxes filled the aisles and each shelf was tagged with names and numbers.

Who had ordered the inventory? Jennifer? Without consulting me? Maybe I'd throw a fit to remind her who was half boss. Still, the information could be valuable if Rick was involved in money laundering. Perhaps it would uncover any unaccounted inventory.

"What are we looking for?" Sam asked.

"I need to find that datebook and the gun." I spotted the three boxes still in the corner of the tasting room. "They should be in one of those boxes."

"Let me look. Why don't you check the office and see if you can find a client list. Or look for billing statements. I saw a copier in his office the other day. Fire it up and make copies of invoices or orders. Between that and the datebook, we might be able to figure out the initials."

The office was as dreary and dusty as the store. I turned on the copier and opened the lower file drawer on his desk and began looking through files. Old bills and invoices were in order and I took one of each from the folders and carried them to the copier. Time seemed to stretch on before I heard footsteps.
"I found the gun," Sam said, standing in the door, brandishing the small weapon. "Not bad. A .38. Got any ammo?"

"It would be in the box. Did you find the datebook?"

He tossed the leather bound book to me. "Is this what you were looking for?"

I caught it and breathed a sigh of relief at

accomplishing something for a change "I'm going to finish the last few pages and shut this down, okay?"

"Sounds good. Let's go get a steak dinner. I need real meat."

"It's a date, old man," I joked.

He disappeared and I went back to copying. A folder toward the back caught my attention. It was marked personal. I pulled it out and was about to open it when I heard a noise from the other room. It sounded like tumbling boxes.

"Did you drop something?" I called.

"Hey!" he said and I heard more tumbling.

"Sam, what are you doing?" I walked into the dim room.

Sam lay on the floor, an open box beside him.

"What happened?" I asked as I approached. Blood spurted from his forehead and I shrieked. Movement came from the corner of my eye and I started to turn, but something hard caught me on the side of the head. Stunned, I tumbled to the hard brick floor.

Time seemed to stand still until I blinked my eyes open. I was only groggy for an instant. Then I heard footsteps and the door slam. I staggered to my feet, called 9-1-1 and leaned over Sam, hands shaking. I wasn't certain how to check for a pulse, but he seemed to be breathing. Blood no longer spurted, but it ran down the side of his head. I darted to the bathroom and grabbed a pile of paper towels, wetting several.

I wiped the cut and saw it wasn't very big, but Sam still hadn't wakened. I sat on the floor holding Sam's head, waiting. My knowledge of emergency medicine was nil and I thought about what Delia had said. I truly was helpless. Finally, in the distance I heard a siren and moments later the ambulance screeched to a halt outside.

Once Sam was loaded and they told me he was going to be okay, I went back inside to close up. I grabbed the folder with my copied material, the folder marked personal, and the datebook. As I turned to leave, I remembered the gun. I looked around, but saw no sign of it. What had Sam done with it?

****

Hank had an anxious look on his face as he hurried down the hospital hall toward me.

"They're stitching up Sam," I said, trying to smile. I hadn't been hit hard, but Sam had a long gash across his forehead. "I gave a statement to your officers."

I was becoming an old hand at this questioning shit. At least this time I was victim instead of suspect.

Hank shook his head, a motion so violent his short hair danced. "That's it, Kimberly. Amateur hour is over! What were you doing there so late anyway?"

I explained about trying to get the information on Rick's client list. "That's why I was at Betty's earlier."

The look on his face told me he'd already known that.

"We don't know this had anything to do with Rick's death," I said. "No one knew we were there."

He held up both his hands to stop me from saying anything else. "I'll check the police report later. You should go home."

Even if I wasn't worried about Sam, I didn't want to leave. "I'll stay here until he's released."

"They're keeping him overnight."

"I don't mind staying." A well lit hospital was preferable to my lonely house. These chairs were as

317

comfortable as my sofa.

Hank's look was skeptical, but he didn't protest.

"I'll get coffee." I stood and took a step, but the floor swam and I staggered back, hitting the plastic chair and sending it thumping against the wall.

Hank caught my arm, his firm grip steadying me. "Whoa. You okay?"

"I haven't eaten all day… Sam and I were going to dinner after we finished…"

He released my arm, but kept a close watch on me as I began to walk. "Let's go to the cafeteria. I could use a sandwich myself."

The hospital dining room reminded me of a school cafeteria, plastic chairs and long tables. We took a spot in the corner though the large room was deserted. He carried my tray where he'd placed a plastic-wrapped roast beef sandwich and a cup of vegetable soup.

"I'm sorry…" I began as we took seats across from each other.

"No talking until that soup is finished plus half the sandwich." He nodded at my tray.

I managed to consume most of the soup and half the sandwich, though I didn't taste either. When I couldn't eat another bite, I lifted my hands like a second grader finishing her vegetables. "All done, Dad."

He smiled, shaking his head. "Not quite the fare you dined on with Miles Brookings, I'm sure."

"Jealous?" I teased.

His face grew somber, tightening into hard lines. "I'm not even going to ask why you would put yourself at risk that way."

It hit me that he took it for granted I'd gone out

with Miles to get information on the case, not because I was interested in the man. But that was why I did it, wasn't it?

"Sam thinks he was setting me up. The interesting thing is Miles thinks I did it. Besides you and Sam, he's the only person who knows I put that glass in the car. He saw me do it."

His head whipped toward me. "Then why did he call…"

We exchanged startled glances. Oh, hell, I'd given away that Miles was trying to remove suspicion from his daughter.

"Maybe he is trying to put the blame on me. Paula thinks that's what I was doing to her with Betty, though I'm not sure why."

He avoided my eyes, and I could sense the wheels turning in his head. "According to Mrs. Gardner, someone called her last night, pretending to be Betty Arguello, saying she had information. When Mrs. Gardner arrived, the girl claimed she never made the call." His fierce eyes challenged me. "Interesting, isn't it?"

"I didn't do it," I protested.

"We're checking phone records."

"You ought to check mine." Enough of this suspicion crap. I whipped out my cell phone and tapped in the buttons for my home phone, hitting keys until I called up the angry, anonymous message. "Sam and I were going to call you with this once we'd finished dinner."

He listened without looking surprised and nodded.

"Well?" I asked.

"Did you give that to Torres or Callahan?"

"Sam thought they might figure I did it or had someone do it."

He eyed me warily. "Uh-huh."

"You don't believe me, do you?"

His blue eyes bored into me. "There are a lot of games going on, and you and your friend excel at games. Let's see. If you were devious, you would first hire a well-known criminal lawyer and then get someone close to the police force to help you. You'd give him enough false leads to send him in another direction and hope he pleads your case to the police force."

His words were like a slap and I drew back. "You son of a bitch! Do you think I'm playing with Sam? That doesn't say much for his abilities. He's too damn smart to be fooled by a scam."

"Even smart men do foolish things and make idiotic mistakes for a beautiful woman."

"Are you saying your dad has a crush on me?" I wanted to smile, but the thought of Sam sprawled out on the brick floor, bleeding, stopped me. "Sam's too dedicated for that. And if you don't realize it, you're underestimating him."

Keeping his eyes on me, Hank got to his feet. "I'm going to call Callahan and have your phone records checked."

It was a game of chicken, and I refused to falter. For once I was in the right. "Did you have Callahan check the license plate Sam gave him for the SUV that followed us?"

His placid stillness nearly unnerved me. "It belongs to a network news producer who is in Israel at the moment. They're getting in touch with him to see if anyone might be driving his car. Interesting that it's a network producer, isn't it? And that he's out of the country?"

"Network..." A horrible suspicion hit me and I felt a sudden chill. "Maybe...you should...check Brad Singer."

"The anchor at your station?"

I didn't want to get Brad in trouble, but I recalled his angry hands on me, and his words, *"We belong together."*

Chapter Thirty-Seven

Saturday, 6:30 p.m.

After parking in a lot near the Mira Loma pier I walked onto the wooden structure ten minutes early. This whole thing felt like a spy movie, but I resisted the comparison. No time for movies tonight. Too much at stake to be silly.

Delia's borrowed money remained in a bag in the trunk of my car. I hated carrying around that much cash. The trip from the bank to my car had been bad enough. Besides with my current luck, I'd accidentally drop it into the ocean.

Families dotted the pier, their fishing rods strung into the water, even though thick clouds shrouded the horizon. I strolled to the end. Was Toby already around? He might not be happy I didn't have the money with me, but I wanted to hear that recording first. I needed to know it was real.

Was I being stupid? What if he had made a copy? Would he come back later and demand more? No. Once the killer was caught, he couldn't. He had to know I might even go after him.

I paced the end of the pier, watching for Toby's approach. Except for the wail of a siren in the distance, the evening was quiet. Checking my watch, I was surprised to see that it was already 7:15. Toby was late to the meeting he'd demanded. Had he gotten a better offer and taken the recording to police? I called his phone, but got only voicemail.

I resumed pacing, but after an hour and a half, I knew he wasn't coming. The sun was totally gone and the crowd had thinned while the fog thickened. I tried his number again but still got no answer. What had held him up? Had he changed his mind? Could I return Delia's money?

Slowly I walked back along the pier toward the parking lot, uncertain of my next move. I stopped to call Delia, but got voicemail. Could she already be on a plane coming home? The possibility filled my head with pleasant thoughts about what we could do to prove my innocence. By the time I reached the parking lot, lights were coming on. The lot was nearly empty and I jerked to a stop. The row where I'd parked was empty.

What the fuck?

This couldn't be happening. Where was my car with its bag containing a quarter of a million dollars?

Oh, hell. Who knew that money was in the trunk? I hadn't told a soul. Was that why Toby had not met me? Had he watched me arrive without anything that resembled the money, and then taken my car out of spite? I started to call Felipe to ask if he'd heard from Toby, but then stopped. He would wonder why I wanted to reach the ex-bartender.

What about the person following me? Had he stolen my car? If police were following me, why hadn't they stopped him? For that matter, where was *Senor Zapato* when you needed him?

Now what? The fog had grown thick and a fine mist dampened my bare arms. I couldn't call the station and ask for help as I might have in the past. Sam remained in the hospital, where I'd spent the previous night on a cot in the hall outside his room. He'd been coherent when I left him several hours ago, but he couldn't come get me.

As I made another pass through the parking lot, my gaze stopped on a small gray sedan near the end. The front bumper was caved in.

Oh hell! Could it be the car that followed me from the Mira Loma Police station the day I was fingerprinted? Was the person who had been lurking in the shadows somewhere nearby?

I wasn't taking any chances. I fumbled for my phone in my purse and called Mira Loma Police. I paced the parking lot as I waited, fearing the person who owned that gray vehicle, but he never showed. When police arrived, I realized I couldn't make any claim about it. At least I copied down the license number.

The interview with police was quick and easy, though I didn't tell them about the money in the car. Better to wait until the car was found. The two young officers recognized me and took the report with a respectful attitude that I'd never received from Callahan and Torres. They even drove me home.

The thought of being alone didn't hit me fully until I walked inside. I locked the door and turned on the alarm system and did a slow check of the premises. What had Sam done with that damn gun? I could sure as hell use it right now.

Part of me wanted to sit in a tub full of hot bubbles and relax, but I knew I couldn't. Maybe I should call a cab and spend the night at the hospital again. As I debated my next step, the doorbell rang. Could it be Toby?

The sight of Hank through the peephole surprised me and set my pulse racing. Had he come to arrest me? Was Torres with him? I couldn't imagine Torres letting someone else handle the job.

I pulled open the door, prepared for anything. Hank wore a light windbreaker, his shoulders hunched against the soft rain that was now falling.

"I hear your car was stolen," he said.

"Gee, good news travels fast in this town. So this is an official call?"

"I was visiting Dad at the hospital and when I called to check in, the duty officer told me. Dad insisted I come over. He was worried, so I'm doing it as a favor to him."

"I see." Naturally Sam would do that, which was precisely why I had not called him. But I was thankful for Hank's presence and Sam's thoughtfulness. It didn't matter why he was here; I was pleased I didn't have to be alone.

"Are you okay?" Hank asked, concern furrowing his brow.

"Sure. Come in before the rain gets worse." Suddenly, I wished I had taken the time to put on makeup or at least comb my hair. I'd done my incognito thing for Toby, not wanting to be recognized at the beach, and I still wore black jeans and a T-shirt.

I led Hank to the second floor and offered him a drink. To my surprise, he accepted, asking for scotch. Finding the expensive bottle I drank with Sam, I retrieved ice and poured us both a drink. After handing him the glass I walked over to pull the drapes. Outside, light rain tapped the windows. In the past I had always left the drapes open, but closing them had become a nightly ritual. The thought of someone watching me had become an obsession.

He sipped his drink thoughtfully before seating himself on the sofa. "We ran the phone records."

"And?"

"The calls to Paula Gardner were made from a pay phone in Pasadena Thursday afternoon. Since you were doing girly things in Beverly Hills, that clears you of setting her up."

"I see." I didn't like the fact that everyone seemed to think they needed to check up on me. "And the calls to me?"

He took another sip of scotch, his eyes never leaving me. "You want to tell me about Brad Singer?"

I drew a deep breath. "I'm not sleeping with him."

His own intake of breath was equally sharp. "That wasn't my question. You gave me that name yesterday. Has he been following you?"

Shock raced through me and I gasped audibly, jerking my head up. "Did you check?"

Hank studied me, but I couldn't read what was in his face. Or maybe he was trying to read mine. "For the past two weeks, he has steadily called your home and cell phone numbers from the station. At least, the calls came from his extension. His private cell called you over and over, quick calls that were a minute long, which means he was hanging up when you answered or your machine picked up."

That explained the strange calls I'd been getting. I put down my scotch, fearing I might spill it as I fought to absorb what he was telling me. "You're saying it's been Brad all along?"

His gaze was steady. "And you're saying you didn't know anything about it?"

My forehead tingled as I realized what he was implying. "Do you think I set that up?"

"Did you?"

"Of course not!" I wasn't certain if I should be furious or frightened. I felt faint suddenly and I put my hands to my forehead and inhaled sharp breaths.

"You okay?" he asked.

I pressed my fingers to my temples. "It makes sense. Brad kept telling me I needed someone to protect me. But…how could he follow me? He's been at work. He was working the night that car followed me from Geneva."

Hank shook his head. "Singer's work has become so slipshod he was suspended on Thursday. He'd been calling in sick, being late to assignments, and the night you interrupted me at Geneva, he never went back to work after dinner."

I recalled Reba's cool attitude toward Brad at the ballgame.

"You told Sam you saw a green car and an SUV following you," Hank continued. "Singer is staying at the condo belonging to the owner of the SUV, and he's been renting a green Ford Fusion."

"And…the gray car?" In a way I liked that idea that he had been lingering in the parking lot. Or had he stolen my car and left his, thinking it meant I would have to see him? Maybe he wouldn't open the trunk.

Hank shook his head. "No luck on that."

I rose on shaky legs and walked over to my purse and pulled out the small notebook I'd made a practice of carrying since Sam came into my life. I ripped out the page with the license plate number.

"This car was in the parking lot where my car was taken. I noticed it because it had a dent in the front. The Monday I was questioned at your police department, a gray car followed me. It got bashed when it tried to make a lane change behind me."

Hank took the note, studied it, and slipped it into his pocket. "You had no idea Singer was following you?"

Perhaps it was time to come clean, even if it got Brad into trouble. He had tried to frighten me about the cars and phone calls. How far would he have gone to get me to allow him to take care of me?

I licked my lips and launched into my story of the night Miles brought me home. I didn't admit he'd kissed me, only that Brad saw him bring me home and grew angry.

"He must have been following us that night," I concluded.

"How did you get rid of him?"

"*Senor Zapato* did it."

"Who?" His head jerked back in surprise.

"He works for Benito Dominguez, the old Mexican mobster. For some reason his bodyguard was watching me. I don't know why. They call him *Senor* Shoe because he likes to kick people."

He wrote down the information and got to his feet. "I should be going. Whoever stole the car couldn't get a key to your house, could they? Please tell me you aren't one of those people who keeps a key under the wheel."

"It was removed when my car went into the shop after Lindy's accident."

He shook his head, but for the first time since he arrived, I saw a hint of humor enter his eyes. "Don't replace it, and don't put a key to your house in the flower pot outside."

My hand shot up in a smart salute. "Aye, aye, Chief."

He ran a hand through his black, rumpled hair. It looked like he'd been doing that a lot in the past hour. "You need to take your safety more seriously."

After the past couple of weeks, I agreed. Given what had happened to Lindy, and the Brad issue…and that nasty voice on my phone.

"Did you check on that threatening call?"

He nodded. "It came from Ken Gardner's cell. Apparently he was unhappy that police questioned him about Wells. He's threatening a lawsuit." He started for the stairs and panic propelled me to my feet. I didn't want to be alone.

"Have you eaten?" I asked. "You were nice enough to feed me dinner last night. I was about to make myself an omelet. Have you eaten?" I didn't even know if I had eggs.

To my surprise and delight, he stopped and smiled. "It might be fun to see you in the kitchen in an apron."

"Don't expect an apron, cop, though I may run upstairs and change. This shirt is damp."

I hopped up the stairs, changed into a jersey sweater with a v-neck that was low enough to show skin and tight enough to show my curves. A long silk skirt with a slit to my knee was both tempting and yet demure. I gave my eyes and lips a light touch-up. No need scaring him.

When I came back down, he was taking eggs out of

the refrigerator.

"I can do that," I said.

"I'll do it. You need to taste my deluxe cheese omelet." He examined my refrigherator and pulled out a chunk of cheddar cheese.

"Okay, how about I open a bottle of wine? I know a lot about wines."

"I'm sure you do."

What a stupid thing for me to say, but I felt giddy as a teen on her first date. All tense and on edge. Excited, yet fearful. What did I want from him? What did I expect? What did I hope for?

Two nights ago I'd dined in a fancy restaurant with one of the most powerful men in the city. Even though he had shaken me up, he couldn't get my heart to pound or my nerves to scream like the man across the kitchen. There might be two yards between us, but I could feel Hank's presence, smell the sandalwood soap on his skin. I'd once licked his arm, telling him I wanted to devour that scent. It still smelled good enough to lick. With a shiver I walked toward the living room.

"How about some music? Still like jazz?" I called.

"You know it."

With the soft sounds of Stan Getz in the background, I focused on opening the wine and setting the table. We worked in silence, lost in our own thoughts. I kept thinking I should tell him about Toby, but I didn't want to compromise him. At least that was what I told myself. The truth was I didn't want to see what his reaction might be.

We changed the subject for dinner, though I could scarcely recall what we discussed—politics, gossip, common friends, anything but the act that had brought us back into each other's lives. When we finished, I stacked the dishes in the dishwasher while he went into the living room and poured brandy.

As I walked over to join him on the sofa, it struck me how wonderful it would be if this could be a simple meeting between old friends. The thought brought sadness and a sudden chill to my bones. I sipped brandy, waiting to get warm. The ringing of the phone jarred us both, but I made no move to answer. It rang two more times before stopping.

"I'll have Singer picked up," he said with a grimace. Despite all the joking, our dilemma returned, quickly constructing a thick wall between us.

I put my brandy on the coffee table, rubbing my cold hands together. "This is so screwed up. They're going to arrest me, aren't they?" It was the first time we'd mentioned the case in two hours. I didn't want to drive him away, but I had to know.

"Well, since 'they' in this case is my department, I can't say."

I inhaled a shaky breath. "Meaning you won't or can't?"

"Probably both."

"I didn't do it, Hank. That's the God honest truth."

"Do you know how many times I've heard that over the course of the years?"

Emotion choked me and I leaned toward him. "You know me. Do you think I could do that? Can you stop being a cop for a minute?"

His gaze was cool. "Is that what you want? Or isn't it more important to find out what I know, what I'm going to do? Be real, Kimberly. Ever since this thing broke, you've been coming to me. Is it because you want to be my friend or is it because you think I can help you?"

His words hurt worse than a physical blow. Tears clouded my vision and I whirled away. If I could have stood, I would have walked away, but my knees didn't feel like they would hold me up. If he believed that, I didn't want to go on. The Queen's reign was over.

Chapter Thirty-Eight

I could feel Hank behind me and I stiffened as his hand touched my arm. His gentle touch calmed me and I drew such a deep breath I knew he heard it.

He took hold of both my arms from behind and leaned close to me, speaking in a whisper. "I'm sorry. I shouldn't have said that."

Was he right? Why did I keep going to him? As his hands ran along my arms, my anger dissolved and a streak of warmth surged through me. His words reverberated in my brain, but in a different way.

"Are you surprised I'd go to you?" I asked, as a smile pressed at my lips. "I mean, you used to be pretty good at getting me off."

"Shit," he muttered and his soft chuckle warmed me all the way to my bones in a way the liquor hadn't. "Ahh, Kimmie, don't do this to me."

I leaned back against him, rubbing my hair against his chin.

"Do you know how hard it is not to..." He drew a quick, shuddering breath and his arms folded around me, pulling me back against him.

An edginess tore through my lower regions. His breath tickled my ear and I wanted him to hold me and never let go. It took all my willpower not to throw my arms around his neck and plead with him to fix this, fix everything.

"Damn you," he said in a gentle, hoarse voice. "You know the effect you've always had on me. I can sense you whenever you're within ten feet of me."

His fingers moved along my arms, teasing me, tantalizing me, and I turned and looked up into his flame-consumed eyes. He lifted his hand to touch my cheek, and I could see the fire burning inside him through the warm glow of his eyes.

There were so many times I couldn't read him, but I could see his passion, and this was real so I gave in to what I wanted. I turned toward him and leaned against his chest, inhaling the scent of sandalwood, enjoying the firm feel of his body against me, knowing he was as likely to fling me away as to hold me.

His fingers burrowed in my hair and I shuddered, whimpering, "Hank."

"Uh-uh," he whispered as though he knew what I was thinking. "We can't."

"One kiss," I pleaded into his neck, my fingers searching his face. "I have to know."

"You tease." He pulled me closer to him, and I could sense the hard tension in his body. "You already know."

I lifted my face to his and his mouth found mine, crushing down hard on it, his tongue forcing its way inside as though he wanted his whole being to possess me. I kissed him back, giving him my mouth.

A soft, needy sigh escaped me and he crushed me to him, laying me back on the sofa. My fingers explored his neck, his hard back, and moved to begin undoing his buttons to slip inside and touch his bare chest.

His hands skimmed over me, setting fires on my neck and then sliding into the back of my sweater to explore the sensitive areas.

Even as I melted against him, he pulled back. "Honey, stop. We can't."

I clung to him. I could feel his lower body hard against me, and I knew what he was feeling. "Hank, I want you."

He lifted his head to look down at me. "You know I want you. I don't think I've ever wanted you more, but we can't do this right now."

"No one needs to know," I whispered, but even as I said that, I knew it was like throwing water over a fire.

He caught my hands and pulled away from me. "I would."

My breath was coming in soft, shallow gasps. "You honorable son of a bitch."

He raised my knuckles to his lips and kissed them. "Yeah, unfortunately."

I stretched up to lean my forehead to his chest. "I hate you."

But we both knew I didn't mean it.

His lips played with my hair and he kissed the top of my head. "I wish I could hate you. It would make things so much easier."

Knowing his feelings made my emotions soar. I felt light as a feather, as though I could float all the way to the upper ceiling. "I think you secretly do. It amuses you to get me turned on and shut me down."

He held my head in his hands, his fingers entangling in my hair. "Let me assure you it's every bit as painful for me as it is for you."

I looked up at him, stroking his cheek with my fingers. "Then let's not suffer. Let's do it now and plead insanity later."

He shook his head. "No. However good it might feel tonight, tomorrow we'd be in pain. At least I would." He kissed the top of my head one more time before releasing me and pushing himself to his feet. "I better go."

The thought of his leaving brought me crashing down to ground level and I sat up. "What if someone has my keys?"

"What do you mean?"

I rose, feeling frantic. "My car *was* stolen. What if Brad made a copy of my key? I don't think *Senor* Shoe is still around."

"Oh, hell." He grimaced and shook his head. "What were you doing talking to Dominguez anyway?"

"He was one of Rick's customers, and I think Rick was seeing Paula Gardner. She's his daughter."

He put a finger to my lips. "Let's not talk about that."

"The truth is I would rather not be alone tonight," I admitted.

"Okay," he said, tipping my face up to his. "Why don't I sleep down here? You go upstairs and lock your door."

"There is no door up there and that couch will kill your back."

He looked around. "Don't you have a sofa bed in the office? I think Dad mentioned one."

"Damn honorable bastard."

"I'll stay there." He gave me one last quick kiss and pushed me away when I reached for him. "I better lock my door," he said with a smirk.

****

Sunday, 8:30 a.m.

Hank stood in front of my chart, examining it. He leaned closer to one of the neon green sticky notes. His brow furrowed into a frown.

I watched him from the door for a minute before tapping on doorframe. "Morning."

"What is this?" he asked, gesturing at the chart.

I walked toward him. "The notes I've been making per Sam's instructions. Hasn't he kept you informed of what we're doing? Do you see anything up there that your guys don't have or haven't pursued?"

He drew a deep breath, touched a name and turned toward me, his face deathly serious. "Tell me more about Dominguez."

While Hank kept saying he didn't want to discuss the case, I sensed his interest in my board. "We know Rick gambled a lot. Maybe the old guy's still working as a bookie, or maybe Rick was laundering money for him. Don't you think that's possible? He may be old and frail, but someone could be running his operation. Maybe even Ken Gardner. Maybe that's why he got so angry at your checking on him. Maybe he's the one who had *Senor Z* watching me."

Hank nodded, betraying no emotion. "During the night I remembered *Senor Zapato*. Reynoldo Lopez. He isn't a man to mess with. He's suspected of several homicides. Of course, no one can prove the people are dead. They simply disappeared."

I thought about what the *Senor* said about kicking people and recalled how easily he had lifted Brad and carried him off. If the man wanted me dead, he could have let Brad start the job and then finished me off. Brad might even have gotten the blame.

"I'm the star of this movie," I said in a sharp, sarcastic tone. "Stars never die, so I can't disappear."

He jerked back toward me, but he wasn't smiling. Instead, he tapped another sticker. "Miles Brookings? You listed him and yet you went out with him? Or did you do it to get information?"

"I've been accused of using people. Why shouldn't I do that to him? He's adamant that he wouldn't have allowed Rick to marry the Bimbo. Who knows how far he'd go to stop it?"

He pointed a fierce look in my direction. "You need to stop playing detective and talk to Callahan and Torres. Tell them about the information you've gathered."

"Will they believe me or think I'm trying to throw out red herrings?"

"Maybe I can talk to them."

I shook my head. "You keep saying you can't get involved, so don't. All I have up there is conjecture. If I come up with something that Sam thinks is solid, I'll take it to them for the dirty work."

He touched another note on the board. "What's your rationale on Bobbi Brookings?"

"Maybe she discovered what a cheating rat Rick was. Miles says she's prone to angry outbursts. She threw a heavy tissue holder at me. Maybe she discovered the truth about Betty or saw her wearing that pendant and killed her too."

His head jerked toward me. "What pendant?"

"Do you know if Betty was wearing a pendant with a diamond heart or if police found one in her jewelry box?" I held up my fingers to show the size. I thought back to what I'd seen at Betty's office. She'd been wearing her gold bracelet and I saw a chain beside it, but I couldn't remember seeing the pendant.

Hank looked confused, so I rushed on, not certain if I was being helpful, but this was information only I might have.

"Rick gave me a pendant when we broke up and the Bimbo had a fit so he asked for it back. Well, the rat gave it to Betty. She was wearing it the last time I talked to her."

He stared at me for a minute and shook his head. "Kimberly, I want you to stop. Maybe Gardner made that call and Singer made calls, followed you, and might have stolen your car. But Wells and Betty Arguello are dead. This is serious business. Whether you like it or not, you're not invincible."

I held up my hands. "I'm going to lock my doors after you leave, and go through the books, okay? I have a whole folder full of material to keep me busy." I didn't admit the folder had been taken from Rick's office. In the turmoil over Sam I'd forgotten about it. Now I was determined to go through it. "If I find out anything I'll take it to your guys, okay?"

"Tell you what," he said with a wink as he walked over to me. He leaned down and kissed me on the forehead. "If you behave all day, I'll buy you dinner at the hospital cafeteria tonight. They're keeping Dad over again. I might even bring you home and kiss you goodnight."

How could I resist an offer like that?

****

Sunday, 4:00 p.m.

"Tell me what you were doing at the pier last

night?" Sam asked. "And don't feed me shit about wanting to go for a walk on the beach. You can do that by stepping outside your house any time you want."

I should have known I couldn't fool him, which was one of the reasons I'd stayed away most of the day.

"Don't you want to hear how I spent the day? I've been matching up the initials in the ledgers with copies of the bills we got at the office. I'm a fourth of the way through."

"Uh-huh. What about the pier?"

"I need to talk to Delia first, okay? I've been trying to reach her all day and her phone is off. I think she's coming home. I promise that once I talk to her, I'll tell you about it."

It was more than losing her money. There was Toby to consider. I'd been calling him all day and never getting an answer. I was beginning to think I'd been right when I theorized that he saw me arrive without a bag and had taken my car in exchange for the money. With so many variables out there, I couldn't risk telling Sam. I knew he'd go directly to Hank.

His eagle eyes remained on me, but for once he let his tenacious curiosity slide. "Okay, what else did you find?"

"So far all the customers and orders are real names and the bills match what's in the books. I found out about the wine shop being closed too. Jennifer ordered the inventory. She's angry about our visit and ready to sue or have me arrested if they can't account for every bottle of wine."

His pale gaze showed no sign of surprise. His response was a question that took everything in a different direction. "Did you hear that girl was killed with a .38?"

"What does that have to do with Rick?"

"What did you do with your gun? Isn't it a .38?" he asked.

"It's still at the shop, I guess. I didn't see it in all the confusion. Did you put it somewhere?"

"I'd just finished checking the damn thing when he hit me. I thought you were behind me and then he socked me over the head."

"I didn't do it," I protested. I was growing so damn used to saying that.

His smile was quick. "I know. I heard you call out from the other room. But you better find the damn gun."

"Why?"

"Just find it!" he urged.

I didn't understand his sudden interest in the gun, but I sensed there was something behind his request. "What's the big deal?"

"You're certain it was in the box with the notebook, but that wasn't where we found it."

"Maybe police put it back in the wrong box."

He shook his head. "Uh-uh. Police never saw it."

Now I was confused. "What do you mean? Of course they did. It was on the inventory list that I gave Hank."

"I saw that in the case file. But I've discovered it was the only thing they never matched up."

"How do you know that?"

He lifted his thin shoulders in a shrug. "I hear things. People come in to visit and sometimes I fall asleep. Hank was here this morning and you know how he checks in. When I was dozing off, I heard him call

Torres so I woke up, but I didn't tell him. Next thing, I hear him talking about the girl being killed with a .38, same as what's registered to you. Hank's all upset 'cause Torres claims they never found the gun you listed on the inventory, like you're going to pretend it disappeared. The thing is, I know it exists. I saw it there. They either missed it or..."

"I put it back..." I finished.

"Yeah? How did you manage to do that when Darryl, Jennifer Roberts, and her husband were there all day and night doing the damn inventory until shortly before we arrived?"

No wonder he had not been surprised about the inventory. He'd already checked. "So what does that mean?"

"I have no idea. What about the necklace? Hank was saying something to Torres about checking on some damn necklace the girl was wearing?"

I warmed to that topic. That was the next thing I needed to tell him. "Not a necklace, a pendant. When you were at Burbank the other day, did you hear anything about Betty wearing a diamond heart pendant?"

"She had a chain on. I heard something about that. It may have been ripped off by the killer. I guess she had marks around her neck from them pulling on it."

Was that the chain I'd seen on the floor? "Do you suppose the killer took the pendant?"

"I don't see how it could have much significance...unless..."

"What?"

"Two possibilities. Crime of passion, like I said from the first, or someone trying to point police in a particular direction."

"At me," I finished for him. "Ken Gardner said he was going to get me."

Sam laughed and waved a hand of dismissal. "Gardner has his own problems. This morning after I heard Hank ask Torres to look into Gardner, I made some calls on my own. The reason Gardner got so angry about being questioned is that he wasn't supposed to be in Vegas that weekend Wells died. And he wasn't alone, which got him into trouble with the Dominguez family. Now the old man has his bodyguard tailing him."

"*Senor Z?*" Could Ken Gardner have been following me Thursday night? Was that why the big bodyguard was outside my door? What had Gardner planned to do? Whatever it was, maybe seeing the *Senor* panicked him.

"I wish we had the damn board here," Sam said glumly.

I grinned and lifted my index finger in triumph. "Let me make you proud of your student, Gramps!" I pulled my laptop from my tote bag and put it on the hospital table. "After staring at the damn thing all afternoon, and then updating it, I wanted to show you what I'd come up with so…" I tapped a few keys and a revised picture of the chart appeared on the screen. "Tuh-duh!"

"Okay, let's start at the top and go through this whole damn list again, one by one," Sam said. "And see how each one ties to Betty."

****

"Not quite like the fare at Geneva," I said to Hank as we sat in the hospital cafeteria later that evening.

I was in a good mood after spending the past three hours with Sam going through our thoughts on the connections to Rick and Betty's deaths. Our efforts were paying off and things were falling into place. We'd given fresh motives to Bobbi the Bimbo and even to Miles Brookings. Given his brush off, we suspected that he might have been trying to set me up with that Thursday night date. He'd probably been the one to have our picture taken!

The discovery of Brad's role in following me put an end to our other fears. The killer might be out to frame me, but we no longer thought he was out to get me as Brad had claimed. Sam would be released in the morning and was coming to stay with me temporarily. He predicted we were on the verge of a breakthrough and while Hank didn't agree, he didn't protest the idea of Sam staying with me.

Now Hank looked across the table at me with his brow furrowed in confusion. "What do you mean?"

"Isn't Sunday your night at Geneva?" I said with a smile.

His lips drew out in a straight grim line. "I don't think I would have gone there anyway. It wasn't the place to be tonight."

"It's good any night."

He put down his sandwich and winced. "A kid from there died last night. Well, not quite a kid. He was a bartender who used to work there. You probably know who he was. Big blond guy named Tony or something like that."

A chill ran through me and my voice shook as I spoke. "Toby?"

"Yeah. Someone found his body in an alley in

Santa Monica. They're thinking it may have been a case of hit and run."

Chapter Thirty-Nine

I dropped my sandwich and realized I was weaving back and forth like I was drunk, or maybe the room was wobbling. I wasn't certain which it was. "I didn't do it."

He started to smile. "Of course not. I was with...hey, Kimmie, you're white as sheet. What is it?"

I leaned my head down against my hand. "Oh, God, Hank. Are you sure it was Toby?"

"Yeah. Why?"

The room seemed to blur and I reach over and clutched his arm. "We need to talk."

The sandwiches were forgotten as I slumped in my chair. He pulled his own chair around and sat in front of me.

"What is this all about?"

I could not look at him as I haltingly blurted out the blackmail scheme and the plans to meet Toby the previous night. "Now the car is missing and the money with it."

"Did you tell the police it was in there?"

"What was I supposed to say? Please find my car because it has my blackmail money?"

He ignored my hysteria. His voice was quiet, measured, the good cop. "He didn't show?"

"No. I waited an hour on the pier before I went back and found my car gone." I could feel his gaze on me, but I couldn't look up. I didn't want to see accusation.

"Was that why you were so jumpy when the phone rang last night?" he asked.

"I thought it might be Toby, calling to tell me he was going to the police."

Hank stood, running his hand through his hair. He was going to go bald at this rate.

"I didn't do it," I repeated. I stared at Hank's hard handsome profile. It showed no emotion. Mr. Police Chief at his finest. When he didn't reply I continued. "You don't believe me? You can't think I would do something like that. Hank…"

Silence was his reply. He stood still as a statue with his hands on his hips. I knew the technique. I used it myself sometimes. If you didn't say anything, the other person would rush on, rambling until he or she said what you wanted to hear.

"Toby was a nice kid. You don't think I'd deliberately run over an innocent kid."

He tilted his head sideways, finally speaking. "He wasn't that innocent, not if he was blackmailing you."

"He hadn't done anything so far."

"And he won't anymore."

"Hank, I could never run someone over! On purpose?" Had Delia and I talked about running over Rick? Was that on the recording? I could barely remember what we'd said that Saturday. It seemed so long ago. Hank's thoughtful gaze remained skewered to me and I tried another tack. "Have you forgotten how upset I got when I ran over a squirrel? I cried, remember?"

"That squirrel never tried to hurt you."

"Neither did Toby. That's why I never told you or

Sam. I was dealing with it."

"By paying him off." He bit off the bitter words. "But your car got stolen. How convenient. Was that what you were going to tell Toby?"

"I didn't know the money was gone until later."

"What about the recording?"

"It…it was on the cell phone. And I don't know where it is," I replied.

****

Hank left moments later and I ate my sandwich because I was starved. When I finished, I looked around the deserted room. What should I do now? Maybe I needed to go upstairs and see Sam. See if he had any ideas. What were we missing? I thought about how he'd looked as I left him—gaunt and thin in his faded hospital gown, but eager to help.

Tears stung my eyes. He'd been hurt trying to help me. Like Lindy. And Toby and Betty were dead. Hell, this was my fault. I was putting people in danger. And I didn't know why.

Enough!

I was on my own. Time for the Queen to stop calling on others. Time for the Queen to become her own Warrior.

I walked to the front entrance of the hospital. Damn! I didn't have transportation. I'd taken a cab over, figuring Hank would provide my ride home. Now I didn't know if I wanted to go home. Maybe I should spend the night in a hotel.

A cab pulled up in front of the hospital to drop off a fare and I flagged it down. I gave him my address, trying to figure out my next step.

My phone rang as I settled into the back seat.

I answered quickly. Static came across the line. "Delia," I shouted hopefully.

"Walter..." came the broken voice.

"Oh, thank goodness. Can I talk to Delia?"

The line crackled again and I only heard bits of his reply. "not here...she didn't come..." More crackling and then the welcome word, "home" came across the line before it went dead.

I drew a sigh of relief. She was coming home! No wonder she didn't answer her cell. She probably had it turned off. Did that mean she was in the air?

"Oh, Delia," I whispered. "Thank you!"

At home I walked inside feeling like I was dragging the weight of the world. I sat at my desk and stared at the chart filled with sticky notes and comments. Had one of them killed Rick, Betty, and now Toby? Who? And why?

I opened Rick's ledger, hoping something might jump out at me. It flipped open on its own to a page in the D's. I hadn't gotten that far yet. I stared at Betty's tiny precise writing. B. D.

One page showed huge payments ranging anywhere from 10 to 25 thousand dollars, totaling more than $300,000 in the past six months.

B. D.? Benito Dominguez? Did the old man order that much wine? Or was this the secret money laundering deal Sam had mentioned as a possibility?

I opened the invoice folder and searched until I found the section with last names starting with D. None matched the ledger. I went back to the beginning of the files. I'd been through the invoices beginning with A and hadn't seen anything to resemble that large amount. I went to the B's and there it was—a series of invoices for wine with large totals that matched the ledger. The invoices showed no indications of vineyards or what wines were ordered, and all the invoices were in Rick's handwriting.

Oh, hell. This was it.

There was no name at the top of the invoice pages—only those damned initials B. D. scribbled in Rick's handwriting.

Benito Dominguez?

I looked at the board and Miles Brookings jumped out at me. B. D. Brookings Development? Why hadn't I noticed that? Maybe he hadn't liked Rick, but he hadn't been averse to doing under-the-table business with him. Or perhaps he didn't want his daughter marrying his favorite money laundering machine. Where did Miles get all his money? But wait, there had to be more. A few hundred thousand a month was pennies for a man like Miles.

Picking up the personal file, I opened it and thumbed through letters, clippings and notes. Many were from me. The damn thing looked like it was years old. Then my skin turned cold. "We're on for this weekend. Call me tomorrow. Love you, Bridget D."

The letters were in a floral scrawl, nearly faded on the page.

I thought about Sam's comments about seeing a note from some woman thanking Rick for a wonderful week. Also signed B. D.

Bridget. I knew no one name Bridget. Or was that a pet name for Paula perhaps? It would be like Rick to give her a funny name, much as he once called me Pumpkin or Diva.

My phone buzzed and I grabbed it and smiled

when I saw Hank's name. Maybe they'd found my car! No, it was more likely he wanted to come over to talk about Toby. Or send Torres.

"Hey, Chief," I began, hoping he'd called to apologize for being so cold at the hospital, but he cut me off.

"I'm probably going to be fired for this, but you need to call your lawyer immediately. They found your car."

I didn't know if I felt relief or fear. "Oh, hell, with the money?"

"No. With the bartender's cell phone."

Shivers ran through me. "Torres is going after a warrant?"

"No. Santa Monica is. They found blood on the dented front bumper. A preliminary test shows the same blood type as Toby. They're going for a DNA workup. But there's more. That gray car you asked about belonged to him, and his name is on your phone records."

I trembled with fear. "Hank, you know I didn't do it. I was with you last night."

"Which is why I'm calling. Call your damn lawyer."

I hung up, not knowing where to turn. I was getting so close to figuring this out, but if police arrested me, they wouldn't pursue my ideas. My car with Toby's blood? Someone had stolen it and used it to kill him.

Someone wasn't trying to kill me.

They were out to get me.

I studied the names on the wall, putting my name into the equation with Rick, Betty, and Toby. What was I missing?

Time! I needed time!

I needed to work through this puzzle, but I had no time before police banged on the door with their damned warrant and a set of handcuffs. Using my phone, I took another picture of the big board and yanked off all the sticky notes and stuffed them, my notebook, and the personal file folder into a canvas tote bag along with my laptop. I needed to get out of here before police arrived.

I had no opportunity to pack a bag. Reba and I had once joked about what we would take if we were one of those viewers warned that a wildfire or flood was approaching and they needed to evacuate.

Now the Queen faced instant exile. What to take? The answer was simple—the crown jewels. I grabbed my Louis Vuitton train case from the hall closet and filled it with all the pouches and boxes from my safe. If worse came to worst, I could hock the shit. The Queen might need financing for her war on evil prosecutors. As I started to close the closet door, I stopped and grabbed a handful of folded Hermes scarves. They were light and could provide an easy source of cash in second hand shops.

I started for the door and stopped. I needed a disguise! If police announced they were looking for me, the Queen could be easily spotted.

Not Kimmie D!

In the office, I grabbed the cranberry USC hoodie Sam used to sit outside in the evening. I also put on my Dodgers baseball cap, pulling it low on my forehead. As I headed for the door, I caught sight of my makeup case that Reba had sent over from work. That might come in handy. It held enough cosmetics to transform me into anything from a sixty-year-old woman to a

Hollywood hooker.

Burdened with my limited valuables and my new Fendi bag slung over my shoulder, I race-walked down the driveway and peered out onto the street. No sign of police and no unknown cars. Still, I felt conspicuous until I reached the end of the residential street and walked onto a main thoroughfare.

Traffic rushed by me and I realized I wouldn't find a cab in this area. I couldn't afford to call one and wait. Police might spot me. A bus with a TV8 logo rolled toward me. It slid to a stop across the street and I waved frantically at the driver. Minutes later I was headed out of town.

I sank onto a seat on the nearly deserted bus, smiling at the image I saw reflected in the window. Who would ever look for the Queen here? But where was I going? I had no destination. I needed to call Oliver, but that would keep until I found a place to hide.

Where the hell was Delia? When was she getting back? She could…it hit me like a light. Her home was secluded. And I had her key! I checked my ring and it was still there, glistening in the glaring light of the bus, providing the promise of a safe hideout.

The bus traveled north along Sepulveda Boulevard and I sat back on my seat, clutching my tote bag with its precious cargo. With a long trip facing me, I drew out the notebook which still held my original suspect list.

Looking over the list again, I went through motives and alibis for each person. I mentally checked off Delia, since her name remained on the list, though her motives were as strong as anyone. She'd been angry over Rick's treatment of me and according to police, he owed her and her husband money. But she and Walter had their alibis.

Betty's name was next, a sad reminder of how stupid some of my early theories had been. She'd become a victim. Sam said her death was a crime of passion. Who would want her dead? And why?

Miles had been opposed to his daughter marrying Rick and had probably given Rick money, but he also had an alibi and no reason for hurting Betty. Unless she knew something? Or maybe he'd been angry about that pendant and arranged to have someone kill her while he was out with me?

Bobbi the Bimbo had a nasty temper and had been angry over the pendant. She'd have a good reason to kill Betty and she'd love to see me in jail. Maybe she was following me and saw Toby hanging around my car. Hell, maybe she'd even had a thing with Toby. She visited Geneva too.

Paula Gardner was possibly having an affair with Rick and might have been as angry as I was over his breaking off with her. What if she'd gone to talk to Betty and they both discovered the other had been screwing Rick?

But why kill Toby?

Carl Edwards might have taken Rick's money and he'd worked with Betty. Maybe she refused to hide or keep silent about the money problems. Again, there was the Toby problem.

Senor Dominguez could be booking bets for Rick, but I didn't see any connection he might have with Betty. Unless it had to do with those big payments that perhaps she also discovered. He might even have heard my conversation in the bar with Del and might know Toby was blackmailing me. He could have had *Senor Z* "take care" of the bartender and arrange to place the blame on me. Perhaps that was even the reason the *Senor* had been following me.

Ken Gardner was the only person who owed Rick money, but I didn't see any connection to Betty or to Toby.

What about Darryl? Maybe he knew something about the money situation.

And what about the mysterious Bridget? Was she lurking out there somewhere?

The bus shuddered to another stop and I realized we had reached Malibu. A lighted strip of restaurants caught my eye. I'd need to catch a cab to take me up into the hills to Delia's house and this was probably as good a place as any to disembark.

Minutes later the cab pulled up to the Lindsay house. The exterior was dark, but lights showed through side windows. That was no surprise. They would have their lights on timers during their vacation. I paid the driver and got out of the cab. I'd make myself a drink, go through the notes and figure this thing out before calling Oliver.

The key worked and I breathed a sigh of relief as I stepped inside. A tall white saguaro cactus sculpture greeted me inside the door. Yuck! Why Delia didn't redo this into a more current style was beyond me. I moved through the marble foyer into a whole world full of Santa Fe style pastel colors, big white-washed log furniture and huge Southwestern sculptures. I'd never liked the style Delia had chosen for her house any more than I liked what she had done to mine, but I welcomed it as my haven for now.

A gasp sounded to my right and I whirled toward it.

I stared in shock at Delia.

Chapter Forty

It was like a dream come true. I dropped my bags and stepped toward her, fearing she was an apparition. Wait, there was something different about her. I couldn't quite place it, but while the eyes belonged to Delia, her face looked different. It didn't matter. Delia was home, and my heart swelled with such joy it hurt to breathe.

"Del," I squealed, glee spilling over as I rushed toward her. "When did you get back?"

To my surprise, she retreated behind a heavy white-washed log chair. "I was about to call you."

I paused at the edge of a sand-colored rug, sensing she didn't want me to come any closer. As she shifted, her hair parted, revealing small flesh colored bandages. I spotted others near the corners of her chin and at the edge of her hairline. "What the hell happened to your face?"

She didn't reply, tilting her head toward me. Her face looked smooth and nearly flawless and the truth hit me like a smack to my own face.

"You had your face done!"

Delia finally spoke, her thick lips barely moving. "This is the third time. You've never noticed before, have you?"

"You told me you did liposuction and botox sometimes and about the boob and nose work, but that was years ago."

Her sudden laugh was mirthless. "Kimmie, you're so clueless sometimes."

I shook off the deprecating humor as I'd been doing since college. "I'm so glad you're here. You wouldn't believe the latest chapter in this never ending saga. Hank tells me they've got an arrest warrant out for me. Hell, I'm officially a wanted woman."

Delia didn't smile at my shaky laugh. "What are you doing here?"

A new predicament occurred to me. "I was going to stay until I can get this thing straightened out. Oliver is not going to do a damn thing if I go to jail, and Sam's in the hospital. I'm on my own, babe, and I better not stay. I don't want to get you into trouble."

This time she did smile, though it was crooked and strained. "That doesn't sound like the Kimmie I know. She lets everyone else do the dirty work."

"No more. I'm becoming self-sufficient. Hell, I've been figuring things out. I've almost got it solved."

She blinked. "You do? Do you want help?"

"I'd love it," I squealed. Then I shook my head. "No. You're my dearest friend. I can't get you in trouble."

"At least let me pour some champagne and tell me what you've got."

I checked my watch. I needed to think, and Delia's clever, devious mind might come up with answers. "Okay, but I can't get silly. I need to keep my wits about me."

"I'll get the Dom."

She walked out of the room and I retreated to the foyer. I picked up the bag with my laptop and hooked it up to my phone to download the latest picture of my chart. Perhaps as I explained it, something new might occur to me.

I frowned at the small size as the picture came up on the screen. "Hey, Del, can we use Walter's computer? I can't see my chart."

"Sure," she called back.

Walter's office was across the foyer and I walked over and turned on the light. The wood paneled office reminded me of an old fashioned men's club, with its heavy furniture and rich wood. Unlike his business office, his home desk was cluttered with papers, and drawers hung open. A Chanel clutch bag sat on one side of the desk.

I turned on his computer and hooked up my phone. Delia returned with two crystal glasses filled to the brim and a bottle of Dom Perignon tucked under her arm. She handed me a glass.

"To the return of the dynamic duo," she said with a laugh, and we clinked glasses.

The champagne was icy and slid down my throat in a welcome journey. Champagne, my best friend, and my bag of jewels. What more could I ask for in what might be my last few hours of freedom?

"Tell me who you think did it?" she asked, leaning over to study the chart on the computer screen.

I stood back and stared at the color coded list and began giving her the lowdown.

"First someone had been giving Rick lots of money. I'm not sure why, maybe for gambling or keeping the shop out of hock. I'm not sure what that means, but here are my suspects."

"Miles Brookings?" she said with a laugh. "Bobbi?

Benito Dominguez?" She turned and blinked at me. "None of them makes sense..."

That was when it hit me. Just like Sam said it would. My clever board with all its cute colors and all those motives had not computed. And for one very good reason. One name flashed in front of my eyes.

"The killer's not on there..." I said, choking.

She blinked. "What? Then who did it?"

"Bridget. The mystery woman who was going to Vegas with him and...giving him all that money..."

She began to laugh and waved a red tipped finger to me. "Of course!"

But something else hit me too, and it chilled me to the bone. "I can't get over your face," I said. "Did you have that done in South America?"

"Hell no! You think I'd let some foreign quack fuck with my face?"

Tears filled my eyes. The shock was so swift, so painful it was as though I had been shot. The other woman—Bridget D. When we were in college we made up names to give to guys. Cute names. Like Gidget or Danielle. Or Bridget? My made up names often used the initials DK, the opposite of Kimmie D. She would be BD instead of Delia Burnett.

My hands began to shake and I turned away, dropping my glass on the desk. The heavy crystal didn't break, but the champagne spilled, dampening my sweatshirt and as I reached forward, my hand hit the bottle and liquid spurted over the desk top.

Delia cursed. "Damn!" She hurried from the room to get towels.

Frantically, I looked around. Now what? Could I be wrong? I reached over and grabbed her small clutch bag and stuffed it inside my hoodie as she appeared from the adjoining bathroom with a wad of towels.

I walked past her to the bathroom. "Excuse me a minute." With the door closed, I reached into her purse with fumbling fingers. I didn't know what I was looking for—maybe proof about when she'd returned home. Or left.

The purse was heavy and I touched something smooth and hard, something metal. I wrapped my fingers around the cylinder and pulled, watching in stunned amazement as my gun emerged.

I unzipped an inside compartment, feeling around, fearing what else I might find. I opened a tiny coin purse with shaking fingers and stared inside. My breath caught. A tiny diamond pendant glistened inside. My pendant—the one taken from the neck of Betty Arguello.

"Kimberly?" Her muffled voice came through the closed door.

I jumped, closing the coin purse and stuffing it back into the Chanel bag. I slid the gun into the back of my jeans, much as I'd seen people do on TV.

Fighting nausea that threatened to overwhelm me, I walked out to confront Rick and Betty's killer. Summoning every ounce of acting skill I'd ever possessed I tried to keep a straight face. Could she have run down Toby? Yes. It explained how my car had been stolen so easily. Delia and I had keys to each other's house and cars.

Delia, who was always taking spa weekends, or maybe they were trips to Vegas with Rick.

Delia, who had not gone to South America. No wonder she would never leave a hotel number.

Delia, who knew my every move.

Delia, who believed in retribution for betrayals.

Yes, it all added up to Delia.

Okay, I'd solved the damn thing. Now what? What came next? Well, it was a mystery, right? Next came the acknowledgment and the fight where the killer tries to do in the heroine.

Wait! Not if she didn't know I had it solved. I would drink champagne until the confession was made, pull out the gun and call Hank. It sounded so simple. I might have slid into a movie mystery scenario, except there was too much at stake. I needed to keep my mind clear. No time for Miss Marple or Sherlock Holmes. I needed to focus.

Delia had cleaned up the mess. She waved at the computer screen. "Fuck that. Let's get fresh champagne and talk this out."

We walked back to the living room, the gun jabbing my lower back. Was the damn thing loaded? What if it shot off my ass? I couldn't sit down. While Delia poured fresh drinks, I paced the room, touching the various pieces of large Santa Fe furniture, the beige and pink sculptures of Native American chiefs, large white pots filled with dried plants. I couldn't live here, even if the furniture looked plush and comfortable.

"You're a terrible detective," Delia said, coming back into the room with a new bottle of champagne. She handed me a full glass and poured one for herself from the bottle. "I've already figured this out. How are you going to find Bridget? That's not her real name, right?"

A burst of air blew past my lips. Was she going to admit it?

Our eyes met and we both recognized what the other knew. We'd spent too many years together when we didn't need words to communicate.

"Why?" I asked, putting down my glass. "That's all I want to know, Del, why?"

Her laugh was pure Delia, but to me, it suddenly sounded evil. "Oh, Kimmie, I'm going to miss you. Maybe we need to figure out someone to pin this on."

The thought hit me. Maybe that was...no... The last few weeks had been hell. And someone had been trying hard to make it look like I did it. I was beginning to understand why she might kill Rick. Even Betty and Toby. But why would she let me take the blame? My oldest, closest friend, BFF, willing to let me take a murder rap. The Queen, stabbed by her most favored Duchess.

"Why?" I repeated, fearing a massive breakdown. The woman facing me was evolving into a stranger. This new face was not my gal-pal.

"Can't you guess?"

I didn't want to. But there was something I needed to know. "How long were you sleeping with him? The whole time?"

She shrugged, showing no remorse. "You knew he was a stud. Why did you think he'd be faithful? Yes, he spoiled you, but that was guilt. You're so damn self-centered, you sucked it in like it was your right. You couldn't imagine anyone preferring another woman to you."

Her voice had taken on the cruel note I often heard her use on others. I'd taken her denigrating remarks toward me as joking, but were they?

"Do you hate me that much?" I asked, my throat

dry.

The thick unnatural lips tightened. "I don't hate you. You're my best friend."

"You're not my friend if you let me go to jail. Was Toby an accident? We can go to Hank. He knows Toby was blackmailing me. He'd understand if he was doing the same to you. Why did you have to hurt him?"

"Toby saw me following you at the pier that night, so I took him on a ride to Santa Monica. And it's not *my* car with blood on it. No one will ever prove *I* did anything." Her laugh was demonic, maniacal. Mrs. Danvers with the house burning down around her in *Rebecca.*

"Hank knows I didn't do it. He was with me that night."

"Like you were with Miles the night Betty died?" She shook her head in disgust. "Why is it you can always get a man whenever you need one?"

"Why did you kill her? Jealousy?"

"Hell no. I knew he fucked around. She knew about me. That was your fault. All your poking around. She left a message after you talked to her, that she was going to tell you about me. She'd figured out I was using a phony account to give him money."

"The BD account."

"And she had that necklace. He used my account to buy the damn thing, but he gave it to her instead of returning it. She was so damn cool about it." Her stiff face contorted in rage as her voice rose to a raspy shout.

Her deranged anger only made me calmer. "Now what?"

The familiar eyes in the unfamiliar face flamed. "I have a gun in my purse. Your gun. The one I took from

Sam. It's the gun that killed Betty. I was going to plant it in Paula's car. If I don't use it to make your death look like a suicide, I may still do that. So it's your choice. Would you rather drink champagne filled with drugs or blow off your perfect face?"

Neither choice excited me. I smiled. "The gun is no longer in your purse and I'm not telling you where I put it." I eyed the glass of champagne. It had tasted different than the first one, and I'd barely touched it. I reached out and knocked over the glass. "Oops, I'm so clumsy."

Again that incredible anger ran across her face, but now there was something else I'd never seen before. Hate? Contempt? It frightened me more than the anger.

"I'm not letting you beat me this time," she said. "The damn Queen is dead. Even if I have to kill her myself."

Chapter Forty-One

Oh, hell. Here came that final scene. The fight to the death. *Mano a mano. Senor Zapato* wasn't going to save me this time. No one knew where I was or that she was home. The gun was in my pants, but I didn't know if it was loaded and I couldn't afford to let her know I had it. I wasn't even certain I could remember how to shoot it.

"Beat you?" I repeated, looking around for a way out.

"Everything goes your way," she said. "You get all the breaks. In college you got the guys and grades. Then you ended up with a great job, making tons of money. Everyone knows you."

Her bitterness overwhelmed me, but maybe we could talk this through. "Del, you have money. You've always had more money than me."

"*Their* money!" She spat the words like a curse, ending my hopes for a sane resolution. "You do whatever you want. Redecorate your house anytime you want. Buy your own jewelry. Take vacations you want. I have to beg for everything. Plastic surgery? Not unless he approves! Jewelry? Only on special occasions. And what vacation does he want? A damn primitive safari!"

Her pleas were sad, but so superficial for the damage she'd caused. Three people dead and another two injured.

"Is that what this is all about? Because he wanted you to go to South America?"

"No. It's about begging. Begging for what I want, while you snap your fingers, you worthless piece of shit! Walter is so pissed he's filing for divorce. I told Rick if he was so damn eager to get married, he should marry me! *I* knew him better than anyone! *I* was the one who saw his faults, but I didn't care. I still wanted the fucker."

"So you went to see him that night instead of getting on the plane…" I prompted. *Damn, why didn't I have a recorder or Toby's cell phone?*

"It was our chance. We could take Walter for every penny and be together."

A wild look entered her eyes, but I didn't want to hear any more. It was time to end this tragedy. I no longer knew this woman.

"I'm going to call Hank."

Disbelief flared in her eyes. Her hand came up and she flung her champagne glass at me. "You will not win this time! I'm not going back into the single world and be forced to compete with you again."

I dodged the heavy crystal glass and it bounced off the sculpture beside me, tipping the glass back toward her and drenching her in champagne. Laughter burst from me. "How could you forget I'm charmed in these catfights?"

"This isn't one of your comedy movie games," she declared. "You're going down, bitch."

Had she felt this way all along? I spotted a clay Navaho vase I'd urged her not to buy because it was overpriced. Picking it up, I waved it at her. "Your decorating taste sucks, and I'm replacing my damn hard sofa."

"You'll never see it again. And don't you dare break that! It's an original. Put it down, you overrated Prom Queen."

"Prom Queen? What happened to Queen of L.A.?" In defiance, I flung it onto the carpet as she let out a little cry. It didn't break, merely chipping so I ground the dull red clay into the pure white carpet. "I'm not afraid of you. And I'm not as helpless as you think."

I kicked the remains of the vase against the marble pedestal of a ceramic statue of a Mexican bullfighter and bull. The vase exploded, and one of the pieces flew up to lop off a horn of the ceramic bull.

She picked up the shard of the horn and approached me, waving the sharp point like a dagger. "You can't do anything without me. You've bounced around like a fucking puppet, and I was pulling the strings. I'm so damn tired of you and your perfect cheekbones. I'm going to chop up your face."

I backpedaled, flashing a teasing smile. "If you cut me, I'm going to bleed all over your expensive carpet."

"It'll be worth it. I've always had to think things through, and you smile and get your way. Now you're going to jail or the morgue. I don't care which." She waved the horn at me again and this time the jagged ceramic brushed my wrist.

Pain raced through my arm as a long scratch filled with a thin line of blood on my forearm. I lifted a Kachina doll that sat on an oversized end table and as she lunged at me, I used it to smack the horn out of her hand.

They crashed to the floor, bouncing. While she whirled away to find a new weapon, I reached around for the gun.

"Hold it, Delia!"

She stared at it and laughed. "The damn thing isn't loaded, you idiot."

I aimed it at a bullfighter ceramic. "Let's just see." I pulled the trigger and the deafening blast stunned me as the statue exploded. My next shot blew up a huge pottery floor lamp. I meant to swing the gun back to her but the second shot jerked the gun from my hand, and it hopped across the carpet out of sight.

"You bitch," she screeched.

I searched frantically for the gun. Where the hell had it gone? Fearing she might find it first, I ran for the front door, but as I reached it, she grabbed me from behind, knocking me to my knees. My head jerked back in pain as she pulled at my hair.

"I'm going to rip your dyed hair out," she cried, though we both knew it was untreated.

Reaching back with my nails, I caught skin. "And I'll rip off your phony face."

She released me with a shriek, but as I dived toward the door again, a hand caught my foot. Reaching out, I hefted my Louis Vuitton train case and spun around, socking her on the head. She grunted and clawed at the bag, grasping the latch and flipping it open. Silk scarves fluttered out along with a jeweled cascade of stones and gold that bounced on the marble floor.

"You bitch!" I screamed and bent forward to scoop up wayward rings and necklaces. She yanked up a long strand of pearls and lassoed me like a cowboy, pulling me to the floor as she tightened them into a choker around my neck.

Gasping for air, I fumbled around, trying to find a weapon of my own. Something pierced my hand, and my fingers grasped a large filigree brooch. I plunged its sharp pin into one of her hands.

"Ow!" she yelped, releasing her hold as I repeated the motion.

Free from her grasp, I crawled toward my purse to get my cell phone, gathering up more jewelry along the way. I needed every weapon I could find.

"When you're dead, I'm keeping all this." She gasped for air.

"When you're in jail, I'll send you pictures of me in the latest fashions," I retorted.

Delia caught the pearl noose again and yanked, but this time the strand broke, showering us both with pearls. "Rick didn't love you!" she screeched. "He was using you."

"All he wanted from you was your money!" I scrambled to my feet and reached for my purse. "And he spent it on bookies, bets, and other babes."

She huddled on the floor, tears streaking her mascara into a long black line down her swollen cheeks. An ugly welt from my scratch cut across her stretched face.

I turned toward the door, ready to make my escape, but my foot came down on a pair of errant pearls and the soles of my shoes spun, plunging me back to the hard tile. My breath whooshed out.

Laughter rang around me, and she flopped on top of me, straddling me. I ripped at her silk blouse, hearing the pleasing tear of material as it fell away from her shoulders. She slapped me hard across my face, stunning me.

"Do you know why I hit him?" she asked, her strange face filled with rage. "He wanted me to talk to you. He said he never realized how hurt you were until that night. He wanted me to get you to forgive him and take the fucker back!"

She slapped at me again, but I jerked my head to the side and her hand smacked the marble floor. The crack was as painful to hear as her howl of frustration.

I twisted out from under her and reached around me for any sort of weapon. My hand came into contact with my makeup case and I opened it and began pulling out small compacts and cases and flinging them at her to keep her at bay. Beige powder showered her, and I heard her curse and blink as it got into her eyes. I fired loose eye shadow compacts at her, dotting her face and hair with brown, blue, and green, but I wasn't doing much damage except to make her look like an artist's palette.

In desperation, I flung the entire case at her. It caught her on the side of the head and I used the time to find my Fendi bag. I groped inside it for my cell phone, but as I pulled it out, my hand stung with pain. She'd taken off her pumps and whacked my hand with a stiletto heel, sending the phone skittering across the tile.

I struggled to get to my knees, but a sudden hissing filled the air and my eyes stung and grew blurry. The scent of hyacinth filled the air.

"You bitch! That's my new French perfume. Four hundred dollars an ounce. I had to special order it."

"You can spend eternity with it. I'll spray it on your casket for you," she screamed.

I reached out blindly, grasped a shoe and hurled it at the sound of her voice.

The clunk told me it hit home, but I still couldn't see where she was. I rubbed my eyes, but the more tears that flooded them, the worse they felt. The smooth feel of silk jerked my hands down, trapping me. A tight pull wrapped my arms around my upper torso. I kicked but she was knotting the silk. Through my blurred vision I recognized one of my scarves. She'd used it to tie me up.

I kicked again, but something heavy and blunt smacked me across the head and stars crossed my closed eyelids. Tears streamed out of my eyes, and I blinked them open. She was removing her bra and as I kicked, she caught my legs and tied them up with her bra.

"Delia, stop this. Let me go." We were both breathless. Neither one of us had been going to the gym recently.

"You're going to hell," she said between shallow gasps of breath. "Tell Rick I said hello." She got to her feet and began to gather other scarves that littered the foyer.

"What are you doing?"

"I'm going to tie you up and hang you from the rafters with your scarves," she said in a gleeful tone. "Poor miserable Kimberly is going to commit suicide rather than go to jail. Obviously you were throwing fits. Look at how you tossed your jewelry around. I'll go away and come back tomorrow to find your cold, dead body."

"Sam will never believe it."

"He will when he reads your suicide note. Remember how I used to copy your writing when we were in school? I'm going to leave a lovely note," she said with a maniacal laugh. "You're even going to admit to killing Rick."

Would Sam believe it? "He knows I didn't do it."

"Everyone else thinks you did! It's been so damn hilarious. I was scared to death until I heard they were blaming you!"

Tears wet the back of my painful eyes. These were emotional tears, not the tears I'd shed over the sting of the perfume. I looked up at the high wooden rafters that crisscrossed the large living room. How was she going to manage to hang me? Was this how my life ended? In a colorful catfight to the death? Done in by a bright array of Chanel eye shadow pots, Dior blushes, and Hermes scarves? Rubies, diamonds, and emeralds winked in the sunlight at me like they shared a giant secret.

No, as I wriggled, I realized one hand was coming free. My gaze moved back to her to make certain she wasn't noticing, and my stinging eyes focused on the statue of a cactus by the doorway. If I could get to that...

I inched my way across the tile. Her attention remained on tying the scarves. By the time I had reached the statue, my whole arm was free. I wrapped it around the base on the statue and yanked. It rocked, but did not fall and the noise alerted her.

"What are you doing?" she cried, leaping to her feet as it rocked again. Delia dropped the scarves and moved toward the cactus. "Shit!" she cried as she stepped on an open pin. She reached out to catch her balance and caught hold of the rocking statue. Her weight carried it to the floor and she landed with a thud as the statue shattered on top of her.

I crawled to her limp figure. Her pulse was strong, but she was out like a light.

"I told you that decor was sooo last century," I said, taking in a deep gulp of air.

Chapter Forty-Two

Hank handed me a cup of coffee and sat beside me. I perched on a low stone wall along the entry to Delia's house.

"How are you feeling?" he asked.

I shrugged, not certain if I would ever feel good again. I thought I'd known Rick and he cheated on me. I thought I knew Delia and she hated me. I wasn't even certain I knew myself.

Hank touched my scratched face with a long finger. "You need to go to the hospital and get checked out."

I leaned toward his hand and a tear escaped my eye. My eyes no longer stung , but tears still threatened every couple of minutes. For weeks I'd lamented Delia's absence. Now it would be pretty permanent unless I wanted to visit prison.

"She hated me. All that time, she wanted a way to get even with me." I looked at him for answers, but saw no emotion in his clear blue eyes. "You hated me too."

"I couldn't hate you. I don't think she did either. She was jealous, plain and simple. She saw money, position, status. For a time that was all I saw." He put his hand on my shoulder and squeezed it. "You can be a hard woman to know, Kimmie."

I drew in a deep breath. Was I? "They said she'll be okay."

"She has a bump on the head, bruises from getting

smacked with various objects and getting tied up with your scarves. You fight a mean battle, lady."

I smiled ruefully. "I wasn't sure how else to keep her tied down until you got here." That had been one of the hardest things to do. Ignoring her pleas to untie her and pretend it was all a grand joke. Before long, we'd be laughing at Geneva.

Now there would be no more Geneva. I could never go there again—not without thinking of laughing with Delia or Toby's adoring smile the day he met us. I glanced toward the house where police still came and went.

"They're picking up your jewelry. I'm surprised you didn't stay to watch," Hank said.

I'd forgotten about it. Strange that it didn't matter anymore. "It's insured."

"You gonna be okay?" His finger traced a line on my cheek.

"That's the same thing Sam asked." He'd sounded so pleased when I called to fill him in on how I'd worked it out and managed to capture Delia.

"And?"

Tears clouded my vision. It was difficult to lose someone and yet not lose them completely because you never knew them. That described both Delia and Rick.

"Do you suppose they would have caught her?" I asked.

Hank's face was grim as he nodded. "There are partial fingerprints on top of yours on the bat. That was the reason Torres held back from arresting you. I have a feeling they'll be hers. We may have witnesses who can identify her outside Betty Arguello's house and leaving the pier in your car with the bartender. There's more I can't tell you, but I'm confident we can build a case."

I was curious about the evidence, but I wasn't going to press him. I'd put his job in jeopardy too many times. "Is that what you told the reporters?"

He chuckled as a smile slid across his face. "Something to that effect."

"So it's over? I can go?"

"TV's down the road." He pointed at the towering microwave poles at the edge of the property.

I glanced at my watch. "They have live shots at 11. And they'll probably be back for the early morning news."

"Do you need me to drive you out of here?"

Emotion caught in my throat, clogging it. The offer from Hank was not something I expected or deserved. Well, maybe deserved. His officers made me look guilty. Yet if I had kept them informed of all I was doing or handled this differently, maybe they would have caught Delia sooner. I'd given her the non-existent alibi.

My phone beeped and I looked down, recognizing Alan's number. Hank got to his feet.

"I'll be back in a minute," he said.

I clicked on the phone and said a quiet hello.

Alan's voice sounded cautious. "Hey, how ya doin', kid? I got Reba at the scene in case you feel like talking."

"Looking for a lead?" I said, fighting back tears.

"You'd be all over it if you were here."

How many grieving widows had I shoved microphones at over the years? How many family members had I tried to get to talk? Would I ever look at victims the same way again?

"So what do you say?" he asked.

"Maybe later. I don't think I'm allowed to speak right now. It might prejudice the case." No one had told me that, but it sounded good.

"Sure, I understand. Got a statement at least?"

"Oliver will send one."

He sighed. "I've told Vincent I want you back on air as soon as you're ready. I warned the SOB that I'll go to the carpet over this. Gwen's moving out of your office and the seat is yours whenever you want it."

I held my breath, my throat closing. The Queen's throne awaited.

"I mean it," he continued. "Vincent knows how valuable you are. The numbers slumped the last two weeks."

"I don't know. Rick left me part of his wine shop. I might get out of the business and run that."

"Now, wait a minute, babe. We got a contract here..."

My phone beeped and I rang off without a reply to go to the next call, expecting Oliver or Adrienne. Miles Brookings surprised me.

"I wanted to let you know how sorry I am for the way I acted the other day."

"No problem." It seemed so long ago.

"I've learned Brad Singer took the picture and released it. He was playing a vindictive game and I'm sorry I let it affect me. May I buy you dinner to make up for being a boor?"

I looked up as Hank emerged from the house. Ten years ago I faced a decision between Rick and Hank. Miles reminded me of Rick. He babied women, spoiled them...

I snapped off the phone as Hank approached.

"Where are you headed now?" he asked.

"Home. Then I may join the family in Mexico. I don't spend enough time with Mom. It's like we don't know each other anymore. You ought to do the same with Sam. He misses you."

He stared at me for a second and then nodded. "Yeah, I know. This case has taught me a lot of things."

"Me too. Like I need to get to know myself better."

Hank leaned over and kissed me on the cheek, grasping my hand. "I might want to do that too, Kimmie."

I squeezed his fingers as I stood. Kimberly delaGarza was no longer Queen. She'd become Warrior Princess, crime solver, crusader for justice. When it was time to jump back into my romantic comedy dreams, Hank Patterson would be where I started. Miles was rich and handsome, but Hank was real. I smiled, realizing there was nothing phony about it. I felt happy all the way to my toes.

"Why don't I drive you home?" he asked.

"I was thinking of taking the bus. It's a good place to think."

He tapped my nose, a playful but intimate touch. "Why don't we think together?"

My pulse quickened as I looked at our joined hands and nodded. *Why not?*

A word about the author...

Rebecca Grace is an award winning former broadcast journalist who spent 30 years working in television newsrooms in Denver, San Diego, Seattle, Las Vegas, and Los Angeles. She writes romance, mystery and romantic suspense for The Wild Rose Press, Inc. She is also a writing instructor and coach. Her most recent work is a romantic suspense novel, *Dead Man's Rules*.

www.rebeccagrace.com

Thank you for purchasing
this publication of The Wild Rose Press, Inc.
For other wonderful stories of romance,
please visit our on-line bookstore at
www.thewildrosepress.com.

For questions or more information
contact us at
info@thewildrosepress.com.

The Wild Rose Press, Inc.
www.thewildrosepress.com

To visit with authors of
The Wild Rose Press, Inc.
join our yahoo loop at
http://groups.yahoo.com/group/thewildrosepress/

www.ingramcontent.com/pod-product-compliance
Lightning Source LLC
Chambersburg PA
CBHW050025030726

47506CB00001B/129